We'd been set up, led into an ambush, but by God, I wasn't losing another partner...

I swept my flashlight back down the body. The clothing caught my eye. The shoes were spit-shined, the pants baggy and cuffed at the ankles. This didn't look right. These weren't the clothes of a vagrant. Then the significance of the silver cross struck me. Dread flooded my mind.

I grabbed the man's thick black hair and turned his face upward. The throat had been slit. My light caught the face in full.

"Whoa!" Perdue said. He leaned over the body and said, "Isn't that the gang guy we—"

Two gunshots roared out of the darkness.

A low grunt came out of Perdue and he keeled forward to the floor as if someone had pitched him off the back end of a moving truck. His flashlight rolled away, the light floundering aimlessly off into the center of the dark warehouse.

I dove to the floor behind *El Perro's* body.

A third gunshot. The bullet *thunked* into a concrete column behind me.

My flashlight remained on, giving away my location. I flipped it off.

The room plunged into darkness except for the distant spray of Perdue's flashlight. I hugged the floor. I tried to lie still, tried to quell my heavy breathing. Any movement or sound could make me dead. Glass or rocks or bits of concrete cut into my stomach and thighs and cheek.

Perdue moaned. His breath was shallow, wheezing. He was struggling for air. *Fuck!* Another partner dying before my eyes. Because of me, again! It wasn't a freakish accident the body in the chair was Willie Flores. This was an ambush. My partner had taken a bullet meant for me.

When Joe Stryker, a burned-out, disgraced 1949 Denver street cop, discovers a body on the railroad tracks with a crushed skull and missing hands, he sees his shot at redemption. He believes the body is linked to the murder of his partner two years before, a murder for which Joe blames himself. But seeking redemption can come at a high price. Joe must not only hunt down a ruthless killer but tangle with Denver's wealthy and powerful, a wannabe mobster, and his own police department, at the risk of his career, his marriage—and his life.

KUDOS for *Murder on the Tracks*

In *Murder on the Tracks* by Bruce W. Most, Joe Stryker is a beat cop in 1949 Denver. He's suffering from PTSD because his partner was killed two years before when Joe failed to act in time. Since then Joe has been determined to catch the killer. He knows who it is, but he doesn't know where he is. Then Joe and his new partner find a body on the railroad tracks and that leads Joe back to the murder of his old partner…Most spins a very good tale, taking you back to a time when police work was done by old-fashioned investigation, knocking on doors, and questioning suspects. The story is well written, the plot strong and exciting. This one will keep you glued to the pages from beginning to end. ~ *Taylor Jones, Reviewer*

Murder on the Tracks by Bruce Most is a historical mystery of the first order. Our protagonist, Joe Stryker, walks a beat on Larimer Street in Denver. Although he is not a detective, he is investigating one case on his own—the murder of his old partner who was killed two years earlier. Joe blames himself for his partner's death and he's determined to bring the killer to justice. When he and his new partner discover a body of a man on the railroad tracks, Joe learns that the man who killed his old partner most likely killed the man on the tracks…I like the way Most writes. His voice is refreshing and unique, like his story, and reminiscent of a simpler time. The plot is full of surprises as poor Joe just can't get a break. You'll be hooked from the very first word. ~ *Regan Murphy, Reviewer*

What a great read! *Murder on the Tracks* reimagines Denver as it was in 1949, with the sights, sounds and quirky characters that make the city hum. Bruce Most has served up a clever, engrossing mystery with twists and turns you never see coming but are thrilled when they arrive. ~ Margaret Coel, author of *Night of the White Buffalo*

ACKNOWLEDGEMENTS

A special thanks to the MWA Rocky Mountain chapter critique group, whose insights and patience greatly improved this novel.

MURDER
ON THE
TRACKS

Bruce W. Most

A Black Opal Books Publication

GENRE: MYSTERY-DETECTIVE/SUSPENSE

This is a work of fiction. Names, places, characters and incidents are either the product of the author's imagination or are used fictitiously, and any resemblance to any actual persons, living or dead, businesses, organizations, events or locales is entirely coincidental. All trademarks, service marks, registered trademarks, and registered service marks are the property of their respective owners and are used herein for identification purposes only. The publisher does not have any control over or assume any responsibility for author or third-party websites or their contents.

MURDER ON THE TRACKS
Copyright © 2015 by Bruce W. Most
Cover Design by Jackson Cover Designs
All cover art copyright © 2015
All Rights Reserved
Print ISBN: 978-1-626943-33-9

First Publication: SEPTEMBER 2015

Published by Black Opal Books **http://www.blackopalbooks.com**

DEDICATION

*To Raymond Chandler, whose mystery novels
inspired me to sow seeds in this genre.*

CHAPTER 1

Denver, 1949:

L arimer Street was where lost souls went to stay lost. It was why I liked walking beat there.

Outsiders found Larimer frighteningly chaotic and foreign. When they drove through in their De Soto coupes or step-down Hudsons, it was only by accident or forced circumstances. They drove with their eyes hard on the road, never looking to one side or the other—and never, never stopping. They didn't see the winos drinking Sweet Lucy in the doorways, or the beggar kids handing over their hard-earned quarters to drunken fathers shadowed in the darkness of alleys. They didn't see the twenty-five-cent flophouses and pawnshops and pool halls and soup kitchens. They averted their eyes from the war veteran who lost his legs to an artillery shell in the battle of Arnhem and who pushed himself in and out of gin mills on a roller board. They were oblivious to the other down-and-out vets who, like me, came out of the war with their legs intact but not their minds. They missed the pushcart vendor selling the best tamales in town, made by his wife from real hog's head and served wrapped in steaming cornhusks. Stuffed in your duty coat on a cold January night, the tamales kept you warm as you walked beat on Larimer Street. The outsiders didn't see or understand, any more than my wife Paula did, that a kind of social order existed amid this chaos of Larimer Street. A social order—as ugly and as violent as it was and as duty-bound as I was as a police officer to extinguish it—that I'd rarely seen since I quit chasing Krauts across Europe.

"Think we'll find that Roadmaster down here, Joe?" my rookie partner asked as we walked our late evening rounds. He asked the question with the irritating eagerness only rookies possessed.

"What Roadmaster?" My mind was on a fight two nights ago in a Larimer Street alley between a Mexican and a Negro. The Mex had ended up running a shiv between the Negro's third and fourth rib. Nothing unusual about that, except people on the street were keeping tight-lipped about this particular fight. I wanted to know why.

"The one that belongs to that rich banker," the rookie said. "The guy who's missing."

"Oh, yeah." A prominent banker had been missing for over a week, and every cop in Denver was hunting for him, as if he came with a finder's fee.

The rookie hunched his muscular shoulders and flipped through his notebook filled with neat rookie notes from roll call. "A 1949 Buick Roadmaster Riviera. Black, two-door hardtop coupe, whitewall tires." His baby face looked up from his notes. "These Roadmasters have a Dynaflow automatic transmission and them new VentiPorts. You seen them? The mouseholes on the sides of the engine?"

"Haven't paid attention," I said. Paula and I were doing good to afford the pre-war Nash I had picked up cheap from a loan shark who had acquired it as payment for a debt, its "Class A" gas-rationing sticker from the war still pasted in the right corner of the windshield.

"Sporty looking for a big fancy car," the rookie said. He returned to his notes. "License AP thirty-eight eighty. The owner is Seth Fitzgerald Rawlins. Read he's one of the richest guys in the state. Tighter 'n Jack Benny with a buck, is what I hear."

I rubbed my left shoulder. The June night was warm and humid, and my old wound always ached shortly before a rain. "We ain't gonna find a shiny new Roadmaster on Larimer

Street, kid. Leastways, not one in its original condition."

I hated breaking in rookies. Especially a rookie like Moroni Perdue. A Mormon named after one of their angels. A rookie tight with our Mormon captain—a captain who for some damned reason had more faith in me these days than I did. The kid was no Jack Mormon, either. He didn't smoke, didn't swear, didn't booze—hell, he didn't even drink coffee. How was he gonna be a real cop if he didn't swear and drink coffee!

The rookie put away the notebook and popped a yellow LifeSaver into his mouth. He consumed LifeSavers the way most people breathed. Must not be on the Mormon sin list. "What do you think happened to the guy?" he asked. "Kidnapped?"

"Probably took a long vacation with some skirt."

"But if he was kidnapped, I bet you could find him. I hear you can find anyone."

Perdue's eagerness was beginning to grate. He reminded me of someone I knew a long time ago. Someone I've been trying to forget.

"I hear you had the best felon arrest record of any rookie in department history," he went on, like a mosquito, buzzing in my ear. "The Denver Kid. Isn't that what they called you?"

I turned angrily toward him. "You been reading the papers too much, kid."

He flinched. "I—I heard it from other cops."

"Trust them even less."

We continued down the street, the rookie blessedly silent for a change, checking out the pool halls and gin mills. Most of the winos were already settled down for the night in the smelly shadows of vacant buildings with fancy window arches and huge signs painted on crumbling brick walls advertising Scotch and cigarettes.

The few bums not already sucking their jug wine still lingered in the string of rescue missions, slurping bowls of chicken-neck soup for the price of an ear-banging. I checked in on the winos I knew and interrogated the ones I didn't. Two of them were in such bad shape we dragged them into a rescue mission to sober up before they drank themselves to death.

"Shouldn't we be getting back to the car?" the rookie said after a while.

"What for?"

He appeared puzzled, as if I had thrown him a trick question. "You know—to patrol."

"Lesson number one, kid—ditch the fucking black-and-white whenever you can."

"Why?"

"Because it's a lame-ass idea bureaucrats cooked up. Every police department in the country is pushing out beat cops in favor of two-man patrol cars with two-way radios. You cruise around until you get a call that something bad's gone down. But by that point, you're just chasing ghosts. You can't see anything from a car."

A mongrel dog dashed by us. It still had its tail. No doubt new to the neighborhood.

"But we can cover more territory and respond faster from a car," the rookie parroted the bureaucrats. "And it's safer."

"It's not safer for the people. You walk beat, you see things. You meet the people. They see your uniform. They know you're here for them—even if they don't like you. You develop sources. You learn who the bad ones are you gotta watch and the good people who can help you watch the bad ones." *You talk to the lost souls like you.*

The rookie didn't take notes, but I saw a flicker of dubious acceptance behind his blinking eyes. Wisdom from his elders.

A few doors later, next to a Mexican bakery, we stopped in front of a bar, *El Sótano*—The Basement. It was one of the most popular Mexican dives on Larimer Street. Always packed. Always a place for trouble. The alley next to it was where the fight between the Negro and the Mex had occurred. We passed a sign reading *No children after 4 p.m.* and dropped into the bar, ducking the low pipes painted black, our feet crunching on butcher shop sawdust and peanut shells. We pushed through a blue cloud of cigarette smoke, the smell of spilled beer, and the sound of mariachi music blaring from a jukebox.

I pulled the plug on the jukebox and the music died. The room instantly fell silent. I strode into the center of the room and said, "Okay, who witnessed the fight in the alley two nights ago? Between the spic and the shine?"

A roomful of brown faces glared at me. Many of them knew me, or knew of me. They didn't like cops. Especially gringo cops. I could feel the rookie beside me, as edgy as a three-legged mouse in a basement of four-legged cats.

"*La lucha! Quién?*" I said louder.

No one spoke. I didn't expect anyone to. I didn't expect someone to raise his hand like an eager first-grader in class yelling, "I saw it! I saw it!" What I was watching for was someone trying to sidle out of the bar or who looked especially uneasy. Someone I could corner. But everyone remained motionless, their faces full of wariness and fear.

I waited a beat longer then headed for a large mahogany bar at the far end of the room. People cleared away as we approached. Someone plugged in the jukebox and the music returned.

The man patrolling the bar, Ruben Castillo, the owner of the place, watched us with sullen eyes. He was a big man who had fought with the Marines in Guadalcanal. He looked as tired as the regulars. "Fightin' them Japs weren't half as tough as running a Larimer Street gin mill," he had told me once.

"Evening, Officer Stryker," Castillo said.

I leaned against the bar, one foot on the slippery rail, and nodded toward the rookie. "Ruben, this here's Officer Perdue. First time 'round the block."

The bartender gave the rookie a cursory nod then excused himself for a moment. He delivered a dark bottle of Negra Modelo to a bristle-faced old man who had shuffled away to the far end of the bar.

I quietly cautioned the rookie to turn around and watch for anyone making any suspicious moves. He faced the room and leaned back against the bar, trying to look casual. But I could hear his ragged breathing. "Rookie lesson number two, kid," I stage whispered. "Never let your fear show."

The bartender returned. He swept away an empty beer glass with one hand and wiped a filthy rag across the counter with the other. "What can I do for you, Joe?"

"Gimme some cigarettes."

His eyes held mine for a moment before he turned and rang up the old cash register guarded by a kneeling nude statue clutching her breasts. He took out some money, slammed the register drawer closed, and dug a pack of unbonded Chesterfields out of a box below a tin sign that said *Celebren El Cinco de Mayo con Schlitz*. He handed the pack of cigarettes to me. I felt the money tucked against the pack. I didn't need to look to know it was a dog-eared sawbuck. Crisp tens never made it down to this part of town. I slipped the smokes and the cash into my pants pocket. I would let the sleazy bar and the penny-ante poker games upstairs survive another week. But I wanted more than money this time around.

"Who was the spic who carved up the shine the other night, Ruben?"

The bartender shrugged his broad shoulders. "Never saw who got into it."

"You got ears."

"They ain't that big."

I hadn't been on duty that night. Rollo Dundee and his partner had caught the call and cleaned up the mess. At least, Dundee's partner had. Dundee had this thing about administering first aid to sliced-up Negros. Claimed they all had syph and you got it from them if you had a cut on your hand. Let the meat-wagon boys handle it, was Dundee's motto.

"The word is, the spic came outa here, Ruben, drunk and belligerent."

He put his big hands up in protest. "*Déme una rotura*, Joe! I run a clean place."

"Yeah, no more than a dozen fights a week. You oughta start charging ring fees, friend. Maybe take up managing. My captain doesn't like those stats showing up on his morning report. Makes him grouchy, and I don't like grouchy captains. Now who was it?"

"I told you, I ain't seen the fight. And folks ain't talkin'.

Just know some niggers lookin' for the cutter."

"Why aren't people talking? What's so special about this fight?"

The bartender glanced to both sides of the bar to make sure no customers were in earshot. The rookie was preoccupied watching the bar crowd. Castillo said something to me in a hushed voice.

"What?" I replied, not quite catching it above the din of the place.

"Word is the cutter was one of the Lopez brothers."

Suddenly I couldn't breathe, as if a giant hand was squeezing my heart.

Lopez!

God, I hadn't heard that name spoken in nearly two years. Not since the Fuller Hotel. Not since Derek's death. A name I had hoped I would never hear again. Its very utterance dredged up a tangle of raw emotions: rage, guilt, sadness, revenge, failure, justice, shame—nightmares.

"You okay, Joe?" the bartender said.

I must have gone pale. I grasped for oxygen and finally found some. I restarted my heart. "Yeah, I'm okay," I said. I hastily dug the keys to the patrol car out of my pocket and handed them to the rookie. "Get the car."

He squinted at me in surprise. "Where we going?"

"Just get it!"

The rookie looked hurt at my abruptness. But I had no reason to tell him about Lopez and the Fuller Hotel, or that Castillo was one of my best street sources. Good snitches were more valuable to a cop than his gun. I would no more give a snitch away to another cop than I would give my wife away to another man.

The rookie hesitated then pushed on out of the bar, glancing warily as angry eyes followed him.

I turned back to the bartender. "You sure the cutter was one of the Lopez brothers?"

"No, I ain't sure. Like I said, people ain't talkin' about it."

"Which one? Angelo or Antonio?"

"Who knows? Their own fuckin' mother can't tell 'em apart under a noon sun."

The Lopez brothers were identical twins. Purse snatching by age eleven, gang violence by age fifteen, burglaries and armed robberies by age seventeen. Both had served time, but it was nearly impossible to pin anything on them short of catching them in the act or getting fingerprints. They usually operated separately to avoid positive identification by their victims. Insolent bastards. Every cop on the force wanted their asses.

I wanted more than their asses. I wanted their souls. "What was the fight about?" I pressed.

"Dunno. Just heard he was lookin' for someone."

"For who?"

"Some boxer. Dunno the name."

"A Negro boxer?" That might explain the fight with the other Negroes.

Castillo didn't know if the boxer was Negro. He didn't know why Lopez was looking for the boxer. "You can bet it weren't to buy him a beer."

"If someone knows where to find this guy Lopez is looking for, how do they get word to Lopez?"

Castillo shook his head. "This is a ghost you don't want to find, Joe. Either of 'em."

"Where, Ruben?"

The bartender relented. "Sometimes you can find them at the *Los Compadres* Hotel. The manager lets the brothers hole up there."

I exited the bar. When Perdue drove up in the black and white, I shooed him over and slid in on the driver's side. Before I could put the vehicle into gear, however, the rookie said, "We got a call, Joe. Somebody reported a body on the tracks near the flour mill."

CHAPTER 2

Abody. Swell. Just what we needed at this hour. I didn't want to deal with a body. Even if it was the boxer Lopez was looking for. I only wanted Lopez. "We got another call to take care of first, kid."

I put the black and white into gear and headed for the *Los Compadres* Hotel.

"But it's a body, Joe."

Eagerness had crept back into his voice, mixed with trepidation. This could be his first body. On his first night of duty. Hell, some rookies didn't catch their first stiff for weeks, months. Personally, I had seen enough bodies as a cop. I had seen enough bodies in the war. I didn't need to see any more.

"It's probably just some drifter run over by a train," I said. "We'll be filing paperwork the rest of the shift. Maybe it's even a false report. People do that a lot these days. Let the next shift find it."

The rookie twisted toward me. "I bet it's that missing banker!"

"The flour mill is down in The Bottoms, kid. What the hell would the banker be doing in The Bottoms?"

Italians had settled The Bottoms in the late 1800s, living in tents and river shanties. The South Platte River's flood plain gave them rich soil for a checkerboard of vegetable patches, and they had scratched out a living, hawking their produce downtown. Eventually they had abandoned the area. Today,

The Bottoms was home to the flour mill, a few decrepit ware-houses, a tangle of railroad tracks, hobos, and Hooverville shacks long abandoned from the Great Depression.

"Come on, Joe," the rookie pleaded. "They told us to check it out."

"If there is a body, it's not going anywhere. We got an ass-hole to catch first."

I pushed the black and white as hard as I could, though that wasn't saying much. It was a vintage Plymouth with enough miles on it to have driven to Normandy Beach and back a few dozen times.

The engine had been overhauled twice, but it still ran like a bad vacuum cleaner.

"Aren't we out of our precinct?" the rookie asked hesitantly after a few blocks.

"Not for this guy."

ℰↃℰↃ

The *Los Compadres* Hotel was the kind of place where if you wanted clean sheets you brought your own. A neon sign with only half its letters glowing hung from the two-story brick building at Walnut and Twenty-Ninth. I parked out of sight half a block down the street and we hoofed it to the hotel.

"There's an alley 'round back," I said as we hurried along Walnut. "Pick a nice dark spot and cover the back of the build-ing. And watch yourself."

"Cover it for what, Joe?" Tension scarred every word.

"For whoever comes out haulin' ass."

I didn't tell him I didn't like hotels and the Lopez brothers. I didn't tell him that the last time I had encountered one of the Lopez brothers in a hotel—I still didn't know which brother—I'd left behind a dead partner.

The rookie disappeared into the darkness. I found the night clerk asleep on a shabby couch in the dinky lobby, a girlie magazine draped over his face. The place smelled of beer and piss. I woke him with my gun barrel. His brown eyes grew huge and stayed that way even after he saw my uniform.

I put a finger to my lips. "What room is Lopez in?" I whispered.

He shook his head and said in a strangled voice there was no Lopez here.

I put my .38 to his nose.

"He's not here," the clerk said tonelessly. "He skipped out yesterday. Without paying."

"Which Lopez was it?"

"Dunno."

"What room?"

"Twenty-seven. But he's gone, I tell ya."

"Give me a key."

"I tell ya, he skipped out. Took the damn key with 'im. Ain't got no key made yet."

I draped the magazine back over his face. "I hear you move from this couch and I'll see you in jail for aiding and abetting a known felon."

I quietly climbed the stairs to the second floor and found Room 27 at the far end of the hallway, next to the fire escape and the community bathroom. The window to the fire escape was wide open, but the hallway was still a sweat bath. I tiptoed to the edge of Room 27 and put my ear to the door.

Nothing. Down the hallway, Benny Goodman's "Stompin' at the Savoy" played faintly on a radio. I cautiously tried the doorknob. Locked. I pressed my back against the wall. My gun felt clammy and foreign in my hands. My breathing muffled Goodman.

The next moment I was in the middle of the tiny room, the door open, dangling from one hinge.

The room was empty. I poked around for clues Lopez might have left behind, though there wasn't much to search: a Murphy bed, a cheap dresser, a sagging stuffed chair.

Footsteps echoed on the fire escape. I bolted into the hallway to the window and aimed my gun at a shadowy figure on the stairs below.

"Hold it, Lopez!"

The man jammed his hands into the air. "Joe! Joe! It's me!

Moroni. It's me! For God's sake, don't shoot!"

Every muscle in my body sagged and I lowered my gun.

"What the hell you doing on the damn fire escape, Perdue? I coulda killed you, you dumb-ass! I told you to stay in the alley."

"I got nervous. You were gone so long I—"

"I was only a coupla minutes."

"Well, it felt a lot longer than that. Then I heard crashing up there. You get who you were looking for?"

"Naw. He's gone."

"Who is this Lopez name you yelled, Joe?"

"Just a shitbird. Look, go on back to the car and bring it around front. I'll be down in a minute."

I gave him the keys and he hurried into the darkness. I prowled around the room until the manager came in, whining about the busted door, and I told him he wouldn't have a problem if he'd quit harboring criminals. When I got down to the black and white, the rookie was standing by the passenger side.

"Can we look for the body now?" he asked.

Maybe that was best tonight. Maybe a body on the tracks would take my mind off Lopez.

"Sure, kid," I said. "Let's go find a body."

CHAPTER 3

We negotiated several dark dirt streets and parked in the shadow of the huge Pride of the Rockies flour mill near the Twentieth Street Viaduct. Our headlights splayed across a double row of tracks twenty yards in front of us. The caller to dispatch had reported seeing the body on the tracks near the mill.

The caller hadn't bothered to leave a name. Nor how he'd happened to have come across the body. Nor why he wasn't going to hang around to show us exactly where it was.

As the dark outlines of the viaduct and mill loomed above us, we walked to the tracks and stood silently for a moment. I listened for the usual sounds on the rails, but the only thing I could hear was the distant rumbling of a lone diesel engine working in the CB&Q coach yards north of us. The air was cooler here than at Castillo's bar, but still warm enough that a light westerly breeze filled our noses with the stench of the nearby river bottom, creosote, and impending rain.

I outlined a search pattern and warned the rookie to watch out for passing trains. "This is CB&Q's main track and those fuckers roar up fast on you. I don't need two bodies out here tonight."

We worked our way south, I on one set of tracks, the rookie on the parallel set. The tracks glimmered from the glare of our headlights and the mill lights. I stumbled along the ties, not well placed for a man's stride. The beams of our flashlights bobbed in the darkness like fireflies. We didn't find much—beer bottles, old newspapers, used rubbers, and a Blackhawk comic book, one of the newer ones where Blackhawk flies jets instead of props.

We walked past the mill to the viaduct, stopped, swapped tracks, and retraced our steps, eventually crossing north beyond the glare of our headlights. The tracks grew darker here under the cloudy sky, and they curved off to the northwest toward the CB&Q yards. We had gone nearly a hundred yards, and I was beginning to figure we were on a wild goose chase, when the rookie gasped loudly.

"Jesus Christ! Joe!—Joe!"

I cut over to his track. The body lay face down on the embankment, a dozen yards south of a single-arm semaphore. Most of the body, anyway. Train wheels had passed over the middle of the skull, severing off the top of the head, which now lay between the two rails.

"Jesus!" groaned the rookie. He popped a LifeSaver into his mouth. "The train musta…" His voice faltered.

"The head looks like a Lincoln penny."

"What?"

"When you were a kid, didn't you and your friends leave pennies on the track for the trains to run over? Flattened the shit outa 'em."

"Jesus."

"Probably the *Denver Zephyr*. All those passenger cars, one right after the other."

"Jesus."

"It okay, you say 'Jesus' like that? I mean, being a Mormon and all?"

The rookie didn't reply except for ragged breathing.

"It's okay, kid, you wanna chuck. All rookies are allowed to chuck once during probation. Especially over a body like this."

"I'm all right," he said, his voice unsteady.

"I won't tell anyone. Just don't toss your cookies all over the stiff. The ME frowns on that."

"I—I ain't gonna throw up!" he stammered, sucking in

deep breaths. He popped in two more LifeSavers. He wasn't looking in the direction of the body.

I flashed my torch on Perdue's face. Pale as celery heart. "Suit yourself. But don't wait until the ME gets here to puke. He loves to razz rookies."

I swung the light back to the body. The head resembled a pumpkin tossed out onto Colfax Avenue a month after Halloween. Dark pools of congealing fluids reflected dully in the light. All that appeared recognizable as a human head was the dark matted hair. I played my light over the rest of the body. Male, probably Mexican, shirtless, in a pair of loose khaki pants and black-laced shoes.

"Is it him? Do you think it's him?" the rookie asked, still not looking at the body, yet suddenly animated.

"Who?"

"The missing banker."

"Naw. Too young. Too poorly dressed. Looks Mexican."

"Nuts."

"Yeah, too bad. You missed your big chance to make the papers your first night. My bet is our vic's a jug heister. You can smell the booze from here. Tried to jump an empty and missed. Let's go call it in."

"Okay," the rookie said faintly. He rustled up his nerves and glanced at the body. Then at me. "Maybe it's that guy you were looking for. Is he a Mexican?"

"Yeah, but—" I stopped. I hadn't thought of someone getting the better of one of the Lopez brothers. Yet if the Negroes hunting for him had caught up with him...

"You got a pocketknife?" I asked the rookie.

"What?"

"A pocketknife! You got a damn pocketknife?"

The rookie dug into his pocket and came up with a knife. I opened the blade and bent over the body. I ripped the blade along the left pants leg, from the pocket seam nearly to the knee.

"What are you doing, Joe?"

I parted the split pants with both hands and twisted the

lower torso to expose the front of the thigh. "Shine your flashlight on this."

"What?"

"Shine your damn flashlight here!"

His light fanned across the exposed thigh, the beam unsteady. The skin under the pants leg was smooth, no scars. I let go of the leg and stood up. That ruled out the Lopez brother I was looking for, though it could be the other one.

The rookie stared at me as I handed back his pocketknife. "Why did you do that?"

"Nothing you need to tell the dicks about."

"You disturbed the evidence," he said, as if *I* were the rookie.

"They won't care about it, anyway. The guy's just a hobo."

The rookie took in a few deep breaths and looked back at the body. Then he said, sudden curiosity in his voice, "Kind of a strange-looking hobo."

"Why's that?"

"He looks in awfully good shape, don't you think?" He cleared his throat to keep from gagging. "I mean, I don't know much about hobos, but I wouldn't think many of them would have a body sculpted like that."

"Coulda been a strong field hand, hitching to another picking site. We've found others down on the tracks that way. Not always dead, but busted up pretty good. Missing limbs, that sorta thing."

"I dunno. I've been around a lotta gyms. Looks like a weightlifter to me. He's too well-defined, too symmetrical. Athletic looking."

The boxer! The boxer Lopez was looking for! Maybe the body could lead me to Lopez. "Athletic or not, it didn't do him much good against a train," I said.

The rookie swallowed hard and stepped closer to the body. He swept his light back and forth across the ties, stopped a moment in curiosity, then began to widen his sweep intently, as if searching for that flattened Lincoln penny.

"What the hell you looking for?" I asked.

"His hands."

"Have you tried at the end of his arms?"

"They ain't there, Joe."

I swung my flashlight to the arms. I hadn't paid attention to them before. The rookie was right. The stiff's hands were missing. The train wheels had cleanly severed them at the wrists, leaving bloody stumps against the rail. Yet the hands hadn't fallen inside the rails. They were gone.

We scoured the area around the body on the chance the train had dragged or thrown the hands, but found nothing.

"I think somebody dragged him to these tracks," the rookie said, studying the earth around the body's feet. "I can make out drag marks." He looked at me in the weak light, suddenly breathless with excitement. "This wasn't an accident, Joe. Somebody murdered the guy."

"That's a helluva leap."

"It would explain the missing hands. He's got fingerprints on file somewhere. Probably a criminal record. Somebody doesn't want us to know who he is. That's why the face is so smashed up, too. I bet there's no ID on him, either."

"You learn all this detective work at the academy?" I had been told the rookie had been the best marksman in his class, but that was all I knew about him.

The rookie looked embarrassed. "It's just what I see, that's all."

"Never jump to conclusions. People do all kinds of strange shit to bodies they didn't kill."

We stood quietly several feet from the corpse, our flashlights dangling limp at our sides, illuminating our dirty shoes.

"It's gonna rain soon," I said, rolling my stiff shoulder. "We better call in the ME and the dicks." I tried to move away from the body but couldn't move my legs. "You call it in, kid."

The rookie hurried off toward the black and white, whose headlights still stared forlornly out into the empty rail yard.

"Hey," I yelled after him. "Tell 'em to alert the railroad people or we'll have another choo-choo running over what's left of this guy. And douse those goddamn lights!"

Long after the rookie had gone, long after I heard him

throw up his LifeSavers in the anonymity of the inky shadows, long after he doused the headlights, I still stood on the tracks, immobilized, as though welded to the iron rails. I was going to stand here until the next train came through and squashed me as flat as the stiff. I wished we had never gotten the call and found the body. It was a good chance the body was linked to Lopez. But hunting for Lopez was a dangerous road to travel, a road that would only bring back the nightmares I had struggled so hard to bury.

Almost against my will, I shined my light on the body again. Jesus, that head. And the missing hands. I had seen worse in the war, of course. Appalling what machine guns and artillery shells can do to the human body.

I thought about Derek Flemming. I hadn't thought of him for months, and I didn't want to start again.

I looked away from the body. I had this thing about stiffs. I never remembered their faces. Once the meat wagon hauled them away, I never remembered their faces. I learned a long time ago in this job—no, I had learned it before that, in the war—that it didn't pay to remember the faces of the dead. Best if you put distance between them and you. Not that this guy had a face left to remember.

I didn't remember Derek's face anymore.

But I remembered what was done to Derek. I remembered who did it.

You would have thought neither of the Lopez brothers would have shown his face in town again, let alone returned and gotten in a crummy street fight. But I had seen such behavior in criminals before, ones who disappeared after they had committed a horrific crime. They went out of town, out of state, went into hiding. Yet inevitably they returned, like moths to flame. They came back because it was where their families or their buddies were, or because it was where they felt at home. They came back because they figured the law had forgotten about them, that we no longer cared what horrors they had committed.

I had tried to forget since The Fuller Hotel. Yet now the Lopez name had returned, unbidden, unexpected. Now this stiff, this murder, which one of them may have committed. As much as I didn't want to, I still cared what they'd done. I cared about what they may have done here. This time I could no longer turn away.

I owed Derek. I owed myself.

CHAPTER 4

I recognized the familiar schlumpy outline of Detective Luther Bock in his trademark fedora as he emerged from his car and picked his way across the tracks. He stopped a few feet from the headless body, not saying a word to us, staring at the mutilated flesh while he fastidiously blew his nose in a white handkerchief the size of a tablecloth. He stuffed the handkerchief deep into a pants pocket and regarded us, casually, as though he had done all he was going to do on this case. He focused on me.

"Dodgers got the shit beat out of 'em by the Pirates tonight, Stryker," he gloated as only a Yankee fan could.

"Still beats having Bucky Harris for a manager."

He harrumphed and looked at Perdue. "This the rookie?"

I introduced them. Bock nodded but didn't offer his hand. He said to the rookie, "Got yourself teamed up with the Denver Kid, eh? Bet he's got the case already solved."

Lou Sheppard, the crime reporter for *The Rocky Mountain News*, had written all that crap about me my rookie year, tagging me the "Denver Kid." He had even sold stories about me to *True Detective* and *Police Gazette*. The prefect way to endear a rookie to the veterans. Now I was an aging gunfighter, trying to live down an outdated, exaggerated legend. A legend that had ended with a bullet in the shoulder and a dead partner.

"We're just preserving the crime scene, Bock," I snapped.

"'Just preserving the crime scene,'" he mimicked. "I like

that, Stryker. Real swell." He stared at the rookie. "Well, kid, keep your eyes in the back of your head when you're 'round this guy." A smirk started to spread across his face, but he abruptly had to blow his nose, destroying the effect. "Some shit's in the air," he mumbled. He stuffed away the handkerchief and dug out a crumpled red pack of Pall Malls from inside his sport coat. "Smokes?" he asked the rookie, making a point not to offer me any. The rookie shook his head.

"The kid's Mormon, Bock. Show some respect."

The detective lit his cigarette and blew out a long stream of smoke through his nostrils. "So what's all this shit about a murder?" he said. "Just looks like a train ran over another fucking bum."

"Ask the rookie. He noticed it." Maybe Sheppard would crown the rookie the new Denver Kid and get everybody off my back.

The rookie explained what we had—and had not—found, though he left out my ripping open the man's pant leg. The dick glanced in the direction of the stiff but didn't move. His eyes blinked rapidly. Like a toad in a hailstorm, my father would say.

"Missing hands ain't no felony," Bock observed with thirteen years of accumulated wisdom on the force.

"It would be if somebody took them away intentionally to cover up a murder, sir," the rookie ventured nervously.

"Betcha it was rats drug off his hands," the dick offered. "Some of 'em down in these yards are as big as Buicks."

"*Both* hands?" the rookie said.

"They work in packs."

A train rumbled through on a nearby set of tracks, shaking the ground below our feet. We had to yell to hear each other.

Bock said, "Maybe it was kids playing down here."

"Right," I said, beginning to feel annoyed. I always got to feeling annoyed around Bock. "You used to do that when you were a kid, didn't you, Bock? Steal severed hands."

"Don't get smart with me, Stryker. Sick bastards do all kinds of weird shit these days. You been around long enough to know that. World's outa whack. Ain't been the same since the war. Guys rape old ladies, kill just for the thrill of killing, fuck the dead. Makes a man wanna go away and become a monk so's he can find some kinda peace. So what's the big deal about stealing some stiff's hands after a train *accidentally* runs over him?"

I rubbed my shoulder. Bock had the mug of a terrier and the disposition of an underfed junkyard dog. He was lazy and often downright cruel—the kind of cop that gave cops a bad name. But I agreed with him on this one. The world hadn't been the same since the war. *My* world hadn't been the same. Like many who came to Denver after the war, I wasn't from here. I had served in the CCCs before the war, mostly in Michigan planting trees and building fire roads. I had enlisted in 1942 and trained at Camp Carson down in Colorado Springs. I liked the Colorado weather and the mountains. When I came back from Europe, I came to Denver for no particular reason, other than the city was a place to start fresh. I couldn't go back from where I had come. Not that it had been a bad place full of bad memories, or had changed in some bad way. I couldn't return to it because *I* had changed.

"We don't have answers, Bock," I said. "Answers are your bailiwick."

"Probably another hobo took 'em. Coupla hands make a mighty tasty addition to the stew pot."

The rookie grimaced.

The dick grinned. "You check for ID yet?"

"We haven't touched the body," the rookie said a bit too quickly.

Bock knelt over the stiff and rifled through the pockets like an experienced dip working a crowd. He didn't say anything about the ripped pants. "Nothin' in here. Ain't no railroader. Can't find a watch. Never knew a railroader without his watch. Even a grease-ball."

"Sir, would a—" The rookie hesitated. "—would a guy empty his pockets before accidentally getting run over by a train?"

Bock looked up. "You're as smart as Stryker here, I can see."

"Come on, Bock, ease up," I said. "It's his first day. Nobody should see shit like this his first day."

The detective glared at me then turned back to the rookie. "The fact is, kid, a grease-ball like this might have had nothing to put in his pockets. Lotta spics 'round here with empty pockets."

"The rookie noticed drag marks," I said, suddenly feeling protective of the rookie. "Which suggests someone dragged him to the tracks. Check his shoe tops for scuff marks."

Bock lifted one foot and shined his light on the toe. I could tell by the way he dropped it and said nothing that it revealed drag marks.

"And another thing," I said. "The way the hands are severed. Both neatly right at the wrist. Like someone laid them there. Not like a drunk crawling his way onto the tracks."

I didn't know why I was arguing with Bock, sticking up for the rookie. It wasn't my job to determine if it were murder or not. If Bock wanted to piss it off as an accident, it made no difference to me. I just wanted to find out if the body might lead me to Lopez.

The detective didn't say anything, but suddenly leaned over and poked around the tear in the man's pants. "Helluva rip in these pants," he said.

"The man was dragged to the tracks, sir," the rookie quickly said. "I'm sure that tore them."

Bock looked at him and said sarcastically, "You're sure, are you?"

The rookie fell silent.

"The man was a hobo, Bock," I interjected. "It's not like he bought his clothes at the Denver Dry."

The detective stood wearily and wiped his nose again. "All right, kid, call the flash boys. Tell dispatch to send some smoke eaters with a pumper and a searchlight on it. Stryker, check out the hobos around here. You know where they hang out. Rustle me up somebody to talk to."

I walked three hundred yards north and flushed out two guys in an open boxcar, sleeping off a Bell jar of homemade brew. I brought them to Bock. They claimed to have seen nothing or anyone suspicious around the tracks. But then they hadn't remembered much of the night. They had unloaded trucks for three hours in the warehouse district, spent the cash on dinner, and bought the jar of booze from a guy behind one of the bars. They didn't remember much after that. One of them threw up looking at the stiff, but that didn't spark any useful memories.

The meat wagon arrived, fresh from patching up two accountants who had gotten into a brawl in their office over a woman. "He's dead," announced one of the attendants as if reporting a final baseball score. He went back to the meat wagon to cool his heels until the medical examiner arrived to make his investigation.

A flash boy arrived and photographed the stiff and the ground around him and anything else Bock pointed to. The detective crudely sketched the scene on a piece of graph paper, directing me and the rookie to walk off distances from the body to relevant landmarks. The ME arrived and, while he sorted out the remains of the crushed skull, the smoke eaters showed up, cursing us for rousting them out of bed in the middle of the night just to look for missing hands. They sprayed the searchlight on their pumper over the tracks and we began combing an area the size of a football field. Two bored cops stopped by, so we recruited them for our search. We found more beer bottles and cigarette butts and old newspapers, but no more Blackhawk comics and no hands or anything suggesting a murder weapon.

I was standing out of the glare of the searchlight, taking a leak, when Lou Sheppard walked up in his rumpled suit and short tie. The reporter's right hand carried his ever-present four-by-five Speed Graphic with its flash attachment.

"Is that what I'm supposed to be doing a story on, Joe?" Sheppard said, pointing to me hanging out.

"Sure."

"Doesn't strike me as particularly newsworthy."

"Some women thought it was."

"Won't rate the front page. Maybe the society section. Of course, a picture would help." Sheppard raised his camera.

I hurriedly zipped up. "You're a fuckin' pervert, Sheppard."

Despite the exaggerated prose he had written about me my first two years on the force, I liked the man. He was a small, hard-eyed police reporter, as quick and smart as police reporters come, which isn't necessarily saying a lot. He rarely slept, and when he did, it was on a table at the police station or in an empty cell in the county jail so he could be ready for a call. Except for the day the deputies locked him up as a joke, Lou was everywhere, day or night.

He had a family, but I don't know when the hell they saw him. Lou had nerve, too. He'd raced to every call on a rickety old motorcycle and had exposed himself to more than one crossfire to get a good photo or a better description of events. Though officially not a press photographer, he always carried a camera with him. "Photographers are never around when you need them," he grumbled. He was something of a lone wolf among his less ambitious and less skilled cronies. Maybe it was why I like him.

"What's with the smoke eaters, Joe?" he asked, motioning toward the fire engine. A dozen silhouettes moved slowly in the engine's harsh spotlight, like a half-formed dream. A light rain began to fall.

"Talk to Bock, Lou. It's his catch."

"Bock's a royal turd. You make better copy."

"Yeah, I got a rookie with me tonight, thinks I'm Wyatt Earp, thanks to you."

"The price of fame, Joe. So you gonna tell me what the hell you guys are looking for?"

I told him about the dead Mexican, what we had found. He scribbled notes, hunched over to keep his camera and notebook dry from the rain. He didn't seem to care much about getting his suit wet, and if I owned a suit like his, I wouldn't care much either.

I asked him whether he had heard that one of the Lopez brothers was back in town.

The reporter jerked his head. "Is that what this stiff is about?"

"I dunno. But I got a tip earlier tonight one of 'em might be around. Don't know which one."

"No shit. News to me."

He started walking back toward the knot of men huddled in the rain. They had turned off the searchlight and hauled away the body. "The hands, Lou," I said, going after him. "Don't write about the hands. That's our little secret. Our little way of screening out the wacko confessors."

"Don't worry, Joe," Sheppard said, and then I lost his words in the rain and the approaching rumble of a switcher.

"What?" I yelled after him.

He waited until I caught up. "I said, don't worry. The stiff's a Mex. He won't rate space in the want ads."

Sheppard scurried off. The rain came harder. It had been a dry spring. Paula and I had driven out onto Colorado's eastern grasslands the week before and everything was parched. I tipped my face skyward and opened my mouth, my arms slack at my sides, letting the rain quench the terrible dryness that had overcome me ever since I had heard the name Lopez.

CHAPTER 5

The rain had stopped and the boxy outline of my house emerged against the dawn sky as I edged my car into the driveway. The house was one of those post-war ranch-style prefabs springing up by the block around town. Paula had wanted to stay in our buffet apartment and stash more money into savings—even with the GI bill, the house payments made our budget look as thin as our newly seeded grass poking up through the burlap bags. Without my working extra hours as a mechanic at Carl's Auto Repair, we'd never have made it. But the way I figured it, a man couldn't properly raise a family without a home. When children finally did come along, I didn't want them living like olives in a jar.

I parked in the garage and slipped into the house as soundlessly as possible so as not to disturb Paula sleeping in the front bedroom. The stale smell of leftovers, cigarettes, and fresh paint lingered in the kitchen. I had worked through dinner at Carl's last night and gone directly from there to pull my shift, so Paula had eaten alone again—broccoli and cheese and half a grapefruit, judging by the leftovers in the sink. A plastic bowl half full of cold, greasy popcorn sat on the metal-trimmed linoleum kitchen table. Paula made popcorn nearly every evening, nibbling at the leftovers the next day.

I munched on several stale handfuls before pushing the bowl aside and sitting down at the table, exhausted. I rubbed my eyes with my knuckles. My back ached from stooping over the tracks and peering into patches of weeds for missing hands. Images of the headless body, the glare of the pumper lights, and Lou Sheppard scribbling on his notepad in the rain tumbled over each other. But I was too tired to want to think about them, about what they might mean for me. I distractedly started flipping through a *Saturday Evening Post*. The cover pictured a man coming in the door from work, his wife puckered up to kiss him as he eyed dinner on the stove. I shoved the magazine aside. The scalloped white edge of a photograph emerged, half hidden under the magazine.

I tugged at the photograph, and with it came a letter dated three days ago. I recognized the small, cramped handwriting. It belonged to Paula's younger sister by two years, Eloise, second oldest in their family of five. I remembered her at our wedding as a small, stern woman—too stern for a woman so young.

Paula had nodded at my observation, remarking that everyone in the family saw Eloise as the reincarnation of their mother, a stern, deeply religious woman who had died of pneumonia when Paula was fourteen. "Eloise is mother's way of keeping tabs on us," Paula had said, with that mixture of love and hate she always conveyed when she spoke of her mother.

While Eloise was the one in the family most profoundly affected by their mother's death, it was Paula, as the oldest, who mothered her younger brothers and sisters, what with her father spending most of his time on the road as a pharmaceutical salesman and whoremonger.

The photograph showed Eloise's husband, Allen, grinning as he helped one of their sons balance on a bicycle, a mixture of terror and delight on the boy's face. I didn't remember the boy's name. They already had three and were probably working on a fourth. They lived in Lincoln, Nebraska. I hadn't seen them since our wedding three years ago.

I set the photograph aside, wondering whether I would ever have children to teach how to ride a bicycle. I picked up the letter and began to read.

Dear Paula:

You haven't written for a while. Are you feeling okay? Are you pregnant? I do so pray you are. Having a child would answer so many of your frustrations and prayers. I know you feel raising the four of us was mother duty enough, that you have other ambitions for your life. But my children have been God's blessing to me. Have you been taking hot baths and monitoring your temperature like I told you?

Your new job as a hospital volunteer sounds rewarding. Perhaps it will relieve some of your boredom. Even with the kids, I'm doing volunteer work at church, and I find it spiritually and emotionally fulfilling. I wish you and Joe would join a good Lutheran church near you. You wrote a while back of not having many friends. A church is such a wonderful source for developing lasting and deep relationships with couples your own age. Most of them have children, too (maybe some of their good fortune will rub off, ha, ha). One cannot deny the need for spiritual comfort, either.

I thought you might like the picture of Allen Jr. learning to ride his bike. Don't you think he's growing into the spitting image of his fath—

I tossed the letter away and went into our bedroom. Paula lay asleep on her side, her legs and arms pulled up around her tightly, though the room was warm and she had only a sheet loosely pulled over her. The book she had been reading lay on the floor where it had fallen off the bed after she had drifted to sleep. *The Naked and the Dead.* Her reading a war novel had surprised me at first, though she had served in military intelligence and she still spoke fondly of her wartime experiences. She said it was a great book and I should read it. Believe me, reliving the war was the last thing I wanted in my life.

On the nightstand rested another souvenir of her war

years—an ashtray full of half-smoked cigarettes. She had taken up smoking, as had many, to take her mind off the boredom and the pain of the war. I understood that. But she had continued smoking after coming home, and I had noticed after I had returned stateside that many women, who had never gone to war, were smoking, too. I understood its attraction, its statement of independence, but damn, it just didn't look right for a woman to smoke.

I moved soundlessly across the room, stepping over a spot where the wood floor squeaked, and pulled the heavy black shades against the strengthening dawn light. Paula refused to pull them when she went to bed—her way of protesting my awkward hours and my work. I undressed in the darkness, the only noise the clink of the belt buckle and the creaking leather of my Sam Browne belt.

I sensed Paula was awake, her hazel eyes silently on me. She rarely spoke until I climbed into bed, as if the creaking of the bedsprings and the rustling of the sheets awakened her. But her breathing was always too irregular, and when she did speak, her voice never sounded convincingly groggy.

Naked, I scratched the hair on my chest, which itched from the chafing of my uniform, and crawled wearily into bed.

Paula moaned dully and rolled against me in a short nightie. "Hi," she said.

"Hi, hon." I fumbled to find her lips in the dark, missed, and ended up kissing her soft brown hair.

"You're home late."

"Breakin' in a rookie." She said nothing, but I sensed she suspected more had gone on tonight than merely breaking in a rookie. "We found a body. Dragged past our shift."

I didn't want to mention the body, but I knew she would read about it in the newspaper, anyway. Sheppard would include my name, even if the story only made the want ads.

She sat up sharply on one elbow. "That missing banker?"

"God, Paula, you're as bad as the rookie. No, it wasn't the banker. It was just a Mexican."

I should tell her the Lopez brothers had surfaced again, that the body on the tracks might be connected to the killer who had changed my life. Our life. But I let it go. It would only upset her. No, it would scare the hell out of her. She feared the name as much as I did. Besides, why worry her over something that might prove to be nothing?

"So what happened?" Paula wanted me to believe she cared about my work. She wanted herself to believe she cared. But the truth was, she hated my being a cop—almost as much as she hated being the wife of a cop.

"I don't want to talk about it. It's late. The man's dead. Talking won't change that."

Like Derek. Talking about Derek would never bring him back either.

∽∾∽

District Two's locker and roll-call room was the usual madhouse at shift change: benches scraping against linoleum, lockers slamming, uniformed and plainclothesmen coming and going in a room the size of a ma-and-pa café.

Sergeant Patrick Mulcahey was holding court from the watch commander's desk, flanked by a large bulletin board covered with thumb-tacked "Wanted" flyers, work rules, and crime reports.

The thin, dark-haired Irishman finished running through the squawk reports from the swing shift.

"Last item," Mulcahey said. "The gang squad's on patrol tonight, fellas, so leave the street gangs alone unless you're called in to assist, or a clear-cut crime is in progress. We sent a few greasers to the hospital the last time we ran this operation, so I think they're getting the message. And for Chrissake, make sure any drunks you pick up aren't our own men—like happened last time."

The room burst into laughter. Benches scraped as our shift headed for the streets.

"I pulled goon squad duty coupla weeks ago," Nathan Tradd said to me and Perdue at the doorway. Tradd had just finished working his shift. He grinned. "A lot of fun."

"Busting kneecaps with batons doesn't strike me as fun," I said.

"Sure as hell is effective. Ever seen a greaser with a busted knee trying to roll a drunk?" He extended a hand and dangled the keys to the black and white in his fingers. "Different car tonight. Engine's got a funny noise."

I snatched the keys. "Maybe you shoulda poured some damn oil into it."

Maintenance on the black and whites was always a game of musical chairs.

Tradd glanced at Perdue with a *what-the-fuck's-his-beef?* rise to his bushy eyebrows, and said, grinning conspiratorially at the rookie, "Hell, you're the mechanic, Joe."

Two quarts of oil stopped the knocking in the car, and the rookie and I hit the street, in short order settling two noisy domestics and talking to an old woman who claimed a man with a missing ear had accosted her. I figured we would be back on one of the domestics before the night was over. He'd have killed her or she'd have killed him. It was a tossup.

I called in a coffee break and drove the black and white to a neighborhood just out of our precinct. "Whattya doing, Joe?" Perdue asked edgily.

"I need to talk to someone."

"Who?"

"A gang leader."

"The sergeant warned us off the gangs tonight."

"This can't wait."

I passed the gas station I was looking for on Marion Street and swung around the block. The vacant station sat on a corner. A streetlight—the only one working on the block—cast a yellowish haze over the cracked driveway where weeds flourished. Graffiti covered the white stucco walls and the plywood covering the windows, warning in that boxy, stilted style so peculiar to graffiti that this was *Vato Locos* turf. They had scrawled VL on walls around for blocks, marking off their territory like a dog marking off his territory with piss.

The rookie nervously popped a LifeSaver into his mouth. "Who you looking for?"

"A guy named *El Perro*."

I'd put out the word I wanted to talk to him.

"What's that mean, *El Perro*?"

"The Dog."

"How will you find him?"

"We don't. He'll find us. If he wants to."

I circled the block one more time before pulling into the station and parking by a set of pumps whose glass dials had been smashed and their black hoses ripped off.

I stared into the shadows of the station. "See anyone?"

"No. And I hope I don't." The rookie's teeth nervously worked the LifeSaver.

I stepped out of the cruiser. Street traffic was nonexistent. Crickets and two distant radios turned up loud were the only sounds. "No flashlights," I warned Perdue as he climbed out.

I walked around to his side of the car and leaned against the hood. We waited. Maybe the goon squad had already found them. Suddenly, shadows in the gas station moved. First one, then two, then three figures appeared. I swore they stepped right out of the walls.

"Keep your hand off your gun," I whispered as the rookie reached for his service revolver.

I suspected two or three more *pachucos* still hung back in the dark. Like a smart general, *El Perro* never deployed all his soldiers in one place at one time.

A story flashed in my mind, one I had heard in 1943 when I was training with the 104th Infantry Division at Camp Carson near Colorado Springs. The story went that a GI had been castrated in a local Mexican bar for making eyes at a senorita, and they had nailed his balls to the doorway as a warning. Smoke by the MPs to scare us away from certain parts of town, no doubt, but smoke that never had completely cleared my head.

The three shadows became two teenagers and a man in his mid-twenties with black hair pushed up in a pompadour. The man stepped forward, the other two hanging back, casually passing a can of beer between them. Gang members were like that. If one *pachuco* had a beer, they all drank from it. They shared everything—cigarettes, cars, shanks, zip guns, women. A regular family, they were.

"You wanted to talk to me 'bout somethin', Officer Stryker," the man said.

El Perro, aka Willie Flores, was big for a Mexican, right down to the steel plates on the toes of his polished, heavy-soled shoes to add a little extra punch to the groin kicks. The padded shoulders of his dark sport coat and the high-waisted baggy purple pants that looked two sizes too large and cuffed tight made him look even larger—an odd clothing style he had brought with him from the barrios of Los Angeles.

Flores had organized the *Locos* when he was thirteen, shortly after moving from Los Angeles. Fathered a girl at fifteen. Now he was an old man in the gang world. When he "retired," the gang would be led by Willie's brother, Jesse, one of the two teenagers standing in the shadows—if Jesse lived that long. His nickname was *Perro Enojado*—Mad Dog. Always looking for another gang to fight. Fighting gave him life. When he couldn't find another gang to fight, he would fight members in his own gang.

"I'm looking for the Lopez brothers, Willie. Word is one of them surfaced again."

"I heard that."

"You know where I can find them, being you were pals once?"

Like *El Perro*, both Lopez brothers had been raised in the gang world—a rival gang to the *Locos*—until they'd moved up to bigger and better gigs, like robbing hotels and killing cops. One of them—who knew which one—had crippled one of *El Perro*'s gang pals. In retaliation, the *Locos* had put some of the Lopez *pachucos* in the hospital. But they'd never touched either of the twins. *El Perro* wanted Lopez almost as much as I did.

"Don't know nothin' about where he is," Flores said. He twisted his back slightly, loosening it. His back had been stiff ever since the surgeon left behind a .22 caliber bullet fragment that lay close to his spine.

"I doubt that," I said.

"One of my *Locos* got his knees broke last week," Flores said.

We'd entered trade talks. I wanted something, he wanted something.

"That's what he gets for rolling drunks and old ladies," I said.

"He never done none of that shit. We don't do that shit. Coupla your goons busted his knees just 'cause he was a *Loco*."

I thought of Tradd. "I can look into it for you."

"That don't mean much."

"The goon squad's taking batting practice tonight," I offered.

The *pachuco* nodded his head in appreciation of the warning. "They been out a lotta nights lately."

"Maybe I can get a schedule for you. Where do I find Lopez?"

"Told you, I don't know."

"This is kinda one-sided, my friend."

"I heard he got in a fight with some niggers."

"That's not news to me."

The *pachuco* turned slightly and the weak street light glimmered off a silver cross that dangled on a silver chain over his creased shirt. "Heard he was lookin' for someone."

"Still old news."

"A boxer."

El Perro was getting to what was on his mind. We just had to do our dance.

"I already found the boxer. A Mexican. A big Mexican. He looked like you except for the fact he was dead."

"He weren't no Mexican."

That was news. "What was he then?"

"Indian."

"Like a redskin?"

"Some kind like that."

"He got a name?"

"Art Red Owl."

The name meant nothing to me. *El Perro* didn't know anything more about him other than the guy apparently was some local palooka who'd been in hiding.

"Hiding from Lopez?" I asked.

He nodded.

"Why was Lopez looking for him? Why kill him?"

The gang leader didn't know. Killing was what Lopez did. A hobby. "But we're looking for him, too," he said. "He owes us a debt he ain't paid."

"Leave him alone, Willie. This man doesn't pay debts, he collects them. If you find out where he is, get word to me. I'll take care of him. That's my job."

Flores shook his head. "My gang is one thing you gringos don't get to control."

"You don't want to go after Lopez, *muchacho*. Either brother. They ain't some knife-flickin' *pachucos* any longer."

Flores didn't say anything. He didn't have to. He wouldn't follow my advice. Retaliation was a badge of honor. He was a man with no fears—and no goals beyond getting even. That didn't take you far in life.

As we drove away, I glanced in the rearview mirror. I had expected the *Vatos Locos* to melt back into the shadows, but I could see *El Perro* and the others still standing in the driveway, faceless outlines. Four more joined them.

The rookie turned to me, puzzled. It was a Lopez I had been looking for the other night at the *Los Compadres* Hotel, he reminded me—*before* we found the body on the tracks. Why had I come to think they might be related?

"His name came up in connection with the fight involving the Negro outside the bar," I said. "When the body turned up, I put two and two together."

At first, the rookie acted impressed at my deductive powers. Then skepticism flashed in his face. He realized I wasn't keeping him informed, partner to partner. But I wasn't about to tell him the real reason I wanted Lopez.

CHAPTER 6

The desk of the homicide detective responsible for investigating the death of the Indian we had found on the tracks resembled all the other desks crammed into the bullpen, only more slovenly: files piled at one end of a green blotter, contents oozing down the stack like a mud slide; a ceramic hotel ash tray growing half-smoked cigarettes; a white coffee mug with black stains ringing the bottom; an open can of shelled peanuts; a small brass-rimmed calendar with each passing day X'd out—a man pushing retirement.

"Detective Griffin?" I asked as the man at the desk hung up his phone.

"Yeah, whattya want?" he asked in a voice as tired as the linoleum floor.

"My partner and I found that body down on the tracks a few nights back, by the Twentieth Street viaduct. Wanted to know what you found out about him."

Griffin scrutinized me with blue-green eyes so bloodshot they made me wince. He smelled of cheap aftershave and cigarettes.

His off-the-rack gray suit looked as if it had spent more time in bed than its owner. "Why? You next of kin?" He broke into a grin.

"Curious, is all," I said evenly.

Griffin swung his chair around to face me, propped one ankle in maroon socks atop the opposite knee, and leaned back.

"I'm sure as hell glad somebody 'round here's got time to be curious."

"It was an unusual death. It's not every day you find a man with his hands missing."

"Got nothin' better to do than nose around in cases that ain't yours?"

"I might have a lead for you."

Griffin narrowed his eyes. "What did you say your name was?"

I sighed under my breath. "Stryker."

His eyes fastened on me as a steam-shovel-sized hand scooped peanuts out of the can. He chewed thoughtfully on them, his teeth grinding them down until nothing was left except enamel against enamel.

He wiped his tongue across the inside of his upper lip. "Stryker. Yeah, I remember seeing your name in the paperwork." Griffin wiggled a finger at me. "You're the guy gets his name in the newspapers more often than the mayor. The Denver Kid, right?" He twisted his head in the direction of a bald-headed man hunched over a desk next to him, scribbling on a report with ink-stained hands. He had the frenzied look of an accountant at tax deadline. "You hear that, Jerry, this here's the Denver Kid. In person!" Jerry stared silently at me. Griffin twisted back in my direction. "You lookin' to crowd in on the headlines?"

I was growing impatient with this bozo's attitude. "There aren't any headlines here. But I might have a lead for you. Do you have an ID on the body yet?"

Griffin studied his pumpkin-colored tie, apparently looking for food stains. Finally he said, "We know he was an Indian in his early twenties and he's dead. That's all we know."

"An Indian?"

"That's what the ME said in his prelim post. Don't know how ya tell. Something about the nose and eyebrow ridges and shit. Didn't say if he was Apache or Crow or Sioux. Report also says he had some false teeth and a coupla ribs broken years before."

So *El Perro's* information had been accurate. That definitely ruled out the dead man being one of the Lopez brothers. Which likely meant it was the man Lopez was looking for.

"Then I have an ID for the body," I said.

"Oh, yeah?"

"An Indian named Art Red Owl. A boxer."

Griffin grinned at his desk mate. "He's doing all my work for me, Jerry. Ain't that nice of him?" Griffin looked back at me. "Without the missing hands, we can't prove nothin'. Could be anybody."

"The body appeared athletic, like he was in training," I persisted, recalling the rookie's observation. "The false teeth and broken ribs the ME found suggest a man who boxed. If you check the local gyms, the boxing—"

"Ain't looking too hard, if you really wanna know," Griffin cut in, shoveling another scoop of peanuts into his mouth. "You're trying to make the dicks, I know. If you do someday, you can do all the fucking legwork you want. Me, I ain't got the time to chase all over the prairie looking to ID a headless Indian. In case you don't read the papers, we got bigger chiefs to find. I catch squeals here about as often as my old lady catches calls from her boyfriends. I got cases I know who the stiff is. I got cases I know who the killer is but can't prove it. So I ain't gonna waste no more of my time on this fucking redskin 'til somebody walks in that door with a positive ID. Find his hands, Stryker. Then we'll talk. Otherwise, in thirty days the city'll plant him in the pines along Clear Creek. I don't give a rat's ass. Now why don't you take that curiosity of yours the fuck outa here?" He swung around in his chair to face his desk.

I was impressed by his impassioned speech. I didn't know the homicide boys had it in them. "Did the ME give a cause of death?" I persisted.

Griffin turned back my way impatiently. "Two Denver and Rio Grande diesel engines and fifty coal cars."

"Any evidence he was murdered? Thrown under the train?"

Griffin's tongue worried one of his molars. "No."

"Somebody took his hands away."

"I like Bock's theory about the rats."

That was the part of it I hadn't doped out yet. Why would a thug like Lopez go to the trouble of crushing the man's face and taking off with his hands? Not his modus operandi.

Had someone hired him to find and kill Red Owl—someone who wanted the Indian's identity destroyed?

"There were signs somebody dragged him to those tracks," I said. "Scuff marks on the tops of his shoes. That should be in the report. And his hands were cut off too cleanly at the wrists to be an accident." I could hear desperation in my voice.

Griffin pulled off a piece of peanut skin from his tongue and flicked it on the floor. "Look, Stryker, there's not a fuckin' spec of evidence somebody killed this guy. You saw the stiff. The ME's having a tough time piecing this one together. His post says the guy was alive when the train ran over him. Don't know how you can tell that, but that's what he says. I figured the Indian either intentionally killed himself or he drank too much Muscatel and fell in front of the train. Why are you so damn convinced somebody killed him?"

"My sources say someone was looking for him."

Griffin rolled his eyes. "*Your* sources. How impressive. Who was looking for him?"

I hated dragging up my past in front of this dickhead. "One of the Lopez brothers. I don't know which one."

Griffin's face stiffened. "Whoa," he said in a hushed voice. "Ain't heard that name in a while."

"I heard it on the street, just before we found the body. A Lopez was looking for a boxer. I've been asking around since and came up with a boxer named Art Red Owl. Apparently he was in hiding from Lopez. I'd wager Lopez put him on those tracks."

This time Griffin got his sorry ass out of the chair and got in my face. "I knew Derek Flemming. He woulda stayed alive and retired if you hadn't fucked up. And at least one of the Lopez brothers would be in jail and this Indian might not be dead and I wouldn't have his damn file stacked on my desk. So quit playing detective and stay outa my cases, Stryker."

Every head in the bullpen turned toward us. It wouldn't be a good time to punch the guy in the face.

"I'll keep looking for the missing hands," I said. "You can sit here on yours and check to see if your old lady is getting any calls from her boyfriends."

Griffin didn't take a swing at me but he wanted to. It probably wasn't a good idea pissing him off like that.

ℰↄℰↄ

Two street cops found the missing banker's 1949 Roadmaster three days after we stumbled over the body of the Indian in The Bottoms. The banker wasn't in the car. Homicide found "evidence of foul play," but provided no details. The car was tucked away neatly in a parking garage at Stout and Fourteenth, unscathed and freshly washed. It even had all four hubcaps. Miracles happened.

"Damn, I wish we'd found him," Perdue muttered for the third time tonight.

The evening shadows of McNulty's Garage on Twenty-Second fell over our car. McNulty's was always a good spot to coop on warm nights when it was late and calls were light. *Repairs: all makes and models* said the red and black sign on the side of the garage.

Perdue tossed the copy of the *Rocky Mountain News* onto the dash. Lou Sheppard's photo of the banker's car and the grinning cops who had found it spread across the front page. No front-page story for the dead Indian. He never even made the want ads in the *Denver Post*, though Sheppard had managed to get him a paragraph on page twenty-five in the *News*. Right below a two-column piece about a white girl on Capitol Hill who had been bitten on the hand by a neighbor's dog and whose father had strangled the pup bitch with his bare hands. The dog's owner was suing.

"You know, I've been thinking, Joe," the rookie said around a LifeSaver. "Maybe one of them flying saucers got him."

"What flying saucers?" I asked, disbelief in my voice.

"No, I mean it, Joe. I—I saw one once. A saucer. Down near Provo. Didn't look like one of them round saucers everybody's seeing these days. More like a giant banana. Could be the Ruskies, you know. They're supposed to be testing some kinda secret weapon."

I let the smoke from my Lucky Strike drift out the car window. What did you say to flying saucers? I listened to the crickets and the distant sound of traffic. I had been thinking about Detective Griffin's warning. If I wanted to track down Lopez, I would have to do it on the sly, right under homicide's nose. Yet I faced some serious risks. I could investigate as much as possible on my own time, but I would have to slide on some of my work at the auto repair shop. Carl wouldn't be happy about that, plus it would mean less pay. Then there was Paula. She would be furious if she found out I was hunting the Lopez brothers. There also was the problem of the rookie. I couldn't do all my investigating off duty, which meant I would have to involve Perdue, as I had done the night with *El Perro*. Yet I wasn't sure how far I could trust him. I didn't trust his connections to the captain. I didn't trust his rookie idealism.

Perdue tapped the newspaper. "I had a cousin who made the front page of *Stars and Stripes* during the war. Killed seventeen Japs in the Philippines. You in the Big One, Joe?"

I didn't want to answer. I thought about lying. But there were few men of my generation who weren't in the Big One. "Yeah," I said.

Perdue faked a cough to remind me that he didn't like me smoking. "I was a marine, myself. Four years in the Corps. Got out a year ago. I bet you were a marine."

"Army," I replied with a certain satisfaction.

Perdue didn't say anything for a moment. Then: "You see any action?"

"A little."

Yeah, a little. The Timberwolves, they called us in the 104th. "Nothing in Hell must stop the Timberwolves" was our motto. Nothing did. Not even the Krauts lobbing .88s at us like boys chucking rocks at a cornered schoolyard cat.

"Wish I had seen action," Perdue said. "Damn war was over before I could get in. Missed it by two months. Even after lying about my age. Never got to fire a shot 'cept on the practice range. Never saw the enemy."

You didn't miss anything. I saw the enemy. They all were kids and they all were dead.

"Where'd you fight?" the rookie persisted.

"Here and there."

Where didn't I fight? Wuestwezel, Zundert, Stolberg, Eschweiler, Lammersdorf, Lucherberg, Bitterfeld.

"They sent me to Guam," Perdue said. "But the only Jap soldiers I saw were a few ragged prisoners. You kill any Krauts?"

How the hell did I know? How did most men in war know if they killed anyone? You shot into the darkness and the terror and you rarely knew if you hit anyone, and you didn't much care as long as you kept shooting and they didn't shoot you or your buddies.

"...that's why I joined the department," Perdue was saying. "I thought if I couldn't fight the Japs over there at least I could fight the enemy over here. You know what I mean?"

Yeah, I knew. I remembered feeling that way when I was a rookie. Joined to save the world. Every cop thought he was something special when he put on a uniform for the first time. A white knight in blue, come to the Round Table.

It had passed in one terrible night.

"I just hope I can be half as good a rookie as you were," Perdue went on. "Though I heard about your partner. That musta be tough for you. What was his name?"

Christ, where did they recruit these guys? At least the cops who came out of the war knew to leave you alone when it came to death. There were things you just didn't talk about to another guy, even in the heat of combat, with death all around you. Angrily, I fished a fin out of my wallet.

"Here, kid," I said, thrusting the five bucks at the rookie.

He stared at the money. "What's this for?"

"Remember the Mexican joint we rousted the other night?

El Sótano? Shortly before the call came in about the body in
The Bottoms?" Perdue nodded. "The owner gave me a sawbuck. For not making life miserable for him. We coulda shut
him down if we'd wanted, for being a public nuisance. Here.
Partners always split their gifts."

The rookie gawked at me, his thin mouth open wide enough
I could have dropped in a bowling ball. A dumb move, offering a cut of my skin to a rookie I didn't know or trust. I had
heard of more than one rookie being planted by a publicity-
hungry politician. We were fair game these days. I didn't like
splitting my money, either. I always put my skin into a bank
account no one knew about but me. For my own auto repair
shop someday, god willing. But the kid was getting on my
nerves with all that bullshit about my being some kind of white
knight. And frankly, if I were going after Lopez, I needed to
know how far I could go with the kid.

"I—I don't want it," the rookie said, looking away as if I
were offering him a picture of a naked woman.

"How much you make a week, kid?"

"That doesn't have anything to do with it."

"How much?"

"Fifty-five."

"You're married, right? Got two kids and a third on the
way." The rookie nodded. "You're poor, right? Mormons gotta
cough up ten percent to the church, don't you?"

Perdue nodded. "I've been thinking about raiding my bish-
op's storehouse."

"See, you can't afford to be principled about this job any
more than the rest of us. Me, I got a wife and a mortgage, and I
hope a kid one of these days. That's dicey on second grade
patrolman's pay. You're ambitious, aren't you?"

"Sure, I guess so. As much as the next guy—yeah."

I waved the fin in his face. "Then take some advice from a
veteran. Nobody likes a clean cop. Least of all, other cops. It
makes you untrustworthy. A good apple spoiling the bad, so to
speak. You won't go far on this force if you're pure and honest."

The rookie's eyes widened.

"Hey, don't get me wrong," I went on. "I'm not talking wholesale corruption here. We still put away the really badasses. We keep the drunks outa sight and the hookers out of the Denver Country Club—the shit the public doesn't wanna see. It's the little shit where we take our cut. Five bucks passed along with the driver's license on a traffic stop or a storeowner who wants to leave his merchandise out on the public sidewalk or a bookmaker who wants his drop left alone. Nothing big. Nothing that'll hurt the public. But the people on Larimer Street expect you to take it. They're contemptuous of you if you do. But they'll hate you if you don't. At least contempt pays. Take it. It's better than being in debt."

The rookie hesitated, looking around as if checking for departmental spies, then took the fiver out of my hand and stuffed it into his shirt pocket.

I would be in deep shit if he confessed to his Mormon captain, the captain who still believed I was worth something. But I didn't give a shit if he did. I didn't give a shit what the captain thought of me.

I flicked my cigarette out the window, watching the bright glow arc in the darkness. I hoped McNulty hadn't left a pool of gasoline lying around.

CHAPTER 7

It didn't take much legwork to find out the dead Indian boxer had a manager well known to local fight fans—Leroy Sunday, the Punching Priest of Broadway. Ran a "church" and dirty little muscle emporium on South Broadway. Saved souls while he taught guys how to bash in each other's skull.

Sunday's gym occupied the second floor above Sam Kitsutaka's dry goods store at the end of a flight of narrow creaky stairs. The rookie and I stood in the doorway under a hand-lettered sign that preached *Your Body Is God's Temple—Worship It*.

We watched two young Mexicans, one in red trunks the other in green, spar listlessly inside a makeshift ring in the middle of a large open space. Three small boys and half a dozen gym rats silently watched the boxers in the torpid evening heat.

A man in shiny black pants, gray short-sleeved shirt, and fuzzy white hair leaned forward against the ropes and yelled at the boxer in the green trunks, "I wanna see some punches, Luis. Quit dancing like Velda Lupe."

His challenge didn't seem to make any difference. The boxers continued to move slowly, their white-laced black shoes squeaking against the smooth ring floor, their gloves slapping against each other like wet towels.

"Use the left. The left. My grandmother woulda knocked your brains out by now, you had any."

Suddenly the fighter in the green trunks, a skull and cross-bones tattooed on his left bicep, loosed a lightning flurry of punches into his sparring partner, a lighter-skinned kid with tufts of hair on his chest and an acre of acne on his back. The kid staggered, swung aimlessly over Luis's head, and took a left uppercut to the jaw. He sank to one knee, glassy-eyed. His nose bled onto the floor. Several of the gym rats roared their approval.

The old man yelled, "That's it, Luis! That's the combination!"

Luis hooked his gloves under the stunned fighter's armpits and lifted him to his feet. "Luis ain't gonna fight no more today, Mister Leroy."

"Okay, okay, hit the showers." The old man split two of the ropes and Luis helped his sparring partner out of the ring and onto a small stool. The kid dangled his head between his knees and wiped at his bloody nose with a gloved hand.

"Hey, take those gloves off before I charge ya for cleanin' 'em," barked the old man.

One of the small boys unlaced the groggy fighter's gloves.

Luis swiped at a patched speed bag and gave us a cursory glance as he headed for a zinc shower stall in a far corner. The others, noticing us for the first time as we moved out from the shadows of the doorway, fixed their eyes on us with a familiar mixture of insolence and wariness reserved for cops.

We approached the old man. He picked up a set of gloves laying on the floor below a wall plastered with scores of fight posters and a large, amateurish painting of St. Martin cutting his cloak in half for a naked beggar. Nearby hung a framed oval dime-store portrait of a beatific Christ. I never realized he'd been a fight fan.

"You Leroy Sunday?" I asked.

"That's me. Used to be a Duvall but changed my name after I heard Billy Sunday preach in Kansas City."

Incongruously bright blue eyes, as delicate as hand-painted

china, blinked once against a humorless face. Up close, I could see he practiced what his hand-lettered sign preached. He had a thick, powerful chest and muscular arms, though the skin sagging in his face betrayed the fact that all of God's human temples eventually crumbled.

I introduced myself and Perdue.

"Welcome to God's temple, Officers," Sunday said with a sweep of his right hand. The tattoo of an empty cross flashed on the underside of his arm. The gym rats began drifting away to flail at a punching bag or jump rope. Sunday jerked his head in the direction of the Mexican boxer stepping under the shower. "Luis there, he's gonna be a champ. That's why they all stopped to watch. Best featherweight I've managed in years—when he uses his left."

"Better boxer than Art Red Owl?"

The blue eyes clouded. "My grandmother, god rest her soul, could beat Lone Wolf. You could beat him and I don't even know you."

"That was his ring name? Lone Wolf?"

"Uh-huh. Full-blooded Indian," he said as he tightened the lacing on the empty gloves. "Found him living with an uncle in Pueblo. Fightin' on some county commissioner's ranch on weekends for twenty-five bucks and beer. Promoters decked him out in a headdress and leathers and bells, and his opponents always wore cavalry pants. They billed it as 'Custer's Last Stand.' Fought like he was beatin' a brick wall. No style, no finesse. Came at you flailing. They don't know crap about boxing in Pueblo. But I saw potential in him. Cruiserweight. Big and strong, anybody could see that. Had the moves, too, given some God-hard work. Golden Gloves material. That's why I brought him up here, to teach him how to box. And to get his life straightened out."

"How long ago was that?"

"About six months." The man's white eyebrows knitted. "Why you askin' about Art?"

"When did you last see him?"

"Dunno. A coupla weeks, maybe. Frankly, I hope I don't see him again."

"Why?"

"He was a no-show for a fight last Friday night on a four-round undercard. Cost me serious bucks." Sunday sighed, as if forgiving the man. "I shoulda known better. He ain't never been dependable. Gettin' him to work out is like pulling teeth. Thinks boxing is something you do in your spare time, like knitting. You gonna be a boxer, you live boxing, eat boxing, pray boxing, and pardon the un-biblical expression, you shit boxing. Now you take Luis there. He listens. He listens good when you put the fear of God in him. He's gonna go far."

The featherweight was out of the shower and drying off with what looked like the team towel for the Dodgers. He talked quietly to his sparring partner who had undressed but looked too groggy to do much else. Sunday walked across the room and stowed the gloves in a small cabinet.

"Know anybody who mighta talked to Red Owl or seen him since you last saw him?" I asked. "Family? Wife? Girl-friend?"

"Hey, I ain't Art's nursemaid."

"I never heard of a boxing manager who wasn't."

"Like I said, I ain't seen him a spell. And I don't know who he might have talked to since then. So why all the flapping about Art? He in trouble again?"

"He's been in trouble before?"

Sunday laughed. "Burglary, vagrancy, theft, numbers, es-caped twice from the State Industrial School and once from County—" Sunday raised his clenched fists. "—assault with a deadly weapon. Look, you still ain't told me what you want with Art."

I told him about the dead man we had found on the tracks and that I believed he was Red Owl.

"Mother of God!" Sunday collapsed onto a slatted wood folding chair at a metal table. The old man looked pleadingly at me. "You sure it's Art?"

I sat down on another slatted chair and pushed aside torn copies of *Ring, Christian Life,* and *Pathfinder.* The rookie re-mained standing and leaned against a wall where a sign read

HOW LONG SINCE YOU WROTE TO YOUR MOTHER?

Next to it, a notice announced the times of worship services at the gym.

"We don't have a positive ID," I said, "but his name came up in the investigation. The medical examiner said the dead man was an Indian. How old is Red Owl?"

"Twenty-three, twenty-four."

"Was he missing any teeth?"

"What boxer isn't? Mennie Maes knocked out four of 'em in a three-rounder in Grand Junction last year."

"He get false teeth?"

"Yeah. I paid for 'em outa my own pocket."

"Ever bust any ribs?"

"Not with me. Before, in Pueblo."

"We also know your boy was in hiding and that a thug named Lopez was looking for him."

I had often seen fear in men's eyes, but the fear I saw enter Sunday's eyes before he looked away went as soul-searing deep as I had ever witnessed.

I leaned toward the old man. "What do you know about his ending up on the tracks, Leroy? Why would your boy be in hiding, and why would Lopez be looking for him?"

Sunday stared at his rough shoes as though they were the only thing between him and eternal damnation. He shook his head and mumbled into the floor.

"What?" I asked.

He spoke up but still kept his head down. He'd lost his preacher's tongue. "I don't know nothin' about him hidin' or about this Lopez guy."

"Try that answer again," I said loudly enough for the rest of the room to hear me.

"I ain't lying. That's a sin."

"Murder is a sin, too, sir," the rookie reminded him.

That was a tough one for the old man, forced to choose between the sin of lying and the sin of murder. "Lopez came here looking for him, didn't he?" I pressed.

Sunday's shoulders slumped. "I don't know his name. He don't give it. I just know he looked meaner than a pissed-off

Doberman. Big and strong. Never make it as a boxer, though. No control. No discipline. More a demon outa hell."

"What'd he look like?"

Sunday's description was vague, but close enough to mug shots I had seen to tell me it was probably one of the Lopez brothers.

"When was this?" I asked.

"A week, maybe. Maybe a little longer."

Before we had found the Indian's body on the tracks, but after the Indian had disappeared. "What exactly did he want?"

"Wanted to know if Art was here. I told him he wasn't."

"Then he asked you where he could find him, didn't he?"

Sunday looked out over his sweltering gym and licked his lips. "I told him I didn't know where he was, that I ain't seen him for a while. Which was the truth." Sunday was still looking away when he said that.

"You must know where your boy lives."

He looked at me. "I didn't tell the man that. I told him I didn't know where he could find him. Which wasn't a lie. I know Art wasn't where he usually lives 'cause I'd gone lookin' for him and the apartment manager said he ain't seen him for days."

"Where was this?"

"The Roxbury Apartments on Bannock. Got a room there."

"This man say *why* he was looking for your boy?"

"No. He wasn't someone who told you anything. You only told him."

"Did he threaten you?"

"He didn't need to."

The old man put his hands into his face and said mother of god again.

"Can you think of anyone in the boxing game who'd want him dead?"

I hadn't mentioned the Indian's missing hands. Maybe that's why his killer cut off his hands and took them away. Like stealing a boxer's soul.

"Naw. It wasn't like he was a contender. At least not yet."

"Got a photo of him?"

Sunday dug an eight-by-ten black and white glossy out of a closet. The Indian held a classic boxing pose: left leg forward, muscular arms up, tight to the head, the right glove higher than the left, ready to strike. The body looked as big and strong as the one on the tracks. The face was remarkably free of a boxer's usual shelves of white scar tissue around the eyes or thick ridges of skin along the cheekbones.

A nice mug any Indian maiden would be happy to invite into her tepee—except for the nose. It was a flattened feature that weaved a serpentine path between wide-set eyes to a thick upper lip traced by a faint mustache. He wore a feathered headdress over long black hair.

"That was his idea," Sunday said almost apologetically. "He couldn't wear it in the ring, of course."

I flipped the photo over. "Lone Wolf" was stamped on the back. "Where was he from originally? One of the reservations?"

"Pine Ridge. Left when he was a kid. He never talked much about it. He was Oglala Lakota. Said Denver was once their seasonal hunting ground. But he didn't talk much about being an Indian. He didn't go for sweat lodges and all that stuff."

"Yet he fought as Lone Wolf?"

"Yeah. We needed something catchy."

I stood up. "I need this photo. I also want you to go to the medical examiner's office to ID the body. The face isn't worth shit, but the rest of it's in pretty decent shape."

The old man paled.

I wrote down the address. "I'll tell them you're coming. If you don't show up, I'll come down here and drag your ass over there myself. I don't wanna see your boy buried in a pine box with no name."

CHAPTER 6

I awoke, startled. The bedroom was dark except for thin cracks of early morning light creeping through the edges of the heavy black shades. The alarm clock on the dresser read 5:23. I had been asleep one hour. I sat up and put my face in my hands.

"Joe?" came Paula's muffled voice from the pillow.

I started to answer but found my throat parched. "Go back to sleep, hon," I finally managed.

She propped herself up onto one elbow and touched my arm. "You're trembling. What's wrong? Are you sick?"

"It's nothing. Just a bad dream. Go back to sleep."

"What kind of bad dream?"

"A dream. A nightmare, you know. Monsters and shit."

"Is it that body you said you found the other night?"

"No."

Paula sat up and stared accusingly at me. "It's Derek, isn't it?"

Yeah, it was Derek. Before Derek died, the nightmares had been about the war. But now they were always about Derek. Trading one hell for another. I thought I had beaten the nightmares—buried them so deep they would never find their way to the surface again. But that damn headless body on the tracks, the Lopez brothers…

I lay back down against the hot wet sheets. "It's okay, Paula. Go back to sleep."

She lay back down beside me, resting her cool hand on my chest. "This isn't okay. When things like Derek happen, it doesn't magically go away, Joe. It can go on for years. It can destroy a marriage. You need to talk to someone."

"A headpeeper? No way. If the department finds out I'm seeing a psychiatrist, I'll be standing in the unemployment line the next day. We went through this back then. I didn't see a doctor then and the nightmares went away. I'm not going to any doctor now. Fuck the doctors. It's nothing. Leave it alone."

Paula pushed up on my chest and stared down at me. "I can't leave it alone! You're not the only one this job of yours affects. I've lived in fear ever since that night, waiting for the shift commander to show up on the doorstep to tell me you're never coming home again. Like he told Derek's wife and kids. No, I can't leave it alone. I won't leave it alone."

"You'll have to. Nothing can change what happened."

"Damn, I wish you weren't a cop!"

She started to roll out of bed. I tried to hook my arm around her shoulders and pull her back down to my chest and calm her, but she pulled free.

"I'm volunteering at the hospital this morning," she said, standing in her nightgown. "Go back to sleep."

She was out the bedroom before I could say another word. Not that there was anything to say but the same old tired words.

I tried to go back to sleep but couldn't. It didn't matter. I found no more peace in sleep than I did in consciousness.

I lay there and struggled to not think about Derek Flemming, about The Fuller Hotel, about the killers in the wet night. I stared at the ceiling, watched dust motes dance in a blade of light. But the memories kept rising to the surface like slippery air bubbles through one's fingers in the water. Memories of a dark-colored Plymouth coupe in the rain. Memories of the hotel lobby and the two drunks and Derek sitting on the stairs with a gun pointed at him by a masked man as evil as I'd ever faced.

I could see Derek's beery complexion, his tired cynicism,

his laziness, his irrepressible storytelling. Derek Flemming taught me everything I knew about being a cop—but I ignored all of it in one night and it killed him.

ᘓᗒᘓᗒ

Later that morning, unable to sleep, I went down to Carl's Auto Repair and put in three hours, most of it wrestling with the transmission in a 1945 Olds. I grew antsy, told Carl I wasn't feeling well, and headed off for the Roxbury Apartments where Leroy Sunday said Art Red Owl had been living. The Roxbury was a shabby place in the Baker Neighborhood. The exterior looked like it had been fashioned out of leftover parts from other houses, a mix of rooflines, gables, and a domed turret. They had chopped the interior into flats.

"You're the second guy come looking for Art," the manager said as he led me upstairs to the back of the house.

I looked sharply at him. "Who? When?"

The guy hadn't left a name, but the manager's description suggested one of the Lopez brothers. The man had come a few days before I found the Indian's body. Either Leroy Sunday had lied about not telling Lopez where the Indian lived or Lopez had found out from another source.

Red Owl's room was barely big enough for a bed and a hot plate. There wasn't even a closet. The bath was down the hall.

"You bring the guy up here?" I asked.

The manager looked offended. "Hell, no. He weren't no cop. He had no right here. I told him I ain't seen Art for several days. Which was true."

"He threaten you?"

The man crossed his arms as if to say nobody would dare threaten him. "No."

The man was lucky. He was a short, wiry man who smelled of herb tea and looked pale from squirreling away in his basement apartment. He wouldn't have lasted a gnat's breath if Lopez had wanted to end it.

The Indian had either left his room in a hurry or had left

with the idea of returning but couldn't. Clothes were strewn around along with a few fight magazines he had probably borrowed from Leroy Sunday. Two of his publicity photos, identical to the one Sunday had given me, lay on a ratty dresser.

The manager said Red Owl had disappeared about two weeks before. Which meant the Indian had managed to stay in hiding a week before Lopez dumped him on the railroad tracks. Where had he laid low?

"Did he have any visitors *before* he disappeared?" I asked.

"He never had visitors."

Probably no room to put them. "He say anything to you before he disappeared? Did he seem afraid? Indicate he might be going somewhere for a while?"

The man shook his head.

I pawed through the Indian's possessions. I figured that after he had been gone this long the manager would have hocked them and rented the room to someone else. It was that kind of place. I told him so.

"He paid up some back rent and next month's before he disappeared," the manager said. "Seemed to have come into some money. Crisp bills, like right from the bank."

"How long had he been living here?"

"A year, maybe."

"How was he managing to pay rent before? Didn't sound like he was making his living as a boxer."

The manager shrugged. "Odd jobs. Probably some shady muscle work. Only thing I heard him talk about steadily was his job at some theater."

"Movie theater? Which one?"

"No, one of them stage theaters. He was a stagehand."

"What was the name of the theater?"

The manager scratched his neck. "Broadway something or other. Run by some New York City hoity-toity. Art was always grumbling about him."

As he told me this, I found a small picture of a Negro woman in the third drawer of the dresser, under some underwear I really didn't want to touch. She was young, pretty in a rough way. I showed the manager the snapshot.

"That's his girl," he said. "She's a hooker, but that's what he calls her, his girl."

"Know her street name?"

"Velvet Knights."

Yeah, a hooker, all right. "She ever come up here?"

The man looked offended again. "I don't run a place like that."

"This neighborhood her territory?"

He shook his head. "Broadway below Colfax."

I didn't bother to ask him how he knew that. I pocketed her photo. Now I had an idea where he might have holed up.

ᏋᎧᏋᎧ

No one on the streets had seen Velvet Knights for days. She had vanished like her boyfriend. I hoped she hadn't suffered his same fate.

But Stella might know. Stella, aka Annie Shaw, knew every "competitor" in town. When she wasn't working the streets, I could usually find her at Edgar's, an illegal after-hours colored joint run by a white-haired Negro woman whose connection to Edgar I never had figured out. The rookie and I parked the black and white on Welton Street by a fire hydrant in front of a four-story brick building. Edgar's was on the second floor, above a second-hand clothing store. During the day, when Edgar's wasn't selling bootleg liquor, the place served as a union hall, accessible by a narrow flight of stairs. After hours, the entrance was up a metal fire escape over an alley that reeked of garbage and vomit.

"Let's take a walk-through," I said to Perdue. We climbed the stairs, our footsteps echoing in the alley. As we reached the second-floor landing and the door to the joint, a familiar voice rang out of the darkness above us.

"Hey, if it ain't Officer Joe."

I looked up. Stella sat several steps above us in a dress hiked up in the warm night, her knees splayed languidly. If it weren't for the clouds that hid a half-hearted moon and the fact

Stella was as black as coal dust, I coulda seen all the way to candy land.

"How you doing, Stella?"

"Livin'."

Her left arm rose and I heard liquid splash against her teeth. She smacked her lips.

"You want some livin', Joe? Still got the best tonsils in Five Points."

"Stell, you know I'm a married man."

"Never stops my customers. How about that cute young stud with you?"

"He's married, too, Stell. A Mormon to boot."

"Ain't never had a Mormon I can recall. Plenty of Catholics and Baptists. Oh, those Baptists! Are Mormons built different?"

"What you're offering is illegal, Stella," I said, more for Perdue's benefit than hers.

"Hey, I ain't selling nothin' people don't want."

The moan of a saxophone seeped out from behind the door. I knocked loudly. A man the size of a beer truck opened the door.

I told Perdue to go on in and check things out. I'd follow in a minute. He hesitated.

"Go on," I said. "Deron here will see no one bothers you."

Perdue meekly disappeared into the smoky, poorly lit interior. I turned to Stella. "I'm looking for a cooch goes by Velvet Knights."

Stella clicked her teeth. "Ain't know no one by that name."

"You know every hooker in town, Stell."

"Maybe she ain't a hooker." She upturned a flask and splashed more liquor down her throat.

"Quit protecting her, Stell. I got reason to believe she might be in danger."

"That ain't never news down here."

I told Stella about Velvet's dead boyfriend, Art Red Owl, and that I thought one of the Lopez brothers had murdered him.

She whistled under her breath and took another drink.

I took one step up from the landing toward her. "Where do I find her, Stell?"

She gave out a deep breath in the darkness. "This Lopez guy was askin' 'round for her."

"When?"

"Coupla weeks ago maybe."

"Which Lopez?"

She didn't know which twin any more than anyone else did.

"I need to find her, Stell. Maybe Lopez doesn't need her now that he's killed her boyfriend. But she might still be in danger for something she knows. Besides, I want to catch the bastard and maybe she can help."

"You don't want to find that wetback, Officer Joe. Even Deron don't mess with him. All the girls are afraid of him. He's roughed up a coupla them."

"Looking for Velvet?"

"No, before that. He likes his *sexo* rough."

"Where can I find her, Stell?"

She paused a long moment before reluctantly saying, "Check out the motels along east Colfax. Dunno which one. She keeps movin' 'round."

"What's her birth name, Stell? She wasn't born Velvet Knights."

"Bessie. Bessie Hayes."

The door to the bar opened up and Perdue spilled out with the music, big Deron right behind him. Perdue reeked of smoke and beer, though I knew he had touched neither.

"Come on," I said to him. "We got some motels to check out."

CHAPTER 9

It took two more days to find Velvet Knights. Abandoning our patrol area frequently to scour motels on east Colfax, instead of covering our Larimer Street beat, was making my rookie partner nervous.

"The truth is, kid, homicide doesn't give a shit about this dead Indian," I said. "They won't even try to ID him unless we find his missing hands for fingerprints. Nobody's gonna solve this case except for you and me. This cooch might help us dope out what happened."

That seemed to appeal to the rookie, even if it was only for a dead Indian. He liked the idea of playing detective. He liked the idea of working with The Denver Kid to solve a case no one else wanted to solve. I didn't tell him I didn't much care about the dead Indian. What I really wanted was Lopez.

We found Velvet Knights in one of the many countless nondescript neon motels that dotted Colfax like a line of heroin tracks, not far from the state capitol building. The manager gave me the room number and a key. We opened the door and walked right in. Velvet was entertaining. I told the red-faced john scrambling into his pants to get lost or a couple of tattooed dicklickers at the city jail would be telling him to drop his drawers and hug the toilet.

"Fuck!" Velvet Knights muttered wearily. She flung a robe around her tall, half-naked body as the john scurried out the door.

We stepped into the tiny motel room. It was hot and stuffy and reeked of sex. "We're not with vice," I said.

"Swell. I needed that money. I gotta eat. So whattya want? A freebie? I ain't givin' no freebies."

"We're here about your boyfriend, Velvet," I said.

"I ain't got no boyfriend."

"You got Art Red Owl."

"Don't know nobody named Red Owl." She hastily pulled a cigarette from a pack of Avalons from atop a scarred dresser. A chipped glass ashtray held several cigs smoked down to the stub. She lit the cigarette and drew on it so hard I thought the entire cigarette might disappear down her throat.

"Sure you do." I held up the picture of her I'd taken from his room.

She blew smoke out hard. "I know lotsa guys."

"Not many who keep your picture in their dresser drawer. Was he a boyfriend, or just a really special trick?"

"Why you wanna know?"

"Because one of the Lopez brothers was looking for you. He was trying to find your boyfriend."

"Well, he ain't found me yet."

"Unfortunately, he found your boyfriend. Left his body on the tracks in The Bottoms."

The hooker's eyes blinked rapidly and she collapsed onto the edge of the bed, onto rumpled sheets I wouldn't have used to wrap dead fish. Her large breasts hung heavy under the robe. Her legs were still in mesh stockings, a rip above a knee where it peaked out from the robe. She started to sob. Not hard, but not fake, either.

She looked too young for any of this shit. I gave her a minute before I said, "Bessie is your name, right? Bessie Hayes?"

Wet eyes pleaded with me. "He's dead? You sure?"

"A positive ID is proving kind of a problem, but I'm sure it's him."

She looked down again and sobbed more. Her left hand clutched her robe, the cigarette now burning unattended in her right hand. Her hands were strikingly coarse compared with the smoothness of the rest of her mocha-colored skin, as if she spent her spare time stringing barbed wire.

"Why was Lopez looking for Red Owl?" I pressed. "Why did he want to kill him?" She didn't say anything. "I need to know, Bessie, or I can't catch him. And if I don't catch him, you might not ever be safe."

That seemed to grab her attention. "Maybe 'cause of what he done to Moretti," she said weakly.

"*Villano* Moretti?"

She nodded and sucked on her cigarette.

"What the hell did he do to Moretti?"

"Art beat him up pretty bad."

"Why the hell would your boyfriend assault someone like Moretti?"

She didn't know, she swore. He never told her.

Perdue stepped deeper into the room. "Who is this Moretti guy?"

"He's a small-time mobster," I explained. "But the biggest one we got in Denver, so we're proud to have him. I've never dealt with the man personally, but I know he runs books, broads, fences stolen goods, loan sharks, fronts an illegal high-stakes gambling club, occasionally rubs out opposition or informants, and sells little packages of juju to kids."

"Sounds like a real nice guy," Perdue said.

"Yeah, so nice, you can go to a Denver city council meeting any month of the year and get all the references you want for Moretti. That's because he contributes generously to Catholic charities and politicians of any religion. He also runs a popular bar and supper club on the northwest side, in the heart of the Italian section. Just about everybody on the city council stood in line to sign his application for a liquor license. His nickname is 'The Fixer.'"

If Moretti's name sounded like something out of a bad B movie, it was. He tried to portray himself as a *paisan*, but legend had it his ancestry was actually mongrel and his birth name was James Newton.

He had grown up enamored with the Italian mafia, however, and in his early twenties legally changed his name to Villano Moretti. "The Fixer" nickname came later. He had earned that.

Moretti claimed close ties with the big boys in Chicago and lower Illinois, but the real mafia considered him a joke. Then again, they considered Denver a joke. But the way local officials looked at it, at least he was our mobster.

The real question was, why the hell had Art Red Owl assaulted Moretti? Was he nuts? Too many punches to the head? Moretti might be a small-time hood but he was still dangerous.

"Did your boyfriend have some kind of personal beef with Moretti?" I asked.

None that she knew.

Whatever the reason for the assault, I could see Moretti seeking payback for the beating. But why send Lopez? Moretti had his own meatballs to do that kind of dirty work. From what I'd heard, Moretti had tried to expand his operations into the Mexican community and he'd hooked up with the Lopez brothers to help run his rackets. But it hadn't worked out. The twins were too crazy to be mob bureaucrats.

"Did your boyfriend tell you which Lopez brother was looking for him?" I asked.

"No. He just said one of 'em was huntin' for 'im and he was gonna stay low for a while. Said I should lay low, too. Nobody needs to tell me twice about that man."

Velvet started to say something else but stopped at the sound of a baby crying in a nearby room. The crying grew louder, more insistent, closer. The hooker stirred uncomfortably.

Perdue abruptly walked past me toward the bathroom and opened the door to a tiny closet. Baby cries filled the room.

Perdue looked down at the floor. "Good god!"

Velvet hastily crushed out her cigarette and hurried to the closet. She bent over and picked up a bundled blanket from a shallow cardboard box. She pushed the blanket from the baby's face and tried unsuccessfully to shush it. She carried it to the bed, rocked it a few moments as it cried its lungs out, and parted her robe.

The squalling baby fell silent as it began to nurse.

"You keep your baby in a *closet*?" Perdue said.

Velvet looked at him with pleading softness in her eyes. "Men don't want us with babies. Just their wives. I put 'im in there if someone comes and I think he'll sleep. Sometimes I leave 'im with someone."

"Maybe you should quit being a prostitute and start being a mother," Perdue said.

She didn't dignify him with an answer. I had been around many people like Velvet Knights. Most of them were simple folks trying to get by the best way they knew how. Some of them shaded over to the wrong side of the law. Not far over. Little stuff, mostly. Nothing compared to the legal crooks who ran the city or guys like Moretti or the really bad asses like the Lopez brothers. People like Velvet didn't have the brains or talent or the chutzpah to get something better. They just couldn't see where else to go. Pious biblical contempt wasn't going to bring them back to the light.

I looked at the baby. "How old?"

"Five months."

"Red Owl's?"

She tickled the baby under the chin as he nursed. "Dunno."

I stared, envious. Everybody seemed to be having babies these days. Even unwed hookers with dead boyfriends. Everybody but Paula and me.

"Where was your boyfriend lying low from Lopez?"

She shook her head. "He said it was safer for both of us if I didn't know."

"Not safe enough."

She said nothing. Tears dripped onto the baby.

"Who else mighta known where he was hiding?" I asked.

"Maybe his manager. Art looked up to him."

"You should stay in hiding a little longer, Bessie," I said. "Until we find Lopez."

She gazed up from her baby who was nursing as if he hadn't eaten in days. She nodded resignedly.

We started to leave the room and she said behind us, "I remember something else."

"What?"

"Art mentioned that man everybody's lookin' for. Said he might need to disappear for a while. Even before he warned me about Lopez. Real scared about it."

"What man everyone's looking for?"

"The one in the papers."

"The missing *banker*?" Perdue cut in. "Seth Rawlins?"

"Yeah, him."

"Jesus!" Perdue said.

"Why was your boyfriend scared about that?" I asked. "He have something to do with the guy's disappearance?"

She looked down at her baby. "I dunno. Just know he was scared."

CHAPTER 10

Villano Moretti's Supper Club was fronted by an off-white stucco façade. A huge neon sign on the roof said Moretti's. The sign was turned off because it was long past the city's legal closing hour for bars. But lights still glowed inside the club and several cars sat in a dark parking lot. I went in through an allegedly bulletproof glass front door. The fact that the place was officially closed for the night or that I was still in uniform, having finished my shift, didn't deter the bartender from asking me what I wanted to drink. He was a dirty-blond-haired kid with a pack of cigarettes tucked under a shoulder of his sleeveless T-shirt. I ordered a Coors draft to keep him happy.

The bartender drew a glass under a photo of that emaciated-looking Sinatra kid and set it on a cigarette-stained bar. I reached for my wallet but he waved me off.

"Hey, we treat you guys right in here," he said. "Smoke?"

I declined. Nothing personal, but I never smoked anything that had been stashed on somebody else's shoulder.

I scanned the lounge. It had a low stage, large enough for a singer and a small band. Two men shot a listless game of nine-ball under a cone of light. A man and woman hugged their beers in a booth, silent, faces featureless. The couple didn't pay any attention to me but the pool players did. The rest of the supper club appeared to be a warren of small dining rooms, cozy alcoves, and dark nooks where one could carry on business undisturbed over white and red checked tablecloths.

The décor was old country. Religious paintings and black and white photos of women stomping grapes, of Pope Pius XII, Tuscany countryside, and Moretti's fake ancestors jostled for wall space. Various statuary, including gold statues of half-naked women, occupied recessed wall niches. The stale smell of garlic and leftover cooking still lingered.

The beer tasted good. I relaxed a little and listened to the click-click of the billiard balls. Muffled bursts of laughter and shouts of encouragement came from somewhere lower in the building. The higher rollers were walking the green.

"Sounds like all the fun is downstairs," I said.

"Depends on what kinda fun you're looking for." The bartender told me this as he stood drying a pony glass with a towel he must have used earlier in the evening while changing the oil in his car.

"Why don't I talk to Mr. Moretti about that? He in?"

The kid eyed me casually, set the glass down, and said, "I'll check."

He disappeared through a set of swinging doors. Rumor had it that Moretti worked out of a small office accessed from a men's room, well-fortified against attacks by hitmen or bombs hurled at him from competitors. But as I stared into the bar mirror I speculated that the mobster was standing behind it, studying me. I wasn't a cop on his payroll and I didn't drop in regularly for free drinks. Who was I? What did I want? I smiled at the mirror.

The bartender returned and said his boss wasn't around.

"Musta left by the back door," I said.

"Yeah, musta."

"Why don't you catch up with him and tell him I want to talk to him about a big Indian named Art Red Owl."

"I don't know no Art Red Owl."

I raised my voice in case he had wax in his ears. "I don't give a shit, friend, whether *you* know Red Owl. Your boss does. Now go find him. Maybe he was taking a piss when you went looking for him."

The kid disappeared again. A few hundred men like him in the army and we would have lost the war.

The swinging doors flapped open moments later, and a fat man in a custom-made dark suit and yellow tie ambled in, trailed by the bartender. I could see why the Indian might have worked him over. Wrap the guy in canvas and he'd make a great punching bag for Joe Walcott.

Moretti made himself at home among the bottles behind the bar, his back to me. He skipped the bottles of Old Grand-Dad and Schenley's with the shot prices scribbled on the labels and snatched a quart bottle of Hennessy cognac. He set the bottle in front of me without a word, dug under the bar until he came up with two tulip-shaped glasses, and set them next to the bottle.

"Ever drink cognac, Officer…"

"Stryker. Joe Stryker."

"Well, Officer Joe Stryker, you ever had cognac?" Moretti's voice was surprisingly smooth for his bulk, as smooth as I imagined the amber liquid he poured into the glasses.

"Once, at an uncle's wedding," I answered.

"Forty-year-old cognac?"

"I didn't ask its age. I was twelve at the time."

Moretti held one of the glasses in his fat hands, warming it. He set it in front of me. I took it, saluted to his raised glass, and slammed the stuff home. My nose caught a wood aroma just before the cognac hit my tongue, shooting darts of heat around the inside of my head and down my spine. I coughed.

Moretti laughed. A Santa Claus laugh. "That isn't cheap whiskey, Officer Stryker. Cognac is made to savor. You don't chug a drink that took forty years to age."

"I'll remember the next time," I replied hoarsely.

Next time came quickly. Moretti poured a second glass for me and sipped from his own, the liquid sliding between thick, wet lips, like those of a river-bottom fish. Dense black hair was slicked back and his dark eyes sank into the folds of his face. His skin had the pallor of a hospital sheet but I caught signs in the dim light that someone had worked him over.

"Johnny here said you wanted to know about some Indian?" Moretti said.

"Art Red Owl. A boxer. Fought under the name of Lone Wolf. One of Leroy Sunday's boys."

"Never heard of him. But then whoever hears of Leroy's boys?"

"He was a big man. Maybe you remember a big Indian in here."

Moretti looked toward the bartender. "You ever see a big fucking Indian in here with that name, Johnny?"

Johnny, who had returned to polishing glasses with the kind of absent motion one makes when one's trying to work yet overhear at the same time, looked up. "No, boss, ain't never seen no big Indian in here."

"Guess you're outa luck, Officer," Moretti said. "What are you looking for him for?"

"I'm not looking for him. I already found him. Down on the tracks in The Bottoms. He went twelve rounds with a passing train and lost."

"I'm sorry to hear that."

"I bet." I sipped at the cognac. "You got a smoke? I'm out."

Moretti shook out a Pall Mall from a red carton. I took it and he extended a nice silver-cased lighter to me. A silver bracelet clamped his thick wrist. He lit my cigarette but before he could snap the lighter shut I grabbed his wrist and thumb, and twisted them and the lighter toward his fleshy face.

The bartender started toward us but stopped when I warned him to stay back. The two men at the pool table headed my way with pool cues. I warned them back, too. Moretti never moved, never took his eyes off me as he told everyone to stay put. It must have been at least two weeks since Red Owl had assaulted Moretti, but in the flickering yellow light I could still see fading evidence of deep bruising and cuts.

I released Moretti's wrist. He snapped the lighter shut and his pale face melted back into the shadows of the bar.

"Looks like Red Owl played you a little chin music," I said.

"I fell down a flight of stairs. All on my own."

"Just naturally clumsy, eh? At least you can take comfort in knowing Red Owl looks a helluva lot worse than you do."

"I still don't see your point."

"I think you sent someone to toss the Indian in front of that train. Revenge for assaulting you."

Moretti calmly topped off his cognac. "If that were true, I'd have been paid a visit by some of your detectives before now. I have a lotta friends on the force. If they got questions, they don't hesitate coming to talk to me. I got nothin' to hide."

"'Cept that puss. If Red Owl coulda worked over his opponents in the ring the way he worked you over, he'd be fighting in the Garden now. But you sent someone after him who was a lot more dangerous than he was. One of the Lopez twins."

Moretti flinched. "You're off your nut! I ain't crazy enough to have anything to do again with either one of them sick fucks."

"One of them sick fucks was looking for the Indian. Everybody within rifle shot of Larimer Street knows that. And you're the only one I've found so far with reason to do the man harm."

A queer expression suddenly crossed Moretti's face, as if he realized something he hadn't put together before. His eyes stared past me, through the supper club's walls, as if trying to divine a message outside in the darkness.

"Was Lopez just supposed to beat him up?" I said. "But got carried away and threw the Indian under a train? He likes to do shit like that."

Moretti returned his attention to me. "If I got problems, I clean up my own yard. I don't hire spic help."

"It seems our dead Indian might be linked in some way to that missing banker, Seth Rawlins. That have something to do with why the Indian worked you over?"

That gave Moretti pause. A slight tremor appeared in his hand holding the glass of cognac. He downed the rest of it, faster than one should drink forty-year-old cognac.

"I've been amused by your company, Officer Stryker, but I have work to do. But please, come back for a drink any time."

"If I come back, it will be to haul your big ass to jail."

念೩೩

Sometimes you got lucky. I got lucky with Villano "The Fixer" Moretti. For all his smoothness and denials, something scared him about a dead Indian boxer named Art Red Owl.

Fifteen minutes after I left the supper club and took up residence in my car up the street, Moretti bolted out a side door as if the US Cavalry was on his ass. He moved pretty well for a tank. He piled into a bright red Packard with white sidewalls and roared off south.

The Packard was easy to follow, though traffic was light at this hour and I had to stay well back. More than once I almost lost him, but he didn't drive as if he feared being tailed. He had bigger things on his mind.

Moretti drove straight to the high rent district around the Denver Country Club, ending up on Marion Street Parkway in front of a large two-story red brick home a nine iron from the thirteenth green. He parked behind a rare 1948 yellow Chrysler Town & Country convertible. I slipped in behind a 1935 Duesenberg a third of a block from Moretti's car and doused my lights. If they noticed my car, they would figure it was the hired help.

Moretti lumbered up stone steps and knocked at the recessed front door. Moments later, the door opened. From my angle, I couldn't see who opened it. Interior light spilled out and Moretti scampered inside clutching a manila envelope.

I waited. I waited a long time. The sun started to come up. It was the kind of neighborhood where the sun came up later than in mine, so the residents could sleep in. As light started to fill the sky, I could see more clearly just how nice a neighborhood it was. The homes were roomy. I could park my house in any one of the garages and still have room for my car. A gardener appeared and began trimming a hedge in front of the house across the street from me. He was so quiet he didn't even wake the birds.

Moretti finally came out, looking around more cautiously than when he had gone in. But I sat slumped low in my seat and he didn't notice my car or me. His hands were empty. He drove off. Two minutes later a tall, well-dressed man in shirt and slacks emerged from the same house. He drove off in the yellow Chrysler convertible.

I waited a few more minutes. No one else came out. I got out of my car and walked across the street to the gardener, a short, wiry man in his forties with a heavily tanned face. He seemed unperturbed that a uniform cop was asking questions at such an early hour.

I pointed to the house Moretti had visited. "You do any work for that house?"

He nodded.

"Who lives there?"

"Mister Lamprey."

"The lawyer?"

The gardener shrugged.

Considering the wealthy neighborhood, I figured it was E. Ezzard Lamprey. How many people, after all, are named after an eel-like fish? I didn't know much about the lawyer, other than he had an ugly-sounding name and he was one of the biggest lawyers in town.

"A man in a yellow Chrysler just left his place. Know him?"

The gardener didn't.

"I wasn't here, got it?" I said.

The gardener nodded, less respectfully.

I got in my car and drove past Lamprey's house. I caught a fleeting impression of leaded windows, well-tended flower-beds, a large porch. I memorized the house number to confirm later that it belonged to Lamprey. Then it was gone as my car moved up the street. A year's worth of "gifts" from Ruben Castillo's bar and all the other gin mills and merchants wouldn't have been enough for me to buy the front door to the place. So why was the biggest, sleaziest gangster in town paying a call to one of the city's biggest lawyers in the pre-dawn darkness? Who was the mystery man in the Chrysler? How were they linked to a dead Indian on the tracks? Maybe even to the missing banker?

All I had wanted to do was find a lowlife named Lopez. What the hell was I getting myself into?

CHAPTER 11

Paula clutched a glass of iced tea in both hands. "You think Hiss is guilty?"

I flipped hamburgers on a small grill as I mulled over her question. She had run an extension cord out to the back porch and plugged in the radio to listen to H. V. Kaltenborn on the NBC evening news as he reviewed the latest testimony at the Alger Hiss perjury trial. I didn't know much about it, except that some guy named Whittaker Chambers had accused some former big shot in FDR's State Department of being a communist spy. That seemed to be going around a lot these days. Now I didn't like commies any more than the next guy, but it all seemed far away to me.

I was more worried about a killer in my backyard.

I sipped from my can of Falstaff. "How the hell should I know? I don't believe any of those people."

"That's a cynical attitude."

"It's all politics and money these days, Paula. It's never about the truth."

My wife sat on the top step of the porch, the balls of her bare feet on the step below as if she were about to rise, her knotted calf muscles giving extra shape to her lean legs. I realized she hadn't painted her toenails once this summer. I liked it when she painted them. They made her look sexy.

She squinted into the low, hot sun and said angrily, "Well, I don't believe this Chambers character. I don't believe he got secret State Department documents from Hiss or that he hid microfilm in a pumpkin on his farm. It sounds totally fabricated."

Kaltenborn's crackling voice had moved on to describe Mao's Red Army sweeping across China. The Nationalists were in retreat and here we were, blacklisting Hollywood writers and arguing over pumpkins stuffed with microfilm.

I poked at one of the burgers. "Everybody's edgy. I see it on the streets. It used to be old men shooting their old ladies, or a coupla guys goin' at it over a woman. Something worth fighting over. Or at least a fight that made sense. Now people seem to kill just for the sport of it. They get away with it, too. That's what I hate. They get away with it."

"I think the Tafties are intent on finding themselves a sacrificial red goat," Paula went on. "Frame Hiss and a few other New Dealers in office and they can start impeachment proceedings against the president. That's who they really want—Truman."

I scanned the fenceless yards. Directly behind us a water sprinkler swished rhythmically. In a yard next to us, a man with no shirt but plenty of belly pushed his lawnmower through thin seed grass, a scowl on his face and sweat dripping from his forehead. In the three months since Paula and I had moved in, he and I had never introduced ourselves to each other or even nodded hello. But then, as a rule, I never had much to do socially with civilians.

Paula rattled the ice in her glass. "They're framing Hiss because they hated the New Deal and they hate the Fair Deal. They don't like Truman's foreign policy, either. In fact, most of them think foreign policy is a disease America contracted during the war and we should get over it as quickly as possible. Of course, if they have to, they'll kill the patient to cure the disease."

"Every time somebody gets away with murder they've chipped away at what little order we've got left in the world," I said. "It leaves the world...unbalanced."

Paula turned down the radio. "By the way, Joe, we've been

invited to a patio party Saturday afternoon. Can we go?"

"*Patio* party?"

"Frosty and Ed Newman. You've heard me mention Frosty. She's a volunteer with me at St. Jo's."

"Right. What's her husband do?"

"He's a big shot in the oil business."

Oil. Swell. I was in the oil business, too, so to speak, working under Mrs. Swain's leaky 1942 Studebaker. Newman and I would be instant buddies.

"I want to meet Frosty's husband," Paula said. "I want to talk to him about getting a job. With my war experiences, I could—"

"We've been over this a dozen times, Paula. You don't need to work. We're doing fine."

"Not on a policeman's salary!"

The burgers were beginning to sizzle. "I got a real good shot at promotion to detective. That'll help. Plus, I got my work at the garage."

Along with the sawbucks passed to me here and there by people who wanted to keep me on their good side.

"I could make really good money working for a man like Frosty's husband," she persisted. "Good enough for you to quit the department and go to college."

"I don't want to quit the department."

"Look at all the guys taking advantage of the GI bill. You could do that. You're a smart guy."

"I like what I do."

Paula rose and walked toward the back edge of the yard. Her backlit body grew hazy in the waning sun. "It isn't just the money, Joe. I'm bored."

"Helping figure out the oil reserves for Hitler's war machine was all well and good during the war. Everybody had to pitch in to help lick the Krauts. But that's past now. I'm hoping you'll get pregnant any day now, honey. You don't want to get started on a job and then have to quit."

"I don't want to sit around waiting to get pregnant. I want to work. I want to go to Newman's party."

I looked back at the burgers and waved the smoke away

with the spatula. "I'll see. I might need to make up some work at the garage."

Paula spun toward me. "On a Saturday night? Why are you making up work at the garage?"

Carl was getting more frustrated with my missed work than I'd thought he would. "The department's got me on special assignment."

"What special assignment?

"I can't tell you. But it's why I'm making up work at the garage."

"What's so damn secret about—"

"Why don't you go to the party without me."

"Because I want you with me. I don't want to go like some widow."

Paula stomped inside to finish the potato salad. I took a long drink from my beer, picked up the morning's *Rocky Mountain News*, and turned to Lou Sheppard's story on page three updating the police investigation of the banker's disappearance. There was little new to update—Rawlins was still missing and there had been no new leads since they'd found his car—except for mine, which I'd told no one about. But Lou had spiced up the story with an unflattering picture he'd snapped of the banker's daughter, Rachel, as she stepped out of a fancy car somewhere downtown. She wore Jean Harlow-styled platinum-blonde hair, her young, pretty face twisted in an angry sneer at his intrusion.

Lou had also provided a few paragraphs of background about her. She was married to an older real estate tycoon named Terry Adler. But the picture Sheppard painted of her was that of a free-spirited woman in her early twenties who loved the party life, drinking, drugs, and who was an "aspiring" actress working in local theater. She'd gone to Hollywood in her late teens trying to become movieland's next Lauren Bacall. The closest she got to getting into the movies was making it into Louella Parsons's gossip column for getting into a catfight in a trendy Hollywood restaurant with a semi-known actress. The actress had accused her of screwing her husband, who happened to be producer of a film Rawlins was trying out for, and Rawlins had attacked her. Gossip was she'd gotten pregnant by the producer, and her father had sent her to Europe for an extended "vacation." She hadn't come back with a baby.

Lou loved gossip.

The phone rang and Paula answered it. I kept reading. Rachel Rawlins was the banker's only child. Adopted. His wife had died several years earlier in a car accident. That seemed to have marked about the time his daughter began to—

Paula appeared at the door, scowling. "It's that reporter, Sheppard!"

I had called Lou earlier in the day and left a message with the flunky who answered his phone. I scooped the burgers onto a plastic plate and handed them to Paula. "What's he want, Joe?" she said, blocking my path to the phone. "Does it have something to do with your *special assignment*?"

"If it did, I'd sure not tell a news hawk like Lou about it."

"What then? I don't trust that man. I thought you left all that stuff behind."

Her voice rose, and the fat man stopped pushing his lawnmower to listen in. I glared at him and he hastily resumed pushing.

"The burgers are ready for cheese," I said, brushing by her. "I'll be right back."

ტ৩ტ৩

"Well, speak of the devil himself," I said, standing by the black phone. "I was just reading your article on Rawlins. His daughter looked none too happy about you taking her picture."

"Too bad. She's news."

"You're all heart, Lou."

The *Denver Post* had been content running a press-release photo of her from her Hollywood days. Not Lou and the *Rocky Mountain News*.

"Whattya want, Joe? I woulda gotten back to you sooner but I was finishing up a piece on a jumper on Fourteenth Street."

"I didn't hear about that."

"Some guy imitated an Esther Williams swan dive off the roof of the Blackburn Hotel. Another despondent unemployed. Your captain's got a toughie on that one—use a putty knife to scrape him up or just pave over him."

"That's why they promoted him. To make the tough decisions."

"Whatever you want must be important. You never call me these days."

"I never called you in the old days. But I need some information."

"And I need a raise. What do I get in return?"

"I don't know at this point if there is a return. But if there is, you'll get the scoop."

"What do you want to know?"

"It's a who—*if* you take a blood oath to keep it out of your typewriter until I release it. If you cross me, I'll take the blood out of you myself."

I sensed Lou sitting straight up in his chair and grabbing a notepad.

"All right, all right. I promise. Who's the who?"

"E. Ezzard Lamprey."

"What do you want to know about him other than you can't afford him? He's not representing some lowlife you arrested, is he? He doesn't do that kind of work."

"A lowlife named Villano Moretti visited him recently."

"So what? Moretti can get an audience with the pope if he wants."

"He visit the pope at three in the morning?"

"Maybe he brought the shyster an early morning pick-me-up. Who the fuck knows. What do you want to know about the infamous Mister Lamprey?"

"Anything. All I know is he's a hot-shot lawyer in town."

"That pretty much says it all. He's got an office on Seventeenth Street. Equitable Building. Same street where most of his retainers work. Gets his name in the papers about once a week for having some pol slap him on the back."

"Clients?"

"Banks, real estate firms, oil companies, some Blue Blood accounts—you know, keep their trouble-making children out of the newspapers. He's a consultant to the Denver Water Department on their water rights case. That's a big deal these days. Beyond that, I don't know much about him. I deal more with the scum you deal with."

"He got a clean rep?"

"Let's say you don't prowl the corridors of Seventeenth Street for long without picking up shit on the bottom of your shoes. Not riff-raff shit, mind you. High pillow stuff."

"I wouldn't call Moretti high pillow."

"Maybe Lamprey's stepped in some deeper shit than he realizes. What's the tie-in? How'd you link him and Moretti at three in the morning?"

Taking Lou Sheppard into my confidence was like taking a snake charmer into my house. But I had to divulge some of it. I had to know why Moretti and Lamprey had met at that hour, along with the mysterious third visitor. What had sent Moretti off in such a panic? What was he carrying in the envelope he left?

I confided to Lou that the dead man on the tracks was likely an Indian boxer named Art Red Owl. I had reason to believe he had assaulted Moretti and Moretti had sicced muscle on the Indian in retaliation. I told him that after I'd confronted Moretti with this information, he'd hustled straight to Lamprey's house.

"I heard Moretti got the shit beaten out of him," Lou said. "But I hadn't heard by who. Or why. Any idea why this Indian would have done that?"

"That's what I'm curious about," I lied. No way was I going to divulge it might be linked to the missing banker. The reporter would have willingly sacrificed all his blood to me for that story, and thrown in his grandmother's blood, too.

"Can't imagine any connection between Lamprey and the Indian," Lou said. "But stranger shit happens in this town. Do I sense the Denver Kid climbing back into the saddle again?"

I ignored his comment and told him about the tall man who

had left Lamprey's house right after Moretti left. The man had driven away in a yellow Chrysler Town and Country convertible. Lou didn't know who it might be.

Paula stuck her head into the living room and impatiently waved for me to come to dinner.

I nodded. When she disappeared, I asked Lou, "Tell me, what do Lamprey's friends and family call him: E or Ezzard?"

"*Mister* Lamprey."

"Thanks for the information, Lou. I gotta eat and go to work."

"Hey, you know who you should talk to?" Lou said. "A guy named Estrada. Emilio Estrada. A Mexican. He's a lawyer, but a clean one. I interviewed him once on a criminal water case. He knows a lot about Lamprey and his cronies."

"Why's that?"

"He's locked in a court battle with Lamprey and the powers-to-be in the city over those water rights I mentioned. You know the reservoir the Water Board wants to build in the mountains near Gold Dust?"

"The Ponderosa Reservoir?"

"Uh, huh. Estrada represents some landowners who've filed a lawsuit to stop the project. Lamprey represents the people and institutions that want it built. They're duking it out in federal district court right now."

"Sounds exciting," I said unexcitedly.

"It's a big deal, Joe. A very big deal. Out here, a lot of money is at stake where water's concerned. You've lived here long enough to know how little moisture we get each year."

I nodded even though he couldn't see me. "I get tired of watering my yard."

"Fifteen inches a year on average. My neighbor's dog pees more water than that on my flowerbed. Fifteen inches might be enough for prairie dogs and sagebrush, but not for a booming city like Denver. Which makes water more valuable than gold. You know how big that fucking dam will be if they build it?"

"Uh-uh."

"Its crest would stretch the length from the State Capitol

Building to City Hall. That's a third of a mile. It'd be three times taller than the tallest building in Denver. The reservoir would cover ten thousand acres. That'll put the town of Gold Dust under three hundred feet of water. Along with good ranch land and some beautiful forestland. It'll also destroy some of the best trout streams in the nation."

"I didn't know you cared, Lou."

"I fish some of those streams."

That was the first time I knew Sheppard did anything but chase cops and crooks.

"Anyway," he said, "Estrada can tell you more about the lawsuit and about Lamprey. Maybe he'd have an idea why Moretti would visit Lamprey. Then you can tell me."

Talking to a water lawyer sounded like a waste of time, but I thanked Lou anyway. I started to hang up when he stopped me.

"You know—" He paused for a moment. "Come to think of it, it is curiously coincidental about you picking up on Lamprey like that, just now."

"Why's that?"

"One of the ranches the reservoir would flood belongs to our city's most prominent missing person."

"Seth Rawlins?"

"You got something you're not telling me, Joe? Something about *Rawlins*? About Moretti and Lamprey and him? I'd give my right nut to scoop the *Post* on that one."

I hesitated longer than I should have. "No, there's no connection I know of. But maybe I do have something for you concerning Rawlins."

"Give it to me." I could envision his pen poised to strike.

"It's from my new partner, Moroni Perdue. That's M, O, R, O, N, I. He's the one with me when we found the Indian's body in The Bottoms."

"I remember seeing him there."

"The guy's sharp, for a rookie, let me tell you. He put me on to the dead Indian."

"Didn't he throw up?"

"He's got a theory about what happened to the banker."

I could hear Lou breathing hard in the phone. "Yeah?" he prodded after I didn't say anything.

"Flying saucers got him."

CHAPTER 12

I was skimming the day's complaint reports looking for a mention of the Lopez brothers when Sergeant Mulcahey told me Captain Donlan wanted to see me before roll call. "What about?" Had my promotion come through?

"He didn't say. But he didn't look happy."

I found the captain sitting behind his spotless wood desk in a buttoned, double-breasted gray suit that went well with his thick dark hair and his burnished face. He didn't say anything at first or offer one of the comfortable-looking chairs in front of his desk. He looked tired.

"You're working late, sir," I said sympathetically.

"More often than I like." He paused before saying, "You're not helping matters, Stryker."

"Sir?"

"I'm getting complaints from homicide you're trying to do their work for them. In particular, from Detective Griffin."

I thought of the slug sitting at his desk in his pumpkin-colored tie. "He needs all the help he can get, sir."

The captain frowned at my sarcasm. "Between you and me, you're right. He's an incompetent short-timer. But I can't have you stepping on their toes like you did before."

"What exactly was his complaint, sir?"

"Seems he warned you to stay out of his case on this head-less body you found on the tracks. Yet he's finding your damn footprints everywhere. Said you were pushing Moretti's buttons about it. That's not smart, pushing Moretti's buttons. Then the other day some old boxing manager shows up at the morgue to ID the body you claimed was…" Donlan consulted a note on his desk. "…some Indian named Art Red Owl."

"Did he?"

"Did who what?"

"Did the manager identify the body?"

"No. He threw up all over the morgue attendant."

"I'm sure it's Art Red Owl, sir. A local small-time boxer."

"I don't care if you're certain it's the mayor. It's Griffin's case, for better or worse."

"He doesn't even believe it was a murder, sir." I hesitated then said, "But I've developed information suggesting the killer might be one of the Lopez brothers."

The captain pursed his lips. "Griffin didn't mention Lopez. Why do you think it involves Lopez?"

I explained the connections I had found so far, more or less. Less being no mention of Red Owl's hooker girlfriend and *El Perro* and the missing banker and the fact Moretti had led me to one of the biggest lawyers in town. I didn't want the captain to know just how much I had been nosing around in Griffin's case. So I stuck to what I'd heard on Larimer Street, that one of the Lopez brothers had been looking for a boxer, including seeking information from the Indian's manager.

"Look, Joe, I know you went through a rough patch after Flemming died. We all did. I understand why you want to nail Lopez. But this is Griffin's case. I want you to lay off. Understand?"

"I understand, sir," I said contritely. Yet in the back of my mind, I mulled over the curious fact Villano Moretti had squealed to homicide about my leaning on him. Which told me he and Lamprey and the mystery man didn't want me digging into the Indian's death. And I always dug where I wasn't wanted.

Donlan leaned back in his chair and crossed his arms. "You know you're up for promotion, Joe. There are people in this department who want to see you make detective."

"I hope to do that, sir."

"You've become more of a team player the last year. You've quit grandstanding since Derek died. We don't read your name in the paper every damn day. That impresses the right people. They know your talent. They think you're a good cop and they want to see you go far."

"I appreciate that, sir."

"Which is why I trusted you to break in my rookie. How's Moroni doing?"

"Fine, sir."

"He handle the body on the tracks okay?"

"He did fine, sir. He's very observant. I think he'll make a fine cop."

If I didn't ruin him first. The captain would not have liked the fact I was regularly cutting the rookie in on my grease and involving him in my efforts to hunt down Lopez. Then, on the other hand, maybe the captain knew all about that. Maybe the rookie had betrayed me and told him about my rooting around for Lopez, about my little bribes. Maybe Donlan was being coy about it for the moment for reasons that were not yet clear to me.

"Good," Donlan said. "Don't fuck it up for him, Officer Stryker. Or for you. I don't want him running afoul of Griffin. Got that?"

"Yes, sir."

"Drop your little side investigation or I'll have you walking Siberia."

∞∞∞

I picked up the patrol car and Perdue after roll call and headed out to our precinct. It was a moonless, hot night, so black the dark pavement soaked up the lights from the buildings and passing cars. The night air was dry and motionless, as if holding its breathe for an impending event it didn't fully understand. I drove stiff-armed, silent, my eyes hard on the road. Even the rookie was unusually quiet, gnawing on his LifeSavers and staring out the open passenger window.

I stopped for a red light on Fifteenth Street, waited as a young couple crossed in front of us laughing and nuzzling each other. The light turned green and I started to accelerate when a dark Chevy flashed into the intersection, crossing in front of us. I slammed on the brakes. The Chevy kept right on going, weaving down Arapahoe, oblivious to us. He was going to end the night killing himself, or someone else. I caught my breath then drove on through the intersection toward lower downtown.

"Joe, that guy's drunk," Perdue said. I kept driving. He stared at the car until it disappeared from view. He turned back toward me. "Shouldn't we go after him?"

"Are you telling Donlan about us?" I said.

"What?"

"Donlan just chewed me out for lookin' into the Indian's death. The dicks are pissed. Donlan said the dicks are finding my damn footprints everywhere. Those were his exact words." I glanced at the rookie. He stared at me as if I were his father who had just revealed he was Jewish, not Mormon. "Did you tell him anything about our investigations?"

"No, Joe. I swear. Why would I do that?"

"You and he are Mormon buddies."

"Joe, I swear, I've said nothing to no one. The captain or homicide."

"Homicide got wind of the boxing manager going to the morgue to try to ID the Indian. You were with me when I talked to Leroy Sunday."

"Joe, I didn't tell anyone about that. Or about the prostitute we saw or that gang guy. I'll swear on a Bible for you. I wouldn't rat on you. I want to learn from you. I want to help you solve the case as much as you do. You gotta believe me."

Panic laced his voice, but I couldn't determine whether it was because I had caught him red-handed or because he was innocent and genuinely feared losing my trust. He didn't tell about Moretti. The mobster had leaned on homicide on his own. The rookie had heard the prostitute link the missing banker to her dead boyfriend, but if he had passed that on to the captain, Donlan wouldn't be playing coy. He and homicide would have been all over me for what I knew. Then he would have ordered me to stay away from the banker case. Far, far away.

"You better not talk to the captain," I said. "I can talk, too."

"Talk about what?"

I glanced at him. "I don't think he'd like hear about the bribes you're taking. About breaking a few department rules here and there."

The rookie's face paled and he looked away. He was hurt. Better that, however, than getting the both of us in a jam.

Maybe the rookie really was telling the truth. But I couldn't be sure. Either way, it wasn't safe to keep the kid involved in my hunt for Lopez. With the links to the missing banker and Moretti and Lamprey, the whole thing was getting too big and too dangerous.

ℰↃℰↃ

My nightmares about Derek Flemming had returned, fiercer than ever. I kept them hidden from Paula, but I couldn't keep them hidden from myself. Sometimes I couldn't sleep. Other times, I slept and didn't want to.

I tried to sort out everything I had learned about Moretti and Lamprey and Lopez and the missing banker, but I kept coming back to Derek.

Derek was an old-timer on the force the day he died, a mere seven months shy of putting in his papers. He was not a man of much ambition by then, but he was one of the smartest cops I had ever known. He had grown up in Denver, and I remember him ranting about the city's exploding growth after the war. "Too many ex-soldiers looking for another war to fight," he would mutter whenever we sat in traffic.

Considering I was one of those ex-soldiers who had invaded his hometown, Derek and I got along pretty well. He took me under his wing, and we worked off and on together for over two years. He may have been a tired cop when we worked together, but he had been a tough sonofabitch back in the thirties—one of the department's best. That was the way it usually went with cops—all dewy-eyed out of the gate, until they realized few people gave a shit. Kept the murderers and rapists off the street and looked the other way when it came to gambling and prostitution. "That's what's expected of you," he used to tell me.

Cynical as he was, Derek taught me how to be a good cop. He taught me all the little tricks, from how to identify and nurture good informants to the best way to search a building without getting your ass shot off by criminals or another cop. I think he got a lot of personal satisfaction watching me those first two years make so many arrests, getting my name in the newspapers, showing up the veteran dicks. "But there are risks," he often cautioned. "There are old cops, and there are bold cops, but there are no old, bold cops."

Derek liked to coop. He could out sleep any man on the force. Whether in the black and white, in a chair, or in a borrowed bed, Derek would flop his head back and be asleep faster than a well-fed baby.

It had been a cold, rainy April evening on foot patrol two years ago when Derek decided he wanted to coop someplace warm. "Assholes don't like the rain any more than I do," he reasoned.

We went to a flophouse named The Fuller on the 2300 block of Larimer Street. The night clerk, a motor-mouth excon named Patrick Kelsey, always kept a spare room for a cop. Actually, he had enough spare rooms for half of Division Two, but that was the hotel's worry, not ours. Kelsey was glad for the company. During the past four months, several hotels on the north side had been robbed, and two clerks had been pistol whipped pretty bad.

Derek tipped Sergeant Mulcahey, the desk sergeant, where we were—they were partners from the thirties—and Derek retired to a second floor room for an hour's sack. I cooled my heels in the lobby with Kelsey and two drunks who sat in their cheap wine stupors near a tarnished brass Greek goddess statue with a chipped knee. Periodically, Kelsey looked up from his three-year-old copy of *Field and Stream* to brag about some humongous pike he had once snagged in a remote Canadian lake or a Dall sheep he had shot in Alaska's Brooks Range, as if anyone believed him, or cared.

I could have napped in my own room, of course, but I was restless, preferring the excitement—it was still excitement to me then—of cruising the streets instead of watching layers of red paint flake off the lobby's cornice. Fifteen minutes of Kelsey's monologues and I was less alert than the drunks, so I put on my slicker and headed out into the rain. I didn't tell Derek. I figured he was asleep.

I walked around for half an hour, rattling storefront doors and checking bars for fugitives. Derek had taught me how to match faces to mug shots and witness descriptions. He had shown me how fugitives could alter their hair color and grow a mustache and dress respectably, yet still not be able to hide their give-away tics and habits. I once caught a disguised escaped murderer because of the way he compulsively combed his hair.

But as Derek had said, rain kept the assholes home, so I wandered back empty-handed to the hotel around 12:45 a.m. As I neared the entrance, I noticed the yellow cast of the lobby lights falling on a dark-colored Plymouth coupe parked in front of the hotel. Its motor was running but no one was inside. I slowed, edging toward the lobby window. I peered in. A bolt of fear shot through me.

Two men wearing black hoods were robbing the place. One was rifling the hotel's cash drawer. The other, a short man dressed in white chinos and a light jacket, his back half turned to me, kept one eye on the night clerk and the two drunks still collapsed in lobby chairs. Most of his attention, however, was on Derek.

My partner was sitting on the bottom of the stairs leading to the second floor, holding his bleeding head in both hands. He must have taken his uniform shirt off to nap. Blood splattered his white undershirt. He was unarmed. The robber calmly aimed a gun at his chest.

Derek would have told me to call for assistance, to remain

outside, to allow the goons to exit the hotel and leave the by-standers out of any line of fire before attempting to arrest them. But while the man pointing the gun at Derek appeared calm, the other robber was agitated, arguing. They clearly had not counted on a cop showing up in the middle of their robbery. I couldn't understand what they were saying, what with the rain beating against my slicker and the fact they were arguing in Spanish. Maybe they were arguing over what to do next. Maybe they were arguing over whether to shoot everybody and leave. Or maybe over whether to shoot Derek.

I couldn't take the time to find out or to call for backup.

I slipped quietly through the outer door of the hotel's vestibule and put my hand on the knob of the inside door. I could hear their Spanish more clearly now, agitated and fast. I took a deep breath, flung open the door, and aimed my gun at the two stickup men.

"Police! Drop your guns!"

For a moment, everyone in the lobby froze like figures in a cheap painting. Suddenly the man with the gun pointed at Derek whirled and wildly fired a shot at me, shattering the glass door behind me. I returned fire. The bullet caught him in the left thigh and he collapsed against the end of the registration desk.

The other masked man pulled a gun and fired at me, the bullet slamming into the doorjamb inches above my head. I swung my gun in his direction and shot twice. The second shot caught him dead center in his chest and he crumpled behind the desk.

The next moment I found myself sitting down inside the vestibule, stunned. I never heard the gunshot. Just felt the blow, as if hit with a sledgehammer. Moments later, incredible searing pain shot deep in my left shoulder.

As I tried to collect myself, the wounded gunman drew a second bead on me. I watched in a kind of helpless fascination as I waited to die.

At that moment, Derek lunged at the goon, wrapping his outstretched arms around a lower leg. The gunman kicked at him, as though trying to shake a dog nipping at his heels.

Derek's action gave me time to struggle to my feet and take better cover in the vestibule. I aimed my gun at the shooter, but didn't fire. I was shaky from my wound and feared I would hit Derek still clinging to the man's leg.

"Drop the gun!" I yelled.

The gunman reached down and pulled Derek to his feet by his thinning hair. He hooked an arm around his throat and pulled him in front of him, turning my partner into a human shield.

The gunman said something to me. I didn't understand the words, but I understood their meaning. He motioned with his gun for me to back out of the vestibule into the street.

"Don't do it, Joe!" Derek yelled.

The gunman butted Derek on the side of his head with his pistol. Another bloody cut appeared.

The gunman again waved for me to back out. I didn't move.

"Just shoot the prick!" Derek yelled.

Again, the gunman barked in Spanish. I held my ground in the protection of the vestibule. Abruptly, he swung his gun arm around and shot the night clerk as casually as a kid plinking crows off a power line with a .22. Blood bloomed on Kelsey's stomach and he went down to the floor, clutching his gut and screaming in pain.

The thug jammed his gun barrel back against Derek's skull. I knew what would happen next if I didn't comply. I began backing out of the vestibule into the street, my feet crunching on shattered glass.

"Don't, Joe," pleaded Derek. "He ain't gonna let me live."

I kept backing out, into the rain.

The gunman limped his way into the vestibule, using Derek as a crutch. I pressed against the wall of the hotel, in the shadows, so the gunman wouldn't have a clean shot at me. He and Derek eased their way out onto the sidewalk. The rain washed off the blood streaking Derek's tortured face.

They stood only feet from me now. In my brief police career, I had met enough criminals to recognize that most of them are scared to death in these situations. Most wave their gun and bounce on the balls of their feet, more likely to accidentally shoot somebody in their panic and fear than in cold blood. Not this bastard. He had an unsettling calmness about him as the rain fell on us. Even through his dark hood, with its tiny crude eyeholes, I could sense him smirking at me, laughing at me. He smelled my fear, and triumphed in it.

"Dammit, Joe, shoot the bastard!" Derek mumbled in pain.

I aimed my gun at the stickup man, my arm outstretched, rain dribbling in my eyes. I didn't have a clean shot. Derek was still in my way.

The stickup man pulled Derek toward the Plymouth. During that passage, which seemed an eternity, the goon moved in such a way that for a brief moment I had an opening.

I didn't shoot.

To this day, I didn't know why. Maybe it was the rain and darkness obscuring the shot. Maybe it was rookie fear. My gun hand was shaking so badly I wasn't sure I could hit the side of the Plymouth, let alone miss Derek and hit the head of the gunman. I had watched men freeze in combat. Maybe I didn't shoot out of naive hope the goon really would not cold-bloodedly shoot a uniformed cop, that all he wanted was to get away.

What I did know was that I didn't take the shot when I had it, and suddenly that brief opportunity was gone, as if someone had slammed a window closed against the storm.

"No, Joe, no," Derek pleaded.

The gunman steered Derek around to the driver's side and forced him in, never once taking the gun from his head. With his free hand on the steering wheel, the gunman made Derek shift into first gear and they pulled away raggedly from the curb. They drove in first gear to the end of the block. The car stopped and the passenger door opened. Derek began to emerge. Relief swept through my body.

As one foot touched the pavement, two muffled shots rang out. To this day, the image of the gun flashes inside the car burn behind my eyes.

Derek sprawled face down in the rain-soaked gutter.

Immediately I opened fire at the car but it was too late. It roared away and around the corner. I raced down the street. Derek lay half on the sidewalk, half in the gutter, rainwater gushing over his still legs. Dead.

I had played it all wrong. Whether I didn't have a good shot or I was afraid to take it didn't matter. Derek knew instinctively the man was going to kill him. His only hope had been for me to take the shot, successful or not.

I had failed him.

I knelt for a minute in the rain, cursing myself. I returned to the hotel and checked the stickup man lying in a heap behind the registration desk. He was as dead as Derek. Kelsey writhed in pain. They had ripped the desk phone's cord out of the wall so I ran half a block down the street to a bar and called in the shooting. I told them to dispatch patrol cars to hunt down the Plymouth coupe whose license plate I had memorized as it pulled away from the hotel entrance. My shoulder began to throb badly. It wasn't bleeding much but every movement was agony.

I walked back through the hotel, past the drunks still huddled terrified behind the lobby couch. They weren't going to move until someone told them it was okay. I went out into the street but couldn't face going down to Derek's body again. I stood in the rain until the first of the black and whites arrived, lights flashing hauntingly in the blackness.

Sergeant Mulcahey made sure my official report never revealed that his old friend had been cooping at the time of the stickup. He personally threw away the half-empty bottle of rye he found in Derek's room. The two drunks were never questioned, and Kelsey didn't speak for days. When he did, Mulcahey made sure his story corroborated mine.

Two men dead, one of them a cop, three wounded. Plus the fact that the robbery was another in the string of recent brutal hotel robberies. It made the front page. Lou Sheppard wrote the story in the *News*. I came off sounding like a hero.

I wanted to strangle Sheppard.

A citywide manhunt failed to turn up the killer. They found

the Plymouth abandoned the next morning two miles away. It had been stolen the evening of the robbery from an elderly couple over on Downing. They found blood on the front seat. The dead stickup man was a Mexican named Munoz. Kelsey swore the other man, the one who had shot him and killed Derek, was one of the Lopez brothers. He had recognized the voice. He knew both of them, including spending time with Antonio in prison. The problem was, he wasn't sure which one was behind the hood. He might not have been sure even without the hood.

We never turned up either one. I never heard their names mentioned on the street again until the night the bartender Ruben Castillo said one of the Lopez brothers had stabbed a Negro in a fight and was hunting for a boxer.

I wrote Derek's family two weeks after he had died, offering my condolences. Derek's job had driven his wife to divorce several years before and she had raised their three boys in Tulsa, Oklahoma, where she had married an oil field roustabout.

Derek had spoken often and fondly about his family. I felt as if I knew them as well as anyone, though I had never met them.

None of them ever wrote back. I had hoped I would hear from Derek's oldest son, Gene. Derek hadn't seen him in over two years, but he had talked often about him, with obvious pride. His son had wanted to become a cop like his old man.

Perhaps his son didn't like to write letters. Perhaps it was too painful. Perhaps he couldn't bear to write to the man who had survived instead of his father. Perhaps he hated me.

I would never be able to change that. I would never be able to alter that night or what I had lived with since. If I had stayed in the hotel lobby, the robbers probably would have passed it by. If I had taken the shot Derek told me to, he might have lived. Instead, he had selflessly sacrificed his life for my failure to act. All I could do now was make sure his sacrifice would not entirely be in vain. All I could do now was to make sure I found Lopez and made him pay.

CHAPTER 13

The next afternoon, I called on the water lawyer Sheppard had told me about, Emilio Estrada. The guy might have all the skinny on his rival E. Ezzard Lamprey and his cronies, but Estrada sure didn't have the skinny on how to make their kind of dough. Otherwise, he wouldn't be slumming in the Danforth, a decrepit black-brick office building near Stout and Fourteenth. I quickly found *Emilio Estrada Atto_ney At La_ 318* on the lobby directory. There weren't many other names to get in the way.

An old Negro wearing a gold-braided cap, showing far more dignity than the open-grill elevator he operated, took me up three flights. As he swung back the grill, he announced, "Third Floor," as if a bevy of attendants would greet me.

I walked the echoey hallway until I found Estrada's name in chipped black letters on a frosted glass door in the middle of a hallway of glass doors with chipped black lettering. I entered a tiny waiting room that tried in vain to rise above its surroundings. Everything was neat and clean, but age had taken its toll, from the worn red vinyl couch to the fading mustard walls. Behind a small clean desk and ancient typewriter sat a Mexican woman engrossed in a book thicker than a suitcase. I started to say something to get her attention but a water pipe behind the walls suddenly rattled like an old woman's dying throat.

When the rattling stopped, I said, "Excuse me."

The woman glanced up, startled, as if I were the first visitor she had seen in weeks. Large brown eyes narrowed on me. The uniform always had a way with women.

She snapped the book shut on a leather bookmark. "May I help you?"

Her voice was frosty enough to cool off an August afternoon. I guessed she was in her early forties, though her shoulder-length unkempt black hair, no makeup, and shapeless yellow linen dress did their best to make her look older.

I introduced myself and said I had an appointment with Mr. Estrada. She consulted the appointment book open in front of her. Out of formality, apparently, as it had only one name written on the page for the day. I twisted my head so I could read the title of the book on her desk. *Principia Mathematica.*

"A little light summer reading, eh?" I said.

She didn't comment or smile, but rose and disappeared behind the closed door to the inner room. I heard her voice in heated Spanish through the paper-thin wall, and then a man's voice cutting her off in mid-sentence. "No Spanish, Mercedes. I won't listen to your damn Spanish." She spoke again in Spanish, then switched to English, in a voice so soft I couldn't make out the words.

She reentered the reception room and said, "Mr. Estrada will see you now."

She ushered me into a small room where light struggled in through a narrow window. She closed the door behind me. A man about the age of his receptionist sat behind a paper-strewn desk. Emilio Estrada didn't rise but extended a strong hand on the end of a thick forearm, so I had to lean across his desk. I glimpsed the shiny metal of a wheelchair.

The lawyer motioned toward the lone faded overstuffed chair fronting his desk. I sat down and studied his face. He had thick wavy black hair and a jaw as formidable as the front end of a coal shovel. Yet there was a boyish quality to his face, especially around the large brown eyes. And even though I had never met the man until this moment, his face was curiously familiar.

My studying must have been obvious, for he said, "You noticed the resemblance."

I twisted my head in the direction of the receptionist's office. "A relative?"

"My sister, Mercedes. One year older and twice as smart. She's read enough to have earned a philosophy degree. She should have been the lawyer."

I turned back. "She looked kinda bored."

"Not much opportunity for a woman who's spent half her life pushing her kid brother around in a wheelchair."

I heard her pecking away at her typewriter. Writing a treatise, no doubt, on how to win friends and influence people.

"So what did you wish to talk to me about, Officer?" Estrada asked. "You were somewhat vague on the phone."

I wasn't sure myself what I was doing here talking to a water lawyer. The Lopez brothers seemed to be growing further and further out of reach the more I probed their possible connections to Art Red Owl's murder. I had gone from a simple body in The Bottoms, to a local "fixer," to a hotshot lawyer, and a very rich missing banker, and now a court battle over water rights.

I couldn't for the life of me figure out where a thug like Lopez fit into all that. Yet the dead Indian appeared connected in some way to the missing banker, and the missing banker seemed to be making many people mighty nervous. So I had to keep hacking my way through the jungle if I had any hope of finding the sonofabitch who'd killed Derek and turned my life upside down.

"It's a police matter," I said. "A reporter named Lou Sheppard said you could background me on a lawyer named E. Ezzard Lamprey."

"I see." Estrada looked at me with eyes as hard as stone. The lawyer leaned forward slightly. "What exactly do you want to know about Ezzard?"

"I understand you two are squaring off in federal court over the Ponderosa reservoir."

"I and three other attorneys. The judge consolidated several lawsuits—over our objections."

"Tell me what you know about Lamprey."

Estrada leaned back and steepled his fingers, bringing them to his lips. "Ezzard is a Harvard graduate, counsel to numerous corporations, special counsel to the Denver Water Board, personal counsel to such illustrious local citizens as Randolph Cornell, Philip Landreau, and Don Pesceone. He's always well prepared. He's an excellent courtroom tactician. He's effective. He'll do anything to win a case. Politically, he's right of Taft, but he wouldn't hesitate to call Uncle Joe Stalin to the stand as a character witness for his client if he thought it would win his case. And he wins most of them. He favors bow ties, eats veal cutlets and drinks a glass of bourbon every day for lunch, and worships that poodle of his, Blackstone. He's married and has one son—the other son, his oldest, died in the war. He doesn't like to talk about that."

"What about friends, acquaintances?"

"They're everyone and anyone of consequence. Name any important social function in the city and he's on the guest list. Though friends might be a misleading word. Even when you talk to the man socially, you get the feeling he's charging you for his time."

"If he's such a big-shot attorney, why would a two-bit local hood named Villano Moretti visit his home at three in the morning?"

That unsteepled the lawyer's fingers and brought him forward in his wheelchair. Nothing moved in his face, but I caught a flinch of alarm in his eyes.

His sister stopped typing.

"Nothing Ezzard does would particularly surprise me," the lawyer said in a low voice, as if Lamprey were eavesdropping. "As for Moretti, he has a lot of friends in high places. Denver Bank and Trust Company carries the mortgage on his supper club. Randolph Cornell is president of the bank and I'm sure he's aware of the loan. Cornell is buddies with Walter Pallas, the councilman who was a principal character reference on Moretti's liquor license application. Ezzard is private counsel to both Cornell and Pallas. That Ezzard and Moretti might know each other or do business together would not be contradictory to the circumstances."

"You seem to know a lot about these men."

"It's a matter of survival. I would add that Moretti has important friends in the police department. I would not make too much out of whatever connection you believe you may have stumbled across."

"Right now it's the only lead I have. Tell me more about this water case Lamprey's involved in. I understand a lot of money is at stake."

"Yes, a lot of money is at stake. In a state as dry as Colorado, water rights are far more valuable than oil and mineral rights. Which makes its supply and distribution a litigious, politically explosive issue."

Estrada backed his wheelchair away from his desk and rolled over to a glass-fronted bookcase full of tattered law books. A dying philodendron in a clay pot sat atop the bookcase, its fallen yellow leaves collecting in drifts on the floor. Estrada pulled a volume from a row of books on Colorado Revised Statutes and wheeled back to his desk. He randomly opened the thick book.

"We have volumes of case and statutory law on water," he said. "As any hydrologist will tell you, most of the state's available water resources lie on the other side of the Continental Divide, in the watersheds of the West Slope. That's where Denver obtains a substantial portion of her water today, via transmountain diversion."

"I thought we got most of our water from the South Platte."

"Oh, heavens no. We get water from the Fraser watershed, for example, which is pumped through the Moffat Tunnel. Which, by the way, was originally built for trains. The Williams Fork collection system is diverted from the West Slope via the Jones Pass Tunnel. We're talking *millions* of acre-feet of water from mountain watersheds. The people Ezzard represents want to add to that by diverting water from the Blue River into the Ponderosa dam project. However, that would have a highly negative impact on the waters of the Colorado River, and it conflicts with senior water rights on the West Slope. Do you know what appropriation doctrine means?"

He probably already noticed my glassy-eyed stare, but I shook my head to confirm the obvious. I didn't have a damn clue what any of this had to do with Moretti's visit to Lamprey. Moretti's only use for water was to dilute his customers' drinks. But it was sure a sore point for Estrada. The lawyer was warming to his subject so much I thought he would rise out of his wheelchair.

"I won't bore you with the fine points of the doctrine," he went on. "In brief, appropriation doctrine is a term used in water rights that crudely means first come, first served. It was developed during the 1800s when water was used in placer mining operations. I and the people I represent believe Denver intends to covertly seize more water from the West Slope than she is entitled to under the appropriation doctrine."

"You're saying they plan to *illegally* take this water?"

A patient smile crossed the lawyer's face. "You need to understand something about western water, Officer. It doesn't flow downhill. It flows toward money. Any relationship to the laws of gravity and the needs of the environment is purely coincidental."

"So people will make a bunch of money if this big Ponderosa reservoir is built?"

"Many people in this city believe Denver has a manifest destiny to grow. To reach that destiny, Denver must drain still more water from the West Slope. A lot more. People like Cornell, the Water Board, real estate developers like Terry Adler, investors—anyone whose fortunes depend on rapid and unregulated growth—see the West as an untapped gold mine. Forty-niners a century later. Only instead of gold, it's real estate and oil. Which is why they hired Ezzard as their chief gunslinger."

I straightened up in my chair. "Did you say Terry Adler?"

"Yes."

"The same man who's married to Seth Rawlins's daughter?"

"Yes."

"Adler's real estate developments would become much

more valuable then, if this reservoir is constructed?"

"Absolutely."

"Even though the dam would flood his father-in-law's ranch in the process."

Estrada nodded, an expression on his face acknowledging the obvious irony of that situation. "A 106-year-old ranch named Lost Coyote. Several thousand acres. A beautiful place. A lake on the property feeds one of the streams that will be dammed."

"Are you representing Seth Rawlins in your lawsuit?"

The lawyer shook his head. "No. He's retained his own contingent of lawyers. They filed a separate lawsuit, though it was consolidated with ours."

"Who exactly are you representing in this case?"

"West Slope interests concerned about loss of water rights and some landowners on this side of the Continental Divide whose property will be flooded by the dam."

"Have you worked with Rawlins or his lawyers?"

Estrada's hand rose and played with a bolo tie, one with a turquoise clasp depicting an Indian doing an eagle dance. "I've talked to his lawyers a few times."

"And Rawlins?"

"I've never met him."

"Have you talked to the attorneys since he disappeared?"

"No. It's been at least—"

Estrada's sister burst into the room. "*Excúseme, Emilio, pero*—" She stopped herself. "I was checking to see if there is anything you need. Coffee or something."

"Nothing, Mercedes," Estrada said. "We're fine."

"It's getting late. You shouldn't work too long. You'll get tired."

Estrada appeared annoyed. "I'm fine. We'll be finished shortly."

She held his gaze for a moment before throwing a withering glare in my direction and leaving the room.

The lawyer shrugged apologetically. "My sister is very protective of my health. Sometimes overly protective."

"It's good you have family to take care of you."

He patted the arms of his wheelchair. "It's hard on her. She lost a baby at birth when she was young and I'm all she's ever gotten to take care of in her life."

I nodded toward his wheelchair. "What happened?"

"I was thrown from a horse while I was checking on my parents' cattle. I was sixteen."

"Sorry to hear that." I looked him in the eyes. "Do you think Seth Rawlins's disappearance might have something to do with this water case?"

"I don't see any connection. It's a federal water case, not some back-alley mugging."

"As you acknowledged, there's a lot of money involved."

He made no reply.

"Ever hear of a man named Art Red Owl?" I asked. "A boxer?"

Estrada looked puzzled. "No."

"How about a man named Lopez? Antonio or Angelo Lopez?"

The lawyer shook his head. "Who are these men?"

I ignored his question. "If something illegal is going on in this water case, it might explain the presence of Villano Moretti at Lamprey's home."

The lawyer smiled mildly, as if I were a slow child who had just figured out the no-brainer answer to the problem on the blackboard.

I rose. "Thanks for your help, Mr. Estrada." We shook hands. "If you hear anything about any contacts between Moretti and Lamprey, call me." I gave him my home phone. Paula would love that. "In the meantime, please keep this conversation to yourself." I looked in the direction of the reception room. "Absolutely to yourself."

"I'm a lawyer, Officer Stryker. I'm sworn to confidentiality."

Mercedes Estrada acted busy when I walked through the reception room. I politely said goodbye and left. She didn't reply.

I stepped out into the empty hallway and headed for the elevator. I was a street cop. I dealt with sharpies, hoodlums, thugs, thieves, dimwits, muggers, drunks, and psychopaths who would make your hair curl. I didn't deal with water barons, missing multimillionaire bankers, real estate developers, and appropriation doctrines. How all this might lead me to Lopez I couldn't guess at this point. I just hoped like hell it did.

CHAPTER 14

To catch a lowlife killer like Lopez meant you worked the sewers. I knew how to work the sewers. If the Mexican lawyer's veiled implications about Lamprey were accurate, however, I would need to come up out of the sewers. Lamprey and his rich cronies were up to something illegal. Exactly what was unimportant. Whatever it was, it appeared tied into Moretti. And the gangster was tied to the dead Indian and Lopez. I sensed that by the way Moretti had panicked when I mentioned Rawlins and Red Owl. Unfortunately, coming up out the sewers meant I would be forced to hunt for Lopez in broad daylight. Get caught by the captain and I would be walking beat in Siberia. Yet keeping a low profile would not be easy with a rookie cop tagging along, either as a spy for Captain Donlan or just some gung-ho ex-marine who wanted to become The Denver Kid, Jr.

Unfortunately, I had no easy answers to any of this. I would do what I could on my own and drag along the rookie when I had no choice.

At least today, I was on my own. One lead I had not checked out yet was the theater where Art Red Owl worked part time, according to the manager of the Roxbury Apartments. The manager only had a partial name, Broadway something or other. I had never gone to a stage theater but it didn't take long to track it down. It was right there in the paper in an ad. The Broadway Playhouse, a summer stock theater. The resident cast alternated plays every other night: Noel Coward's *Blithe Spirits* and some hot new drama, *A Streetcar Named Desire*.

It was Saturday night and *Streetcar* was playing. I had relented earlier and gone with Paula to the "patio party" at Frosty and Ed Newman's. I was as out of place as a vagrant at a society ball. Cops usually felt that way among civilians. Especially well-heeled civilians.

Ed Newman and I didn't talk oil. But Paula did, cornering him about job possibilities in the oil industry. Maybe I needed to let her get a job. It might get her off my back about my job. The party dragged into early evening and, finally, I told Paula I needed to leave—police work. She was pissed and refused to go, so Mrs. Newman agreed to take her home.

ɛ৲ঽɛ৲ঽ

The Broadway Playhouse was located on the northwest side of town, not far from Moretti's supper club. It was a large, rambling structure resembling a poorly designed barn. Still, the parking lot was full, including many vehicles that would have fit right in at the Newman party.

The play was already underway, so I went around to an open stage door where a man leaned in with a cup of coffee in one hand and a cigarette in the other. He was dressed in greased-stained seersucker pants, a dirty undershirt, and theatrical makeup.

I flashed my badge. "You one of the actors?"

"Yeah." He took a drink of coffee. "I'm Steve tonight. Not a nice guy. Hot tempered. Beats his wife. Drinks and gambles. Totally unlike my charming self in real life."

"You know a stagehand here named Art Red Owl?"

"The Indian?"

I nodded. "When was the last time you saw him?"

The man thought about it as he sipped again at his coffee, which smelled sweetened with Old Fitz. "Geez, I dunno, better than two weeks maybe. I haven't seen him since his fight with the Mad Hungarian."

"The Mad Hungarian?"

"Victor King. The impresario of all this. The Muses' gift to Denver. From New York City," he said with a theatrical flourish of an arm, as if that explained everything.

"King doesn't exactly sound Hungarian," I said.

"It's his theater name. His real name is Kárpáthy. Is that Hungarian enough for you? Claims to be from Hungarian royalty. Of course, nobody with any theatrical ambitions would use the name Kárpáthy, so he changed it to King. Worked out well."

"How's that?"

"He became a successful character actor on Broadway. He could play anybody. Did radio, too. Could do a million voices. He still has some serious connections back there. It was a coup to bring *Streetcar* to a backwater town like Denver. The play just won the Pulitzer Prize and it's still on Broadway. We're drawing big crowds."

"You said you hadn't seen the Indian since his fight with this King guy. A physical fight?"

"Oh, hell no. Victor may be an egomaniac, but he's no fool. Nobody here would take on the Indian. The man was a professional boxer, for chrissake. No, it was a verbal fight."

"Over what?"

"I dunno. I heard them in Victor's office, behind closed doors. Probably over money. We all have that argument with Victor."

"Anybody come around looking for the Indian before he disappeared?" I asked.

The actor shook his head. "Hey, I gotta get inside. Miss my cue and the Mad Hungarian will live up to his name."

I followed the man into a stifling, hot backstage. I caught of a whiff of marijuana, but I wasn't here on a vice raid. The actor nodded toward a man I presumed was Victor King and quietly disappeared behind a set of curtains.

"Dammit, he blew that line again!" King yelled to no one in particular, but loudly enough some of the actors on stage must have heard it. "I'm going to ship that bumbling Lothario out to

Hollywood. He can sit on a damn horse and mumble his lines along with the Duke."

None of the half-dozen people in the wings said anything. The director fell silent, watching the action on the skeleton set, his long fingers tightened around a curtain rope. He was a tall, angular man, late-thirties, looking snappy in a double-breasted, pinstriped suit with a red pocket-handkerchief which matched his tie. A Fancy Dan, my father would have called him. A man so useless on the farm he couldn't drive nails into a snow bank.

I gazed past King and the stage into the darkened audience. The place looked packed. I observed the production for a few minutes before stepping forward to speak to King, who hadn't seemed to notice me. But at that moment, the act ended and the curtain dropped. The cast scurried off stage as the stagehands scurried on. No large Indian among them.

King ignored the actor he had criticized earlier, focusing instead on a young woman in platinum-blonde hair and red satin robe.

"How many damn characters are you trying to portray out there?" His outburst appeared to startle her, as if her mind were elsewhere. "One minute you're Jezebel, the next Joan of Ark. You're supposed to be Blanche DuBois. If this were New York, Mr. Williams and the critics would have left an hour ago."

"This isn't New York, Victor, however desperately you want it to be," she snapped in a Katharine Hepburn nasal-twang, her flush face burning through a thick layer of pancake makeup. Suddenly I recognized who she was. Made up to be a much older woman, she appeared well beyond her tender twenty-something years.

But I recognized that same angry expression from Lou Sheppard's front-page photograph of the woman coming out of a car.

Rachel Rawlins, the missing banker's daughter, stomped off toward the dressing rooms.

King noticed me for the first time and said, "Who the hell are you and what are you doing on my stage?"

I introduced myself, showed him my badge, and said we needed to talk.

Cool gray eyes narrowed in annoyance. "Can't this wait? It's obvious we're in the middle of one of the great plays of the twentieth century—even if my actors don't realize it."

"No, it can't wait."

The director sighed. "I can't bear to watch their acting, anyway."

I followed him to a small office cluttered with stacks of bound plays, jazz records, and props. Playbill covers and yellowing newspaper reviews plastered the walls along with photographs.

Many of the photos showed King posing with groups of actors, an arrogant expression always on his face. The other photos documented scenes from plays or individuals in theatrical poses, autographs scrawled across the corners.

The photograph of a patrician-looking man with an arched eyebrow caught my eye.

Its faded inscription read: "To Victor, From Noel."

"What exactly is this police matter?" King said. He leaned against a desk, as if intending his stay to be brief. In the harsh light of the room, his pale, sharp-boned face was not that of a handsome leading man. Yet it had an arresting coarseness to it, an intensity I suspected many women found irresistible.

"I'm investigating a homicide involving one of your employees," I said.

King crossed his arms. "My actors may be killing this play, Officer, but I doubt any of them would actually be involved in such a sordid affair."

He spoke with a New York accent. Not Hungarian, not foreign, unless you considered a New York accent foreign.

"It's not one of your actors. He was a stagehand named Art Red Owl."

"Ah, our Indian." He slowly shook his head. "I should have known. He's a bruiser. He's killed someone?"

"We think he was the victim."

The man's eyebrows rose in the kind of exaggerated way of

actors. "I find it difficult to imagine Art was a victim of any-one. He was a boxer, you know." He paused. "What do you mean, you *think* he was a victim? You don't know?"

"We're trying to establish a positive identification of a dead man we found on some railroad tracks. I believe it's him."

King looked puzzled. "Didn't his fingerprints confirm who he was? He had a criminal record, though I hired him anyway. He deserved the break."

"As I said, we're still trying to confirm ID. But I'm work-ing on the premise it's him."

The director put his hand to his mouth to muffle a cough. "I'm saddened to learn of his possible demise, but I'm not sure how I can help you."

"I understood you two had an argument shortly before he disappeared."

"Ahhh," he said. "So that's it. There's no such thing as a private conversation among theater people."

"What were you two arguing about?"

"He wanted more money. Everyone here wants more mon-ey. Unfortunately, a theater like this operates on a Spartan budget." King waved his hand around the room. "I've sunk every penny I had into this place. Are you from here?"

"No."

"This was a well-known theater once—forty, fifty years ago. Some big names played here in the summers: Sarah Bern-hardt, Douglas Fairbanks, Harold Lloyd, Ethel Merman. But it was an abandoned dump when I came out here three years ago. The only actors by then were the mice, a stray cat, and two bums using one corner of the stage for a toilet and another cor-ner to cook over small fires. It's a miracle the place hadn't burned to the ground."

His speech sparked a minor coughing fit. When he quieted, I asked if Red Owl had physically threatened him over their pay dispute.

"He got noisy, not violent."

"Nobody's seen him since then. Did you fire him?"

"No. He just left. Picked a bad time. Right at the start of our run."

I told the director the date of Red Owl's death and asked him where he was that evening.

"Right here. A dozen people can vouch for me."

I spotted a revolver laying on a wood table beside a Tiffany lamp. I picked it up and checked it. It wasn't loaded. The director answered before I could ask.

"It's a prop," he said. "A replica. It has no firing pin."

"Looks damn real."

A thin smile crossed the director's face. "It's supposed to look real."

I set the gun down. "Do you know the name Villano Moretti?"

"Only by reputation. Some kind of local criminal, isn't he?"

"We suspect Red Owl may have recently assaulted Moretti. Did you hear anything about that?"

"No."

"Did anyone come by looking for the Indian around the time he disappeared?"

King brushed long thin fingers through thick black hair neatly clipped. "No, not that I recall. Do you think his death has something to do with this Moretti fellow?"

"He ever talk about his life—friends, family, enemies, boxing?"

"I didn't know him well, Officer. He was a stagehand. It's not as if we went out for beers."

"We have reason to believe Red Owl went into hiding before he was murdered. Any idea where he might have gone? Or why?" King shrugged. "He ever mention a man named Lopez?" I asked.

The director cocked his head. "No. Is he your suspect?"

"I'm not at liberty to discuss case details. How long had Red Owl worked here?"

"Six months, perhaps."

"It's an odd job for someone like him."

"I'd put out an ad for stagehands. The work can be heavy. He is—was—a big boy. And he actually had an interest in acting." The director coughed again, harder this time. Suddenly he exploded in a flurry of raspy, body-racking coughs. I stepped forward to help him but he fiercely waved me off. He finally caught his breath.

"You oughta take that in for repairs, friend," I suggested.

"Emphysema," he said. His voice wheezed. "The doctors told me if I didn't move out West I wouldn't see mid-century. Frankly, I'm not sure which is the worse fate—dying an agonizing death from emphysema in New York City, or trying to establish legitimate theater in this philistine town."

"Your theater looked full."

"Oh, people come. There was almost no theater in this town until I arrived, let alone decent theater. But they prefer pap *Harvey* or a farce like our alternating play *Blithe Spirits*. I'm trying to educate them in what constitutes real theater. Someday the nation's best stage actors will come here again."

"One of your actresses is the daughter of Seth Rawlins."

He gave me a limp smile. "I have to work with what I have."

"You didn't sound pleased with her a few minutes ago."

"She needs to get that Hollywood crap out of her head and stay concentrated."

"You are aware her father is missing?" I reminded him.

"Of course. It's what she should be drawing on out there on the stage, her fears and anxieties. She isn't. Or can't. I don't know which. I always try to get my actors to pull their emotions, their own lives, into their characters."

It was a wonder we didn't find King dead on the tracks instead of Red Owl. "Do you know if Mrs. Rawlins had any kind of relationship with Art Red Owl?" My leads were beginning to loop back on themselves. Art Red Owl to Lopez to Moretti to Seth Rawlins, now to the banker's own daughter. "Relationship? What kind of relationship?"

"Anything beyond stagehand and actress."

"No. I doubt I saw them exchange two words. Why? What could that have to do with the Indian's death?"

"Curious."

"You have an odd sense of curiosity, Officer."

"Yeah, it's what usually gets me in trouble."

CHAPTER 15

Frank Sinatra was singing to his horse. I stared through the windshield of the Nash at the Sky-Hi Drive-in movie screen, trying to keep my eyes focused on this gawky, greasy-haired kid all the rage among the bobby-soxers. I tried, but couldn't. In desperation, I turned down the volume knob on the tinny speaker as low as it would go, but it didn't help. The kid still sounded as though he were singing from the bottom of a swimming pool.

"Turn that back up," Paula protested. She sat with a bag of homemade popcorn in her lap, a bare leg sticking out the open passenger window.

"I can't stand this guy."

"Well, I can, so turn the sound back up."

Reluctantly I did. "What the hell is the name of this movie?"

"*The Kissing Bandit.*"

"Maybe Sonja Henie will skate into the picture—you know, give it a touch of class."

Paula ignored me. She was a hopeless romantic when it came to musicals, no matter how awful they were or what skinny kid starred in them.

The heavy night air lay as motionless as the movie's plot. Couples sat in front of their cars in lawn chairs fanning themselves while hordes of kids played on the swings at the base of the two-story-high screen. Teenage boys in cutoffs and Brando

T-shirts lounged on car hoods watching the girls stroll by. In my rearview mirror, a sullen quarter moon rose just beyond the blinking neon arrow above the ticket booth.

"What do the kids see in this *dago*, anyway?"

"He's not a *dago*, Joe. Now will you be quiet."

"Any jerk who hangs out with Lucky Luciano oughta be banned from making movies."

"That's all lies in the gossip columns."

"Well, I heard he was bought by the mob. And I can see why. He sure as hell couldn't have made it on his own."

Sinatra had stopped serenading his horse, much to the relief of the horse. Now Kathryn Grayson was forced to listen to him.

"I wonder which end of the horse he kisses at the end of the movie," I said.

Paula stifled a giggle. I leaned over and tried to nibble her ear. She swatted at me with her hand as if I were a mosquito.

"The guys at the department who moonlight at these places say a lot of *S, E, X* goes on," I said. "Everybody around us is having babies. Let's join 'em."

"Shhhh," she said. I tried nibbling again but she pushed me away. "I'm not an hors d' oeuvre, Joe."

"Then let's go right to the main course." I slid my hand across the front of her shorts. Her thighs were sweaty from the heat. She pushed away my hand and clenched her thighs together. She was still angry with me for skipping out early from Newman's party the evening before.

I sighed audibly and grabbed the front section of the Sunday *News* off the dashboard. I could see the print by the lights of the concession stand. Lou Sheppard had scooped the *Post* again, breaking the biggest story yet about the Seth Rawlins case. A ransom note—amount unknown—had been delivered two days before to the missing man's daughter, according to Lou's unidentified police sources. Neither Rachel Adler, her real estate husband, her father's lawyers, nor the dicks on the case would publicly comment on the validity of Lou's story, but his police sources were usually reliable.

I tossed the newspaper back onto the dashboard and

scooped a handful of stale popcorn out of the bag. Lou's story didn't make sense. He likely had his facts straight, but the facts didn't make any sense. Why would the kidnapper take so long after snatching Rawlins to send a ransom note? He would want to get his money and vanish as quickly as possible. Rawlins himself probably wrote the damn note. He was off with some bimbo, and this is his way of covering his ass. Or maybe homicide or the daughter was using the note as a ruse to draw out the old man.

On the other hand, there remained the connection between Rawlins, the dead Indian, and Lopez. It couldn't be coincidental that Lopez likely killed the Indian who had worked at a theater where Seth Rawlins's daughter was a principal actress. It couldn't be coincidental that Red Owl had allegedly assaulted Villano Moretti, a mobster connected to a big-time lawyer who just happened to have been working on a water case that involved Seth Rawlins's property and the banker's son-in-law. How all these connections fit I had no idea. Frankly, I didn't care how they connected other than how they might lead me to Lopez.

I tried to let the whole damn business slip from my weary mind. I watched a woman tote a basket of laundry past us toward the Laundromat located behind the snack stand. At least one person was making good use of her time.

Mercifully, the movie finally ended. Kathryn Grayson didn't have to share Sinatra with his horse at the end of the movie—she got Sinatra all to herself. If you ask me, the horse got the better of the deal. The lights came up before the next movie started—some Roy Rogers two-reeler. I flicked on the radio, hoping to catch a Dodger score, and fiddled with the dial until I found KOA, just in time to hear that the Bums had beaten the Phillies 5-1. Pee Wee had gone three-for-three and Preacher Roe had tossed a two-hitter. The Preacher's change-up must have been changing right tonight. It couldn't have been his fastball. My mother could spit faster into a headwind. But the Dodgers never were pretty when they won.

Paula said, "Did I tell you Frosty's husband told me at the

party there was a good chance I could get a job with one of the oil companies? He says I've got the background. I could start with somebody like Sohio for more money than you're making now at both jobs. He's going to look into it for me and let me know if—"

"We've been over this, Paula."

"Not over it enough."

"There's nothing to discuss."

"I want to—"

"Wait a minute!" I held my hand up for silence and cranked up the radio volume.

"...as we reported earlier tonight. Shortly before sunset, Ponderosa County Sheriff's deputies pulled a badly decomposed body from a small lake located on the Rawlins mountain ranch, Lost Coyote. The body was discovered by William Gannon, the ranch foreman, who was fishing in the lake. Sheriff's officials had dragged the lake the week before, but had found nothing."

The agitated voice of a young man came on. "I thought I had snagged a log at first. Then the hook gave free, and when I reeled it in I found a piece of dark cloth on it, all covered with moss. I knew it was Mr. Rawlins. I knew it."

"Law enforcement officials are saying little," resumed the announcer, "and formal identification of the body is yet to be made. But all expectations are it is the missing banker, who has been the subject of a massive statewide police hunt. Unconfirmed reports indicate the body was tied to a small motor boat sunk in sixty-five feet of water. The condition of the body suggests it had been in the lake from around the time Rawlins disappeared. Neither the Sheriff's Department nor the Denver Police Department will say if they have any suspects or leads. We'll keep you updated on further developments as soon as they are available. This has been a KOA special news bulletin."

"Jesus Christ!" I said so loudly an elderly couple in the car next to me glanced annoyingly at me. I scrambled out of the car.

"Where you going, Joe?"

"I gotta make a phone call."

"I thought you didn't have anything to do with that Rawlins case?" she said angrily.

"I'll be right back."

There was a line at the pay phone and it took me several minutes before I was able to call Lou Sheppard. He was still on his way back from the lake, according to the city desk. Knowing Lou, he had beaten the dicks up there.

The quarter moon rose behind me as I made my way back to the car. Keeping my investigation low profile had just become a whole lot more difficult.

CHAPTER 16

Despite the poor condition of the rotting corpse at the bottom of the mountain lake, the Ponderosa county medical examiner didn't have much trouble confirming it belonged to one prominent missing banker, Seth Rawlins. He still had his hands. Meanwhile, the body of the Indian still lay officially unidentified in the city morgue. Art Red Owl deserved better. Plus, his hooker girlfriend's nervous remarks appeared to link him to the banker's murder. I decided to visit the Rawlins spread. It was a risky move, sticking my nose so visibly into the banker's murder. If Denver homicide or Captain Donlan got wind of it, I would be toast. Yet I was convinced that somewhere between the Indian's murder on the tracks and the banker's murder in the lake, I would find the Lopez brothers.

The Lost Coyote Ranch was actually one of several ranches Rawlins owned in Colorado and Wyoming. It lay on the other side of Loveland Pass, in a wide valley covered by pine trees, fierce stands of aspen, and meadows blanketed thick in wildflowers. At the south end of the valley rose a bowl-shaped mountain, patches of snow still clinging stubbornly to its shadows and feeding a coarse stream that snaked down to the Blue River. I turned off the paved highway onto a narrow dirt road that followed the stream for over a mile, past barbed wire and pinkish-purple patches of fireweed where the forest had once burned out.

A large grass-fringed lake appeared on my left just before the road ended at the main building, a modest one-story log cabin of rough dark timbers dotted by several stark bleached antlers. A barn, corrals with a few horses, and an icehouse stood nearby.

I pulled up behind a big yellow Chrysler Town & Country convertible parked in front of the cabin. I got out and walked along the car, running my hand across the soft leather interior and wood sides. It appeared identical to the car I had seen parked in front of E. Ezzard Lamprey's home the morning I trailed the hood Villano Moretti from his supper club.

A cowboy approached on horseback from behind one of the barns. He reined in a few feet from me. "Help you?"

"This the Rawlins place?"

"Yep. I'm Bill Gannon, the foreman. Checkin' fence on the south pasture. Saw you drive in."

Gannon was a young man, though his face was already deeply tanned and furrowed. He wore a cowboy shirt with pearl buttons and long sleeves rolled up to the elbows, scarred chaps, and a stained brown cowboy hat with a brim large enough to shade him and his horse.

I wasn't in uniform, so I flashed my badge and introduced myself. Gannon dismounted, his leathers creaking as he stepped down. "Told the sheriff everything I know," he said. "Talked to a coupla city detectives, too."

Officially, the case of Seth Rawlins rested in the hands of the Ponderosa County Sheriff. Publicly, the Denver Police Department was providing assistance. Privately, according to what Lou Sheppard had told me, the Denver dicks figured the sheriff for a backwoods yokel who couldn't track a cow through a field of manure, let alone track down a murderer.

With the pressure from the city leaders to resolve the case quickly, every detective in the Denver PD put in at least some time on the case running down leads, fielding phone tips from cranks, interviewing the weirdoes who confessed to every homicide they read about in the papers.

"New evidence we need to check out, sir," I said. "Recognize this man?" I held out the boxing photo of Art Red Owl.

The foreman squinted, then shook his head. "Never seen him before. He a suspect?"

"We think he may be connected to the case. His name is Art Red Owl. Did your boss ever mention that name?"

"No."

"What about the name Lopez? Antonio or Anthony?" The man shook his head. "You work long for Rawlins?" I asked.

"Six years. I used to work at his ranch down near Pawnee Buttes. Then he asked me to run this place. Just needs one man. Only summer a hundred head of cattle. He's got thousands at his other ranches."

"Your boss come up here often?"

"Most every weekend the weather was decent enough. Come here Friday evening straight from the bank. Loved to ride and fish. He woulda come up even more but the bank and the water lawsuit kept him pretty tied down. You know about that, the lawsuit?"

"A little."

The man shook his head in obvious disgust. "Denver and them other cities wanna build a damn just so city folk can grow grass where it weren't never meant to grow. Mr. Rawlins opposed it. Guess it don't make much difference now."

I surveyed the ranch. "Will all this be under the reservoir?"

"Damn right!" Gannon pointed to a stand of lodge pole pine that shot seventy-five feet into the blue sky. "See them trees there? Those tops will be two hundred feet under the surface, though they say they'll log the timber first. Sad. This ranch's been in the Rawlins family over one hundred years. This is elk and deer winter range, too."

"Maybe his daughter will carry on the lawsuit."

The foreman didn't reply, but his expression clearly indicated no hope lay with her.

"There are others fighting it," I said, trying to be encouraging.

"They don't carry the power Mr. Rawlins did. They don't have his stubbornness. He was a man as set in his ways as a rusty nail in a barn door. A good man, though." His eyes hardened. "I hope you guys catch the bastard who done it."

Gannon took off his hat and wiped his pale forehead with the back of his hand. He stared vacantly south toward the lake a hundred yards away. A rowboat floated serenely next to the wood dock jutting into the shimmering waters.

"That where you found him?" I asked.

"Yeah." Gannon's voice went thick. "Pulled out a calf once who'd been in a stream a coupla weeks. It weren't the same."

"Rawlins fish the lake often?"

"He preferred streams. We used to ride back up that ravine there—" The foreman pointed into the sun. "—and fish for brookies. But sometimes he fished the lake. That's where I was fishing, where it's real deep, where Mr. Rawlins used to catch lake trout. The lake's deeper'n she looks. There's some big ones down there. Maybe I was lookin' for him, I dunno. That's where I found him, real deep."

I thought about the old man at the bottom of the lake, roped to his motor boat. On the way up here, I'd mulled over the possibility that Lopez had committed the murder. Normally, I would never have connected the two. It wasn't Lopez's kind of crime. He was more into acts that brought immediate payoff, like robberies or assaults. I couldn't see him snatching the old man, sinking him to the bottom of the lake, and weeks later sending a ransom note. Yet Art Red Owl appeared linked to Rawlins, and Lopez was likely linked to the Indian. Had Red Owl known something about what had happened to Rawlins, and Lopez had murdered the Indian to keep him quiet? Lopez had gone to the trouble of cutting off the Indian's hands. Sending Rawlins to the bottom of the lake suggested a similar deliberateness not associated with either of the Lopez brothers. But deliberateness for what reason?

"You see your boss the weekend he disappeared?" I asked.

According to the newspapers, Rawlins's secretary had last seen her boss at 2:30 p.m. Thursday afternoon. He had told her he would not be in on Friday but didn't give a reason why. She presumed he was spending time at his ranch. Three business acquaintances told detectives he had failed to show up for a scheduled luncheon date Friday, and he was not a man prone to missing appointments.

"I was gone that weekend," Gannon said. "He called me out of the blue Thursday and told me to pick up a load of hay the next day in Brush and take it to his ranch up by Steamboat Springs. I didn't get back here until mid-afternoon Sunday."

"Was he still coming up Friday night?"

"That's what he told me. But he wasn't here when I got back. Come Monday morning his secretary called me. Said he hadn't come in for some appointments. I checked with his daughter but she hadn't seen him neither, though that ain't unusual. I decided I better call the sheriff."

"Any signs he'd been here that weekend?"

"Yeah, little things. But his car wasn't here or nothin'."

If the banker was at the ranch that Friday, he was back in Denver Saturday.

Witnesses had seen him at a bar, a feed store, and driving in his Roadmaster in his trademark rumpled cowboy hat with a small feather in the hatband. Plus, his car had been found in town.

"When was the last time you saw your boss?" I asked.

"The weekend before. We drove a coupla horses down to his Pawnee Buttes ranch."

"Did he say or do anything during that trip that was unusual? His mood strange?"

Gannon thought for a moment. "He didn't say nothin' unusual, but I could tell he was upset."

"About what?"

"His daughter, Miss Rachel, had come up that morning, and I overheard 'em arguin'. Don't know what about. She tore outa here right after that, as mad as a wet hen. I figured that was what was bothering him."

"Did he say what they were arguing about?"

"No. But he kept them things pretty much to himself. Just 'tween you and me, she's a high-strung filly, and I think she wore on Mr. Rawlins."

"Anything else unusual that day?"

"On the way to the ranch we stopped at the town cemetery

just outside of Pawnee Buttes. Small place no one's taken care of for years. Mr. Rawlins walked around looking at the grave-stones for a few minutes."

"Why was that unusual?"

"We'd driven by that cemetery a hundred times and never stopped before."

"What was he looking for?"

Gannon shrugged. "He walked it alone. When he got back in the truck, I asked him and he said he had relatives buried there. Didn't say nothin' else."

"What about visitors here? Besides his daughter. Bank clients, that sort of thing?"

He shook his head. "Visitors were rare. This was his re-treat." He stared down at the ground, as if suddenly trying to tease out a memory. A moment later, he found it. "There was someone up here two or three weeks before he disappeared. A Saturday, I think."

"Who was it?"

"Dunno. I was just getting back from doctoring cows. Saw Mr. Rawlins helping a man out of his wheelchair and into his car."

"His Roadmaster?"

"Yep. He put the wheelchair in the trunk and they took off."

My mind reeled with the image of the man in the wheel-chair. Emilio Estrada! The crippled lawyer had told me he had never met Rawlins, only his attorneys. Yet he had been with the man, on his ranch, where few visitors came. I remembered he had described the Rawlins ranch as "a beautiful place." He had seen it in person.

Then something else struck me. The cops had found the banker's abandoned Roadmaster within a block of the lawyer's office.

"No idea who this person was?" I pressed, struggling to keep the shock out of my voice.

Gannon shook his head. "Like I told the sheriff and some of your investigators, I was too far away to see who it was. Nobody seemed to have any idea, neither."

"Was anyone else with them?" I asked, thinking of Estrada's sister, Mercedes.

"No, I'm pretty sure it was just the two of them."

"You ever see this person up here before?"

"Nope." The foreman stopped to collect his voice again. "Like I said, visitors were rare."

I nodded toward the Town & Country convertible. "Then whose car is that?"

"That belongs to Miss Rachel."

I raised my eyebrows. "She's here?"

He nodded toward the cabin. "Arrived an hour ago."

Rachel Adler definitely was not the man who walked out of E. Ezzard Lamprey's house early one morning and climbed into the same convertible. Which meant it must have been her husband, Terry Adler, meeting with Lamprey and Moretti that morning. So Moretti was clearly playing with the big boys. The question was, why were the big boys playing with Villano Moretti?

"Her husband, does he come up here much?" I asked.

Gannon looked at me and snorted. "Never. Mr. Rawlins couldn't stand the bast—"

Suddenly his eyes darted toward the cabin. I turned to see Rachel Adler standing on the porch by the bleached skull of a pronghorn antelope. A silky-coated apricot-colored Afghan Hound stood by her side. She wore an apricot-colored dress and a black-veiled apricot-colored hat tipped rakishly to one side. The veil was drawn up and she blew cigarette smoke out hard. She stared at us but said nothing.

"The police, Mrs. Adler," Gannon offered.

I doffed my light-brown snap-brim hat.

"God, what a bore. Handle it, Bill." Her words came out slightly slurred.

She spun abruptly to go back inside and I called after her. "Excuse me a minute, Mrs. Adler." I cut around the yellow convertible and onto the porch. "Officer Stryker of the Denver Police Department."

"I've already talked to the police and the sheriff."

"We have new evidence, ma'am. I need to talk to you."

An exasperated sigh escaped through apricot-colored lips and she retreated into the cabin with the dog. I followed her inside, my eyes on her black and white suede pumps and the silk stockings whose seams ran true up her nicely rounded calves.

CHAPTER 17

A kerosene lamp on the mantle above a stone fireplace struggled to light the dim interior of the cabin's main room. Dark, musty furniture sat under a low knotty pine ceiling and rough timbers. Mounted hunting trophies and several oil paintings of Western landscapes crowded the walls. Through an open doorway, I saw a Majestic wood-burning cook stove and what appeared to be the original blue and white diamond pattern linoleum floor in the kitchen. A closed door led to what I presumed was a bedroom. That was about all there was to the place. No room for guests. A modest cabin for a man of such wealth. Maybe it was all he wanted. His retreat, as Gannon had described the place.

"Nice place," I commented to Rachel Adler.

"Yes, real rustic charm. My father stabled his horses in here." She picked up a glass of booze perched on the mantle and knocked back the last gulp. Even through the smoke, I could smell a heavy lavender perfume. The dog settled near her feet.

"I gather you don't come here often," I said.

She looked at me, annoyed, and dragged on her cigarette. "I came up to go through some papers my father kept here. I was just about to leave, in fact."

"I saw you at the Broadway Playhouse the other night."

"You came all this way for an autograph?" Her nasal twang was more pronounced than when I first heard her at the theater.

Maybe it was the liquor.

I shook my head. "We believe there may be a link between your father's death and a man murdered around the same time in Denver."

She blew out a long plume of smoke in the lamplight and stared at me with clover-colored eyes as dry as Colorado's high plains. She was a small woman whose figure any man would have trouble finding fault with. If I had to be picky, I'd say her mouth was a little too large. One should be so picky.

I held out the photo of Art Red Owl. "Do you recognize this man?"

"He's a stagehand at the theater. Art something. He's an Indian."

"Art Red Owl is his name."

"People said he was a professional boxer and he had a criminal record." She paused in sudden realization of my inquiry. "Do you think he—"

"We found his body shortly after your father disappeared. His name has subsequently been linked to your father's disappearance, but we don't have much beyond that."

Her eyes widened. "He's dead?"

"Murdered. Did you ever talk to him at the theater?"

"Rarely."

"Would your father have ever spoken to him?"

A strangled laugh hung in her throat. "I'm sure he didn't. My father hated the theater."

She moved to a coffee table in the middle of the room and tossed her half-smoked cigarette into a rare-looking Indian pottery vase.

"Red Owl no doubt knew you were the daughter of a wealthy man," I said. "Did he ever ask you anything about your father? Any details?"

"No. You think he kidnapped my father, killed him, and then sent the ransom note?"

So Lou Sheppard's story claiming the ransom note was accurate. Which left a puzzling scenario. The Indian kidnapped Rawlins with the intention of ransoming him, then something went wrong and he killed him. Which would explain why, according to the hooker Velvet Knights, Red Owl was so nervous about the citywide hunt for Rawlins. Yet it didn't explain several other things, including the fact the Indian had been murdered well before Rachel Alder had received the ransom note. Had Lopez and Red Owl engineered the kidnapping together, then had a falling out? Would that explain why Lopez had killed the Indian? Had Lopez then sent the ransom note? If so, why weeks after Rawlins had vanished?

"We're exploring multiple possibilities, ma'am," I offered.

She poured another drink from a cut-glass decanter—Scotch, I'd guess. She didn't offer me any. She moved unsteadily away from the coffee table, barely missing a pair of dirty cowboy boots standing next to a bootjack. Then she moved back to the table, as if not wanting to be far from the booze.

"You know how my father wanted to die?" Her voice was hard.

I would guess not the way he did. "No," I said aloud.

"When it was his time—that's what he called it, his time—he wanted to be tied to a horse on his Pawnee Buttes spread. Some old lame critter named Old Guts or Old Glory or something like that. Tied to the horse and sent packing off alone into the prairie."

"I'm sorry he didn't get his wish."

"The horse isn't."

I walked over to the fireplace. Several framed photographs, some new, some old, lined the mantle. I didn't recognize most of the people, but one was of her and her father. I studied it by the glow of the kerosene lamp. It had been taken when she was younger, perhaps in her teens. Her hair was black then, long, peeking out below a cowboy hat two sizes too large. She wore slacks, long-sleeved western-cut blouse, and cowboy boots—definitely not Hollywood. Seth Rawlins also looked far different from the more formal portraits run in the newspapers. He wore a corduroy jacket, plaid shirt open at the collar, and his trademark tan cowboy hat, a rumpled affair with a tiny feather in the hatband. He had steady eyes, a firm chin, grizzled sideburns that curled up in front of his ears like tumbleweed against a barbed wire fence.

Both sat on horses, posing for the photographer. Rawlins held his reins slack, relaxed, while his daughter gripped hers tight. She wore the smile of someone who wanted to be anywhere but atop a horse.

I held the photograph toward her. "You resemble your father, Mrs. Adler. Not weathered, of course. But the same eyes."

"Yes, that's what everyone says." Anger reared in her voice like a spooked horse. Yet her anger sounded edged with hurt. I had often seen such anger in the relatives and friends of murder or accident victims. As if they blamed the victim for dying before their time. As though the person had intentionally died out of spite as a way to irritate the living.

She crossed her arms. "I presume you are aware I'm adopted."

I nodded.

"Which explains the similarities." She studied me for a moment, as if gauging whether I was bright enough to understand what she was saying. From my blank expression she apparently figured I wasn't. "Adopted children take on the features of their adoptive parents. You know, like dogs start to look like their owners after a while."

What could I say? A heart-warming analogy I'm sure her father would have deeply appreciated. I had been around people before like Rachel Adler. People who seemed to have burned the skin right off their emotions. But never around one so wealthy.

She set down her Scotch and lit another cigarette. In the flash of movement of her arms, her long sleeves pulled up and I spotted freshly healed razor marks on her wrist.

She noticed my observation and quickly readjusted her sleeves.

"My father never kept my adoption a secret, but he didn't broadcast it, either." Her eyes suddenly paled and her voice softened. "He always introduced me as his daughter, never his *adopted* daughter. He never thought of me or treated me as anyone but his real daughter."

I reexamined the photo. I could see the differences: her higher cheekbones, the darker skin, the slightly wider nose, the smaller chin. I set the picture back on the mantle.

"You were your parents' only child, correct?"

"Yes. My mother couldn't have children. Or my father. I don't know which one. Maybe both. I'm the only child." She paused, as if the reality had hit her for the first time. "I'm the only one left."

"You inherit your father's entire estate, is that correct? Twenty-six million dollars?"

I swore her eyes flared with fire in the shadowy interior. "Are you accusing me of murdering my father for his money?"

"No. I was merely clarifying who inherits his estate."

She took a belt of Scotch. "Well, it's not exactly that simple. I am the sole beneficiary. But the money is in a trust, and I don't receive a dime unless I agree in writing to the trustees to give up acting. Forever."

"Your father put that in his will?"

Hurt returned to her voice. "He disapproved of me acting. He refused to even see me in *Streetcar*."

"Do you know anyone who would want to kidnap and murder your father?"

"Thumb through the social register—or anyone who needs a million dollars."

Now I knew the amount of the ransom note.

"He made a lot of enemies?" I asked.

Her anger swelled again. "He was a selfish man who never compromised."

I couldn't keep up with her moods. I couldn't tell if it was all play acting or just the confused world of a young, immature woman whose life had taken a dramatic, horrible turn.

I peered out the front door. "That car, Mrs. Adler. Do you or your husband usually drive it?"

"My husband. Why?"

"Does he know a lawyer named E. Ezzard Lamprey?"

"He's Terry's business attorney. What does any of this have to do with my father's death?"

"Do you know a man named Antonio or Angelo Lopez?"

"No. Who are—"

"Villano Moretti?"

"I recognize the name. I don't know him."

"What about an Emilio Estrada?"

"No. Who are these people?"

"Did you ever see a man in a wheelchair here?"

"No. Why are you asking about these people?"

I ignored her question and asked her why her father would stop at a cemetery near Pawnee Buttes. She took another drink and said she had no idea. "I don't know why he did a lot of things he did."

"Your foreman said your father was upset about something the weekend before he disappeared. Any idea what he was upset about?"

Her eyes looked away. "No."

"He said you were here that same weekend. You appeared upset. What went on between the two of you?"

She glared at me. "Fuck you!" She grabbed her purse and bolted through the door, the dog in tow. Moments later, her car roared away like a hound outa hell.

CHAPTER 18

When I left the Rawlins ranch, I wanted to go straight to Emilio Estrada's office. I wanted to confront him about why he had lied about never meeting Rawlins. But it was late afternoon by the time I got back to the city and I figured he would have left his office by then. So I grabbed a bite to eat at home and dressed for my shift.

One guy I knew would be around in the evening was Art Red Owl's boxing manager, Leroy Sunday. Something the hooker had said as she'd sat on the bed nursing her baby had stuck in the back of my mind and it had finally dislodged. It meant bringing along the rookie, but I had to take the risk.

Leroy's gym was quiet, except for a guy slugging a heavy bag as if it were his mother-in-law and two guys in the ring who would not be mistaken for contenders. The Punching Priest of Broadway raised his eyes from an open Bible as Perdue and I approached.

"I went to the morgue like you asked," he protested.

"Yeah, you threw up on the attendant. You didn't even ID the body. Your Indian's gonna end up buried in a pauper's grave with no name."

"I—I couldn't do it. His head—" Sunday's body shuddered.

I leaned both arms on the table in front of him. "So now you can atone for your sins. Tell me where Red Owl was hiding before he was killed."

"I told you, I don't know."

"I think you do. I think he told you because he looked up to you, he trusted you."

The old man licked his lips and mumbled something.

"Speak up," I pressed.

"He mighta been hidin' out with his cousin."

"What cousin?"

"Some cousin he knew from the reservation. Called him He Who Rides Thunder. Ridiculous name. I think his real name was Rodney McNeil."

"Where does this cousin live?"

"He don't *live* any place. Mostly he camps down in The Bottoms with the rest of the alkies."

"That's where we found the Indian's body," Perdue interjected.

"Art didn't tell me he was going there," Sunday said defensively. "He didn't tell me where he was hiding. I swear. I'm just guessin' he went there."

"Did you tell Lopez this?"

Sunday glanced down at his Bible, as if hunting for the right scripture for the occasion.

I reached across the table and flipped the book shut. "You aren't gonna find refuge in there, Leroy. Not tonight."

The old man jerked and looked up with a face beseeching forgiveness.

I recalled our previous conversation, when I had told him his boxer had turned up dead on the tracks and the man who had come asking where he could find Red Owl was likely the man who killed him.

I'd mistaken the old man's response at the time for sadness and fear. Now I knew the response had been one of comprehending guilt. He had made a terrible mistake in judgment for which god would never forgive him.

"Did you tell Lopez about the cousin?" I repeated slowly.

"I dunno. I mighta." His words barely leaked out. "He scared me." The old man looked down again. "And I was mad at Art. Figured he'd gone off on a bender with his no-good cousin and skipped his fight. Stuck me with the no-show money."

"You told us Lopez didn't say why he was looking for Red Owl. You wanna change your story now?"

"No. I was tellin' ya the truth. The man wouldn't say. But I knew it weren't for no good." Sunday looked up, as if pleading his case before God. "I didn't know the mug—what did you say his name was?

"Lopez."

"I had no idea he'd kill Art. I wouldn't have said nothin' about The Bottoms if I'd known he'd do what he did." Sunday shuddered. "I kinda hoped he'd put the scare of the Lord into Art. You know, set Art right."

I straighten up in disgust. "Yeah, that's Lopez. Doing God's work."

Perdue and I headed back out of the gym. When we reached the stairs to descend to street level, I stopped and told him to wait. "I forgot to ask Sunday something."

Leroy Sunday flinched as I approached, as though he expected me to slug him in the face.

"Did Red Owl say anything about assaulting Villano Moretti?" I asked.

The old man blinked rapidly. "No. But I heard. I asked him about it but he wouldn't talk about it. I swear to God, that's all I know."

"Did he ever mention the dead banker? Seth Rawlins?"

Sunday's eyes opened wide. "No. He got somethin' to do with that?"

I left and caught up with Perdue. As we went down the stairs, he asked what I'd forgotten to ask Sunday.

"Whether he thought he was going to hell."

∽∾∽

Perdue stewed silently as we prowled The Bottoms not far from where we had found the body of the Indian. I couldn't blame him. He sensed I hadn't told him the truth back at Leroy's gym. He didn't know about Moretti and his links to

Red Owl and Lamprey, and it was best for both of us to keep it that way. Still, it was tough putting your life in the hands of a fellow cop who didn't trust you.

Then again, prowling The Bottoms at night would make any man nervous. Even an armed cop. A half-moon spilled light, but most of the people who lived down here camped out where the moon's glow didn't reach, deep in the brush and trees on the land between the railroad tracks and the South Platte River. Only scattered campfires and our flashlights lit our way as we thrashed through the underbrush.

The Italian shanties, which had once occupied this river land, were long gone. The squatters who stayed down here slept on open ground or under tarps, makeshift lean-tos, or ragged canvas tents. Few women stayed in The Bottoms unless they had a protective boyfriend. The place was dangerous even for the men. Drunk, drug-crazed, hungry, broke, loony, or just plain mean, the inhabitants of The Bottoms would turn on each other without warning, like rabid dogs. Predators and prey, and it was never clear at any given moment who would be which.

I felt certain Red Owl's murder had come at the hands of one of the Lopez brothers, and his death was in some way mixed up with Moretti and the dead banker. Yet as we searched The Bottoms, I couldn't entirely rule out the possibility of a simpler answer. One of The Bottoms' inhabitants had killed him over something as inconsequential as a bottle of dago red.

We moved through smothering fetid air. Discarded tin cans, broken booze bottles, remnants of clothing, and torn newspapers littered the ground. The area stank of human waste, booze, and despair. Unrecognizable meat browned over campfires. "Maybe we should look for those missing hands while we're down here," I joked to Perdue.

We questioned sullen faces stained red from the campfire or alcohol. We shined flashlights into dark tents and poked the tips of our shoes against lumps in sleeping bags that I half expected to find dead. We asked where we could find an Indian named He Who Rides Thunder, what they knew about Thun-

der's cousin found dead on the tracks, and a Mexican named
Lopez who might have come through The Bottoms hunting for
Red Owl. A few believed Thunder was around, but they didn't
seem to know where. Even fewer had heard of the dead Indian.
Nobody owned up to seeing the hulking Mexican.

Finally, a man at a campfire pointed us in the direction of a
lean-to "that redskin claims is his." Perdue and I pushed
through brushy stinking ground for thirty yards before we
stumbled on to a chest-high lean-to built out of scrap lumber
and canvas tarp. The underbrush had been cleared from around
the entrance. I threw back the canvas flap and found a man
asleep in a flannel shirt and green hospital pants. His shoed
feet lay toward the entrance, ready to bolt at a moment's notice. He lay on his side, motionless. Except for his light snor-
ing, I might have mistaken him for dead. Perdue shined his
flashlight at his face and yelled, "Hey, wake up." The man
didn't stir. I kicked the sole of a foot.

He awoke suddenly, startled, and rolled over on his back, a
long-bladed knife in his hand.

"Whoa, friend," I yelled, one hand palm up, the other on
my holstered gun. "We're police."

The man kept a grip on his knife, either unsure we were police or unsure of reality.

"Put the knife away," I said. "Now."

Slowly he placed the knife atop a small shelf of canned
goods. Perdue swept his flashlight through the interior of the
lean-to. The beam glinted off a cardboard box of empty beer
bottles and cans, and a cracked mirror hanging from the ceiling. The light fanned over a large duffel bag, a pack of cigarettes, a tattered army jacket, a folded blanket, and of all
things, a two-drawer dresser. All the comforts of home.

"I try to keep it clean and organized," the Indian said with
genuine pride as we searched his home.

"Sit up," I said.

He sat up and rubbed his face. An Indian's face, not unlike
the one in Red Owl's publicity photo. Except where Red
Owl's boxer-flattened nose ran a crooked path, this man's
hooked nose ran due south.

Dirty, stringy hair framed his face. He reeked.

Perdue's flashlight caught the spidery veins of a whiskey nose.

"Your name He Who Rides Thunder?" I asked.

"Yes, sir."

"We have questions about your cousin, Red Owl."

"You know where he is? Is he okay?"

I told him what we suspected.

The man's head sank to his chest—less in surprise than in the sadness his worst fears had come true. He said they had come from the rez two years ago, after Red Owl's father had died. First to Pueblo, then to Denver. His cousin wanted to be a professional boxer—had since they were little kids. But it had never worked out all that well for him. For either of them. He Who Rides Thunder had feared it would end this way for his cousin.

"Why?" I asked.

The man grew agitated and began to scratch nervously all over his flannel shirt, as if lice were crawling on him. He reached for a half-empty bottle of beer but I snatched it away.

"Was he hiding here before he died?" I asked.

The man nodded forlornly. His cousin needed a place to stay.

"Why?" I asked. "He had his own apartment." Two men would have been cramped in the lean-to, especially with a man as big as Red Owl.

"A bad man was lookin' for him."

"A guy named Lopez?"

The Indian shrugged.

"Did your cousin tell you why this bad man was looking for him?"

He Who Rides Thunder shook his head and eyed the beer bottle in my hand. I wondered whether he had been too drunk most of the time to have understood or remembered anything, even if his cousin had confided in him.

"Did you talk to the man who was looking for your cousin?" I prodded. "Did he come through The Bottoms?"

The Indian shook his head hard. In fear or denial, I didn't know.

"When did you last see your cousin?" Perdue asked.

He wasn't sure. He probably wasn't sure what day it was. "Weeks maybe," he replied.

Red Owl had stayed with him several days. One evening his cousin went off to get food and never returned. He Who Rides Thunder later heard someone had died on the tracks. He wondered if it was his cousin. He wondered if the bad man had gotten him. He asked around but nobody knew. Or would say. He never went to the police. He hoped his cousin had simply decided to leave. Sometimes they wouldn't see each other for months.

"But I kept his bag for him," the Indian said. "In case he come back."

"What bag? Let's see."

He dug into his duffle bag. "Some personal stuff," he said. He unearthed a small canvas bag and placed it in front of me. I set down the beer bottle outside the lean-to, knelt, and opened the bag. Inside were jeans, a single dirty shirt, one piece of underwear, a few personal items.

"No booze," the Indian said brightly. "My cousin didn't drink. 'Cause he was a boxer. Always in training."

Too bad you aren't in training, I thought, though I was surprised he hadn't thrown away the bag or hocked its meager contents for food or a Mason jar of rotgut. His cousin must have been special to him. I felt paper and pulled out a manila envelope. "Give me some light," I said to Perdue.

Inside the envelope, I found several papers: a birth certificate, a few letters, some legal papers related to his boxing, and a five-by-seven black and white photograph. I held up the photograph. Perdue's light shimmered off the glossy surface and I angled the photo to cut the reflection. It wasn't a publicity shot of the boxer. The picture was slightly soft and grainy, obviously shot under dim light. I could make out a man, an older man, probably in his fifties judging by streaks of gray in his sideburns. A white man, not an Indian. His eyes were half shuttered. He appeared to be sitting on a couch, naked. A woman's head was face down in his lap, but I couldn't see her face, only black hair and naked shoulders.

"What the hell is that?" Perdue asked. "Is she…"

I held the photo out toward He Who Rides Thunder. "Who is this man?"

The Indian shook his head. He eyed the beer bottle.

"Your cousin ever say anything about this photo?"

He didn't think so.

Why was a photo of this mystery man getting his Johnson blown so important to Red Owl? Why the hell keep this photograph yet leave the snapshot of his hooker girlfriend in his apartment? Had Lopez been hunting for the photo instead of Red Owl?

I stood up, keeping the picture in my hand.

"I'm sorry about your cousin," I said.

The moment we turned away, He Who Rides Thunder grabbed the beer bottle. I could hear him chugging the rest of the liquid as we plowed our way back out of The Bottoms.

᭞᭞᭞

"What are you going to do with the picture?" Perdue asked as we neared our black and white.

I tapped the photo on my fingertips. "Find out who the guy is."

"Aren't you going to turn it over to the detectives?"

"Why would I?"

"It might be evidence."

"Evidence to what?"

"The Indian's murder."

"The dicks don't believe it was murder. They didn't even bother to ID him. They don't give a shit."

"It's still evidence."

"Yeah, evidence that will end up buried in a case file or tossed in the trash. Besides, the captain warned me to stay off the case and to keep you outa trouble. Turning in this picture would put both of us in a hole."

❦❦❦

After I finished my shift and Perdue headed home, I went upstairs in the station house and pored through mug shots until my tired eyes blurred and I caught myself dozing off. The man in the picture in the Indian's bag didn't match up to any known criminals.

The next evening, Perdue and I took the picture to Leroy Sunday, but he claimed he had no idea who it was, and I believed him.

The next afternoon I took the picture to a photographer acquaintance. I had cropped off the woman with black paper, so only the face of the man showed.

The photographer raised his eyebrows but didn't ask any questions. He copied the picture and handed me a reproduction suitable for framing. An hour later, I met Lou Sheppard outside the offices of the *Rocky Mountain News* and gave him the copy. The move was fraught with risks, but one I needed to take.

Sheppard stared at the photo. "Who's this?"

"I was hoping you'd know. You know everybody in town."

"The city's gotten too big for that."

"Then dig through your newspaper morgue. Ask the other news hawks. Just don't tell them where you got it."

"I need some kind of clue about who I should ask, Joe. Something to work with."

"I don't have any. I have no idea who this person is or where the photo was taken."

"Then why do you want to know?"

"It's official business. I can't tell you."

Sheppard rolled his eyes. "Official my ass. You don't do anything official. The last thing the police department would want from me is something official. This got something to do with what you were asking me about earlier? Lamprey, Moretti, Lopez, that dead guy on the tracks? What are you holding back from me, Joe?"

"You took a blood oath, Lou, remember?"

Sheppard didn't say anything for a moment. Probably calculating the minimum amount of blood he needed in order to sustain life. He studied the photo again. "This is a copy of another picture, isn't it? You cut something out."

"I knew nothing would get by you."

"Why's the guy's eyes half closed? He got a bowel problem?"

"Just find out who he is. As soon as you can."

"I hope it's big," Sheppard said. He disappeared into the building.

That was what I feared, that it would turn out to be big. Too big for me. So big Sheppard would risk severe blood loss and break a big story. So big Captain Donlan would demote me to traffic patrol, if not outright fire me. So big I would lose control of my investigation and lose forever my chance to find Lopez and nail him for what he had done to Derek—to me.

CHAPTER 19

I pushed my way through the smothering mid-July heat, disoriented from lack of sleep. I had missed so much work at the garage lately I skipped going home after my last shift and went straight to the garage to overhaul a 1944 Hudson. I worked all morning, my tired, warped senses struggling with the greasy stubbornness of the engine. By mid-afternoon, I gave up, leaving scattered oily parts on the garage floor and Carl's threats to fire me hanging in the dim interior of the garage.

I had a crippled water lawyer to see.

But first, I walked the first floor hallway of the Danforth Building where Estrada's office was located. Half the offices were vacant and the remaining should have been. I showed what few people I found a picture of Seth Rawlins I had clipped from the newspaper, but nobody remembered seeing him in the Danforth.

Nobody except the geologist.

Howard Jennings, Geologist, said the black letters on the frosted glass of the open door. I stepped inside to a large room containing two worktables, one cluttered with rocks, microscopes, and small hammers, the other holding a large map pinned down at the corner with fist-sized rocks. Large trunks, a bookcase, an empty hat rack, a gray metal desk, a glass case full of unmarked rock samples, and rolls of maps protruding from two waist-high boxes occupied the rest of the office.

Nobody was around. I turned to leave when a sunburned, red-bearded giant of a man strode in.

"Oh, didn't expect anyone," he said. He extended a hand larger than Roy Campanella's catcher's mitt. I put him in his mid-thirties. "I'm Howard Jennings. Sorry I was out when you came in. Visiting the little boy's room. What can I do you for?"

I identified myself and he cracked in return, "Don't tell me. You need a geologist to testify about what kind of rock was used on some poor slob's noggin."

"No, I—"

"Most any rock is effective, though granite is probably the best bet."

I grinned politely and showed him the newspaper clipping. "Ever see this man in this building?"

The geologist squinted at it as though he were assaying a rock under a harsh sun. "Is that the missing banker guy—uh, Rawlins?"

"Yes. Only he isn't missing any more. They found him at the bottom of a lake on his mountain ranch."

"Oh, yeah? Jeez, I hadn't heard that. But I've been back in some pretty isolated country for three weeks. Just returned two days ago. Don't read the papers much when I am here."

"So, as I was asking, have you seen this man around here?"

"Yeah, I have, actually. He stopped in several weeks ago asking directions to someone's office. Said the number was missing on the directory, which didn't surprise me."

"Whose office?" I suspected the answer but I had to ask anyway.

"Emilio Estrada. He's a lawyer on the third floor. I gave the guy directions and sent him on his way."

"You're sure this was the man who came in here?"

Jennings looked at the picture again. "Pretty damn sure. Older guy. Had a face like an abandoned house. Wore real expensive clothes. Not surprising I guess, him being a rich banker and all. Though he wore a cowboy hat with a small feather in the hat band, which I thought looked kinda strange with the clothes."

"Do you recall what day this was?"

The geologist started pawing through the rock samples scattered over one of the worktables as if the answer lay under one of them. "Let's see, it was a Saturday morning, I remember that. I hate working Saturdays, but I had to finish a report."

"Which Saturday?"

"Uhh, back in June. I remember I was working on some core samples that day." He hefted a rock in his hand. "The Lubell report, that was it." He dug through a stack of files on a desk, eventually pulling one out and rifling through it. "Yeah, I turned the report in June sixth," he said. He consulted a full-year calendar hanging on the wall. "That was a Monday. The Saturday was the fourth. Yeah, I'm sure it was then."

The same weekend Seth Rawlins disappeared. The same weekend he was likely murdered. The same Saturday other witnesses reported seeing him around town. He had told his foreman he was going up Friday to the ranch. Had he changed his mind and stayed in town? Had he gone to the ranch and then driven back to meet Estrada? If so, what was so urgent he would leave his mountain retreat to see the lawyer?

"Any idea if Estrada was in the building that morning?"

The geologist chewed on it. "Yeah, he was. I happened to be in the lobby when he came in. He's in a wheelchair, in case you didn't know. His sister was pushing him. Cold number, that one. I said hello and they went on up the elevator. I remember it because Emilio rarely works on Saturdays. He isn't exactly overwhelmed with business."

"What time was this?"

"I dunno. Nine, maybe. I'd been working since dawn on the report. Slept overnight here, in fact. Right there on the floor. Sleep better on a hard floor than a bed. Get that from camping out a lot, I guess."

"When did you see Rawlins?"

"Maybe half an hour later."

"Did you see him leave the building?"

"No."

I stared at the large map laid out on the worktable, a meaningless swirl of lines and splotches of green. "Did you ever see the banker in here before that day?"

The geologist thought about it. "No. But Emilio met him at his bank a few months back."

I looked up sharply from the map. "How do you know that?"

"I took Emilio to the guy's office. I help him out now and then, if I'm around and he needs to go someplace and his sister has to cover the office. I've done occasional jobs for him, too. In fact, one was a groundwater study up by Gold Dust. Part of the water lawsuit over the Ponderosa Reservoir. Not far from where that banker has his ranch. Emilio specializes in water law. He's involved in the case. Me, I'll do anything: basin studies, core analysis, well sites, hard-rock exploration, groundwater." The geologist paused and grinned. "Pay me enough, I'll study the rocks in your mother-in-law's head."

This was getting more entangled by the minute. "When did you take him to the bank, exactly?"

The geologist leaned his back against the worktable. "Hell, I don't know. Back in the spring sometime. I picked Emilio up at his office. He told his sister he was going to the state law library, but when we got into my car, he asked me to drive him to this guy's bank. Told me not to tell Mercedes. Thought that was kinda strange."

"He met with Rawlins personally?"

"Yeah. We went up to his seventh-floor office. Huge place. I've seen smaller oilfields. The secretary rolled Emilio on in while I waited outside."

"How long was he in there?"

"Fifteen, twenty minutes."

I stared back at the map. That made the third time the two men had met.

"Did he say anything about their meeting?" I asked.

"No. But he seemed pretty upset." The man pushed off the worktable. "Is Emilio in some sort of trouble over this dead banker?"

"Just pursuing leads, Mr. Jennings." I shook his hand. "Thanks for your help. Oh, by the way, this conversation was just between us. Don't say anything to anyone, including Estrada."

"Hey," the geologist called after me as I reached the door. "Emilio gets a little too caught up in his work, but he's a good guy. I can't see him messed up with this dead banker."

But he was messed up with him. And I needed to find out how.

CHAPTER 20

I checked the lobby directory on my way to Estrada's office. His name and office number were there as I had seen them three weeks ago. The "r" was still missing from attorney and the "w" from law, but the number 318 stood out clearly. I don't know why Rawlins had to ask for directions. I doubted the directory had been touched for a long time.

On my way to the third floor, I showed the banker's photo to the Negro elevator operator working the last time I came here. He usually worked Saturdays, he said, and had a good memory for faces. But he had never seen the man, except in the papers. Maybe the man took the stairs, he suggested. He solemnly announced we had reached the third floor, and I stepped off.

Mercedes Estrada rose like a sentry from behind her desk as soon as I entered.

"My brother's very busy," she said. Her long black hair was pulled off her neck, and I saw a beauty to her face I hadn't noticed before. Still, she wore a gray dress as shapeless as the last one I had seen.

"I'm busy, too," I said.

"What do you want with us? Why do you keep persecuting my brother? He's crippled. You can see that for yourself."

"I'm not persecuting him, Miss Estrada. But he hasn't been straight with me."

"He's not a well man. He—"

"Mercedes!" snapped her brother's impatient voice from his office. "For God's sake, show the officer in."

The lawyer sat in his wheelchair by the narrow, dirty window, staring at Fourteenth Street below. A law book lay open in his lap. His sister closed the door behind me, and the echoing click of the latch swiveled Estrada's large brown eyes in a slow arc from the window to me.

"How's the investigation going, Officer?" His voice sounded distant and he did not move away from the window. I sat down in the overstuffed chair by his desk.

"It's taking on some curious twists."

"Such as?"

"Such as your relationship with Seth Rawlins you told me you didn't have."

The statement brought a sharp sound from the other side of the wall. A chair scraped against the linoleum floor. The distraction almost caused me to miss the flash of resignation in the lawyer's face.

"You were seen with him at his ranch at least once this spring," I said. "A witness put a man in a wheelchair there. You also visited Rawlins at his bank office at least once earlier this year."

The lawyer sighed. "We wanted our working together on the water case to remain a secret from Lamprey's team."

"When did you two last meet?"

"Two weeks before his disappearance."

"Here?"

Estrada hesitated, then said, "No, his ranch. He never came here."

"Then explain why he was in this building heading for your office on the weekend he was last seen alive."

Estrada's face pulled back in puzzlement. "I never met Seth here that weekend."

"A tenant saw him in this building that Saturday morning. He asked for directions to your office and the tenant told him. The witness also saw you and your sister in the building shortly before Rawlins arrived."

"I don't see why Seth would need to ask—" The lawyer

suddenly stopped. He rolled his wheelchair to his desk and set down the law book.

"What was the date?"

"June fourth."

"Mercedes," Estrada called toward the door, "bring me the appointment calendar."

His sister brought in a loose-leaf desk calendar. She lingered, her hands holding each other. Estrada dismissed her silently with his eyes. She turned obediently and left.

The lawyer flipped through the pages until he found June fourth. "Yes, we were here that morning. I remember now. It was a no-show."

He spun the appointment book around and pushed it toward me. "Kenneth Morrisey, 9:45," was written in a neat feminine hand on the Saturday page.

"Who's Kenneth Morrisey?" I asked.

Estrada leaned back in his wheelchair. "I don't know. He called Friday night at my home. I don't know how he got the number. He apologized for the lateness of the hour, but insisted we meet the next morning at my office."

I scribbled the name and date in a notebook. "About what?"

"He claimed to have information proving the Water Board's efforts to obtain additional water rights on the West Slope were illegal."

"Illegal how?"

"He wouldn't say until we met."

"But he never showed?"

"No. We got here about nine-thirty and waited until eleven. Then we went home." For a split second, his eyes glanced toward the other room. "We were there the rest of the day."

"Did you ever locate or talk to this Morrisey guy later?"

"No. I checked around but no one had ever heard of him. He never called back."

"And you never saw Rawlins that morning? He didn't come to your office?"

"No. I'll swear an oath on that."

"You may need to. Police found his missing car parked a

block from this building. Which strongly suggests he came here but didn't leave on his own."

"Let me understand you, if I can, Officer Stryker. You believe I met Seth here and killed him. Then somehow, I—a man confined to a wheelchair—drove his body to his ranch and dumped it in the lake. Or I rode with him in his car to the ranch and killed him there. Then I managed to drive his car back to town. In either scenario, I foolishly parked his car a block from my own office."

He was right, of course. He could no more kill Rawlins and dump his body in the lake than could my ninety-five-year-old great grandmother. But there was another possibility.

"Your sister was here that morning."

Fear rose in his eyes. "Leave my sister out of this!"

I rose and walked around his desk to his window. I stared out at Fourteenth Street and watched people walk by.

An idea was brewing in my mind. I wasn't sure I would carry through with it. I wasn't sure I should. Yet parts of this attorney's story smelled as bad as a hobo on a Friday night binge.

Estrada wheeled his chair around to watch me. "Why would I have murdered Seth Rawlins? We were working on the same side."

"Maybe you weren't working together as well as you liked."

My idea didn't prove as difficult as I thought it might. The lawyer wasn't a heavy man. I stepped behind his wheelchair and twisted it to one side before he could protest.

Emilio Estrada spilled to the floor like a sack of coal.

He was too stunned to say anything at first, but his sister crashed through the door and began clawing at me.

"What are you doing!" she screamed, scratching at my face. "What are you doing to him!"

I caught her hands by the wrists and held her back, though she was far stronger than she looked. She began kicking at me with her black pumps, so I twisted her around until her back was to me and her hands crossed behind her head. I steered her around the desk and forced her into the chair. "Stay there!" I yelled. She started to get up but I pushed her back down. "I'll handcuff you to a damn steam pipe, if I have to. Now sit and I'll help your brother up." Out of the corner of my eye, I watched Estrada struggling to right himself to a sitting position. Slowly I released my grip as his sister calmed down to heavy gulps of air. I walked around the desk, hoisted the lawyer up under the arms, and set him back in his wheelchair.

Mercedes started to get out of her chair but I scowled at her and she sat down again. "Why?" she said, breathing heavily. "Why did you do that?"

"A truth test," I answered.

"You think he sits around in that damn wheelchair all day as some kind of joke?" Her voice was bitter.

"People have been known to fake being in a wheelchair to ply on other people's sympathies. And you're always around to guard the door to give him time."

"It's sure a dumb move for a lawyer, Mr. Smartass. Clients prefer lawyers who can stand on their own two feet."

Estrada winced at his sister's remarks but said nothing.

"I'm convinced he really is paralyzed," I said.

I had counted on surprise. A healthy man would instinctively have tensed his legs when I dumped the chair, if only for an instant. Estrada had not. His legs had folded under him like well-cooked spaghetti.

"You go around the city checking out all the wheelchair cases?" she hissed. "You push little old ladies into the street? Kick away canes? We'll file a lawsuit for this tomorrow morning."

"Don't push me! At the moment, I'm the only person who can link your brother to the wheelchair at the Rawlins ranch. You might want to leave it that way."

She started to yell at me again but bit her tongue.

I glanced at Estrada. He was breathing heavily, flushed from his fall. "I don't believe you're telling me all you know about Rawlins. You better start soon, Estrada. Or they're gonna be wheeling you into the gas chamber."

CHAPTER 21

"Phone, Joe."

I rolled out from under the belly of a '46 Packard and stared upside down into the big, grease-stained face of Carl Nelson. A shambling hulk of a man, Carl stood with his hands stuffed in the black pockets of his overalls. He never looked liked a garage owner to me. He looked like a farmer, or one of the itinerant hands my father used to hire for threshing or corn picking.

I stood up, still half a head shorter than Carl, and wiped sweat off my forehead. Even with the large doors open at both ends of the garage the place simmered like the back of a bakery.

Carl glared at me as I walked to the telephone. He was not one for interruptions—even from customers—and he certainly didn't like me chitchatting on the phone, official police business or not. With all the work time I'd already missed, this would not be good. I picked up the black telephone, not bothering to wipe my hands. Nobody but a greasy mechanic would touch our telephone. "'Lo," I said.

"Officer Stryker?" The voice at the other end was smooth and Eastern and edged with banked anger.

"Yeah."

"We need to meet. This afternoon."

"Who the hell is this?"

"Terry Adler."

That gave me pause. Why the hell was Rachel Adler's husband calling me? I finally said, "I'm working this afternoon, Mr. Adler. I have a second job. Your taxes don't pay enough for a cop to live on."

"Meet me in one hour and we can remedy that situation."

"I said I'm working. Right up to the start of my police shift. By the way, how the hell did you find out I work here?"

"It's urgent we meet," Adler said, not bothering to answer my question. *I guess power doesn't need to explain how it accumulates its information.*

I didn't like the idea of giving in to his demands. On the other hand, I had several questions for him. I looked over toward Carl. He was humped over the engine in a Ford pickup, but I sensed he was listening. He wouldn't be happy about this.

"Where?" I said to Adler. He gave me directions to a location several miles south of Denver. I wrote them down on a dirty pad. We agreed to meet in an hour.

I told Carl I had to leave because of police duties. I promised I would finish the Packard after my shift, and start on the Chevy with the busted rod. I had a key to the place so I could work nights when I pulled a rare day shift. Carl said he figured if he couldn't trust a cop, who could he trust? Sometimes it paid never to tell people the truth.

"Joe, you're a helluva mechanic," Carl said, barely containing himself, his hands wringing a fifthly rag. "But it doesn't do me any good if you're never around. I got customers complaining."

"I know this has been a bad stretch, Carl. Trust me, it'll be over soon. I'll get these cars done."

Carl threw the rag on a workbench. "You better, Joe. Or you're done."

e⁄ɔe⁄ɔ

Terry Adler's directions took me to a lonely dirt road and a huge swath of barren land with a realty sign stuck in it. *Front Range Ltd* it said in green letters against a stylized mountain

backdrop. I didn't know what the hell he was selling here. The
land appeared too worthless to farm and too far away for city
folk. I hooded my eyes against the glare of the mid-afternoon
sun and surveyed the sun-bleached, wind-scoured surface with
its low patches of lavender-green sagebrush and prairie dog
mounds. The little beggars had built quite an impressive city.
Every few holes a chubby prairie dog popped up, watching me
alertly, chattering in high-pitched squeals to each other.

"Hot sonofabitch, ain't it," I commented to the nearest sentry. He chattered back amiably.

I waited several minutes, listening to the motionless heat
kill off what little was left alive. Finally, a familiar yellow
Chrysler Town & Country convertible with wood exterior and
white walled tires drove up. A tall pale man emerged. He wore
a bone-white linen suit, white shoes, and a boater with a brown
band that Fred Astaire might wear, as if he had wandered off a
movie set into the Land of the Lost.

He was the guy who had walked out of E. Ezzard Lamprey's house after Moretti's early-morning visit.

Adler slammed the car door and walked to within a few feet
of me, real casual like, his hands deep in his trouser pockets.
He glanced at my clothes—I was still in my dirty mechanic's
clothes. Then he stared past me, his eyes surveying the horizon
where the sky and the earth met and left a seam. "It doesn't
look like much, does it?" he said.

"No, it doesn't."

"But this will be prime real estate in a few years. Mark my
words."

"I didn't realize prairie dogs qualified for mortgages."

His eyes settled on mine. They were as blue as the sky,
with long eyelashes, set apart by a narrow, angular nose. A
pencil-thin blond mustache slashed over thin lips and a trian-
gular chin. Reddish blond hair and sideburns crept below the
hat. Clean-shaven, pinkish skin. A long, smooth neck ended at
his tie, a silly affair with tiny blue umbrellas on a red background, white water droplets raining on the umbrellas. A
matching breast pocket handkerchief stuck out of his suit,
which didn't have a wrinkle in it, despite the heat. He looked

well into his forties—twice the age of his wife. Why a dish like Rachel Adler would trade wedding bands with a fop like this was beyond me.

A smug smile crawled across Adler's face like a cat stalking a mouse. "You sound as skeptical as my father-in-law did. But that's all right. Doubters like you are why visionaries like me get rich. All this land needs is water and this place will be crawling with swimming pools, paved streets, noisy kids, and crabgrass."

"Your father-in-law's ranch sorta stands in the way."

"Not for long."

"Too bad. It's a pretty ranch."

"He sat on that ranch like an old hen on a dead egg. Ran his bank the same way. His policy was that a bank should never loan more than thirty percent of its assets. Back East we call that regressive banking. Unfortunately, he persuaded most of Seventeenth Street to go along with him, which is why Denver is finding it so difficult to grow. There's no capital available. Hell, I couldn't get a damn bank loan for my business when I first came to town. This city could boom tomorrow, given sufficient financial resources."

"He's dead. Maybe you'll get your way and get even richer."

Adler canted his head. "What exactly are you after, Officer? What's your game? You barge onto my father-in-law's ranch, harass my wife, and—"

"I would hardly call it harassment, Mr. Adler. I questioned her because we are investigating—"

"You can dispense with the 'we' shit. I've had you checked out. You are not assigned to my father-in-law's case. You're not even a detective, though you misrepresented yourself as one to my wife."

"I never told your wife I was a detective. She may have mistakenly assumed I was, but I never claimed it."

"You're a *patrolman*, Officer Stryker. The Denver Kid, they call you. Assigned to Larimer Street. A real up and coming area, though a little far from Lost Coyote Ranch."

"A murder in my precinct led me there."

"That's what my wife said. A stagehand at the theater where she acts. How exactly do you think his death is linked to Seth's murder?"

"It's what I'm investigating."

"You accused my wife of killing her father for his money. I won't have that."

What was he planning to do, punch me?

"Either she or you aren't getting your stories straight," I said. "I didn't accuse her. But their relationship was obviously strained. I also find it curious it took three weeks after his disappearance for a ransom note to show up. Puts the kidnapping scenario a little off."

Adler bristled. "Don't bother my wife again. She's under enormous stress. She's fragile."

"You dragged my ass all the way out here just to tell me that? You coulda told me that over the phone."

"Impressions are stronger when made in person."

The man reached into his inside coat pocket. I tensed. For a moment, I feared he was going for a gun. Not a real gun. One of those toy things, a little Derringer. That would fit him. Still, he was close enough to me it could prove fatal.

He came out with a new pack of Fatimas. He ripped off the cellophane and tossed it to the ground, shook out a cigarette, and tapped it hard on an ivory lighter before lighting it. He didn't offer me one.

He blew smoke out his mouth and I caught the strong aroma of the Turkish blend.

I didn't believe he hauled me all the way out to this godforsaken country just to have a smoke and chew me out for bothering his wife. More was on his mind. He and Lamprey wanted to assess how much I knew. Maybe a sample would spark their interest.

"Do you know a thug named Lopez?" I asked.

"Of course not."

"I believe he's responsible for the Indian's murder. I believe he's linked to a gangster named Villano Moretti. You are acquainted with Moretti, aren't you?"

Adler pulled hard on his cigarette. "I never met the man."

"You sure? You see, I visited Moretti early one morning at his club. Had a little chat with him about the dead Indian and Lopez. Mentioned your father-in-law, too. Made him kinda nervous. Right after I left, he took off like a bat outa hell. I followed him to the home of your business attorney, Lamprey. Nice house. Moretti stayed quite a while. When he left, you came out right after him." I nodded toward Adler's car. "Got in your yellow car. But perhaps you were in the bathroom when Moretti dropped by and you missed meeting him. Too bad. He's a swell guy."

I wasn't sure if that was the kind of information the real estate developer and Lamprey wanted to know I knew. Maybe it was more than they wanted to know because as difficult as it was to tell in the bleached sunlight, Adler's pale skin paled another shade.

He started to say something, but I kept going, my hands swirling by now, as though stirring up some concoction. "I start nosing around and come to find out Lamprey's working for the Water Board on this big federal water case over the reservoir that's gonna flood your father-in-law's ranch. The dam he objected to. And all that water that will pile up behind the dam will make the right people in Denver stinking wealthy. Or wealthier in your case. You get my point, don't you? It all just sort of mixes together in a big bucket—you and Lamprey and Moretti and a dead Indian and your dead father-in-law and water. Lots of water. And I don't quite know what to make of it all, but it sure as hell *smells* suspicious."

"What is it you want?"

A prairie dog yipped at us.

"On the phone you said you could remedy the problem of my having to work a second job to survive."

Adler smiled triumphantly. "I heard you're a man open to monetary persuasion. How much?"

A chill went down my spine, even under the hot sun. The man had dug deep on me. How the hell had he learned about my petty bribes? Perdue? Had the rookie ratted me out? Was it one of people who paid me? Or was Adler just guessing, figuring most street cops take a little graft?

I looked away and scanned the vacant land to hide my confusion. "Lemme see, if this place is gonna be worth so damn much money someday, how about a cut? Say fifty-fifty?"

"I see you don't take this seriously."

"No more serious than your offer to bribe a police officer."

Adler hurled his cigarette in the general direction of a prairie dog hole. "Stay away from my wife, Stryker. And stay away from me. You're out of your league. Bother us anymore and I'll make sure you lose both of your jobs."

"I may be out of my league, Mr. Adler, but I know things you don't want made public."

I looked down at a chattering prairie dog as Adler walked away. "I think your days are numbered, buddy. If Adler gets his way, they're turning your front porch into crabgrass."

Adler drove away, dust swirling on the horizon. His bribe attempt confirmed that I was onto something—if only I knew exactly what, and how it would lead me to Lopez.

CHAPTER 22

As soon as I got back to town, I called a guy named Preston at a title company whom I had met during an investigation of an assault. I asked him about Terrance C. Adler.

"Why about him?" he asked.

"I'm thinking of going into real estate with him."

The man laughed. "You can't go wrong there. Everything Adler touches would put Midas to shame."

Preston said he would do a little digging. He called me at home the next afternoon. Paula was doing her charity work at the hospital, so I didn't need to be discreet on the phone. I leaned against the kitchen counter as he spun out the man's bio.

"Adler founded Front Range Limited shortly after he moved to Denver, eight, nine years ago. It's already the largest realty company in the state. Property management, syndication, development—you name it, he's got his fingers in it. Owns a healthy chunk of downtown and much of the suburbs."

And future suburbs, if Adler was right. "Where'd he come from?"

"St. Louis. Didn't waste any time making himself a mover and a shaker here, though. Even got himself appointed to the Denver Board of Water Commissioners about a year ago, which upset a few natives."

"Why?"

"They don't like outsiders telling them how to run their water supply. Very touchy subject. But as I said, Adler's a mover and shaker. Getting on the Water Board was a smart move, too. Several developers have made water service contracts directly with the Water Board for projects outside the city limits, which is a highly questionable practice. Adler's been the silent partner behind several of those deals."

"Sounds illegal."

"Most certainly is."

"But Adler's business attorney is the Water Board's lead attorney in the Ponderosa reservoir lawsuit," I added.

"Incestuous little town, isn't it? Adler and a lot of other people stand to make a fortune if they can get the dam built."

Preston rattled off an impressive list of Adler's real estate holdings. He stopped and paused before he said, "Two things caught my eye when I researched his holdings."

"Yeah?"

"Seems our city's favorite gangster is secretly invested in several of Adler's properties."

I pushed off the kitchen counter. "Villano Moretti?"

"Yep."

"How did they get hooked up?"

"Rumor is Moretti bankrolled Adler when the guy first came to Denver and set up his real estate business."

"A pact with the devil's retarded nephew," I said.

I remembered Adler lamenting he couldn't get a bank loan when he first came to town because of his future father-in-law's "regressive" banking practices. The spurs off the railroad tracks where we had found the dead Indian were all leading to Moretti, and I suspected from there to Lopez.

"Ahh, but it gets more interesting," Preston said. "One of the properties Moretti invested in with Adler is the Broadway Playhouse."

"Where Adler's wife is an actress."

"Who also is the daughter of Seth Rawlins."

"Interesting, but so what? Her rich husband bought her an old playhouse for her mediocre acting talent."

"Ahh, but guess who's paying the rent on the theater to Ad-

ler? And covering most of the operating expenses, I'm told."
Preston seemed to enjoy teasing this out.

"I'm guessing not the guy who runs the theater...uh, King."
The Mad Hungarian, one of his actors had called him. "Is it
Moretti?"

"Nope."

"Okay, I bite. Who is it?"

"Not who is. Was."

"Was?"

"Well, unless they've opened a branch bank at the Fairmont
Cemetery."

"*Seth Rawlins*?"

"Bingo."

☙☙

Victor King's theater was quiet, except for a carpenter
working on the set. I found the director in his office reading
play scripts. "Have you confirmed the dead man is our stagehand?" he asked, clearly annoyed at my arrival.

"Not officially. But I'm more curious about a coupla things
involving your playhouse."

"What?"

"Your leading lady's husband, Terry Adler, owns this
building. How did that happen?"

His brow wrinkled. "When I first moved here, I ran a little
theater out of the basement of an old house. I met Rachel there.
But I had my eye on this place. My parents played here one
summer, and I saw potential in it. When I learned her husband
was a wealthy real estate developer, I persuaded him to buy
it."

"Adler has a silent investor in this place, the gangster Villano Moretti. You told me you didn't know him."

King put aside the scripts. "I've heard those rumors, but
I've never met the man. I deal with Terry."

"You pay the rent to him."

"Yes. Terry doesn't do anything for free. He may have

bought the theater to showcase his wife, but he still expects rent checks."

"Yet you don't actually pay the rent, do you, Mr. King? Seth Rawlins paid the rent on this place, along with much of your operating expenses."

King rose, walked to a small, green, boxy Magnavox phonograph on a brass wire stand, and put on an album. "You like jazz, Officer?"

"I don't listen to it, no. About Seth Rawlins."

The director shook his head in disapproval. "You should listen. Jazz is America's greatest contribution to music. Only contribution, actually. I don't count musical theater." He gently set the needle. The scratchy sounds of a saxophone began to wail. "Sonny Rollins," he said. "Incredible player. Incredible. Someday I'm going to write a play built around his music. Not a musical, god forbid. Something which seriously examines the artist."

The frantic sound of the saxophone engulfed the room, along with the incessant rhythm of the bass and the spare notes of the piano. King stood with his eyes closed.

"About the Seth Rawlins," I persisted.

He opened his eyes and threw up his hands in mock surrender. "I confess—he funded most of the expenses on my theater. Most theaters are funded by patrons. Ticket sales rarely cover expenses. But I don't know what any of this has to do with your investigation of the Indian's murder."

"He musta been a pretty damn silent patron. His daughter says he hated theater and hated her being an actress."

"Yes, Seth disliked theater. Even musical theater. His idea of a musical was three cowboys and a guitar around the campfire."

"She claims he disliked it so much his will stipulates she doesn't inherit until she vows to give up acting forever. Like some kinda nun."

"Which she melodramatically reminds me daily."

I leaned against the door. "Then why foot the bill for your theater? Including paying rent to his son-in-law, whom he detested."

He sighed heavily. "I didn't want any of this to get out. The truth of the matter is, he—"

A hard cough suddenly rattled in the director's throat, and I wondered if he would be seized by another hacking fit like the one he experienced the first night I came here. He regained his composure, however, and sank into his chair.

"Seth covered our expenses because he loved Rachel. As looney as she is, and as much as they fought, I think he liked her spirit. He didn't want her becoming an actress, but he was willing to see she got a fair crack at it. He wanted her to have the best, and I was the best director west of the Hudson. He didn't like me but then, I'm from New York, and he disliked anyone from New York."

"Then why the secrecy? Why the inheritance clause? Why not openly support her?"

"He didn't want Rachel to think she was getting acting jobs because her old man was buying off the director. Don't tell her that, please. It didn't influence me. As for his will, she's free-spirited and undisciplined—and a rich, pampered bitch who doesn't have to *do* anything. I believe he wanted to see how serious she was about acting. She never takes much of anything seriously. Unfortunately for her, he died before he could change the will."

"He told you he was going to change it?"

Sonny Rollins went into a new song.

"No. But I believe he intended to. She was his only child. He wouldn't cut her off. She'll inherit under the terms of the will, regardless. She's too much of a strumpet and has much too drama in her own life to dedicate herself to the stage."

"*Strumpet*? What the hell does that mean?"

The director gave a smug smile. "She's a slut. Rachel will fuck anybody crazy enough to take her on."

"Does that include you, Mr. King?"

He shook his head slightly. "Not anymore."

☙❧☙

"Says here Allied aircraft delivered over two hundred 'n

fifty tons of food and supplies into Berlin in June," I said to Paula above the low murmur of Edward R. Murrow on the kitchen radio. "It's a record."

I sat with the *Rocky Mountain News* and a Bud on a metal stool in a corner of the kitchen, inhaling the pleasant aroma of chuck roast, potatoes, and carrots while Paula dressed a salad.

"My friend Frosty has a food drive going to Berlin. I gave her some cans of soup."

I put down the paper. "Frosty can afford that kind of stuff, Paula. Hell, they could donate a whole damn grocery store. We can't."

"I know." A cigarette smoldered in an ashtray next to her. "I had to pay fifty-seven cents a pound for this chuck roast."

I fell silent, retreating back into the headlines about the fighting in Greece and the bloody riots in the Bolivian tin mines. Paula pushed aside the salad and moved a heavy black sewing machine and some brightly flowered material from the kitchen table to an empty spot on the counter next to a box of Rinso.

"What are you sewing?" I asked.

"A dress." Her voice was curt and harsh. She leveled her eyes at me. I could tell she had been stewing on something since I had gotten home from King's theater. "Carl called late this afternoon from the garage. He asked where you were. I thought you were there."

"I couldn't go in. More of my special assignment."

"He was angry, Joe. He said you missed work yesterday, too. You were supposed to make it up after you finished your shift, but you didn't."

"Oh, yeah," I said, shaking my head. I had forgotten all about the '46 Packard and the Chevy with the busted rod. I was so tired I'd come straight home after pulling my shift.

Paula went on. "Carl said you're missing a lot of work these days. He said he'll have to fire you if you don't start showing up. What's going on, Joe?"

"This special assignment."

She stared at me. "We can't afford for you to lose your job at Carl's."

"I know, I know. I'll straighten it out with him. It'll be okay. I'll talk to the shift commander, too."

We sat down for a silent dinner. The phone rang a few minutes later. It was Lou Sheppard.

"I got an ID on that photo," he said.

I avoided Paula's glare as I asked, "Who?"

"Not over the phone," the reporter said. "In person. I got some questions and you owe me some answers."

ℰↃℰↃ

I caught up with Sheppard at the Press Club's bar a half hour before my shift started. He hung on to a trolley car strap dangling from an overhead brass rail for the benefit of those who found the floor unsteady. His other hand held a sour mash.

"Hey, Joe," he said, his voice as murky as the bar's smoky interior. "You know what's the driest martini on record?"

"No."

"The Bikini Martini."

"If you say so."

"Seriously. Remember the atoll in the South Pacific where they tested the Bomb right after the war? The scientists packed the bomb casing with a bottle of vermouth, and when the damn thing went off, they extended their glasses of gin out the window of the observation post. One part gin to one-billionth part vermouth."

"That's swell, Lou. Let's find some place private."

I helped him disentangle his hand from the strap. He held on to his sour mash and grabbed his Speed Graphic camera from the end of the bar. We went downstairs, but the poker table and the pool table were packed with people I recognized as reporters and local politicians. We went outside. The downtown office bees had gone home and the streets were quiet, except for the occasional drunk and couples holding hands on a warm summer's night.

Sheppard sat down on the bumper of a Packard parked in

the lot next to the Press Club. He put his head between his knees.

"Who's the person in the picture?" I pressed.

He pulled the photo out of the inside pocket of his wrinkled sport coat. "Tell me where you found this picture and why you're interested in it?" As drunk as he was, he still could play the reporter.

"Not yet."

"I can't keep sitting on this."

"Sitting on what? You got nothing here but a picture. Not much more than a mug shot. It means nothing by itself. Now who is it?"

"All right, but you better come through for me, Joe. You owe me."

"Who is it, Lou?"

"His name is Benjamin Glazer."

"Never heard of him."

Sheppard rolled his droopy eyes. "*Judge* Benjamin Glazer. The federal judge presiding over the Ponderosa reservoir water case."

I stopped myself from letting out a whistle, but I couldn't stop myself from blowing air out through my lips. What the hell was the dead Indian doing with the picture of a federal judge getting a blowjob?

"Which I find curious, Joe," Sheppard said.

I tried to appear innocent. "Why?"

"Curious because you called me asking about Lamprey—who's arguing the Water Department's case before this very judge. You linked Villano Moretti to Lamprey. You linked Moretti to the body on the tracks. I sent you to Emilio Estrada, also a lawyer on the case. Our murdered banker's ranch is goin' underwater if the dam gets built. Then by the grace of the Virgin Mary you end up with a mysterious picture of the judge presiding over that very case."

"You're doing a lot of speculating, Lou."

He took a drink. "You obviously didn't get the picture from Lamprey or Estrada. They coulda told you who it was. Plus, I doubt they keep this kind of picture with them under their pillows. Where'd you get this photo? What'd you crop out? Our illustrious judge appears to be enjoying himself."

"I told you, I can't tell you. It's under investigation."

"What investigation? It sure as shit isn't the department's investigation. You're on your own here, Joe. What the hell are you doing?"

It was what I kept asking myself.

CHAPTER 23

I dropped the photograph on Emilio Estrada's desk. I hadn't waited this time for his sister to make her usual attempts to block me.

I had simply bulled by her and her protests into his office.

The lawyer stared at the photo of Federal District Court Judge Benjamin Glazer. It was the original version, uncropped, the mystery woman's head in the judge's lap. The attorney glanced at me, then back at the photo.

He studied it a while before I said, "Ever see the photo before?"

His face held the expression of a man who knew the rest of his day would not go well. "No. But we knew photographs existed of the judge and a woman, *in puris naturalibus*, shall we say."

"We? You and Rawlins?"

"Yes."

"Any idea who's the woman?"

"No."

"She's definitely not the judge's wife?"

"Definitely not. His wife's hair is prematurely gray."

"How did you two find out about these photographs?"

"I didn't. Seth did. I don't know how."

"You said there are other photos."

"I haven't seen them. I understand they're quite—*explicit*. Judge Glazer has a reputation for womanizing. Especially young women, and especially young married women. Apparently he gets a thrill from it."

"Which makes him ripe for blackmail," I offered.

Estrada nodded.

I flashed on the gangster Villano Moretti carrying an envelope to Lamprey's home in the middle of the night. "My bet is Lamprey paid Moretti to do the dirty work," I said.

"We believe they're also bribing the judge with undeveloped land Terry Adler owns," Estrada said.

Maybe I shoulda taken Adler up on his offer for a piece of the action. Hell, if a federal judge could, why not me?

"Didn't you take this information to the feds?" I said. "It's a federal crime to blackmail a federal judge."

The lawyer looked away, like a little boy who knew he had done wrong.

"Bringing corruption charges against people like Lamprey and Adler would have been a nightmare. Too many officials in their back pockets."

"Let me guess. You two sent an Indian named Art Red Owl after Moretti to beat the shit out of him and retrieve the photos. An Indian you told me you'd never heard of."

"Seth never told me what he was doing until after it happened. I had nothing to do with the Indian. I'd tried to persuade Seth to use his financial leverage to pressure Lamprey and the others, not violence. But he was adamant about handling it his way. Unfortunately, his method was crude, clumsy, and ultimately ineffective." The lawyer glanced at the photo again. "Where did you get this?"

"From Red Owl's possessions."

"How do you get onto this?"

"I found the Indian's body on the railroad tracks several weeks ago. In my precinct. He'd been murdered. His name came up linked to Rawlins's disappearance."

Color drained from the Mexican's face. "My god. You think this had something to do with Seth's murder, too?"

"I think so. I'm convinced a thug named Lopez murdered the Indian. Probably in retaliation for his assault on Moretti." I tapped the photograph. "And to retrieve this photo. He may have killed Rawlins, too."

The lawyer's eyes widened. "Who is this Lopez?"

"Someone who shouldn't be allowed to walk this earth." I leaned back in the chair and crossed my arms. "Then again, maybe I got this all backward."

"In what way?"

"Maybe you and Rawlins blackmailed the judge, not Lamprey and his friends."

The lawyer stiffened in his wheelchair about as much as a man in his condition could stiffen. "That's a preposterous—"

"Maybe the Indian snapped the photos. Lamprey learned about it and sent Moretti after him to retrieve the photos. The Indian beat the shit out of Moretti, so Moretti sent Lopez. He killed the Indian and recovered all the photos but this one."

"We did not blackmail the judge. Lamprey did."

I stood up. "Maybe. But you've already lied to me about your relationship with Rawlins. I don't trust the lot of you."

∽∾∽

Moretti's Supper Club was quiet for a mid-afternoon, except for two prowl car boys I recognized sitting in a corner in street clothes, several empty beer bottles scattered in front of them. I nodded to them but didn't stop to chat. I went directly to the bar. The presence of the two cops worried me. I didn't want word getting back to Detective Griffin and Captain Donlan, another sign of my "footsteps." Yet I needed to talk to Moretti.

I ordered a beer. The bartender was a different man from the jerk I had encountered the first time. I gave him my name and said I needed to talk to his boss. Moretti appeared soon afterward, not needing a second invitation this time. He spotted my untouched beer.

"No cognac?" he said.

"Not unless you're treating."

"Once around is enough. What do you want?"

I eyed the bartender, who politely shuffled off to do whatever bartenders do when they're not wanted. I set the photograph of Judge Glazer down on the bar.

"You missing this one?" I said.

Moretti stared at the photograph longer than he needed to. Finally, he looked up with wet, bulging eyes, like frog's eyes. "I don't have anything to do with smut."

"No, you're more into shakedowns."

"You need to leave, Officer Stryker."

"You see, I think this photo is part of a collection you took of Judge Glazer. I think you took them on behalf of a lawyer named E. Ezzard Lamprey. To blackmail the judge into ruling in favor in the Ponderosa reservoir. Seth Rawlins found out, however, and sent the Indian to get the photos. He beat the shit out of you in the process. He must have come away with at least this photo, maybe more. You sent Lopez to get them back." I picked the photo up from the bar. "Lopez killed the Indian but he didn't find everything. I suspect Lopez has something to do with the banker's murder, too. Which would put you in a jam even your politician and cop friends won't be able to bail you out of. The dead Indian is no big deal, but the banker is. You panicked when I showed up asking about Red Owl and Rawlins and hauled ass with the rest of the photos to Lamprey's home."

Moretti's big wet eyes retreated into his sockets. "I don't like you coming here squeezing me," he said.

I leaned across the bar and said quietly, "Give up Lopez and I'll forget about the blackmail. I'll forget you even exist. I just want Lopez."

"I told you, I didn't hire either Lopez brother. I have no idea where they are. I want nothing to do with them."

"Then send your meatballs to find them. That'll get me off your back. Just warn them to be careful if they want to come back with all their body parts intact."

I left my beer untouched and walked out, nodding to the two cops still adding to their collection of beer bottles. They nodded back with suspicious eyes.

I drove away and parked in an alley to watch for signs of

Moretti's red Packard speeding away. This time he was smarter. He wasn't leading me to anyone today.

∽∾∽

The next day, I buried Art Red Owl in a pine box at my own expense in Riverside Cemetery north of downtown. Well, not entirely at my own expense. I got a discount from the funeral home whose owner owed me for keeping him out of a jam once. I dipped into my payoff stash and hit up a little harder the lawbreakers I let skate on various infractions. For a good cause, I told them. I hit up Leroy Sunday, as well. It was the least the Indian's manager could do.

I could have let the city bury Red Owl, of course. I hadn't come up with his missing hands for fingerprints and Detective Griffin was too busy X-ing out his days to retirement and keeping an eye on his wife's boyfriends to ID the Indian. But the city would have buried him as John Doe or Chief What's-His-Name. That wasn't right. People should be buried with their given name. So I buried the big Indian as Art Red Owl. I'm not sure he would have wanted the name on his small gravestone. He probably had an Ogallala Lakota name he preferred, but it was what he got. Better than Chief What's-His-Name.

Only Perdue and I showed up for his burial. I couldn't find his cousin down in The Bottoms, and Leroy Sunday begged off.

After the burial, Perdue asked again about the photograph we had found in the Indian's possessions. I wasn't about to tell him it was the federal judge presiding over the Ponderosa water lawsuit because that would open up a whole new world of my investigation I didn't want him to know.

"It turned out to be a nobody," I said.

"What do you mean a nobody, Joe? He's somebody."

"His name is, uhh, Stanley Hague."

"Who's Stanley Hague?" he said around a LifeSaver.

"A...a car salesman."

"Why would Red Owl carry around a picture of a car

salesman with a woman's face in his lap?"

"It, uhh, turns out this Hague guy makes money on the side doing smut. The Indian musta bought one of his pictures."

Perdue's face registered dubiousness. "How did you find this out?"

"A reporter friend checked it out for me."

"If the guy in the photo was a nobody in some smut racket, how did the reporter find out?"

"Because he's is the kinda guy who keeps up on this shit," I said.

"Maybe Red Owl was involved in this smut ring and we should be—"

"Quit asking so many questions, kid," I snapped. "The point is, the guy's a nobody and the photo doesn't lead anywhere. Drop it."

CHAPTER 24

My pulse quickened as I stared at the *Rocky Mountain News*. Spread across the front page was a photo of Emilio Estrada being wheeled through the front entrance of police headquarters by his sister, her head ducked from the photographer. The photographer, naturally, was Lou Sheppard. Below beamed a banner headline in thick black type.

Police Link Mex Lawyer to Banker Slaying.

Under it ran a smaller headline in thinner type.

Ransom Note Matches Lawyer's Typewriter;
Banker Last Seen near Lawyer's Office

I dropped the paper on the kitchen table and settled in a chair with my cup of coffee. Paula was off volunteering at the hospital. The cover story started on page three, under Lou's byline.

I began to read with a growing sense of betrayal.

The ransom note received by the daughter of prominent 17th Street banker Seth Rawlins shortly before the discovery of his bludgeoned body at his mountain ranch has been linked to a local Mexican lawyer, Emilio Estrada, according to exclusive Rocky Mountain News *sources.*

An eyewitness also placed the banker in Estrada's office building the weekend Rawlins vanished, while a second eyewitness reported seeing someone resembling Estrada at the banker's mountain ranch in the weeks before he disappeared.

"This is the big break we've been looking for," said an anonymous source in the Denver Police Department.

The police brought Estrada in yesterday afternoon for extensive questioning.

Police have not officially released any information regarding a link between Estrada and the ransom note. Based on information gathered from sources within the DPD, however, along with additional independent reporting, the News *has unearthed several key facts.*

The break in the six-week-old case, which has stymied several law enforcement agencies, came in the form of a tip to the Denver Police Department from an as-yet unidentified source. The source claimed the 41-year-old Estrada was responsible for the murder of the banker. Estrada is wheelchair bound from a horse accident at age 16.

Exactly what the informant told police is unclear. But according to News *sources, their investigation is focused on a typewriter confiscated at the attorney's office. Crime technicians believe the typeface on the ransom note matches the unique typeface characteristics produced by the Remington Royal typewriter recovered from Estrada's office.*

Police and Rawlins's daughter, Rachel, married to real estate mogul Terry Adler, have refused to confirm the existence of the ransom note, reported previously in this paper. Sources close to the case, however, have indicated the note, delivered three *weeks after the banker disappeared, demanded $1 million in return for his release.*

In another major development, police sources said William Gannon, the foreman at Seth Rawlins's Lost Coyote Ranch near Dillon, told investigators he saw Rawlins with a man in a wheelchair at the ranch weeks before Rawlins vanished. Gannon was unable to identify the man, but Denver police and the Ponderosa County Sheriff's office believe the man was Emilio Estrada.

The foreman discovered the banker's badly decomposed body 11 days ago lashed to a small boat at the bottom of a lake located on his mountain ranch.

Police sources also revealed that the previously reported "evidence of foul play" they found in the banker's abandoned Roadmaster was a lengthy piece of bloody pipe. The blood type on the pipe matches the blood type of the dead banker. Shortly after the banker's disappearance, police found his Roadmaster abandoned a block from the office building where Estrada works.

Additional independent investigation by this reporter led to a witness also linking Estrada to Rawlins. Rawlins was reportedly last seen at his bank June 2. Howard Jennings, 36, an independent geologist and tenant in the office building where Estrada's law firm is located, told the News *a man he identified as Seth Rawlins stopped at the geologist's office asking directions to the Estrada office the weekend the banker was last seen alive. Jennings reported seeing Estrada and his sister, Mercedes, who works as her brother's secretary, in the building earlier the same morning.*

Jennings also revealed he had taken Estrada to Seth Rawlins's office at the Prairie Guarantee and Trust Bank several weeks before, where Estrada met with the banker for roughly 15 minutes. Jennings said he did not know the nature of their meeting.

Although a small-time lawyer by 17th Street standards, Estrada is considered one of the state's foremost authorities on water rights laws. He represents several landowners in a lawsuit filed in federal court opposing the construction of the Ponderosa Dam and reservoir being pushed by the Denver Water Board and other water interests. Rawlins also had filed a lawsuit against the project, whose reservoir would flood the Rawlins mountain ranch.

E. Ezzard Lamprey, the attorney representing the Denver Water Board in the case, said he was shocked to learn that the Mexican might be involved in the banker's death.

Said Lamprey, "Knowing the character and the circumstances of Emilio Estrada, I find it highly unlikely he could be involved in any way with the unfortunate demise of Mr. Rawlins."

℘℘℘

I found Sheppard at his desk on the second floor of the *News* building chattering to a red-haired guy wearing a stockman's hat.

Lou started to introduce the man but I cut him off. "Who tipped off the dicks about Estrada?"

Lou stared at me a moment, then waved away his companion. He casually leaned back in his chair. "You know I don't reveal sources."

"Come on, Lou, this is a frame. You can't believe Estrada is physically capable of murdering Rawlins and sinking his body in a lake. Someone set him up."

Lou took a bite from a hot dog and spoke with his mouth full. "I have no idea who tipped off homicide. They don't, either."

I had a suspicion of the identity of the snitch, but I wasn't telling Sheppard. "Tell me what you *do* know?"

"That I got the scoop and the *Post* didn't." He grinned at

the thought. "Witlaw is sitting at the Press Club bar right now crying in his Irish Mist."

"C'mon, tell me what you're not reporting. Homicide give you any plausible scenarios how Estrada pulled off this murder?"

Lou leaned forward in his chair. "What am I gettin' in return? I get an ID for you on the mysterious photo, but I get nothing back. The photo is lookin' more and more interesting, considering the subject being the federal water judge on a case involving a water lawyer the dicks are looking at as the prime suspect for the murder of a man suing the Water Board. There's a big connection there, Joe, and I want to know what it is."

"The sooner you tell me what you know, the sooner I can solve what I need to solve. Then you'll get your story."

He looked at me skeptically. Of course, police reporters looked at everyone skeptically. He took another bite of his hot dog. "Homicide's got two theories. One, no water was found in Rawlins's lungs, so he was dead before he was sent to the bottom of the lake. They think it's possible Estrada used the steel pipe they found in the car to whack Rawlins to death."

I rolled my eyes.

"It's possible if Rawlins was sitting or kneeling by the wheelchair at the time," he said. "Wheelchair people have strong arms."

"How do they figure a man who can't use his legs drove the guy's car down to Denver?"

"He used the pipe to work the brakes and the gas. It's one of those new-fangled automatics. No clutch to work."

"Jesus, what a stretch, Lou. What's their second theory?"

"His sister was involved. They like that theory even better."

I would, too. It would explain many of the physical hurdles. Plus, Mercedes Estrada was an icy bitch. But I asked Lou the same question Estrada had asked me.

"What about motive? Why the hell would Estrada—and maybe his sister—murder Rawlins? They were on the same side of the water case. They were working together."

"Perhaps they saw their opportunity to make serious bucks kidnapping him. Beats being a poor, obscure water lawyer."

"Then why wait weeks after killing Rawlins before sending a ransom note?"

"They're amateurs at this sort of thing. Amateurs make mistakes. Besides, the typewriter is pretty damning evidence."

"Somebody could have broken into their office and typed the ransom note."

"Back to the frame job, huh? Any ideas on that one, Joe?"

I shook my head. But my own hunch was Villano Moretti. He or one of his meatballs could easily have broken into Estrada's office, typed up the ransom note, delivered it to Rachel Adler, then tipped off his buddies in homicide.

The reporter munched more on his sandwich. A spot of mustard stuck to his upper lip. "Homicide does have one kink in its theories on the Estradas," he admitted.

"What?"

"A fingerprint they can't account for. A thumbprint on the dash of the Roadmaster doesn't match up with Estrada, his sister, or anyone else. They even checked it against the mechanic who maintained the car. The steering wheel was wiped clean. So was the bloody pipe. They found stray prints around the rest of the car, but they belonged to Rawlins or his foreman. But they can't account for the thumbprint."

"Which proves Estrada was set up."

"You seem awfully protective of this Mexican."

"Homicide seems bent on going after him. Consider the information they leaked to you. I bet they tipped you when they were bringing him in to headquarters. So you could get a front-page picture and burn it into the mind of every future juror."

Sheppard didn't respond, but he didn't deny it either.

"Estrada is their fall guy," I said. "They got no one else."

Sheppard picked up his hot dog and took a bite. "What I think is, you know a helluva lot more than you're telling me. You talked to Estrada before all this broke. You talked to the geologist in Estrada's building. He happened to mention to me he'd talked to a cop earlier about seeing Rawlins in the building. Didn't say the cop's name. Maybe homicide would like to know that bit of trivia."

"Fuck you, Lou. And fuck the mustard on your lip."

CHAPTER 25

Moroni Perdue hunched sullenly over his coffee and blew it cool, ripples sweeping across the black surface like waves across a dark pond.

He hadn't spoken since we had sat at the counter in a hash house near division headquarters shortly before the start of our shift. Between us lay a tattered copy of the *News* with Sheppard's front-page picture and story.

"You gonna drink that or just blow on it all night?" I said.

He took a sip but didn't say anything.

I took my own sip. "Besides, I thought Mormons didn't drink coffee."

The rookie pushed away his cup and tapped the newspaper. "Did you tip homicide to this Mexican lawyer?"

I stared at him. "Why the hell would you think that?"

He half leaned toward me and said in a low voice, "'First the dead Indian's name came up with the banker. Now this Mexican lawyer seems connected. I know you're digging around without me. I figure it was you who tipped homicide."

"Well, you figured wrong, kid."

"You're up for detective." He said this with an edge.

"You figure I did this to score points?"

He stared into his coffee. "Makes sense."

"The captain warned me to stay out of the Indian's case, remember? Wouldn't be real smart of me to tell them anything I turned up."

He stared at me. "What have you turned up, Joe? What ain't you telling me about—"

He fell silent as a rough-shaven young man lugging a rack of clean glasses approached us. He slipped the rack in under the counter and nodded toward the newspaper. "Whattya you two officers know about all that?"

"Nothing!" I snapped.

He settled the rack in place and said, "You ask me, they should fry that crippled spic. Got it comin', killing the old man like that."

"We didn't ask you."

"Didn't mean no disrespect, sir. Just think it's a waste of taxpayer money. They oughta just wire the guy's chair to 220 and save us the expense of a trial."

"Hey, dickhead, he ain't even been indicted yet." I glowered at him until he went away.

Perdue swiveled on his stool toward me. "After I read the story this morning, it got me curious. I went to the library and searched old newspapers to learn more about this Ponderosa water case."

"That must have been exciting."

"It was. I came across a picture of the judge who's presiding over the case. A guy named Benjamin Glazer."

I stared into my coffee, not daring to look toward him.

Perdue leaned closer to me and said in a hushed voice, "I recognized the judge. He's the guy in the photo we found in the Indian's possessions. The guy you told me was a car salesman named Hague mixed up in a smut ring."

"Lookalikes, that's all."

"No, Joe. It makes more sense Red Owl would have the judge's photo than the photo of some car salesman. Is it what led you to this Mexican lawyer?"

I glared at Perdue. Hurt, anger, and determination burned in his eyes. "What are you after?"

"You haven't been straight with me, Joe."

"It's for your own protection."

And for mine.

"Why are you doing this, Joe? Why are you risking your career over this Indian?"

"It's the right thing to do. No one else is going to do it for him."

"You're saying I shouldn't be helping you do the right thing?"

"Drink your damn coffee, kid. I'm not someone you should be trying to help."

❡❡❡

Perdue and I weren't long into our shift when we picked up talk on Larimer Street that two men were seen fighting in a nearby abandoned building. Nobody knew what the fight was over—a bottle of booze, food, possessions, territory, shoes. Nobody cared. But apparently the loser had been left for dead.

The problem was, nobody knew which building. Several abandoned structures littered the surrounding blocks and we hardly had time to search all of them. Finally, at a soup kitchen a description came up that I recognized—a three-story warehouse on Market Street often occupied by vagrants.

We parked the black and white by the brick warehouse and circled the place once on foot. Most of the windows were boarded up, and what few still held glass were so grimy our flashlights couldn't penetrate. Finally, on the alley side we found a door studded with rusty nails jimmied open, inviting us in.

We drew our guns, climbed several concrete steps, and entered. Inside, our footsteps crunched on broken glass. We froze. The air smelled dank, the building dead still except for the echoes of water seeping from the ceiling. We swept the beams of our flashlights around in the pitch-blackness. We were in a narrow entryway. Ghostly images came and disappeared: a broom standing in a corner, piping, a concrete stairwell descending into a black hole, a wall of peeling paint, as if slashed by the claws of a ferocious animal.

My chest tightened and my breathing turning hard. Old terrors resurfaced from across the years as if they were yesterday.

The rookie started creeping down the entryway, his flashlight sweeping back and forth across the trash-littered floor like a blind man sweeping his cane. I held back. When Perdue didn't hear my footsteps behind him, he froze. "What's wrong?" he said in an edgy whisper.

"Nothing," I said.

But something was wrong. I had been in too many an abandoned dark building like this, and every time it was wrong. Every time haunting fears choked off my breath. During the war, I often was assigned to squads clearing buildings of Nazis. Those were the most frightening times for me—Krauts, booby traps, mines, and other horrors lurked behind doors and walls, in shadows and darkness. At least there, I could toss a grenade into a suspicious room and follow it with the deadly spray of a Thompson submachine gun. Here, I had only a flashlight, my .38, and a rookie. I made it out of those buildings with my life—but not my sanity.

"Just be careful, kid," I whispered. "It's damn easy to get disoriented in these buildings. The floors can cave in. You got empty elevator shafts, open pits, sharp objects. People die in these places."

The rookie swallowed hard. After several moments, he moved out into the main floor. Darkness swallowed up his beam of light.

I willed myself forward.

The warehouse on the main floor consisted of one huge open room, broken only by large concrete support columns. In the inky blackness, our flashlights struggled to provide bearings. It was like lighting a lone match to illuminate the interior of a giant cave. The warehouse appeared empty of whatever contents it once held, though we saw numerous signs vagrants had taken up residence. Our flashlights snagged glimpses of broken liquor bottles, stained mattresses, a wood chair, a lone boot with the sole torn away, empty cans of beans and Sterno, the bones of a cooked animal.

If two men had fought here, the victor no doubt was long gone, along with any witnesses. Still, we moved cautiously,

ten feet apart, our footfalls echoing on grit and pools of standing water, every column providing potentially lethal cover for
someone who didn't want us there. Every few feet we stopped
to listen for sounds beside our own footfalls and nervous
breaths. We heard the patter of rats scurrying, but nothing
more. When we spoke, we whispered like schoolgirls behind a
classmate's back.

Suddenly the rookie sucked in his breath as his flashlight
brushed across an object white and man-sized. We hunched,
our guns raised. Almost as quickly we realized the object was
a urinal. The bathroom walls around it had been ripped away.

Slowly we worked our way toward what we sensed was the
far end of the vast room. It was difficult to tell in the darkness
where we were. Electrical wires sagged from the ceiling like
old clothesline. My breathing grew tighter. Only two more
floors to search, I thought grimly.

At that moment, my light caught a man's thick-soled shoe.
The shoe was attached to a foot and the foot to a leg and finally to an entire body.

"Perdue," I said, no longer whispering.

He came over and we painted the body with our flashlights.
The man sat in a wood chair. Electrical wire bound his ankles
to the chair legs and his wrists and arms to the back. His head
lolled forward, so we couldn't see his face. A silver cross on
the end of a silver chain dangled from his neck. He was shirtless. Swaths of dried blood smeared the neck region and his
chest, though little blood stained the wood floor. Burn marks
dotted his upper body. Frenzied knife slashes crisscrossed his
chest and stomach.

"God," Perdue said, "somebody tortured him."

I swept my flashlight back down the body. The clothing
caught my eye. The shoes were spit-shined, the pants baggy
and cuffed at the ankles. This didn't look right. These weren't
the clothes of a vagrant. Then the significance of the silver
cross struck me. Dread flooded my mind. I grabbed the man's
thick black hair and turned his face upward. The throat had
been slit. My light caught the face in full.

"Whoa!" Perdue said. He leaned over the body and said, "Isn't that the gang guy we—"

Two gunshots roared out of the darkness.

A low grunt came out of Perdue and he keeled forward to the floor as if someone had pitched him off the back end of a moving truck. His flashlight rolled away, the light floundering aimlessly off into the center of the dark warehouse.

I dove to the floor behind *El Perro's* body.

A third gunshot. The bullet *thunked* into a concrete column behind me.

My flashlight remained on, giving away my location. I flipped it off.

The room plunged into darkness except for the distant spray of Perdue's flashlight. I hugged the floor. I tried to lie still, tried to quell my heavy breathing. Any movement or sound could make me dead. Glass or rocks or bits of concrete cut into my stomach and thighs and cheek.

Perdue moaned. His breath was shallow, wheezing. He was struggling for air. *Fuck!* Another partner dying before my eyes. Because of me, again! It wasn't a freakish accident the body in the chair was Willie Flores. This was an ambush. My partner had taken a bullet meant for me.

Fuck! Fuck! Fuck!

Another shot out of the darkness drew my attention. It was difficult to determine in the disorienting blackness where the flash impression of the shot had come from. But it appeared to have come from my left, in a corner, low to the floor.

Quietly I raised my gun and fired two shots in that direction, blindly, as I had done into those dark buildings during the war. I wanted a damn grenade. I wanted my Thompson submachine gun. I wanted to kill Nazis!

No return fire. After a several heartbeats, I quietly stretched out my left arm with the flashlight and aimed where I thought the shots had come from. I flicked it on, flicked it off.

A shot rang out.

I fired two rounds in the direction of the flash. One bullet ricocheted off something metallic.

Silence.

Perdue moaned again, followed by a faint crunch, the sound of a soft footfall. I fired into the darkness. Rapid footsteps now, fading as they retreated. The shooter was on the run. I bolted in the direction of the sound and quickly came to the corner of the floor. A stairwell dropped down. I eased to the edge and shined my flashlight into it.

Clear.

I tiptoed down the stairwell. More footsteps, distant now, the rattle of a chain-link fence.

The stairwell led to a ramp where trucks once pulled in to deliver their loads. Fencing ran across the ramp entrance to keep out trespassers, but I found a section peeled back.

I wouldn't find the shooter now. He had vanished into the labyrinth of the city.

I raced to our patrol car to call an ambulance for Perdue.

Time was bleeding out of him.

CHAPTER 26

On my way to Captain Donlan's office two days later, Sergeant Mulcahey stopped me. "Got something for you, Joe," the desk sergeant said, waving a small, fancy envelope in his big hand. I reached for it, but he playfully held it back. He ran the envelope under his nose and rolled his eyes. "No mash notes at the station. We don't condone improper behavior by our officers."

"Maybe it's from my wife," I said.

"If it is, have her get in touch with my wife." He handed me the envelope. A familiar strong lavender caught my nose. A feminine hand had scrawled my name and the address of police headquarters at Thirteenth and Champa across the soft, pebbled paper with an exaggerated flourish. No return address, but I had a hunch who had sent it.

I slipped the envelope into my pants pocket. I was already late for my meeting with the captain.

The sergeant's fleshy face turned serious. "That was real bad, what happened to the kid."

"Yeah," I said, my voice thick. I had been dwelling a lot since the warehouse shooting about how I had pushed the rookie away, how I had lied to him about my real motives for finding the Indian's killer. It was not what I wanted the kid to go to his grave with.

"Still touch and go the last I heard," Mulcahey said.

"Yeah, that's what I heard too."

One of the shots had struck his right lung. After calling for an ambulance, I had done what I could to stanch the blood until the medics arrived.

The doctors told me he was lucky he hadn't bled to death on the warehouse floor. They got him into surgery and repaired the lung, but he had yet to regain consciousness and remained in critical condition.

I turned for Donlan's office but the desk sergeant stopped me again. He leaned over a stack of papers and spoke softly. "You and the captain seem to be meeting on a frequent basis, Joe."

"Yeah."

"From where I've sat all these years, that's never good."

☙☙☙

"What the hell happened in there, Stryker?" demanded Captain Donlan. "I told you to keep the kid safe!"

"I'm sorry, sir," I said as apologetically as I could.

"I just got back from the hospital. We nearly lost him. We may yet."

I had been over to the hospital myself earlier in the day, but there was nothing to do. I wasn't even allowed into his room.

"Tell me what happened," Donlan said.

I glanced at the papers on his desk. The statement I had given the detectives lay on top. He followed my eyes to the papers then looked up, hard. "I want to hear it from your mouth."

I told him as straightforward as I could about investigating the report of a fight between vagrants in an abandoned warehouse, about finding the body, about the ambush in the darkness.

"You couldn't identify who shot at you?" he asked.

"No, sir. It was pitch black in there. I couldn't see anything but the gun flashes."

Investigators had found no blood by the stairwell or the fence. All my shots had missed.

"You said the word on the street was there'd been a fight between two vagrants," Donlan said.

"Yes, sir."

"If that was the case, why'd the winner hang around and ambush the two of you?"

The ambush wasn't aimed at the two of us, it was aimed at me. Aloud, I said, "I don't know, sir."

"Does this have anything to do with the Lopez brothers?"

"Sir?"

"You told me a while back you thought one of the Lopez brothers was involved in the death of the man you and Moroni found on the tracks. Does this shooting have anything to do with him?"

"I didn't see the shooter, sir. I have no idea if a Lopez was involved."

The captain gave me the skeptical look everyone seemed to give me these days. From the moment I recognized the victim as *El Perro* and the shots rang out, I knew the shooter had been a Lopez. The rookie had been an unfortunate bystander, stepping into the line of fire at the wrong moment. What I didn't know was whether the ambush was Lopez's doing alone, in an attempt to rid himself of a nuisance cop hunting for him, or whether he ambushed me on orders from someone else. It probably wasn't a coincidence that only days before, I had flashed the picture of the blackmailed federal judge in Villano Moretti's face.

The captain frowned, pulled a piece of paper from another stack on his desk, read it for a second, and looked up. "The dead man you found was a *pachuco* named Willie Flores, aka *El Perro*. Not exactly your typical vagrant. You know him?"

"We've crossed paths a few times, sir. I recognized him in the warehouse."

"What the hell was a *pachuco* doing in that building alone? Where was his gang?"

That had been my question, too. I'd tracked down *El Perro*'s brother, Jesse Flores. He claimed he had no idea how his brother had come to be murdered—but like me, he suspected Lopez. The gang had received a tip they'd catch one of the

Lopez brothers doing a drug deal that night by the Greek Amphitheater at the Civic Center Park right after dusk. Jesse and two other gang members had gone with his brother. They observed several drug deals go down, but none involving either Lopez brother. *El Perro* told his brother he had other business and left. It was the last time they saw him.

Damn, I had warned Willie not to go looking for a man as dangerous as Lopez.

"I interrogated the victim's brother," I told the captain. "He didn't know anything."

Donlan frowned. "See, that's exactly the kind of maverick investigating I warned you to stop doing. Homicide investigations belong to the detectives."

"Yes, sir."

The captain's voice softened. "I understand your anger at your partner being shot." He paused. The death of Derek Flemming hung between us. He pulled out a file and opened it. "Prelim from the ME says our victim wasn't killed there."

That had been my guess, too. The killer had slit Flores's throat, yet little blood stained the warehouse floor.

Donlan went on from the report. "The victim was tortured extensively before being killed. Somebody used a cigarette to burn him, and a pretty hefty knife to slice him."

"Yes, sir, I saw the marks."

"A rival gang? Usually they don't torture each other. They stomp each other to death."

"I don't know, sir."

"His own gang turn on him?"

"I wouldn't know, sir."

"You don't seem to know much of anything, Stryker," the captain said in a tone suggesting he suspected I knew everything.

സ്ന

After leaving the captain's office with another stern warning not to conduct my own investigation into the shooting of my partner, I stopped to open the perfumed envelope Sergeant Mulcahey had given me. My hunch had been correct. Rachel Rawlins had sent it. Or Rachel Adler. Whatever name she went by these days.

Tucked inside was a note and an engraved invitation to a party this coming Saturday night. Not at her home, but the home of Randolph Cornell, the banker whose name I had stumbled across several times, with connections to Moretti and Lamprey and the water case.

The invitation was generic. My name wasn't on it. But the note was personal, written on delicate blue note paper in a feminine but unstable handwriting.

> *Officer Stryker:*
>
> *I owe you my sincerest apologies for the crass-ness with which I spoke to you at my father's cabin. I appreciate the fact you were seeking to solve the murder of my father and were only doing your du-ty—even though, according to my husband, you have no official role in the investigation. Please present this invitation at Randolph's home at 8:30 p.m. Sat-urday. It is urgent I speak with you regarding the murder of my father. This invitation is for you only. Dress in your best.*

She'd signed the note simply Rachel, as though we were in-timate friends. What puzzled me more, however, was why, when she knew I wasn't a detective or officially involved in her father's case, she was inviting me to a top-hat party at the home of one of the men who may well be mixed up in her fa-ther's murder?

❧❦❧

"Emilio's not in," snapped Mercedes Estrada. She stood by the open fire escape window at the end of the clammy hallway in their office building smoking a cigarette. I moved down the hallway to her, past the open door of their office. The door to her brother's inner office stood open, the room empty.

"He's at police headquarters again," she said. "In one of those little rooms where they use the rubber hoses. I'm surprised you're not there."

"I didn't know. Actually, I came to see how the both of you were doing."

"That's magnanimous, considering you're the reason he's become their number one suspect."

"How do you figure that?"

"You were the only person bothering us up until now. You're the one who linked Emilio to Rawlins. You're buddies with that sleazy reporter, Sheppard."

"I didn't tell homicide or the reporter anything about your brother, Miss Estrada."

She dragged on her cigarette, unimpressed. True, my investigation had unearthed suspicious links between them and Rawlins, but someone else had seized the opportunity to frame the man.

"It didn't help that you two have not exactly been truthful about all this," I said. "It wasn't me who lied about not knowing Seth Rawlins. It wasn't me in a wheelchair at his ranch. It wasn't my office he came to visit."

"Would our being truthful have made a difference in any of this?" she said.

"It would have to me."

She flicked cigarette ashes out the window. A slight breeze brought in rancid odors from the alley. She wore her black hair long and loose today, its ends brushing the shoulders of her striped print cotton frock. A warm vulnerability managed to seep through her usually cool exterior. Suddenly she turned away and brushed by me. I trailed her into the office.

"Why aren't you with your brother at the police station?" I asked.

She crushed out her cigarette in a stamped brass ashtray on her desk. "Emilio told me to go home. They said it would be a while."

"This isn't home."

"I have work to do." She stared at her empty desktop. "Of course, I don't have my typewriter. And they took files. I don't know which ones, or why. They just took them. 'Impounding potential evidence,' they said. Emilio says it was illegal."

"I don't think your brother expects you to work at a time like this," I offered as sympathetically as I could.

A scornful smile parted her unpainted lips. "You don't know my brother very well, do you?"

"He didn't strike me as a slave driver."

"Let me tell you something about my brother. Our father came from Mexico. He spent much of his life here—married, raised a family on a dirt-poor ranch. But his heart always lay in Mexico. Not Emilio's heart. Emilio thinks of himself as a gringo. He's even adopted the gringo ways. He refuses to speak Spanish, even to Mexicans who can't speak English. 'I'm not a wetback,' he says. Work has become his middle name. He works even when he doesn't have a case to work on."

"That's how people get ahead in this country."

She stifled a laugh. "That's what Emilio believes. He believes he has it made. He lives in the big city instead of some backbreaking farm. He's better schooled than our father ever dreamed of. Even as poor as we are, he makes more money in one year than our father made in ten. For that, he thinks he's Anglo. He thinks he's climbing the economic ladder. What he doesn't realize—no, refuses to realize—is that nobody else in this city treats him like an Anglo, and that ladder just keeps getting taller and he's still at the bottom of it along with the rest of us Mexicans." Suddenly she stopped, as if embarrassed by her outburst.

"Look, one of the reasons I came by was to ask you something."

"You've asked enough of us. Get out."

"Was your office broken into before the police received the tip about the ransom note?"

The question stopped her. "No. Why?"

"Could someone have gotten in without you noticing it? The door doesn't look very secure."

"I suppose. But if they did, we never saw any signs of theft. Nothing is missing."

"Oh, they didn't come to steal anything. They broke in to use your typewriter."

First puzzlement, then realization washed over her face. She looked down at where her typewriter had sat, but hurriedly look away.

"I think Villano Moretti or one of his thugs broke into your office and typed the ransom note," I said. "Likely under the orders of Lamprey and Terry Adler. In order to destroy your brother and improve their chances in the lawsuit."

Her eyes found mine. The idea that Moretti and Lamprey might have framed her brother seemed to have caught her by surprise. I would have thought she would have found hope in my speculation. Instead, she said. "Please, leave. Leave me alone. Leave us alone!"

"For what it's worth, Miss Estrada, I don't think your brother is guilty of killing Rawlins."

"Your views are worth nothing." Anger flushed her face. "Emilio's already convicted. The rest is just show."

"But if we can find some evidence that—"

"Two hours after the story about my brother hit the streets, the people he represented dismissed him from the case. You've already destroyed him."

CHAPTER 27

After my confrontation with Mercedes Estrada, I wasn't exactly in the mood to go to a fancy party. But Rachel Adler's invitation to Cornell's home said it was urgent she speak with me about the murder of her father.

I was getting dressed in my "best" as her note had requested when Paula entered the bedroom. I had told her two days before I would be on special assignment tonight, which she was not happy about, it being on a Saturday night. That was always our night. When she saw me in the suit, she demanded I tell her what the hell kind of special assignment I was on.

"I can't," I said.

She didn't buy it this time. She knew what my "special assignment" was about, she yelled, why I was so hush-hush about everything, why I was missing so much work at Carl's garage. She spit her answer at me.

"The Lopez brothers!"

I stopped cold. How the hell had she found out? I had been so careful not to give her any hints. Had I mumbled the name in my troubled sleep? Was she just making a lucky guess? The truth proved more mundane. Paula had met Moroni Perdue's wife three days after the shooting, over dinner while I pulled a shift. Paula had arranged it, which surprised me. She disliked mingling with other cops' wives. It reminded her too much of the job she hated.

They had talked and cried for a long time, about the shooting and how much Moroni looked up to me. Mrs. Perdue had brought up the body we found in The Bottoms, and about my side investigation. Somewhere in there, the Lopez brothers had come up.

Perdue had made a rookie mistake. Never tell your loved ones about your work.

I left for Cornell's party with Paula sitting silently in a living room chair holding a gin and tonic. A large gin and tonic.

೮つ೮つ

Randolph Cornell's house sat in the country club district, not far from E. Ezzard Lamprey's house. I pulled my car to a stop in front of a huge wrought iron gate with a large letter C emblazoned on the grillwork and waited for a burly man in a dark coat to inspect my invitation. Behind the gate and a high brick wall rose a three-story tan brick house, bathed in bright exterior lights.

The guard swung the gate open and I drove up to the house. A valet took my car and I watched him park it at the far end of the curved brick drive so it wouldn't mix with the gleaming Caddys and big Buicks and fancy foreign models. Piano music and the aroma of food wafted out the front door. I decided the doorman in the striped vest and gilt buttons wouldn't bite, so I went on in.

It must have been fun growing up in the huge house. On rainy days, you could roller skate indoors or play a baseball game if you invited over enough friends.

I wandered around for several minutes—long enough to realize there were enough guests to pioneer a good-sized town, the chief of police and the mayor among them, and that I had bought my suit in the wrong store. I learned Cornell had brought in a piano player from San Francisco and a twenty-piece orchestra would begin playing soon on the third-floor ballroom. I also discovered that Cornell collected museum-quality paintings—nudes, flowers, and royalty, mostly—and the food the white-shirted waiters carried around on fancy silver trays was almost large enough to feed squirrels.

I stood staring at a wet bar bigger than what you'd find in most gin mills when a woman's voice behind me said, "You actually came, Officer Stryker." I turned to see Rachel Adler holding a glass of champagne in one hand, a black satin clutch bag in the other. She smiled. "I would have been hurt if you hadn't."

"I was surprised by the invitation, Mrs. Adler."

"Don't be so formal. Call me Rachel."

"Your exact words the last time we spoke, Mrs. Adler, were 'fuck you.'"

She shrugged as if the words had belonged to a different person. Perhaps one of the characters she played on stage. She snatched a glass of champagne from a passing waiter and handed it to me. I took it to fit in, but didn't drink.

"It's excellent champagne," she assured me.

"I don't drink when I'm on duty."

"It's Saturday night."

"With you, I think I should stay on duty."

She laughed. Her laugh sparkled like the champagne. She gave my brown gabardine suit the once over. What could I say—it was the only suit I owned.

She, on the other hand, wore a long silk taffeta apricot evening gown with padded shoulders and a tight waist. Earrings designed like wild animals dangled from below her platinum hair. Surprisingly, her apricot-colored Afghan Hound was nowhere in sight. Probably out back with all the other purebreds.

"I'm sure I'm not on Cornell's guest list, Mrs. Adler. Do you often invite people to other people's parties?"

"All the time. It's fun. I like fun." She looked around at the guests. "Their stuffy little world needs more fun. I thought having a police officer here would be fun."

"The chief of police is here," I said.

"He doesn't count. He's a bureaucrat. You're a real live policeman."

I was growing annoyed with her nonsense. "Your note said you urgently needed to talk to me about your father's murder."

She raised her champagne glass. "You just got here, Joe. Enjoy the party."

"Your father, Mrs. Adler."

She frowned and leaned in toward me. Her breath smelled like the bottom of her glass, though the rest of her smelled like the perfumed invitation she had sent.

"I know who killed my father," she whispered.

I pulled back and stared at her. She looked earnest, even if she was drunk. "Who?" I asked.

She stared into her champagne, as if trying to divine the answer trapped in the bubbles working their way to the surface. "Maybe I shouldn't say anything," she finally said.

"Then I have no reason to be here." I turned to leave.

"No, wait," she said. Desperation edged her voice.

I stopped. I scanned the crowded room. "Maybe we shouldn't be discussing this here, Mrs. Adler. Is there a quieter room we can go to?"

"Hell, let's leave. The party is boring, anyway."

She clumsily put her arm through mine and awkwardly steered me toward the front door.

I glanced about. "Where's your husband?"

"He's out of town on business."

"His friends are here. They'll see us leave together."

"Terry has no friends. Only business associates."

"I guarantee he'll find out I left with his wife."

"I don't give a shit," she slurred.

I did. The thought that her husband might send Lopez after me again chilled me.

We ran into our host on the way out. Randolph Cornell was a tall, elegant-looking man in his fifties, with a slight paunch his white dinner jacket couldn't quite hide and hair so silver it made you want to take out your handkerchief and polish it. His white teeth gleamed when he saw Rachel and he broke away from a conversation with two men. One of the men was the police chief, the other a tall man in a bow tie whom I didn't recognize.

Rachel introduced me by name and said I was a police officer helping her find her father's killer. Swell! Now her husband would definitely find out I left with his wife.

Cornell shook my hand and thanked me for helping find Seth's killer. He proudly added that his bank had posted a ten thousand dollar reward. He acted as though he didn't recognize my name. Usually guys like him flick guys like me off like a bad loan. But his eyes and a tightness along his jaw line betrayed him. He shouldn't have recognized my name, of course. Not if he were an innocent man.

ᘓᘓᘓ

The valet brought up Terry Adler's big yellow Chrysler convertible, its top down. Rachel handed me her champagne glass. "Don't spill any." She went around to the driver's side and got behind the wheel.

"Where are we going, Mrs. Adler?" I asked, remaining outside the car.

"For a little drive."

"You shouldn't be driving. You're intoxicated."

"I sure as hell hope so."

Like a fool, I got in, careful not to spill her champagne or mine. Soon we were cruising on West Colfax, headed toward the light dying behind the western foothills.

I let her drive in silence for a while. I couldn't grill her like some Larimer Street lowlife. She would get to her father's killer on her own sweet time, a time no one else was on.

She drove us out of the city, past the mesa that overlooks the city of Golden and the Coors Brewery and the mobile homes that flank its shoulders, past rock shops advertising gold and polished agates and Indian arrowheads. She stayed in her lane better than I thought she would and she even drove at a speed vaguely resembling the posted limit.

The wind kicked at my face. It was the first movement of the still, hot air I had felt for days.

"My father loved me," she suddenly said as we passed yet another rock shop.

"I'm sure he did."

"No, you're not sure. No one is sure. My father called me his frisky filly. Corny, I know. He was cornier than people realized. He called me a few other things I won't repeat, but I was always his favorite frisky filly."

"I'm sure you miss him."

She turned toward me. I wasn't sure if the damp eyes were genuine or something she had conjured up on cue. The car drifted over the centerline and I drew her attention to the road. She settled back into our lane and said, "My father hated me for going to Hollywood, for acting, for the baby. You know about the baby, don't you?" I didn't reply. "Of course you know. That ugly reporter for the *News* mentions it every damn time he writes about me. He should be a Hollywood gossip columnist." She paused. "He—they never tell you but I always knew my baby was a boy—he would have been three last April."

Where was she going with all this? I was beginning to feel like a psychiatrist, not a cop. An impatient psychiatrist.

"Tell me who you believe killed your father, Mrs. Adler," I finally asked.

The car went faster, but she said nothing. Her hair whipped about her face. The road narrowed to two-lane US 6 and we began to climb snake-like up through the parched foothills, the velvet-black shadows, and a gap gouged through red rock.

"Do you even know?" I demanded.

When she didn't respond, I told her to take me back to Cornell's house. She only drove faster, too fast for me to risk hitting the brakes and grabbing the steering wheel from her. I would have sent us straight off the road.

We came up behind an ancient pickup on a blind curve, but she never slowed. She whipped around the pickup, ducked back into the right lane to avoid a honking oncoming car, and sped up the hill. I think I spilled champagne.

"Slow down!" I yelled.

Rachel laughed and goosed the powerful engine.

"Pull over and I'll drive!"

"Oh, hell, you're no fun."

She abruptly turned off onto a graveled road that led to Lookout Mountain and Buffalo Bill's grave. Or one of his alleged graves. Cody, Wyoming, claimed his body, too. She parked thirty yards later. We were among the pines now, the air cooler. The Rocky Mountains spread out before us, their peaks fading into ever-deeper shades of purple. She snatched her clutch bag and one of the champagne glasses from my hands, and flung herself out of the car. I turned the motor off but left on the headlights. I felt safer that way. I got out and leaned against the front grillwork, holding my champagne glass just in case she needed a refill.

She chugged the rest of her champagne and hurled the glass into the darkness. Glass shattered against a rock. She dug into her clutch bag and lit up a hand-rolled cigarette. A light breeze carried the sweet smoke to me. She wasn't smoking any ordinary tobacco.

"That's illegal, you know, Mrs. Adler."

She defiantly took a puff, held it, tipped her head up, and slowly exhaled into the air. "Are you going to arrest me, Officer Stryker?"

"I should but it would be a waste of good jail space."

"You're a bastard!"

"And you're poison. Pretty, but still poison."

The last remark was a dumb-ass line. She closed in on me as if I were spider's prey, pinning my body against the car. She leaned in so close her eyelashes made butterfly kisses on my check and her boozy marijuana breath burned hot on my neck. She moved her face in front of mine and smeared scarlet lipstick across my mouth while her tongue tried to introduce itself to my tonsils. I let her kiss linger longer than I should have before I pushed her arm's length away.

"Your husband warned me not to see you again, Mrs. Adler. I can understand why."

She pouted. "Can't we have a little fun? I'm wearing apricot panties."

"I'm a married man, young lady."

"I like married men," she said with a wiggle in her voice. "Especially older ones."

"I'm not that much older."

"You'll do."

"I came at your invitation to talk about your father, Mrs. Adler. Now either tell me what you know about your father's murder or give me the damn car keys and I'll drive us back."

The come-hither look evaporated and she pulled away. "It's my husband."

It took me a few moments before I said, "You're claiming your *husband* murdered your father?"

She took a drag on her tea stick. "Yes."

"Why would he kill your father?"

"For my inheritance."

"Your husband's already rich."

"Men like him are never rich enough. My father was never rich enough."

"What evidence do you have he murdered your father?"

She tipped her head slightly to one side, as if it might dump out the words she wanted to say. "He's impotent."

"Impotent?" I repeated stupidly like a puzzled school kid struggling over a word.

"Impotent. You know, he can't get up the old—"

"I know what it means. Why the hell do you think—"

"I bet you're not impotent, are you? You don't look impotent."

"Why would you think impotence is evidence he murdered your father?"

She stared at me as if I were the village idiot. "Because murderers are always impotent. The sex drive is sublimated by the need to kill. Surely you know that. You see those cases all the time."

At this point, all I could think of was my wife home alone getting drunk because she didn't trust me, while I was stranded on a mountain side with a stoned nympho nut-job.

I threw the champagne glass off into the weeds and said, "Give me your keys, Mrs. Adler. This is a waste of my time."

She suddenly looked older. Sadder. "No, no, I'm serious."

"If you weren't so high, and drunk, Mrs. Adler, I might believe you're serious. By the way, where'd you get the juju?"

"I'm in the theater. It's always around in the theater."

"You get it from that director of yours…King?"

"It's none of your business."

"He hinted you two were once lovers."

She shrugged. I doubt she ever thought of her men as lovers.

"Okay," I said. "Do you have any evidence—besides his impotence—that your husband killed your father? You told me at the ranch a lot of people had reason to kill him."

"He was blackmailing my father."

"How do you know that?"

"My father told me. Shortly before he—before he died."

"He said your husband was blackmailing him?"

"He didn't say who, exactly. Just that he was being blackmailed. But it was Terry, I'm sure."

"What you *think* is not evidence, Mrs. Adler."

Her shoulders slumped. "I thought you would believe me."

"Forget the evidence for the moment. Do you have any idea what your husband might have used to blackmail your father?"

"What do you mean?"

"He had to have had something on your father, something he didn't want made public."

She took another puff on her tea stick before answering. "I have no idea."

For an ambitious actress, she was doing a lousy job of lying. "I can't help you if you don't tell me."

She looked away. "I don't know. Honestly."

"Your husband supports the proposed dam that would flood your father's ranch. Was he blackmailing your father in order to get him to drop his lawsuit?"

She shrugged. "Sounds logical. Whatever it was, my father told me he would take care of it."

"Take care of it how?"

"He wouldn't say. But I think he confronted Terry and Terry killed him."

That Terry Adler might have blackmailed and murdered her father was not beyond the realm of possibilities. But more like-

ly Lopez did the actual dirty work on orders from Adler—or
Adler and his buddies Lamprey, Cornell, and Moretti. Still,
something puzzled me about her ratting on her own husband.

"Why are you telling me this, Mrs. Adler?"

"I want you to prove Terry killed my father."

"Then tell the homicide boys, hon. Hell, let's get back to
the party and you can tell the chief of police in person. He
hasn't collared an asshole since Hoover was president."

"They won't believe me."

"But I would?"

"At the ranch you seemed a man hungry for the truth.
You've been investigating on your own. Why are you so interested in my father's murder?"

"As I said, go tell homicide."

"They already have a suspect. That Mexican in the wheelchair."

"Estrada is his name," I said, feeling the man should have a
name.

"I don't believe he did it."

Well, at least that makes two of us, even if one of us wasn't
running on all eight cylinders.

"I'm not investigating your father's death for you, Mrs. Adler," I said firmly.

She came toward me again. "I can make it worth your
while."

I put my hands up for her to stop. "Give me the car keys."

I had a lot to think about on the drive back down to Cornell's place.

CHAPTER 28

Perdue had recovered enough for me to visit him at Denver General Hospital. They had moved him from intensive care into a sterile white ward of a half-dozen beds. Heavy curtains shuttered every window, the room lit by garish fluorescent lights. My nose crinkled at the overpowering smell of antiseptic and bleach.

"How ya doin', kid?" I asked, standing at the foot of his metal-framed bed. He sat propped up slightly on pillows. A glass bottle half full of clear liquid hung from a nearby pole, rubber tubing running to a needle taped to the back of his left hand.

"I'll be back to duty in a shake," the rookie wheezed through dry lips. He looked pale. The doctors said he was out of danger, but it would be weeks before he would be cleared to return to active duty.

"I bet you will," I said. "They treating you okay?"

"Yeah, fine. How are *you* doing? You got a new partner?"

"They got me patrolling alone for the moment. Just waiting for you."

That, and the fact no one wanted to work with me. I was the touch of death.

Perdue reached for a glass of water on a nightstand. I quickly stepped forward and picked it up for him. He took a few small sips through a straw and I set the glass back.

I noticed an unopened bag of LifeSavers. I offered him one but he declined.

"They got any ideas yet who shot me?" the rookie asked softly.

"No."

The rookie nodded slightly. "Captain Donlan told me they didn't, but I wasn't sure if he was holding something back."

"He wasn't. But I—"

A nurse in a starched white cap and white apron padded by on soft shoes, smiled, and stopped at another one of the beds. I pulled the privacy curtain along the overhead rod, closing us off from the rest of the ward.

Perdue nodded toward the window near his bed. "Would you open the curtains for me? They keep this place as dark as a morgue."

I opened the curtains. Bright morning sun washed over his bed. I pulled up a chair next to him. I spoke quietly, so adjoining patients wouldn't hear me—so maybe I wouldn't hear myself.

"I owe you an apology, kid."

He wrinkled his brow. "For what?"

"Because I'm the reason you got shot."

"It's not your fault. They told me I just happened to lean over the body at the wrong moment. I—I don't remember any of that. But if the bullet hadn't hit me, it woulda struck you."

I didn't say anything for a few moments. I became acutely aware of the annoying buzz of the fluorescent lights and the slow whoosh of a ceiling fan trying to push the stuffy air in the ward. I became aware of the guilt coursing through my soul.

"That's why it was my fault," I finally said. "That bullet was intended for me."

"Why? You think God had meant for you to—"

"God had nothing to do with it. It was an ambush. The shooter was—" I leaned closer. "This is just between us."

"It won't go anywhere. You can trust me, Joe. I know you don't, but you can."

"I believe the shooter was one of the Lopez brothers."

The rookie's eyes widened. "Why do you believe that?"

"Remember the body we found in the warehouse, moments before the shots?"

Perdue weakly shook his head. "The last thing I remember was entering the place. Nothing after that. But the captain said the victim was that *pachuco* named *El Perro*. I remember him. He gave us the name of the Indian."

I pulled back, my face tense.

"Don't worry, Joe. I didn't tell the captain we talked to the guy weeks ago. I figured you wouldn't want him to know."

My face relaxed and I half smiled. "You're a good man."

Perdue adjusted himself on the bed and pain remolded his face for a moment. "So why do you think it was an ambush?"

I told him about *El Perro* disappearing after he and his gang had staked out an alleged drug deal with Lopez in Civic Center Park. I said Lopez had likely lured Flores there with a fake tip and grabbed him when the opportunity arose. He tortured Flores, murdered him, and propped his body up on the chair in the warehouse, like a taunting prize. Then he spread the rumors about two guys fighting in the warehouse during our shift so we'd take the bait.

"He was aiming for me when you were shot," I said. "Lopez wanted *me* dead."

"Because you've been trying to catch him for the Indian's murder?"

"That's part of it." I leaned forward with my elbows on my thighs and my hands clasped. I stared at the thin but clean white sheets. "But there's more."

"What?" Perdue said after I didn't say anything.

I wavered on telling him anything—then I told him everything. I told him the truth about why I was after Red Owl's killer, about Lopez killing my partner. I told him about Moretti and Lamprey and Estrada and Adler, about their connections to Rawlins through the water case. I told him about Rachel Adler and the ranch foreman. I told him about showing the photo of the judge to Moretti in an attempt to get him to give up Lopez, and that I believed he sicced Lopez after me—perhaps on orders from Lamprey or Adler.

I told him more than I should have told a wounded man. Through it all, I watched his face for reaction, for a sense of betrayal.

But he listened silently, with half-lidded eyes. He appeared exhausted when I finished.

"That's why I owe you an apology," I said. "My obsession with Lopez has clouded my judgment. I didn't tell you the truth of it. If it weren't for me, you wouldn't need to be here."

I gave Perdue another drink of water.

"You don't owe me an apology, Joe. Lopez deserves to be hunted. He's an evil man."

I shook my head. "I've put you in a bad place, kid. I don't mean just the warehouse. I put you in a bad place with the captain and with homicide. I lied to you and now you've lied to them. I put you in a bad place with the—" I lowered my voice. "—with the little payoffs. I shouldn't have done that."

Perdue wasn't the only person I had put in a bad place these last weeks. Paula, Emilio Estrada, his sister. Myself.

"I made my choices, Joe. We Mormons believe strongly in free will." The rookie's voice was stronger than I deserved. "I've known for some time one of the Lopez brothers probably killed your partner. That wasn't difficult to find out. I kinda suspected it was what was really driving you about the Indian."

I stared at him, stunned. "Why didn't you say something?"

"I wanted to hear it from you. I wanted you to trust me enough to tell me."

For the first time in my life, I realized what true shame felt like, what it meant. I realized it to the core of my being. I hung my head. "I'm sorry. You're absolutely right. You gotta be square with a partner." I looked up. "You're a good kid, Moroni. I like your spirit. I had your spirit once. You'll make a good cop if I stay out of your way."

"I like being your partner."

"You don't want to hang around me. You don't want to become like me. We need cops with enthusiasm, idealism, integrity. *Clean* cops. This job's tough enough as it is. It's easy to get burned out on it. It's easy to get cynical, to not trust people. To not trust yourself."

The rookie looked at me with tired but steady eyes. "You're a good cop, Joe."

Derek Flemming had said almost the identical words to me, before I failed him and he died. "Once, maybe," I said.

"You still are. You just don't want see to it anymore."

I got up and pulled back the privacy curtain. "Get some rest, kid. Get well. I'm going to need a partner again."

Perdue lifted a finger for me to wait. I leaned forward slightly. "You catch Lopez," he whispered. "You catch the sonofabitch before he kills again."

CHAPTER 29

I remained convinced Rachel Adler and I were right in our belief Emilio Estrada did not murder her father. But the Mexican attorney was making it as difficult as possible to hold on to our belief. Estrada had told me a horse riding accident had put him in his wheelchair. Lou Sheppard's latest front-page story painted a far different, far more troubling picture.

Emilio Estrada had been paralyzed in a gun battle during a bitter land dispute with the Rawlins family.

Sheppard had gone digging around Pawnee Buttes where Estrada and his sister Mercedes had grown up on their family ranch on the northeast Colorado grasslands. Lou had inspected sheriff records, talked to locals, and combed through old issues of a local newspaper. According to his lengthy article, Estrada's father, Rodolfo, had crossed the Rio Grande near El Paso in 1904 and worked as a farm hand throughout the Southwest, eventually working several years for an old widowed ranch woman near Pawnee Buttes. She willed Rodolfo the small ranch when she died. It was the only Mexican-owned ranch in a 200-mile radius—a ranch bordering the Rawlins spread.

For several years, the Estrada family raised sugar beets, a few cattle, and a crop of debts. By the summer of 1924, the pressure to sell was enormous, pressure particularly from the Rawlins empire. The Rawlins family had eyed the Estrada place because it held valuable water rights they needed in order to expand their already humongous cattle spread, one of several ranches the Rawlins empire owned, from Montana to the Mexican border, 850,000 acres in all.

Although a young Seth Rawlins ran the Pawnee Buttes spread, the real pressure to buy out the Estrada ranch came from his old man, Clay, known for his ruthlessness. Clay Rawlins bullied the local bank into calling up Estrada's loan, in effect foreclosing on the ranch. Rawlins bought the place for a song and kicked the family off.

According to the article, shortly before the foreclosure, Emilio Estrada, then sixteen, rode out to the Rawlins ranch armed with his father's 30-30. Several Rawlins cowhands intervened and a gunfight broke out. Versions of who fired the first shot differed, but the result was that Emilio ended up in the sagebrush with a bullet in his spine.

Soon after, the Estrada family moved to Grand Junction where their father died in a paint factory fire in 1937. Their mother died of an undetermined illness in 1943. The rest of Lou's article examined how the paralyzed attorney managed to put himself through law school with the help of his sister, moved to Denver, and build his modest career as a water attorney.

The story added nothing in the way of evidence proving Emilio Estrada murdered Rawlins. The implications were clear, however. Estrada and his sister had a deep-seated motive to murder the man whose family had destroyed their family's ranch and put Emilio in a wheelchair.

∾∾∾

It took me two hours to catch up with Lou Sheppard by phone in the newsroom. I wasn't sure he would talk to me. The last time I had talked to him, I had told him to fuck the mustard on his lip.

But Lou was in an upbeat mood, having scored yet another coup on the rival *Denver Post*.

"The only thing Witlaw can do now is report Estrada's arrest," he said smugly.

"The sheriff has already arrested Estrada?" I said, surprised.

"They're drafting the paperwork as we speak, is the word I got from a guy in the county DA's office."

"They got the wrong man, Lou."

"You've claimed that before, but it's a compelling motive. Those folks around Pawnee Buttes say it was a bitter feud between the two families. The dicks like the story. Desolate damn place. You ever been out to the grasslands?"

"Why the hell would Estrada wait twenty years to kill the old man's son? It was Clay Rawlins who was the prick according to your story."

"DA figures Estrada never had the opportunity. Clay Rawlins is dead, but the water case put Estrada and Seth Rawlins in contact again, so he took advantage of it."

"I still say there's still no way Emilio Estrada could have killed Rawlins on his ranch, sunk his body in the lake, and driven his car back to Denver."

"You're forgetting his sister."

"Then why aren't they arresting her, too?"

"They got no legal basis to arrest her at the moment. They figure her seeing her crippled brother hauled off to jail will ultimately make her more cooperative when they do bring her in."

"I still haven't seen proof, Lou."

"The Estradas are Mexican, Joe. They don't need more proof than that."

CHAPTER 30

The Dick Jurgens orchestra played "Cruising Down the River" as Paula and I turned a slow circle on the Trocadero's crowded ballroom floor. Over her shoulder, I watched one of the roving chaperones tap a warning on a man's shoulder for dancing cheek-to-cheek with his woman.

No one was going to tap me on the shoulder tonight.

Paula was in no mood to dance at all, let alone cheek-to-cheek. But I had persuaded her to go to our favorite ballroom in an attempt to apologize for making a hash out of things. Earlier in the week, Captain Donlan had demoted me to walking beat in Siberia. I wasn't surprised. It had been only a matter of time—and not much time at that—before he had learned of my appearance with Rachel Adler at Randolph Cornell's party. Most likely from the police chief himself. Homicide also had learned I had talked to Gannon, the foreman at the Rawlins ranch, and to Jennings, the geologist in Estrada's office building. My "footprints" were everywhere. Donlan didn't bother to ask for an explanation. I had disobeyed his direct order. He said people—he didn't bother to say who—wanted me "quieted down" and he was going to do just that. I needed a "change of scenery," he said. Any chance for a promotion to detectives was put on hold—maybe permanently.

A day later, Carl fired me from my part-time mechanic's job.

Yeah, I had made a hash of things.

"I love this tune," I said as we moved with the mass of dancers swaying counterclockwise around the Troc's huge hardwood floor.

"We shouldn't have spent the money to come here." The tenseness in Paula's spine burned through her summer dress.

"We need a night out," I said. I squeezed her tighter, hoping to get her to relax.

"We need the money more."

I looked away, around the cavernous interior of the Troc with its ornate mauve and pink decorations, recalling when I used to come here on the weekends during the war. I would buy the nickel dance tickets and stand nervously in the stag line behind the iron fence watching the guys with dates out on the floor. We had more GIs than girls, but it beat sitting back at the barracks spit-shining boots. Dances had grown considerably more expensive since then, but the money was the least of it tonight.

"We're fine," I said. I had tapped my bribery stash to cover the evening.

"No, we're not fine."

"Don't worry, I'm a good mechanic. I'll find a job soon."

Paula shook her head. "We're not fine until you stop hunting the Lopez brothers!"

The light on the dance lantern above us blinked from waltz to fox-trot as the orchestra broke into a bouncy version of "A-Tisket, A-Tasket."

"Let's get outa here," I said. I steered Paula toward one of the Troc's open stucco arches. The music followed us out into the warm summer air of Elitch Gardens, mixing with the bark of the carnies and the screams of young girls on the roller coaster and the smell of corn dogs and popcorn.

We hadn't walked far, in silence, when I stopped at a vendor selling cotton candy. "What flavor do you want?" I asked Paula.

"I don't want cotton candy."

"You love cotton candy."

"Joe, we need to talk about this. There's something I need

to tell—" Her voice dropped as she eyed the vendor swirling light blue cotton candy onto a cardboard cone, his face hopeful for a sale.

"What flavor would you like, miss?" the vendor said. "We have orange, peppermint—"

Paula took off. So fast, I almost lost her in the crowded midway as we passed game booths and more food vendors. I caught up with her and grabbed her waist to slow her down.

"What do you need to tell me?" I demanded.

She turned and faced me as people swirled around us, like water skirting a boulder in midstream. Not a good place to talk, but she seemed bent on it.

"Joe, I love you. But this obsession with Lopez isn't just about losing your job or your promotion. It's destroying our marriage."

"If I don't catch Lopez, our marriage won't survive, anyway."

"Let someone else catch them. They'll slip up. You tell me criminals always do."

"One of them tried to kill me in that warehouse, Paula."

"Because you were hunting for them!"

"I wouldn't describe it as—"

"It was obvious from Mrs. Perdue that you'd been after them for *weeks* before the shooting. She blames you for what happened to her husband."

I didn't add that my "obsession" with the Lopez brothers had put an innocent man in jail. Just as Lou Sheppard had predicted, the Ponderosa County sheriff's office had arrested Emilio Estrada for the murder of Seth Rawlins. I didn't tell her I owed my wounded partner and my dead partner. I didn't tell her catching Lopez was the only way to rid myself of the nightmares of my mistakes. "I don't have a choice now," I merely said.

"Of course you do!"

"He's not going to quit coming after me until one of us is dead."

The cold reality of the line made Paula blanch.

Behind me, one of the barkers yelled, "Step right up, gentlemen! Show your lady you got the arm of Bob Feller. Knock over the bottles and win your lady a prize. A winner every time."

I snatched Paula's hand and dragged her over to the Milk Bottle Throw booth.

"Ahh, I see a man who wants to win one for his lady," the barker said with a grin that made my spine crawl. He looked as if he had eaten several of the huge stuffed animals perched on shelves behind him. He repeatedly tossed a baseball in his fat hand and gave a "dare you" look. "All ya gotta do is knock over three lousy bottles," he challenged. "I can tell that's a piece of cake for a feller like you."

I pointed to a large teddy bear on the top row of prizes and told Paula I would it win for her. She loved teddy bears.

"I don't want a bear," she said.

I paid the barker my money anyway and he tossed the baseball to me. I stared at the white-painted wooden milk bottles, one stacked on the other two. I reared back and hurled the ball, knocking off the top bottle but leaving the other two standing.

"Close, sir, so close," taunted the barker. "But I have a consolation prize for you."

"I don't want a consolation prize," I said.

I paid for another throw. This time I hit the three bottles squarely in the midsection. Two fell over, but the third one remained standing.

"*Ohhhh*, I thought you had it, sir," the barker said.

"I hit it dead center."

The barker shrugged, as if it were the fault of the gods. I eyed him. I knew they often rigged the midway games. I paid for another throw, anyway.

"Joe!" Paula said.

I threw again, hard, but missed badly.

"Let's go, Joe," Paula said, tugging on my sleeve.

"One more," I said.

I paid again. The barker had a shit-eating grin by now. He lived for suckers like me. Time to try something different. I stepped to a forty-five degree angle to the bottles and threw hard at the base of the stack. All three bottles scattered across the table.

The barker frowned, but only for a moment. Bystanders were watching. He broke into a big forced grin. He reached up and pulled down the teddy bear I had singled out to Paula. He tossed it in a high arc to me, so everyone would see.

"We have a winner, folks! We have a winner!"

I handed the bear to a scowling Paula. Behind me, the barker went into his spiel again. "Step right up, gentlemen! Knock over the bottles and win your lady a prize, just like that man did. A winner every time."

Paula and I reentered the flow of the crowd. She kept steps ahead of me, squeezing the life out of the big stuffed bear. Suddenly she whirled toward me. She took several deep breaths. Uncertainty and fear laced her face.

"I'm pregnant!"

She almost spit out the words. Passers-by glanced at her, smiled, elbowed each other. I simply stared, stupefied. I glanced at her belly, hidden by the bear, and finally managed to stammer, "That's *wonderful*, honey."

I stepped forward to hug her, but the bear was in the way. I grabbed it by the scruff of the neck and held it as I wrapped my arms tightly around her. Her arms lightly touched my back. I stepped away and glanced at her belly again. "When did you find out?"

"Yesterday."

Tears streaked her cheeks, but I sensed they weren't tears of pregnancy or joy. I didn't ask why she had waited a whole day to tell me. I knew it had been news she didn't want to learn. Still...

I reached out and touched an arm. "This is wonderful news, dear. It really is. This will be good for both of us."

She yanked the bear back from me and squeezed it. "Don't you see now, Joe? You've got to drop this Lopez business. If not for me, if not for our marriage, then for your baby. You need to start thinking like a father, not like a cop."

I swallowed hard. The child I had wanted for so long suddenly seemed so far away. I hesitated, and she jumped in before I could speak.

"We need the money. I can't get a job now, and I don't want you getting killed. I don't want your baby growing up without a father."

"I'm not going to get killed, Paula."

"You just said it was him or you." She began moving again.

"Paula," I called after her.

She spun back abruptly. She wiped tears from her eyes. The din of the midway enveloped us.

"You know what's really wrong here, Joe. You wouldn't tell me what you were doing. You wouldn't tell me the real reason you were missing work. You wouldn't take me into your confidence. You haven't been honest with me, Joe. You don't build a marriage on that. Even if you do stop Lopez."

"It was for your protection, Paula."

Her face hardened. "No, it was to hide what you were doing! You knew I wouldn't approve."

"I'm sorry. You're right. I should have told you. But it's too late now. I can't just drop it."

"I won't accept that. You have a choice, Joe. Stop hunting for Lopez, get yourself another mechanic's job, and get yourself back in the good graces of the department." She thrust the teddy bear into my arms. "Or I won't be here when your baby is born."

CHAPTER 31

I avoided lawyers at all costs. They gave me headaches. Unfortunately, I sometimes had no choice but to deal with them. This was one of those times.

E. Ezzard Lamprey's office was located in the Equitable Building on Seventeenth Street, a red sandstone structure that housed behind heavy oak doors the accountants, lawyers, and financial wizards who served the corporate moguls. It was a long way from Emilio Estrada's office building.

On my way to Lamprey's sixth-floor office, I ran my hand along the shiny bronze handrails smoothed by thousands of passing visitors and gawked like a kid at the Tiffany windows. My footsteps echoed in the green marble hallways. The place was as hushed as a church, and about as spiritual.

I wore my only suit and flashed my badge at Lamprey's secretary. She said he was busy and couldn't be interrupted. I said I was working a murder case and didn't care if he was in with the governor. She ushered me into a high-ceilinged, book-lined office. A nice cozy room. Spread a few inches of rich Iowa soil over the lush green carpet and I could have started myself a respectable-sized farm.

A man in his fifties with thick wavy black hair sat alone at the end of a long mahogany conference table eating veal cutlets and smothered asparagus spears from a china plate with gold-plated flatware.

A half-finished glass of amber liquid sat on the table—a

fondness for bourbon, Estrada had told me. Yeah, the man was real busy.

His secretary apologized for the interruption but said I was a police officer who urgently needed to speak to him. She suddenly realized she didn't know my name.

"That's okay," I said. "Mr. Lamprey knows who I am."

We had seen each other before, at Randolph Cornell's party. He was the man in the expensive bow tie standing next to the chief of police when Cornell had broken away to speak to Rachel Adler. Lamprey wore a bow tie this time, too, with a dark blue three-piece suit with narrow chalk stripes and a white shirt.

His secretary apologized again and Lamprey dismissed her with, "Just make sure no one else interrupts us, Margaret."

She meekly fled the room and closed the door. Lamprey tossed the cloth napkin from his lap onto the table and stood up. But instead of coming forward to shake my hand, he picked up his drink and moved to an imposing carved antique desk that would have taken half a dozen weightlifters to move.

"We can talk while you eat, Mr. Lamprey," I said.

"I never discuss business over food," he said in a courtroom-sized voice as he settled behind his desk. "Improper digestion produces deleterious effects on the brain. Unfortunately, it's increasingly difficult to find people willing to sit down for lunch merely for the pleasure of enjoying food. Everybody's been in a rush since the war. When I was a young man in my first law firm, I used to sit around with the senior partners discussing the finer points of law. Who the hell does that today? Time is money."

He casually sipped his drink. Apparently booze didn't produce the same deleterious effects on the brain as did interrupted lunches. "How may I be of assistance to you, Officer Stryker?"

He didn't offer a chair and I didn't take one. I began walking around his office. I took a certain enjoyment making the lawyer wait. A manicured Yorkshire Terrier, whose long coat matched the steel blue of a Smith & Wesson, lounged on a dark leather couch. It didn't bother to acknowledge my presence. Nearby on a lamp table I spotted a Florentine gold-framed photograph of a young man in an air force uniform. I remembered what Estrada had told me. I walked over to the photograph.

"I was in the war, Mr. Lamprey. I'm sorry about your son."

I think that caught him off guard, that I knew about his son's death. Or that I cared. Which I did.

"His B-twenty-nine went down over Berlin," he said. The polish went out of his voice. "I think the Ruskies have him. They have a lot of our boys over there."

"I've heard rumors like that."

"But you didn't come here to talk about my son or the Ruskies."

Down to business, I guess. Apparently time was money for him, too. I walked back in front of the gargantuan desk. "There's a man in jail who shouldn't be there, for a murder he didn't commit."

"Yes, as I told the media, I was shocked Emilio would be accused of such a heinous crime. Though I understand you helped put him in that position."

"Not as much as you did. But you can get him out. You can make those charges go away."

Lamprey clasped large-bonded fingers in front of him. "I have no idea what you're talking about."

"I think you had Villano Moretti type up the Rawlins ransom note using Estrada's office typewriter and then you fingered Estrada to homicide. You did this to knock out one of your courtroom opponents—and to cover up the blackmail and bribery of a federal judge."

If lawyers had wraiths from hell they summoned when they were angry, Lamprey looked as though he had just subpoenaed his. He stood up behind his desk. "You need to leave immediately."

I pulled the compromising photo of Judge Glazer from my jacket pocket and laid it on his desk. Lamprey glanced at it but didn't touch it, as if it were infected with some form of plague.

"That's not the judge's wife," I said. "But you already know that, don't you?"

The lawyer glared at me. I could understand why witnesses might wilt under the gaze of his brown eyes. "This is supposed to prove what?"

"I believe Moretti took this photo and several others. I believe he showed up one bright morning in the chambers of the honorable judge and handed him a nice eight-by-ten glossy of His Honor's under-the-bench activities and offered to print free of charge a dozen extra prints just in case His Honor thought the Bar Association or the Boy Scouts or his wife or the press might like copies. Moretti sweetened the deal by offering the judge ownership in cheap prairie land Terry Adler owns—land that will become very valuable once water starts flowing to it. That's the judge's job, to ensure delivery of that water by ruling favorably for the Denver Water Board."

Lamprey sat back down and tried to look relaxed in his high-backed executive chair. "Those are slanderous, unsubstantiated accusations, Officer. I'm a man of evidence—as are the courts."

"Oh, I don't need evidence. I just need a hungry newspaper reporter and a story that sounds plausible. Blackmailing a federal judge is bad for business, even for guys like you. Plus, this ties into the Rawlins murder and the murder of a man named Art Red Owl. And that's going to dirty your shoes, even if they don't nail you for the charges."

Lamprey took another drink, slowly, just to show me his nerves were steady. "I understand you were recently demoted, Officer. Should you persist in your efforts to threaten me or disparage my reputation in the newspapers, I'll ensure your permanent departure from the police department."

"You'll have to get in line for that. Your bigger worry is not me. It's Moretti. You're working with a loose cannon there. I had a little chat with the man and he panicked and ran to your house at three in the morning carrying incriminating evidence of blackmail. If he hadn't done that, I wouldn't have connected you to him. Not a sign of a stable guy. I guarantee you, when Moretti goes down, his fat ass will drag a lot of you with him."

Lamprey left his drink alone this time. He worked his square jaw and I saw fear flinch behind his eyes.

❧❧❧

Following the arrest of Emilio Estrada, his sister Mercedes dropped out of sight. She closed up their office and didn't answer whenever I knocked at their home, deep in the Mexican neighborhoods on the west side of town. But I watched the alley behind the house whenever I had the time and, late one afternoon, I saw her drive up and park in the detached garage. She came out carrying a sack of groceries.

"Need some help?" I asked from the gate of the waist-high wire fence that enclosed the backyard. The lawn hadn't been mowed in weeks, the flowerbeds were overgrown with weeds, and grass sprouted through the cracks of the sidewalk leading from the garage to the house.

Mercedes glared at me in the sun and frowned. Her eyes were swollen and red. Her hair hung limp and tangled, as shapeless as the pale brown dress she wore. "Why don't you leave us alone? Why do you *persist* in meddling in this case that's not even yours?"

"Because I'm trying to catch the asshole I believe murdered Rawlins and another man. I know it's not your brother."

I had lost all leads to Lopez, ever since the ambush. But I felt sure he was hiding somewhere under the rich and powerful who ran the city. It was only a matter of time before I turned over the right rock.

"Would you rather talk out here in broad daylight, or inside?" I said.

She sighed resignedly and headed for the house, a small, square, one-story, yellow-framed structure with lime green shutters in need of fresh paint. I hurried through the gate and reached the back steps just as she did.

A reinforced section of plywood covered half the steps, wide enough for a wheelchair. I held the screen door open while she juggled the sack of groceries in one hand and unlocked the door. I followed her in before she had time to change her mind.

"Shut the door," she commanded. "I don't want any reporters or sightseers knowing I'm home. They're like...leeches."

The *Post* and the *News* had been duking it out on their front pages, trading headlines like a couple of punch-drunk fighters. Both papers had standing offers to pay handsomely for any "evidence" private citizens turned up. The *Post* came up with a tip from a fifty-three-year-old fisherman from Buena Vista who found a bloody cowboy hat along the edge of a gravel road three miles from the Rawlins ranch. Good front page stuff, that.

Six days later it ran two paragraphs on page thirty-four admitting authorities had determined the blood was animal, not human.

The *News* reported a tip from a tenant in Estrada's office building who swore Estrada and his sister ran an illegal babyselling operation using unwed Mexican girls smuggled across the border. Sheppard later checked out the tenant.

Turned out the guy was a down-and-out dentist who had been kicked out of Waco, Texas, for practicing without a license and who had moved into the office building only four days before the police had arrested Estrada. The paper also carried a report about a car stolen from Denver the evening Rawlins was believed to have disappeared. Law enforcement found the car at a roadhouse a scant mile from the entrance to the Rawlins ranch. But other than returning the car to the idiot who had left it running while he dashed into a store, nothing came of it.

The newspapers had found the Rawlins story so entertaining and profitable the *Post* hired the famous mystery writer Erle Stanley Gardner to write a series of stories on Estrada, his family, and the intrigues of the Rawlins empire.

Not to be outdone, the *News* brought in a New York criminologist named Schreiber to administer a polygraph test to Estrada.

The lawyer initially refused to take the test, then changed his mind, then failed it.

I closed the door and found myself in a tiny dim kitchen. The interior was hot and clammy, with the smell of over-ripened fruit.

I moved quickly through the rest of the house: two bedrooms, a modest living room, and a dining niche barely large enough for the two-person drop-leaf table. Stairs led to a basement. Every shade and curtain in the house were drawn, the place in a self-made twilight for such a bright afternoon.

Mercedes was putting away groceries in white metal cabinets when I returned. "You lied to me about how your brother was paralyzed," I said. "Are there other things you lied about?"

"Does it make any difference?"

"Your brother's being railroaded into the gas chamber by a bumpkin county sheriff, the media, and most of the Denver Police Department."

"What do you want me to say? It won't make a damn difference. They need a sacrificial lamb. A crippled Mexican makes a good one."

"Why is your brother being so stubbornly silent? He's refused to make a statement, he refuses to cooperate with detectives. He acts like he *wants* to be found guilty."

She jammed a box of crackers in a cabinet and turned to me. "He does."

"You're saying he really did murder Seth Rawlins?"

"No. He's trying to protect me."

"Because the police suspect you were his accomplice?"

"No. Because he believes I killed Seth. All by myself."

It took me a moment to digest her assertion. "Did you?"

She put away more groceries. "No."

"Why does your brother believe you did?"

"Because I was furious when I found out Seth had secretly hired Emilio."

"*Hired* him?"

She finished putting away the groceries and turned to fill the sink with soapy water. "Those West Slope interests and other landowners Emilio represented were something of a sham. Real plaintiffs, but it was Seth covering their attorney's fees to Emilio. He wanted as many lawsuits as possible brought against the reservoir. He also hired Emilio to do research for his own attorneys on the case. Emilio is the real water-law expert."

"How did you find this out?"

"Whenever Emilio would meet with Seth and his attorneys, he would tell me he had a meeting with some hush-hush client he couldn't talk about. He always went without me. One afternoon I was out of the office, but returned early. I found Seth with Emilio."

She yanked a cast-iron skillet from the Roper gas range and plunged it into the soapy water.

"Your brother said they never met in your office."

She dug out a Brillo pad and began scrubbing off the encrusted food. "Well, he lied."

"What happened when you found them together?"

She stopped scrubbing and looked at me. "I screamed at Emilio. What do you think I would do? I couldn't believe he was working with that bastard. I couldn't believe he would betray his own family—betray me. Betray even himself. All he said was we'd talk about it later. Seth shut the door to the office and they continued meeting."

"What did they talk about?"

She returned to scrubbing. "I wasn't in there with them."

"Those walls are so thin you can hear the leaves fall off the plants."

"I left. I couldn't stand being in the same building with the man."

"So when Rawlins turned up murdered, your brother suspected you?"

"Seth and his family ruined our family. I hated him for that, for being responsible for crippling Emilio."

"How exactly does your brother think you carried off this murder?"

She kept scrubbing, not looking up. "He didn't detail it to

me. But I wasn't with Emilio part of the day Seth was seen in our office building."

"The Saturday you were supposed to meet this Kenneth Morrisey who never showed?"

"Yes. After I dropped Emilio at home, I ran errands. I think Emilio believes I went to Seth's ranch instead and killed him."

"Can you prove you ran errands? Can anyone vouch for you?"

"No. It was just shops."

She kept scrubbing, though I was pretty sure the frying pan was clean.

"If you drove up there in your own car and killed him, does your brother have an explanation for why you would drive the Rawlins car back down here and park it a block from the office? And how you got yours back?"

"I think Emilio theorizes I arranged to meet Seth somewhere in town and went from there to the ranch in his car."

"Why would you two have done that?"

She glared at me. "I don't know. Ask my brother. It's his theory." She returned to the pan.

"Yet he's willing to go to jail to protect you. Maybe go to the gas chamber."

"He knows his practice is destroyed, even if he's acquitted. So if he believes there's a chance I killed Seth, he might as well protect me by getting himself convicted. He has nothing left to lose."

"Not every brother would do that for a sister," I said.

"It's not a debt I asked for or wish to bear."

She kept scrubbing the pan. Scrubbing it raw.

In the darkening stillness of the room, the buried anger in her voice emerged like a long-hidden ghost. I had an image of her standing in the kitchen and eating alone each evening, in the dark, anger boiling like hot oil inside her. Suddenly I knew.

"You didn't kill Rawlins," I said. "But you were angry enough at your own brother for working with Rawlins that you framed him, didn't you?"

She stopped scrubbing. Her expression contained many emotions, but surprise wasn't one of them.

"*You* faked the ransom note on your own office typewriter," I went on. "*You* gave up your brother to homicide. Even at the risk of imprisoning yourself."

She looked at me. Even in the twilight, I could make out the pain and self-loathing in her eyes. Then a strangled laugh came out of her, from deep inside her. "The thought had never crossed my mind until Seth disappeared and you showed up asking Emilio questions about Lamprey and that blackmail photo. I began to see the possibilities, see how Emilio might be linked into it."

"You need to tell this to homicide, Mercedes. You can't let your brother rot in jail."

"Yes, I can."

I walked out of the darkness of the house, leaving her alone with her hate.

CHAPTER 32

Another night walking Siberia. Another night waiting to be shot by Lopez. Angelo or Antonio. Whichever one had murdered Art Red Owl and maybe Rawlins, had killed *El Perro*, and wounded Perdue at the warehouse.

Lopez would certainly know by now from Moretti and Lamprey that I'd been exiled to The Bottoms. I was a sitting duck walking beat here, alone, at night. No patrol car, no partner. A patrol car dropped me off at the start of my shift, like one tossed out an unwanted pet in the woods. Nothing down here but warehouses, mangy dogs, and the occasional burglar. And shadows from where one could shoot unseen. A few boneheads brought girls down for a little humping in the back seat. But not many. Even sluts found Siberia too spooky.

Whoever had designed the beat on Siberia had taken perverse pleasure in planning it. They had put the call boxes far enough apart and the reporting times close enough together so it was all one could do to walk from one box to the next in time. No way was one going to coop on this beat. This beat was a forced march. A lesson in humility watch commanders employed for fuckups. They assigned the recalcitrant officer a week or two or three on Siberia, to remind him who was in charge. Like prisoners in isolation.

An unusually strong, chilly wind blew for a July evening. My fingers curled stiffly around my flashlight as I swung the muted beam along the front of a warehouse. I spotted some

concrete steps and sat down, tired. I couldn't stay long. I needed to reach the next call box on time. A few minutes grace.
They gave you a few minutes grace, just in case you happen to
nab a burglar along the way.

My thoughts turned to Paula, as they had done often since
she'd broken the news to me that she was going to visit her
sister Eloise in Lincoln.

"For how long?" I had asked.

"A while."

"How long's 'a while'?"

"I don't know. A while."

She had told me this at dinner, over pot roast, mashed potatoes, and creamed corn. She could have saved the news for
dessert, but I don't think she wanted to make a big deal out of
it.

I got up and walked to the next call box. I checked in with
division and moved on. Headlights suddenly flared behind me.
I doused my flashlight and ducked into a shadow, my heart
quickening. I put my hand on my holstered gun. Cars didn't
wander down here accidently. It couldn't be Tyler and
Klosowski. The two cops who had dropped me off weren't due
to pick me up for another three hours. Maybe it was a dumb
couple down to hump in their car.

Or maybe it was Lopez.

The vehicle slowed and I realized it was a black and white.
I emerged from the shadows into the headlights and shivered
in the wind. The car stopped.

"You look cold, Joe," Allan Klosowski said, grinning
through the slightly cracked passenger window. He'd flipped
on the interior light. The car looked as inviting as a fireplace in
a snug log cabin.

"You gonna sit there and jaw, friend, or you got something
important on your mind?"

Klosowski flashed a mouthful of teeth again. "Get in the
car. We'll drive you to the next box."

I opened the rear door and hopped in before they had a
change of heart.

Klosowski's partner, Tyler, who always reminded me of a not-too-bright uncle in Texas, stared at me as if I were some freak from another planet. "Didja hear the news?"

"Of course he didn't hear the news, you knucklehead," Klosowski said. "He's been down here."

I blew on my cold, cramped hands. "What news?" I said.

What more good news could I get? My wife had left me, I'd been demoted, I'd put an innocent man in jail, and I was further from catching Lopez than I when I'd started.

"Somebody—" Tyler started to say but Klosowski interrupted him.

"Drive the car. I'll tell him."

Tyler put the car in gear and we inched forward.

Klosowski leaned over the front seat toward me. "Somebody torched Moretti's supper club—with Moretti in it."

"You're shitting me!" I said.

"Bet his fat ass cooked up real nice," Tyler said.

"They're sure it's Moretti?" I asked.

"The ME ain't officially identified the stiff," said Klosowski. "But they found a body in what was Moretti's office. You know, the supposedly bomb-proof room. Think he died more from smoke inhalation than being toasted. Guess they found a special silver bracelet on the body, something he wore all the time."

I recalled seeing the bracelet the first night I went to his supper club and confronted him about the Indian beating the tar out of him.

"Bartender said he'd closed up early and Moretti was the only one left in the building," Tyler added. "Probably tried to torch his own place for the insurance money and was too fat to get out the door."

"Don't think so," Klosowski said. "The word is whoever started the fire jammed his office door shut from the outside, to make sure he couldn't get out."

A local rival mob? A hit ordered from Chicago? Or had Lopez killed him on orders from Lamprey and Adler because Moretti knew too much? I had told Lamprey the gangster was a bigger risk to him than I was. Maybe the lawyer took my warning to heart. But why burn the place down? It wasn't as though Moretti was storing the blackmail photos of the judge in his office. I had watched him take them to Lamprey's home.

Or was he holding something else they wanted destroyed? Rawlins was dead and Estrada was in jail. What the hell were they worried about?

Tyler stopped at the next call box. I thanked them and stepped out into the wind.

"We'll check back," Klosowski said. "You need lookin' after, Joe."

I watched as their red taillights and all of what had made sense about the Rawlins case disappeared in the distance.

ℰↃℰↃ

I couldn't dig up a whisper about Lopez. He had gone to ground, as he had done after killing my old partner. He would resurface eventually, but it could be weeks, months, even years. Meanwhile, Moretti's murder continued to puzzle me. Worse, with The Fixer dead, my best link to Lopez was severed.

For the first time since I had started hunting for Lopez, I seriously considered suspending my investigation.

ℰↃℰↃ

I called Paula in Lincoln several times. Her sister always answered the phone, assured me Paula was fine, but that she didn't wish to speak to me just yet.

About the only person willing to talk to me was the rookie. Perdue had improved well enough to leave the hospital and go home for more recovery. I had visited him several times at his apartment since his release. His wife barely tolerated my presence, though Moroni seemed to enjoy my visits. But he still refused to blame me for my mistakes, the bastard.

I served my time in Siberia and returned to Larimer Street, though still without a partner. Frankly, I liked it that way. I didn't want a new partner bugging me with questions or giving me the wary looks other cops at the station gave me, or worse, making me worry my next decision would get him killed.

Being alone also gave me time to mull over everything I had learned since that first evening the bar owner Ruben Castillo dropped Lopez's name. As I rattled doorknobs, checked alleyways and drunks, and scanned the streets, I turned and twisted each facet, each bit of evidence and conversation. Nothing stepped forward and gave me the answer. But what it did tell me was I couldn't give up. I might not catch Lopez soon, but I had a new problem to solve. The wrong man was sitting in jail for killing Seth Rawlins. I helped put him there and I was the only one who could free him.

෴

I went looking for Rachel Adler. I had questions for her. What had happened between her father and the Estrada family twenty years ago? Did she know he had been secretly meeting with Emilio Estrada? Had he mentioned Estrada's sister, Mercedes? Had he said anything about Moretti's blackmail photos of the judge or whether he had used a stagehand in her own theater to try to retrieve the photos? Did she know her own husband was likely involved in blackmailing the judge? Was she certain her father had never mentioned Lopez?

I went to her home, hoping her husband wasn't around. A maid told me she'd left two hours before, upset. Over what, she didn't know.

I went to Victor King's Broadway Playhouse on the chance she might be there. As I passed through the front entrance, I stopped to examine the photos of the resident company cast plastered on a wall by the ticket window. I didn't spot Rachel at first, until I realized her photo showed her in dark hair instead of her usual platinum blonde. A glint in her eye told you she was not to be trusted.

I went inside. A cough echoed from the stage. I found Victor King examining part of the set.

"Is Mrs. Adler here?" I asked as I came down the center aisle toward the stage.

The director stepped to the front of the stage. "She was here an hour ago. Stormed in and stormed out."

I thought of the maid informing me Miss Rachel had left the house upset. "Any idea what was she angry about?"

"No. She wanted to get into the prop room. We keep it locked. I was busy so I just gave her the key."

"What did she want in the prop room?"

"Said she left something personal in there. She dropped off the key a few minutes later."

"I think we'd better check the prop room."

The director looked puzzled, then alarmed. I followed him backstage. He unlocked the door to the prop room and we went in. The place looked like a messy attic. Crap sat piled everywhere on the floor and on shelves. I didn't know where to start. "Was she carrying anything when she left?"

"Just the handbag she came in with."

We began pawing through stuff: lamps, a mirror, racks of costumes, swords, rope, baby dolls, masks, fake paintings, chairs, tables and table settings, a door, a ratty suitcase, a bookcase of fake books. I had no idea what if anything was missing, especially something small enough to fit in a handbag. I picked up a tan cowboy hat and a skull appeared. I jerked back.

"That's Yorick's skull," King said. "From *Hamlet*," he added condescendingly when it became obvious I had no idea who the hell Yorick was.

I covered up dear old Yorick with the hat and kept on digging. I came across several wigs on manikin heads. I said to King, "I noticed a picture of Mrs. Adler in the entrance. She had dark hair instead of platinum. Is that for a new role?"

"No, it's her natural hair. That photo was taken before she started doing *Streetcar*."

Dark hair. I returned to rummaging through the prop room. A dark thought was beginning to surface when I spotted a large cardboard box marked "guns." I pulled down the box and began digging through a haphazard collection of pistols and rifles. My heart quickened.

"Check this out," I said to King. "Tell me if anything is missing."

The director pawed through the weapons, pausing once for a coughing spell. Finally, he said, "We're missing a handgun. One of those colt detective specials."

Small enough to drop into a purse. "A prop gun?"

King shook his head sheepishly. "No. It's real. The only real one we have."

"Why would you have a real gun?"

"It was part of the prop collection when I started running the place. Remember, I said this was a theater long before I took it over. There were still a lot of useful props in here, and we have too small a budget to buy much."

"But a real gun on stage!"

"We only have blanks for it. We don't keep live ammunition here."

Ammunition would be easy to buy—but why would Rachel want ammunition?

"When she left here, did she say where she was going?" I asked.

"No."

I thought about it for a few moments. I thought about her dark hair. I thought about the photograph I had found in Red Owl's possessions. I thought about Emilio Estrada telling me Seth Rawlins had wanted to recover the blackmail photos his own way. Then it struck me. I raced out of the playhouse for my car without so much as a goodbye to King.

෨෮෨

Terry Adler's Front Range Limited company occupied the entire third floor of a shiny new downtown office building. When I exited the elevator, I found an office in chaos.

Several police officers milled about, and knots of staff huddled in hushed conversations and shaken crying amid a warren of offices and desks. I was out of uniform but flashed my badge at a uniformed officer standing a few feet from the elevators. He nodded perfunctorily for me to pass. I would have asked him what had happened but then he would have wondered who the hell I was and what the hell I was doing there. I walked by him as if I belonged and found an attractive, short-haired redhead sitting vacantly behind a desk near an office that anchored an entire corner of the floor. Adler's office, I guessed.

On the wall behind her hung a large artist's rendering of what I presumed was a future Adler development. The embossed walnut nameplate on her desk said Annette Haversham.

"What exactly happened, Miss Haversham?"

She looked up, pale and red-eyed from crying. "What?"

I flashed my badge. "What happened here?"

She blinked and glanced toward the corner office. Two hand-carved doors, big enough to wall one side of my house, were closed. I could hear muffled voices and movement inside.

"Terry—Mr. Adler—has been shot."

"How bad?"

"I don't know." Her lips quivered. "She shot him in the chest. There was a lot of blood. They rushed him to the hospital."

"She?" I knew who, but I didn't want to lead my witness.

She blinked. "His wife, Mrs. Adler."

"Tell me what you saw."

She glanced toward the closed doors. "I already told them what happened."

"We always double check with different officers," I lied. I hoped the dicks didn't come out of Adler's office before I was done. Otherwise, even my days walking Siberia would be over.

Miss Haversham looked at me and shivered. The room felt cold enough to store ice cream. I had read this was the first office building in Denver to be fully air-conditioned. But I didn't think she was shivering from the cold. She looked downright toasty in a natty dark blue business suit, light blue shirt, and a light maroon man's tie.

"Mrs. Adler came in and headed straight to his office. I said hello to her and asked if Terry—Mr. Adler—expected her. But she didn't say anything. She just walked right by me and right into his office and slammed the door."

"You're his private secretary?"

Her eyes glanced away and down. "Yes."

Apparently with an emphasis on *private*. "Then what?"

"I heard them arguing. Very loud."

"Arguing about what?"

"I couldn't understand their words. The doors are thick. But they were yelling at each other. Everyone in the office could hear them. She was the loudest."

"And then?"

"I heard a sharp noise! Muffled but definitely a noise. Then a crash. Mrs. Adler came storming out of his office and hurried to the elevators. She left the office door open and I immediately went in and found Ter—Mr. Adler. He lay slumped on the floor behind his desk. Blood was everywhere." She shuddered again. "That's when I realized the sound I'd heard was a shot. I've never been around guns—god, it was awful."

"Did anyone stop Mrs. Adler?"

"No. By the time I realized what had happened, she was gone. Some people said she went down the stairs instead of waiting for an elevator. I don't think the police have caught her yet."

"Was she carrying a small gun when she came out of his office?"

"I didn't see one."

I got out of there before the real dicks came out of Adler's office. As I walked back to my car, I could guess more or less what had happened. I knew almost from the moment I learned a real gun was missing from the prop room.

I recalled the night Rachel and I had left Randolph Cornell's party and driven into the foothills. She was convinced her husband was blackmailing her father and had killed him when her father attempted to "take care of it." At the time, I chalked it off as the talk of a crazy woman. She had offered no evidence, other than the preposterous claim her husband had killed because he was "impotent." While I still doubted Adler himself murdered Rawlins, I couldn't rule out the possibility he had blackmailed him. The real estate mogul was already part of a group blackmailing a federal judge. Why not black-mail Rawlins? Before, I couldn't figure out what leverage Adler would have on his father-in-law. Now I believe I knew. It answered why Rachel had shot her husband.

Her picture at the theater showed her in dark hair—her natural hair color, according to King. I recalled the picture of Rachel and her father sitting on the mantle of his mountain ranch home. She had dark hair then, too.

Dark hair like the hair of the woman in the photo I had found among Art Red Owl's possessions, a woman whose head was in the lap of the federal judge.

I could see what might have played out. The judge liked young women, and Rachel Adler, as she had made plain to me the night of Cornell's party, also liked older men. And they both liked them married. I could see them at the same parties. I could see Terry Adler introducing his wife to the judge and giving the judge a gentlemen's "wink-wink" to go after his own wife. I could see Moretti's camera work taking it from there. A married judge with another married woman. Perfect blackmail material!

Seth Rawlins found out the federal judge not only was being blackmailed for being *in puris naturalibus* with someone other than his wife, but the "someone other" was his own daughter. That would explain why the banker went after the photos so aggressively by using Art Red Owl, over Estrada's objections. When that effort failed, Rawlins tried to "take care of it" himself.

Somewhere along the way, Rachel must have learned about the photos. It wouldn't have taken her pretty little head two seconds longer to figure out her husband likely had something to do with setting it up. She had lied to me the evening of Cornell's party when she claimed she didn't know what secret her husband could have used to blackmail her father.

After that, it was a simple matter for Rachel—an unstable woman under the best of circumstances—to snatch a real gun from the theater's prop room and plug her husband.

God, for being such smart, rich people, it was a damn wonder they didn't kill each other off.

I'd take the lost souls of Larimer Street any day.

CHAPTER 33

The next day, I drove to the Ponderosa County Jail to talk to Emilio Estrada. I wanted to find out where his sister was and why he remained in jail.

The front-desk deputy inside the two-story red brick building asked for the purpose of my visit with Estrada. I said I was investigating another murder for which I believed Estrada had information, which bore some resemblance to the truth. The man hesitated, but finally had me sign in. Word would get back to Denver homicide about my visit, but there was nothing I could do about it, and frankly, at this stage I didn't care.

A deputy ushered me into a visiting room with two white picnic-like tables and benches anchored to a pitted cinderblock wall. I sat at the end of one of the benches, listening to the echoes of catcalls and cell doors slamming shut. Ten minutes later, footsteps approached and the deputy opened a gate of thick iron bars. Estrada rolled into the room in his wheelchair. The door clanked shut and we were alone.

We didn't shake hands. He looked shrunken, as if he had already spent ten years in isolation in maximum security in Canon City. I needed to catch the real killer of Seth Rawlins soon or Emilio Estrada would be dead by Christmas.

"How are you holding up?" I asked anyway.

The attorney's lifeless eyes searched my face. He looked wan and motionless in his frayed jail clothes. "What do you want?" His voice barely reached me.

"I want to help free you."

He didn't exactly perk up at the prospect.

"I know your sister framed you," I went on. "Faked the ransom note and steered the police to you."

The lawyer revealed no surprise at my statement. He obviously had already figured out she had been responsible for his arrest.

When he said nothing, I said, "She refuses to tell the police what she did."

He spoke this time. "I told her not to."

"Why?"

"They wouldn't believe her. They would insist it was merely a stratagem to free me. It would only cause trouble for her."

"No, that's not why. You told her to be silent because you're trying to protect her. You believe she killed Rawlins, don't you?"

A flicker of emotion—what emotion I wasn't sure—snapped in his eyes, but vanished almost the instant I saw it. He looked down at the floor and said nothing.

"She may have thought about killing Rawlins when she learned you were working with him," I said. "But I don't think she did it."

Estrada looked up. A mixture of doubt and hope filled his eyes. He wanted to believe me, but hell, I was the guy who'd helped put him in jail.

Just then, the deputy strode by. I waited until he moved on before telling Estrada about the recent murder of Villano Moretti—he'd heard the news—and reminded him of the murder of the Indian. I insisted those murders were tied into the banker's death, and behind those murders were Lamprey and Adler and god knew what other movers and shakers in Denver. His sister was not mixed in any of that. Then I told him my theory that Rachel Adler was the woman in the blackmail photos, that she believed her husband had killed her father in a fight over those photos. I told him she'd just shot her husband.

Estrada had yet to learn about that shooting. He looked alarmed and leaned forward anxiously, his voice suddenly strong. "Have they caught her?"

"Not yet. But they will. She doesn't have the talent to stay lost."

That didn't seem to comfort the attorney. "You need to find my sister right away. You need to find her and protect her."

"Why?"

"Because Rachel Adler may try to kill her, too."

I stared dumbfounded at him. "Why?"

"Mercedes told me a few days ago she was certain a woman was watching her. She saw her several times by the house and once outside the office. She thinks the woman was Mrs. Adler."

It was possible homicide had put a rare female tail on Mercedes, because they suspected she'd helped her brother kill Rawlins. Still, I couldn't entirely dismiss the lawyer's concern. "Your sister didn't happen to say what the woman was wearing?" I asked.

"Always something light orangeish. That's what caused Mercedes to notice her."

That would be Rachel. She would be difficult to miss in apricot. "Why would she be stalking your sister?" I said. "Why would she want to kill her?"

"To avenge her father. I'm in here and Mercedes is out there. She's accessible. It's obvious this Rawlins woman is of unsound mind."

"Rachel believes her *husband* killed her father. That's why she shot him. She told me she doesn't believe you did it. I presume that would include your sister."

Estrada rolled his wheelchair to the end of the table where I sat. He glanced toward the room entrance and said in a hushed, trembling tone, "I think she has another reason to kill my sister."

He explained that after Mercedes learned he was secretly working with Rawlins, she'd begun leaking inside information about their lawsuit strategies to the Lamprey team. She wanted Rawlins to lose his mountain ranch to the Ponderosa reservoir just as the Estrada family had lost their ranch to the greedy Rawlins empire—and for her own brother to lose the case because he had chosen to work with Rawlins. Emilio had gotten suspicious and confronted his sister. She'd admitted it, without a trace of regret.

"I suspect Rachel found out what Mercedes had done," he said.

"How? Through her father?"

"I didn't tell Seth. I should have. It was the ethical thing to do. Her betrayal badly compromised our case. But she was my sister. I couldn't bring myself to do it. It was my fault she had betrayed us."

"Then how did Mrs. Adler find out?"

"I don't know. Maybe her husband said something."

"That's still not much of a motive for her to kill your sister."

Estrada looked away. Pain creased his face. "I think Mercedes may have revealed something else to Lamprey. Something that *would* provide motive for the Adler woman."

The deputy strode by again. "You two about done in there?" he said. "It ain't as if you're his lawyer."

"It's an investigation," I reminded him.

"Well, hurry up. He gets dinner soon."

The deputy moved on and Estrada spoke softly. "There's more to the story about how I came to be paralyzed than what you read in the papers."

Why was I not surprised?

Estrada said his sister became pregnant when she was seventeen years old. When she could no longer hide her pregnancy, she told her family the father was a kid at school, whom she refused to name. The baby died at childbirth and was buried in the Pawnee Buttes cemetery.

Only later did Emilio begin hearing rumors from kids at school that the father was Seth Rawlins, then well into his twenties. When Emilio confronted his sister, she confessed, though she swore him to never tell their parents. That's what drove him to barge out to the Rawlins ranch, a rifle in hand, and end up in a gunfight that crippled him.

He had gone to confront Seth Rawlins over the pregnancy, not the fact the Rawlins empire drove his family into bankruptcy in order to obtain valuable water rights.

"Mercedes was a very impressionable kid at the time," he said. "She looked up to Seth. But after the baby died, he would have nothing to do with her. Like it had never happened."

Now I understood why Estrada believed his sister had deep motives to murder Seth Rawlins, even after all these years.

"I think Mercedes told Lamprey about the pregnancy," the lawyer went on. "As one more way to put the screws to Seth. She denies telling them, but I think she did. I'm sure Lamprey and Adler used this information against Seth, along with the blackmail photos."

"Rawlins ever say anything about it to you?"

Estrada shook his head. "When you told me about his daughter shooting her husband over the photos, it struck me she also may have learned about them using the pregnancy to blackmail her father. Maybe her father told her, or she found out somehow. She also must have found out it was Mercedes who put that information in Lamprey and Adler's hands. So she would blame Mercedes for aiding the blackmail conspiracy and the resulting murder of her father. That would explain her following her. And now that she's shot her husband…"

It was a stretch based on a lot of suppositions, but not an implausible stretch.

"You need to find Mercedes," he implored me again.

Fear filled his eyes. His sister had landed him in jail and he had a good chance to fry because of it, despite his innocence. Yet he was more worried about her than about himself.

"Rachel Adler is on the run," I said. "She doesn't have time to—"

Estrada vehemently shook his head. "Find my sister and you'll find Rachel Adler."

CHAPTER 34

That evening, while pulling a graveyard shift on Larimer Street, I finally caught up with Lopez.

But not in the way I expected.

Not in the way I wanted.

It was luck, really. Dumb luck. I happened to be in the patrol car when I heard the call over the squawk box about a fight involving "twin brothers" near Welton and Twenty-Seventh. Within minutes, I pulled up in front of a pool hall on Welton, one of several that littered the street. A ten-year vet named Billy Flexner was interviewing a knot of witnesses. I stepped out into the warm evening air. The muffled riffs of a jazz band drifted into the street from the Rossonian Hotel a few doors away. Flexner's partner, a red-haired ox named McKee, stood in an alley flanking the pool hall, his flashlight trained on two men in the shadows huddled against a brick wall. I went into the alley.

"What the hell you doin' here, Joe?" McKee said.

"I heard you needed backup."

"We didn't call for backup. A meat wagon, but not backup."

I stopped a few feet from the two men huddled against the wall. One man was sitting down, cradling the other man's limp body in his arms, rocking him, murmuring over and over in a soft, motherly voice, "*Hermano, no mueras. Mi hermano. No mueras.*"

In the glare of McKee's flashlight, I could see they were Mexicans, dressed in short-sleeved shirts and chinos. It was difficult to determine whether they were twins. The face of one of them had been beaten almost beyond recognition. But I immediately recognized the conscious man as one of the Lopez brothers. I recognized him from staring at their mug shots over the years. Antonio or Angelo, I didn't know. I didn't care. Now both were in front of me, ghosts come to life.

"He dead?" I asked McKee.

"No, but he might as well be. He'll be a vegetable if he makes it to morning." McKee looked out the mouth of the alley. "Which he won't if the fucking meat wagon doesn't get here." He looked back at the unconscious man. "His brother bent a fucking pipe over his head. *Bent it.*"

McKee swung his light to a foot-long metal pipe lying near the wall. The pipe was bent at a thirty-degree angle. Washes of fresh blood glistened on its rusty surface.

"Shouldn't you have the other one handcuffed?" I said. The last thing I needed now was for him to escape.

"Does he really look like he's goin' someplace?" McKee said, softness in his voice. Sometimes the brutality and senselessness of human beings left us more with ache than anger.

"Which brother is which?" I asked.

"Don't know." McKee didn't need to ask me why I wanted to know.

"Checked ID?"

"Neither one of 'em got any. But when we fingerprint 'em we'll know."

I leaned over into the face of the conscious brother. "Which brother are you?"

He kept rocking his brother's body. "*Hermano, no mueras. No mueras.*"

"Which brother?" I yelled.

McKee grabbed my arm. "Back off, Joe."

I shrugged off his arm and stepped back. The man rocking his brother didn't even look up at me.

Flexner showed up and told us witnesses said the two

brothers had been drinking heavily in the Rossonian Hotel bar and had started a fight over something. No one seemed to know over what. No one cared. An argument like any other bar argument. Two voices yelling past each other. The fight had spilled out into the alley. Most of the people in the bar had probably watched, had done nothing to stop it. Cheap Friday night entertainment, well worth the price of a ten-cent beer.

"Look what we took off the loser," McKee said. He held out a five-inch switchblade. "One of them Filipino jobs. Found it in his pocket. Don't know why he didn't pull it."

I took the knife from McKee and found the release button. A double-edged blade snapped viciously in the darkness. I leaned over the limp body and grasped a chunk of the baggy chinos around his left thigh. I sliced open a hole.

"What the hell you doin', Joe?" Flexner said. He reached for me but I shrugged off his hand.

I gripped the hole with a finger and ripped open the pant leg along the inseam.

"Joe!" McKee said. The other brother stopped chanting and stared at me, but did nothing beyond that. No one moved to stop me.

I told McKee to shine his flashlight on the inside of the man's thigh. In the light, I could see it. A few inches above the knee, across the inside of the thigh, ran an ugly, two-inch-long scar.

I stood up. I was vaguely aware of someone taking the knife from my hand. I shivered in the warm night. Someone asked a question.

"You okay, Joe? What the fuck was that all about?"

"He's the bastard who killed Derek." I shivered again.

"How do you know?"

"'Cause I put a bullet in the asshole's leg that night, and I know the asshole was one of these two brothers. I just didn't know which one." I looked down at the two men. The conscious brother had picked up his singsong lament again. I didn't want to wait for fingerprints.

I wanted to know now which Lopez he was. I wanted to put a name on my nightmare.

"Which brother are you?" I repeated, but the conscious one said nothing.

The meat wagon finally arrived. McKee chewed out the attendants but they snapped back that they'd had to make another run first. It was Friday night, after all.

I watched them work on the unconscious Lopez. I wasn't sure what to feel, whether I wanted him dead or alive by morning. He had destroyed my career and possibly my marriage. He had cost Derek his life. He had reached into my soul and tore a chunk out of it.

My long hunt was over. Justice had been served, even if only in its own strange way. A stain on mankind had been removed. Yet I did not feel the elation and relief I had believed it would bring me. Only a weariness and a sense of disappointment, a hollowness. It had not been me who had taken down Lopez. It had been his own brother, in just another senseless act of violence, like the one that had taken Derek's life. What sense of justice was there in that? Irony, but not justice.

I knew, too, my nightmares would not end here. I would always be responsible for Derek's death, and the apprehension of his killer would never absolve me of that sin. Moreover, while Paula would be relieved Lopez had been caught, I feared my obsessive hunt for him had created a rift between us I could never close.

McKee and Flexner hauled the conscious brother to his feet and handcuffed him. The meat wagon attendants prepared to haul the other brother off on a stretcher, though they seemed in no particular rush, as if they knew they were attending to a dead man.

Then the full implication of the beaten brother struck me, the other half of my nightmare. I still couldn't be certain which of them had killed Art Red Owl and *El Perro*, had tried to kill me, shot Perdue, and had possibly murdered Moretti and Rawlins. Each brother was capable of the crimes. But if the killer was the vegetable, I'd lost a valuable link to the person or people behind him. For I remained convinced Lopez was only the messenger of death in all this, that someone or others were behind his actions. I'd lost a chance to free an innocent Emilio Estrada from jail and put the right ones behind bars.

The conscious Lopez was nearly to the patrol car when I caught up with him. I leaned into the Mexican's face.

"Did you kill the Indian? Did you? Or was it your brother?"

He blinked back with cold eyes. Probably didn't understand English. Or maybe at the moment, he didn't understand life.

CHAPTER 35

The narrow tar-patched highway stretched listlessly in front of me, across shriveled grasslands shimmering in the stark afternoon heat. West, a thunderstorm brewing over the mountains gathered power as it spilled out onto the plains, lightning snapping against the deepening blue-blackness. I kept my foot hard on the gas, driving past sagging buildings and rusty Ford pickups abandoned since the Great Depression, past knots of cattle shading under clusters of cottonwoods, past listless windmills the breath of the storm hadn't yet touched, past sagebrush drifted three wires high along the side of the road. Ahead, I could see the hazy outline of the small town of Pawnee Buttes. Beyond it rose the butte itself, a striated rock monolith rising out of the flat of the land as though God had rammed up the eraser end of a pencil from below.

It was a long shot, coming here. Emilio Estrada didn't know where his sister was, but he had guessed she would come here, to Pawnee Buttes. "It's where we lost everything," he said. "She wants to find what we lost."

I nearly missed the small cemetery on the outskirts of town. Weeds shrouded most of the headstones and the black iron entrance that said *CEMETERY* barely caught my eye. I hit the brakes and slowed to a stop in the middle of the empty highway.

According to Estrada, his sister's illegitimate baby had died at birth and was buried here.

I parked along the gravel shoulder, walked to the cemetery, and pushed through a squeaky iron gate. I tramped around pushing aside tall grass to read the headstones while watching warily for rattlesnakes. I finally found it, a small headstone, rough on all sides, stuck away in a corner. I knelt and used my fingertips to brush the dirt out of the grooves cut into the stone until I could read it clearly.

Javier Estrada
Born and Died August 23, 1926

By itself, the baby's grave meant little. But Rawlins's foreman, William Gannon, said he and his boss had stopped at this cemetery while taking horses to the ranch not far from here. The last time he saw his boss alive. He had described Rawlins as upset, the same day he had overheard Rawlins arguing with his daughter back at their mountain ranch. Stopping at the cemetery was odd. They had never stopped here before, and all Rawlins did was walk for a few minutes alone among the gravestones. Gannon didn't know what his boss was looking for.

Now I knew.

ɔ∕ɔ∕ɔ

I drove into Pawnee Buttes. Judging from the layout of the scattered buildings and the dirt streets, the town once sprawled over four blocks square. But it long ago had passed its prime. The sign at the edge of town said a population of 382, but I would wager that included those in the cemetery. Several of the businesses on the main street were shuttered.

Abandoned cars rusted in front of vacant homes. People walked the streets, but they had the look of sleepwalkers, the forgotten, their relatives and friends gone in the wind to Denver and other growing cities. The soldiers I knew in the war who had been raised on farms and in small towns weren't going home. Like me, the war had changed them and they couldn't find their way back.

I stopped at one of the few signs of life, a small general store. A middle-aged clerk with burn scars on her left arm recognized the name Javier Estrada.

"I remember that poor little boy's name 'cause I do stone rubbings in the cemetery," she said. "Real sad, dying the day you're born."

She didn't know much beyond that, other than the baby was the out-of-wedlock child of the Estrada girl. "That ain't official, mind you. They didn't publish it in the paper. Just talk."

"Did the talk say who the father was?"

"Some say it was the Rawlins son, Seth. The one they found dead on his ranch in the mountains."

"Would you recognize Mercedes Estrada on sight?"

"Doubt it."

I described Mercedes and asked if she'd seen such a woman in town the last few days. She had. The woman had been in the store to buy groceries, though she'd given her name as Mary Hall. "Didn't look like a Mary Hall to me, if you know what I mean."

"Where can I find her?"

The woman shook her head but then wrinkled her brow as if two pieces of a puzzle had come together accidently. "I have heard folks say they've seen someone out at the old Jackson place. It's been abandoned for years, but folks swear they've seen lights in the house. Spooky, if you ask me. But it might be true if it's her."

"Why?"

"That's where the Estradas lived back in the 1920s. Bought it from a woman named Jackson. The Rawlins family took it over before the Depression and used it as a line ranch."

Emilio Estrada had been right. His sister had come home.

The clerk gave me directions to the Jackson house, a few miles north of town.

I took a picture of Rachel Adler out of my pocket, the one

Lou Sheppard had snapped for the *News*, and asked the clerk if she'd seen this woman also in town. Yes, the woman had been in the store two days before. Hard to forget a woman driving a big yellow convertible and dressed in apricot-colored clothes. "Had a big dog with her, too. Useless lookin' thing."

This didn't bode well. "Did she ask about Mercedes Estrada?"

The clerk shook her head. "Didn't say nothin' about her. Just wanted to buy a bottle of gin. Now does this place look like it sells gin?"

ひふひふ

I found the isolated Jackson house north of Pawnee Buttes, right where the clerk said it would be. The house was shaded under a thin stand of wind-rippled cottonwoods, the only trees around as far as the eye could see in an ocean of prairie grass. It was a gaunt one-story structure with several rambling additions, fitting together in ways you wouldn't have expected.

I drove the short driveway in from the gravel county road and parked near the house. A gray weathered barn stood nearby. The half-dozen cows browsing in the front yard petulantly moseyed away. I got out. The prairie grass began to stir from the approaching storm. The cooling air on my skin felt dry and electric.

I stepped over sagging barbed wire fence which had seen too many hard winters. I called Mercedes's name, but only the wind answered. I stepped onto the front porch, gingerly testing each step for fear it would cave in, and knocked on the door. "Mercedes!" No answer. I walked around the back of the house. A 1942 Chevy sat parked under a high arching cottonwood. Fresh tire tracks told me it hadn't been there long. No signs of a yellow Chrysler Town & Country convertible.

I went up to the back door and banged on it. "Mercedes!"

I opened the screen door. The unlocked inner door gave with a slight shove and I found myself in the kitchen. The house was hot and muggy. I sensed rotting wood everywhere. Large brown water stains streaked the flowered wallpaper. The old stove looked unused. Yet the kitchen floor had been swept and the counters wiped clean. I traced a finger across the kitchen table covered with yellow oilcloth, like the one I used to do my homework on, writing my spelling words on the cloth and wiping them away once my mother had checked them. My finger showed no trace of dust.

I moved into the living room and that's where I found Mercedes.

She sat motionless in a rocking chair facing the dirty window. She had watched me pull in and knock on the front door. She kept staring out the window. She looked as old as the house. Then she spoke.

"Are you some sort of plague God keeps sending down on me?"

❧

Lukewarm cider was all Mercedes Estrada had to drink. The house had no running water. But I was so dry the cider tasted good. I had stupidly driven out onto Colorado prairie without water.

I wouldn't have made it as a pioneer.

I sat on a lumpy couch across from her. Whoever had abandoned the place had thoughtfully left the furniture. Mercedes had dusted the living room, too, though she had left the front windows encrusted in dust so passers-by would be less likely to notice someone inside.

"I expected to find you dead," I said.

"Why?"

"Your brother said Rachel Adler has been following you. You both believe she wants to kill you for the murder of her father. She was seen in Pawnee Buttes two days ago. Has she been here?"

Mercedes Estrada stared out the window. "No."

"You're making it easy for her, staying here."

She said nothing.

"I explained to your brother why I don't think you killed

Seth Rawlins. He doesn't need to protect you any longer. You need to tell the police you framed him."

"How is he?"

"He'll be dead by Christmas if I don't find the real killer."

I told her what I had told her brother, about Art Red Owl and the rest, why I didn't believe she murdered Rawlins.

Her hushed voice fell like dust in the room. "God knows, I thought about it. After I saw Seth with Emilio, killing him is what I thought about all the time."

"I stopped at the cemetery. I saw your baby's grave."

She quit staring out the window and turned toward me, an expression of unease lining her face. A sound echoed from behind a closed door leading from the living room. A movement, a scrape of a shoe. Panic filled Mercedes's eyes.

I set the glass of cider down and moved toward the door, drawing my gun from a side holster hidden under my loose shirt.

"Come out!" I said. "It's the police."

Mercedes started to rise out of her chair, her eyes wide, but I sternly motioned for her to stay put.

"Out of there!" I yelled. "Hands where I can see them."

The door opened slowly. I backed to one side, gun drawn. Rachel Adler emerged, pale, shaking. Her hands were empty.

"Where's your gun?" I demanded.

"What?" Her voice trembled, the spoiled arrogance left behind.

"The gun you used to shoot your husband."

"It's in there." She nodded back into the room, a bedroom.

We went in and she pointed to a nightstand. I found it in the drawer, a colt detective special, the one Victor King described as missing from the prop room. Her purse lay on the nightstand and I searched it for a second gun. I scanned the room.

"Where's your dog?"

"In the barn. With my car."

I marched her into the living room and sat her down near Mercedes. I holstered my gun, pocketed Rachel's gun, and sat opposite them.

I didn't understand what I was looking at. Rachel had come

to kill Mercedes Estrada, and here she was hiding with her. What the hell was going on?

"How long have you been here?" I asked Rachel.

She lit a cigarette. A real one, not one of her tea sticks. "Two days."

I looked at Mercedes. "Do you know what she did?"

Mercedes glanced at the young woman next to her. Her eyes held no fear. "Yes. She shot her husband." She turned toward me and said almost proudly, "Because he killed her father."

I remained unconvinced Adler had done the actual killing, but I didn't want to get into that just yet.

"Is he still alive?" Rachel asked.

"The last I heard, he was."

"Shit!" She looked down at the floor in disappointment. "I should have practiced first."

"What are you doing here?" I asked. "You were stalking Mercedes in Denver. You were looking to kill her. Why didn't you?"

She looked up at the woman sitting next to her, her eyes softening. "I didn't want to kill her. I—I wanted to talk to her. It just took me a while to get up my nerve."

"Talk to her about what? Whether she killed your father?"

"To tell her she's my mother."

CHAPTER 36

Each of us had moments in our lives when we discovered secrets about ourselves we wished we had never learned. Unfortunately, we couldn't return those discoveries as if we were returning defective merchandise to customer service. We were stuck with them, however painful they were. Watching Rachel Adler pace the small living room in the yellowing light and bitterly explain how she had discovered Mercedes Estrada was her real mother, that her adoptive father had been her real father, it was apparent her discovery was one she wished she had never made.

Not that a part of her wasn't happy to learn the identity of her biological mother—she often stole soft glances at Mercedes as she spoke. But the life-long betrayal by her father must have been more than her fragile soul could bear.

Rachel explained he'd confessed to her shortly before his death that she was not his adopted daughter but his biological daughter—by a woman he refused to name.

He and his father had arranged a phony adoption through a private adoption agency in North Dakota, though he insisted his wife never knew they had adopted his own biological daughter.

Rachel had begged him to tell her the name of her real mother, where she could find her, but he had refused to tell her anything. It was best, he said, for all concerned.

That was what the ranch foreman had overheard them arguing about. That was why she had stormed out of the ranch that day—the last day she saw her father alive.

As she told her story, I came to understand why, at her father's ranch, her fits of molten anger had burned through her grief, and why, the night at Cornell's party, she had insisted her father had loved her, that he had called her his frisky filly.

"You never had any inkling before then that you were his real daughter?" I said. "Something he said or when people told you how much you two looked alike?"

She blew smoke out her nostrils and stared at me, a pain so deep in her eyes I knew it would remain there forever. "Of course I never suspected! Some parents never tell an adopted child they're adopted. The child grows up believing they are his real parents. But what sick parent raises his *real* child yet lies that she's not his!"

In her bitter moments like this, I could see her murdering her father. She physically could have done it. God knew she had motive. But as with Mercedes, it didn't explain the other murders I felt certain were linked to the banker's death. I could imagine neither a reason nor the cold nerve for Rachel to murder Art Red Owl and steal his severed hands, or torch Moretti inside his own supper club. Besides, as the dramatic shooting of her husband demonstrated, she was not a woman who would kill in secrecy. She would not have surreptitiously sent her father to the bottom of the lake. She would have killed him on stage, dramatically, for an audience to witness.

A gust of wind rattled the house. Dust infiltrated everything. The storm was closing in.

"Why did your father tell you this?" I asked "After all those years?"

For a moment, her face betrayed her wish that it had been because he had finally summoned the strength to acknowledge it was the right thing to do, to admit to the cruelty of rejecting her true heritage all these years, depriving her of her very being. But the expression melted and hardened into something children should never have for their parents.

"He wanted to regain control," she said, her voice balancing on edge. "My father was a man who always demanded control. You're not in control when you're being blackmailed."

"If you believed he was being blackmailed over this, why not tell the police after he disappeared?"

"What, reveal to the entire world how my father loved me so little he lied to me and everyone else about who I really was?"

"I think there's evidence he loved—"

"I wasn't even sure at first I believed him," she cut in. "I thought it might be a cruel joke. I *hoped* it was a cruel joke."

She stared at the floor and dragged on her cigarette.

"If he didn't tell you who your real mother was," I asked, "how do you know this woman next to you *is* your real mother?"

She looked up. "I didn't know for certain, not until I came here. But I began getting suspicious after the article in the newspaper about the shooting of her brother at our ranch—which I knew little about growing up. Then I saw pictures of her in the paper when they brought in her brother. I—I just thought she looked like me."

"That's not much to go on."

"I hired a private detective and he found out about her dead baby, about the grave, about the rumors she had become pregnant from my father. He checked the adoption agency in North Dakota, too. It was gone by then, but he learned authorities had shut it down for fraudulent adoptions."

"Still not proof," I persisted. I turned to Mercedes. "Do you believe she's your daughter? Do you have any proof?"

"Yes. I'm positive now. I had my own suspicions once, right after she was born." She looked at Rachel, begging forgiveness. "But I had given them up over the years."

Mercedes explained that she had delivered her baby at the office of the only doctor in town, Doc Graham, a gruff old man who hated Mexicans. He had refused to let her family stay, telling them he would get word to them after the baby was delivered. As was common practice then, he had sedated her with morphine and scopolamine, which had left her in a kind of twilight sleep through delivery. When she had awakened, he coldly informed her the baby was stillborn.

"I swore I heard a baby's cries during delivery," Mercedes said. "But Doc Graham and his nurse insisted it had been born dead. I was young and scared, so I believed them. I assumed the cries were because of the sedation, that I *wanted* to believe my baby had lived."

I thought to myself that it was hardly a surprise Seth Rawlins and his father had wanted to hush up the illegitimate birth, a birth involving a wealthy white family and a dirt-poor Mexican family, a family whose ranch stood in the way of valuable water rights. As Rawlins grew older, perhaps he grew to care less about what the world thought about the birth. The Estrada family was long gone, the ranch swallowed up by the Rawlins empire. By itself, the illegitimate baby was not blackmail material to stop his fight over the Ponderosa reservoir. But by then, the lie to his daughter about her true heritage must have grown large within him, a boulder in his soul.

Mercedes went on: When she learned Seth and his wife had adopted a few months later, her suspicions had resurfaced. It seemed too coincidental. Yet the adopted child was a girl, and Doc Graham had said her dead baby had been a boy. She had cornered Seth in town shortly after the adoption, but he swore Rachel was not her daughter. She never spoke to him again until the day she surprised him in her brother's office.

Meanwhile, the Estrada family moved away after the loss of the ranch, so Mercedes never saw Rachel grow up as a child. She later saw society pictures of Rachel in the newspapers, but any resemblances by then seemed tenuous at best.

I mentally did the math on the date on the headstone in the cemetery. The baby had died in 1926—twenty-three years ago. Exactly Rachel Rawlins's age. "But the baby in the cemetery," I said. "Who did you bury? Who's Javier Estrada?"

The wind was blowing steadily now. The house groaned to the point I thought it might fall in on itself.

"There is no Javier Estrada," Mercedes said. "A dog is buried there."

"A dog!"

Doc Graham had told Mercedes after the delivery it was best she never see her dead baby. He had put it in a tiny box and nailed it shut. That's what her family buried in the cemetery.

"I gave him a name," Mercedes said. "Javier, after an uncle. I wasn't going to bury my baby without a name."

"But how do you know it was a dog?" I pressed. "How do you know what he'd done? Did you dig up the grave?"

They never knew for certain until yesterday, Rachel explained, when they talked to Doc Graham's nurse. After Rachel found Mercedes at the abandoned Jackson place and revealed her belief that she was her daughter, that she in fact had survived childbirth, Mercedes realized Doc Graham and his nurse had lied to her and her family. Graham was long dead, but his nurse still lived in Pawnee Buttes, married with three children and a grandchild. The two women confronted her and she broke down, confessing everything.

Seth Rawlins's father Clay had hatched the scheme, according to the nurse. His initial plan was to ship the baby off to some orphanage. But Seth had objected. So they had come up with a scheme—convince Mercedes and her family the baby had died in childbirth, have it secretly taken care of for several months, and then run it through the sleazy adoption agency in North Dakota.

Mercedes looked toward her daughter, her eyes brimming with tears. "They stole my baby!"

I said to Rachel, "You came here *after* you shot your husband, to confirm all this?"

"Yes." She shrugged like a lost little girl. "I didn't know where else to go."

"How did you know where to find her?"

"I was pretty certain she'd seen me following her in Denver, so I had the detective follow her. He's good at that sort of thing. He trailed her here when she left town."

"You musta scared the hell out of her when you showed up," I said.

Everyone fell into silence. Finally, I rose and motioned for

Rachel to stand. "I won't handcuff you if you promise to sit quietly in my car on the way back to Denver."

The young woman nodded and rose, and Mercedes immediately stood with her. "Don't take her back!" she pleaded. "She and I could go away. Disappear. She did the right thing, shooting her husband."

I looked sympathetically at Mercedes. "Maybe if it were another time and another place and under other circumstances. But your brother is sitting in a jail for a murder he didn't commit. I helped put him there. Your daughter can free him."

Mercedes looked at her daughter with fear of someone about to lose a precious gift she had just received. She threw her arms around Rachel and began to cry. For a few moments, Rachel didn't hug back. A bewildered expression marked her face. I don't think anyone had hugged her in a long time. Then her arms slowly went up her mother's side and she lightly hugged, then suddenly hugged her hard and began to cry. Finally, they broke apart.

"I wouldn't worry about the shooting charges," I said to Mercedes. "If Terry Adler was blackmailing her father and was involved in his murder, she won't serve a day in prison. It will be a crime of passion." I turned toward Rachel. "Hell, it might even be good for your acting career."

She scowled at my remark. "I shot my husband because he deserved to be shot."

CHAPTER 37

Rachel rode silently much of the drive back to Denver, staring dispiritedly out the window, sulking, sometimes crying inconsolably. I think she was angriest with me for making her leave behind her Afghan Hound, though her mother—if that's who Mercedes really was—wouldn't need to take care of it for long. When we passed through Pawnee Buttes, I stopped at the sheriff's office and told them where they could find Mercedes, the dog, and Rachel's car.

Yet now and then the young woman suddenly turned talkative, almost elated. Her moods seemed controlled by an unseen hand on an unseen light switch. During her unpredictable talkative moments, I tried to learn more about her conviction her husband blackmailed her father. Some points troubled me.

"How did your husband find out you were your father's real daughter?"

She had a theory. It turned out she and her mother were not the first people to talk to Doc Graham's nurse. A Denver police detective had shown up in Pawnee Buttes several months before looking into the same story. He had tracked down the nurse and told her he was investigating a case involving Seth Rawlins. He wouldn't provide any details, but he had made it clear she needed to tell him everything about the illegitimate baby or she could go to jail. Frightened, the nurse had told him what she later told the two women.

The description of the detective didn't match Terry Adler,

but Rachel didn't believe the man was a Denver detective, either. "I think he was a private investigator my husband hired."

"But how did your husband become suspicious about the phony adoption in the first place?" I pressed. "If you didn't know until your father told you, how would your husband have found out enough for him to send the private dick?"

She dug fingernails into the palm of her hand, as if searching for pain. "I don't know. I just knew it was Terry the moment my father told me about the blackmail."

"Maybe if you wouldn't shoot people, we could find out some of these things."

She retreated to her sulking and I returned to watching the heat ripple off the asphalt highway. The storm had passed through while we were still at the house, but it had been a dry storm, leaving no satisfying rain. Now a strong crosswind leached out what little moisture clung to the soil.

Things that made sense about this case were drying up, too. On the one hand, it sounded logical that Terry Adler blackmailed his father-in-law over the secret of his daughter's true parentage in exchange for him dropping the water lawsuit. This would have been the one thing the old man feared above all—letting his daughter learn he had betrayed her in a way no parent should ever betray a child.

Yet if that was what the blackmail was over, it had been a failure. Rawlins ultimately confessed to his daughter. Had he told Adler there was nothing left to blackmail?

Plus, the banker was still pushing the lawsuit up to the point of his death. Was that why they finally just murdered him?

Then there was the matter of the judge's blackmail photos. Why had Rawlins gone to the desperate lengths of using a thug like Red Owl to get the photos, presumably to protect the fact that his daughter was in them, yet stubbornly not give in to Adler to protect a secret far more devastating than those photos?

Farther down the road, after Rachel had dozed a while and then awoke, I asked her, "Did your father tell you about some photos being used to blackmail Benjamin Glazer, the federal judge presiding over the lawsuit?"

Her eyes widened. "No."

"But you know the photos I'm referring to, don't you, Mrs. Adler?"

She turned toward the window. "I don't know what you're talking about."

"Your husband and Lamprey, and maybe your buddy Cornell and god knows who else in this town, used some compromising photos to blackmail the judge to rule in favor of the reservoir. The photos showed the judge having sex with a young woman who was not his wife. You were that woman, weren't you?"

She said nothing, but her body trembled. The searing emotional pain of the past days and weeks had drained her acting skills.

"The photos!" I snapped.

She jumped and pulled away from the window. "Yeah, yeah, okay, it was me."

"Did you help set it up?"

"Hell, no! I didn't know they were being taken. I wouldn't have done that."

"How did you find out?"

"A fat, creepy man came to my house and showed them to me."

I jerked my eyes off the road and stared at her. "What creepy man?"

"He wouldn't say. He was just a fat, creepy man who wanted blackmail money for making sure my husband never saw them."

I asked her to describe the man. Her description fit Villano Moretti.

I was certain Moretti had left the blackmail photos at Lamprey's house. Had I been wrong? Or had he held some back or made copies? Had he been working both sides of the street? It made sense. The payoff from Adler and Lamprey for taking the pictures probably wasn't much—cash and maybe future greasing of the wheels for his dirty enterprises. Pennies compared with blackmailing a woman potentially worth $26 million. I told her who the man was. "When did he come to you?"

"Two weeks ago."

Moretti had overreached trying to blackmail the wife of one of the men who had hired him in the first place. Only days after the mobster had come a callin' on Rachel Adler he had turned up crispy in his own supper club.

"Did you pay him?" I asked.

She stared out at the prairie. Dry lightning had come through with the storm and smoke from a small prairie fire spiraled in the distance. "Only a little."

"You don't pay a man like Moretti only a little."

"Victor said I should pay him *something*."

"Victor King? Your director?"

"Yes." Suddenly she looked very young, like a little girl. "He was the only one I could talk to, that I could trust. He said I should pay the man. He said the photos would be bad for the judge. I don't think he cared whether they were bad for me."

"Did you tell the judge about the creepy man?"

She shook her head.

"How about your husband?"

"Of course I didn't."

"But you suspected he was involved in those photos, didn't you? Is that what compelled you to shoot him?"

"Oh, I'd thought about shooting Terry right after they found my father. I would have, too, if I'd had a gun handy. But Terry doesn't own a gun. I thought about buying one, but I was afraid he was having me watched and would have me killed. That's why I asked for your help."

"You should have waited longer."

"I tried. Then that fat, *creepy* man came by."

And pushed her over the edge on which she always seemed to teeter

❦❦❦

"How does a man do that?" Rachel Adler asked as we approached the outskirts of Denver. She looked at me as if I could provide great insight into my gender.

"What, kill your father?"

"No. How does a man use his own wife to blackmail a federal judge?"

I didn't bother to point out it was she who had cheated on her husband in the first place, even if he had orchestrated the opportunity. Screwing a federal judge presiding over a lawsuit involving her father, no less. Irony escaped people like Rachel Adler.

"Your father cared about those pictures," I said.

"He knew about them?"

I told her I believed he hired Art Red Owl to take the photos by force from Moretti. She turned away toward the window and fell silent as the tires of my car hummed on the asphalt. She began to cry softly. I hoped somewhere in there she would find something good about her father.

I stared at the road and rehashed in my mind what she and Mercedes had told me. I kept coming back to the baby's fake death, to the "police detective" who had threatened the nurse, the use of that secret to blackmail Seth Rawlins. Images of the Lopez brothers, one rocking the other in his arms, began to play in my mind. Identical twins no one could tell apart until one had beaten the other one into a bloody pulp. It started me thinking about the odd fact of Seth Rawlins walking into Estrada's office building and asking the geologist for directions to the lawyer's office—an office Mercedes said Rawlins had visited only weeks before. Or why Rawlins never actually arrived at Estrada's office, where Emilio and Mercedes waited for a mystery man named Kenneth Morrisey who never showed.

I still couldn't figure out how Art Red Owl fit into the murder of the banker and Moretti. By the time we pulled up in front of Denver police headquarters, however, bits and pieces had begun to fall into place, and I realized how wrong I had been about so many things. But my thoughts were quickly ripped away as reporters and photographers mobbed over us, Lou Sheppard among them. The sheriff in Pawnee Buttes must have alerted Denver police, and the press had picked up on it. Fear rose in Rachel's face.

"You'll be okay," I said to her.

She sucked in gulps of air. I wondered if she did that each time she prepared to go on stage. "My husband deserved to be shot. He killed my father."

I wanted to agree with her. I wanted to reassure her. I had believed her husband was mixed up in her father's murder. But not any longer.

"You shot the wrong man, Mrs. Adler. Your husband deserved to be shot, god knows. But you shot the wrong man."

CHAPTER 38

Dusk slipped into night as I trailed *El Perro*'s little brother Jesse "Mad Dog" Flores and three other *pachucos* as they left a bungalow on Humboldt Street and cruised north *bajito y suavecito*. They had just made a drug buy, something Mad Dog's dead brother would never have approved of. Still, for having just bought drugs, they made an easy target to follow as they laughed and drank beer in their low-riding Chevy. Jesse wasn't nearly as bright as his brother, though Willie had been none too bright getting himself killed by Lopez.

I trailed them to the vacant gas station on Marion Street. The lone streetlight still worked, still cast its yellowish light over the station's weed-infested driveway and graffiti-covered white stucco walls. The crickets still sang in the evening air. But everything else had changed since Moroni Perdue and I had last come here to *Vato Locos* turf, to hear *El Perro* drop the name of Art Red Owl.

Flores and his *pachucos* parked behind the gas station and I parked half a block away. I stood in the deepening shadows of a nearby pawnshop and observed them unloading several packages from the trunk of their car. They went inside and I let them settle in. Soon one of the *pachucos* came outside to stand as lookout, a beer in one hand, a cigarette in the other. I watched the glow of the cigarette as it arced from his side to his mouth and back to his side. I waited until the kid turned his back and began to piss beer on a stucco wall. He was pissing so loud he never heard me come up behind him.

"*Tranquilidad, muchacho,*" I said softly. He looked at me wild eyed as I held my gun up and put a finger to my lips. Though I wasn't on duty, I had dressed in my uniform, just so no one accidently got confused about who I was and took a shot at me.

I marched him inside where Jesse and the other two worked over a large table in the middle of what once had been the garage portion of the gas station. The table was covered with bottles of beer and several large brick-sized packages wrapped in burlap and tied with string. Two of the packages were open and the *pachucos*, when they weren't guzzling beer and laughing, divided the contents, and wrapped them in smaller packages of tinfoil.

"*Mierda!*" said Jesse when he saw me. The other two slowly edged away from the table, as if hoping to disassociate themselves from its contents.

I pushed the pisser into the middle of the room and motioned with my gun for everyone to move to the garage door side. I walked up to the table and poked the brown, gummy substance.

"A little Mexican Mud, *muchachos*?" I said.

Nobody responded. What could they say standing around a table cutting up pounds of brown heroin?

I frisked them one at a time and found three knives and a .22. I dumped the weapons on top of the heroin, then told everyone but Jesse to get the hell out. They hesitated, looking to Jesse for orders, but I said, "You don't have a choice here, fellas, unless you all want to do time."

Jesse wisely motioned with his head for them to leave.

When they were gone, I said to Jesse, "Your brother would never have put up with this shit if he were alive."

"Well, he ain't alive."

"You won't be either, pushing dope like this."

Jesse hadn't earned the nickname Mad Dog for doing nothing. But at least his brother had reined in the kid's worst impulses. The *pachuco* flexed his bare, heavily tattooed forearms. "You gonna arrest me, Officer Stryker, or just talk priest to me?"

"I'd fucking love to arrest your ass, but you're gonna do something for me instead."

He narrowed his eyes. "What?"

I put away my gun. "It's real simple. You're going deliver a message to someone."

"That's all?"

"That's all. Do it right and this—" I waved toward the Mexican Mud. "—goes away. Like it never happened."

Jesse clucked his teeth, a habit I had noticed before when he tried to think real hard. "A message to who?"

"I'll tell you that when it's time."

"What kinda message?"

"You're going to tell this person he's going to post bail for Antonio Lopez."

Flores stiffened. "Lopez is the mothafucker who killed my brother."

"Not the one in jail. That's Antonio. He beat the shit out of the one who killed your brother—Angelo. Angelo now has fewer working brain cells than a head of cauliflower."

Fingerprints had finally sorted out which twin was which. I had persuaded homicide to check their fingerprints against the unidentified fingerprint in Rawlins's Roadmaster. Homicide was surprised I knew about the fingerprint, because it had never been publicly revealed. Moreover, they detested the idea of helping me nose around in their case. But my arrest of Rachel Adler made it too difficult for them to tell me to fuck off. The press continued to report about her arrest and the aftermath, and Lou Sheppard naturally made me look like god's gift to the Denver Police Department.

The front-page pictures of me escorting her into police headquarters didn't hurt. Homicide and Captain Donlan were going to have to deal with me, at least until the commotion settled down.

The fingerprint in the car didn't match either Lopez brother, which further confirmed my suspicion of the banker's real killer. Angelo had killed Red Owl, Willie Flores, and probably Moretti. But he hadn't murdered Seth Rawlins. That was someone else's evil. No one had come forward yet to bail out Lopez and I didn't expect anyone to. Everyone on the street, even the bad guys, felt safer with one brother behind bars and the other in the hospital. Now I was counting on the fact the twins never told people which Lopez they were.

"I still ain't gonna help the other fucker get out," insisted Flores "He's still a Lopez."

"Then scoop up the heroin and bring it out to my car and we'll ride down to headquarters together. Maybe you and Lopez can share a cell."

The *pachuco* rocked on the balls of his feet. "That's all I gotta tell this person? That he puts up bail for Lopez?"

"He won't pay the bail personally. That would put him in a bind with the police. Tell him you'll take the money for him and bail out Lopez yourself. He'll want to know why he should trust you. Your job is to convince him he has no choice but to cough up the money."

"How am I gonna do that?"

"You're going to tell him you're a friend of Lopez and that Lopez told you that if the guy doesn't bail him out, Lopez will sing to the police about who ordered him to kill a man named Seth Rawlins and a guy named Art Red Owl."

"Red Owl," mused Jesse. "My brother told you about him."

I didn't tell Jesse that if his brother hadn't told me about Red Owl, his brother would likely still be alive. I didn't tell him the man he was taking the message to was the man behind the Lopez who killed his brother.

"The man is going to demand proof you in fact represent Lopez," I said. "So you're going to tell this guy three things. Think you can remember three things, Jesse?"

"Yeah, I can remember three fucking things."

"I'll tell them to you now and I'll repeat them when it's time to go see the guy, just so they're stuck inside that thick skull of yours."

First, he would tell the man that the fact he knew who to

deliver the message to confirmed he was working with Lopez. Second, Lopez knew where the police could find the missing hands and he could tell the police why they're missing. Third, Lopez knew about the blackmail of the banker.

Flores stared at me. "I don't understand none of that."

"You don't need to understand it, Jesse. It's better, in fact, that you don't. All you gotta do is pass it on accurately to the guy and persuade him to put up the bail. Under no circumstances do you say my name to this man. *Comprehende?* You tell him you and only you are dealing with Lopez."

"Who's this guy I give the message to?"

"I'll tell you when it's time. No point in getting ahead of ourselves."

"That's all I gotta do to get outa this?"

"You gotta get him to buy it, Jesse. You don't, you're going to jail for pushing dope."

Flores glanced longingly at the table of heroin. There was a lot of money lying there.

"Don't even think about it, Jesse. You're not seeing that dope again." After he left, I would anonymously call the police from a pay phone and tell them where they could pick up a nice stash of Mexican Mud. "Now get outa here. Just make sure I can find you when it's time."

⌁⌁⌁

I met Moroni Perdue on a stretch of the South Platte River maybe a mile below The Bottoms where we had found Art Red Owl's body. A few shanties and industrial sites dotted this stretch, but mostly century-old cottonwoods shaded the river's edge. I found Perdue under one of the trees. He was fishing. I never knew he fished until we arranged to meet here.

"Hey, it's Headline Man," he said as I approached.

He looked much healthier than the first time I'd seen him in the hospital. Color was back in his cheeks. That was good. For what I had in mind, I needed him healthy.

"Headline Man?" I said.

"That's what I hear they're calling you around the department."

I rolled my eyes.

"They're just jealous," he said, like a kid speaking proudly of his father. "You showed 'em up again, Joe. Tracking down the Rawlins lady was a great piece of detective work."

Yeah, the homicide boys were thrilled.

I sat on a nearby rock and watched the river tumble over a wall of boulders. "Catching anything?"

"Naw. Too hot for the fish. I'm not much of a fisherman, anyway. It's just something to do to get away."

He was nestled comfortably between two rocks. He looked more like a man settled in a hammock than a fisherman. I didn't ask what he was getting away from. Maybe I should take up fishing.

"You think the Adler lady's husband murdered her father?" he asked. "Like they're suggesting?"

Rachel had already been bailed out of jail. Not surprising, considering her money bought the best of lawyers. It also didn't hurt that the press was portraying her as the aggrieved daughter of a murdered father. Her lawyers were hinting that powerful people in town, including her husband, might be responsible for the death of her father, and as a consequence she was justified in shooting him. Lou Sheppard was dashing off stories claiming authorities were looking into rumors Terry Adler and others had blackmailed the federal judge presiding over the huge Ponderosa reservoir lawsuit, and that they also might be tied to the recent murder of well-known local mobster Villano Moretti.

I'd seen no mention of the blackmail photographs and that Rachel Adler was the woman in the pictures, or that she was the *real* daughter of Seth Rawlins and Mercedes Estrada. But it would come.

The stories had made no mention of Art Red Owl, who was the key to it all. But there was nothing I could do about that for the time being. I needed to get proof first. For that, I needed the rookie's help.

"No, I don't think Terry Adler killed Seth Rawlins," I told Perdue. "That's why I want to talk with you. I need your help, partner."

The rookie's eyes lit up. "Really?" Then he turned somber and said, "Don't tell my wife. She doesn't know I'm meeting you. She wouldn't like that."

"Let me give you a piece of advice about that, Moroni." I leaned forward to emphasize my point. I told him Paula had left me, at least temporarily, and no small part of the reason she had left was my secrecy about my work. "Don't make the same mistake, kid."

He fell silent and reeled in his line. He checked the night crawler on the hook and recast into the broken waters of a back eddy swirling at the base of the boulders.

I asked how he was feeling.

Officially, he couldn't return to duty for another two weeks, but he felt rarin' to return tomorrow. "I want to work with you again, Joe. What kinda help do you need?"

"We're going to catch the guy who's behind all of this—the murder of the Indian and Seth Rawlins, you getting shot, the murder of Moretti, everything."

He looked puzzled. "Don't you already have Lopez? I read in the paper one brother's in jail and the other's all beat up in the hospital. You said one of them shot me."

"I'm talking about nailing the bastard behind Lopez."

"I'm in, Joe. You can count on me."

I watched an empty soda bottle shoot over the boulders.

"You need to understand, kid, there may be some personal risk in what I'm planning. And professional risk. We could make some people in the department very unhappy."

Perdue looked steadily at me, the gleam still in his eye. "You're talking about catching the man who killed that banker, Joe. That's big stuff. Isn't that what our job is all about?"

Once it was. Maybe it would be again.

∽∾∽

Two days later, Perdue and I stood by my car near the entrance to the Denver city jail. Jesse "Mad Dog" Flores had done his job and come up with the bail money. I expected Lopez to be released any minute.

"How do you know this Lopez isn't the one who killed the Indian and Moretti?" the rookie asked. "Maybe the Lopez who killed your old partner isn't the same one who killed the Indian."

I explained that after they had identified which brother was which through fingerprints, I found out the one who beat his brother to a pulp had been in jail in Colorado Springs when Art Red Owl was killed. That meant the vegetable brother, the one with the scar on his thigh I'd put there two years before, was the one who killed Red Owl and *El Perro*, and likely Moretti. Justice had been served by his own brother.

"You know what they were fighting over?" I asked Perdue, who was fidgeting under a hot sun. He didn't. I told him the vegetable, Angelo, had posed as his brother Antonio in order to have sex with Antonio's girlfriend. She realized the ruse when she noticed he didn't have a particular tattoo like his brother. When she tried to leave, Angelo raped her. Antonio took his revenge in the alley.

Perdue shook his head and then said, "So let's go over one more time what I'm going to say to Lopez." He was nervous, and I wished I could meet Lopez myself, but he would recognize me, especially after all the publicity over Rachel Adler. I couldn't use Flores, either, since Antonio would not have trusted the brother of the man Angelo murdered.

I really needed the rookie's help.

"You're going to tell him you represent the man who bailed him out and that you've arranged a meeting with the man for tomorrow night," I said.

"Who is this mystery guy?" Perdue asked.

"You don't need to know any more than Lopez does at this point. It's better that way."

"Okay, if you say so."

"Now Lopez naturally is going to ask who the hell the man is and why he bailed him out. Tell him he doesn't need to know his name yet, but the guy has a job for him. A good-paying job. Just make it clear to Lopez he has no choice in this matter. The man bailed him out. He owes him. He either meets with the man or the man revokes his bail and he goes right back to jail. That's all Lopez needs to know."

I told Perdue exactly when and where Lopez was to come for the meeting. The rookie nodded more than he needed to.

I put my hand on his shoulder. "You'll be fine, partner. If you feel you come off too nervous with Lopez, tell him his benefactor is not someone to mess with. Tell him your ass is on the line, too, if Lopez doesn't follow your instructions exactly."

I spotted Antonio Lopez walking out the door of the jail, blink his eyes several times in the brightness, and turn his face up to the sun. I ducked into my car.

"That's Lopez," I said to the rookie. "I'll be covering your back, Moroni, don't worry."

CHAPTER 39

L opez shifted uneasily on the balls of his feet in the deepening shadows of a furniture warehouse. The man he was scheduled to meet hadn't showed and, from my vantage point inside a nearby shanty, I was beginning to fear my carefully laid trap wasn't going to work.

The rookie had done his job and convinced Lopez to come to this spot to meet with the man who had bailed him out. Jesse Flores had carried a message to the same man earlier in the day. He was to bring $8,000 in cash to ensure the Mexican's permanent silence and his promise to leave town immediately. Flores gave the man the time and location and didn't ask for a yes or no. He had issued it as a demand and left, just as I had instructed him.

I squeezed my tired eyes. Today had been a workday for me, but I had traded my graveyard shift for the day shift with a cop who owed me a personal favor. I had pulled last night's graveyard followed directly by the day shift, so I had not slept for nearly 24 hours. Now it all looked like it might be a damn waste of time. Maybe much more than that. I had staked Emilio Estrada's life, the capture of the real killer of Seth Rawlins, and maybe my career on making this work.

I moved slightly to loosen my tired body and accidently bumped a metal can with my foot. The Mexican snapped alert and looked in my direction. I was a mere 15 yards from him, observing through cracks inside the low, corrugated-roof shanty. Perdue had taken a position in a similar structure across the street, well before Lopez had arrived.

I had chosen the location for two reasons. We were just around the corner from Inca Street, an unpaved block leading to the railroad tracks not far from we had found the brutalized body of Art Red Owl weeks before. It was a none-too-subtle message Lopez possessed information worth paying for.

I also liked the location because we were less likely to trip over vagrants. Nearly all the Hooverville shanties down here, some of them covered with tires or bricks holding down tar-paper, were in such disrepair even the vagrants avoided sleeping in them for fear the shanties would collapse. Two drunks had wandered by while we waited, each hitting up Lopez for spare change. Each time the Mexican told the drunk to fuck off.

Lopez started toward my shack to investigate the noise. But at that moment, another wino staggered around the corner from Inca. Lopez stopped and turned to see if this time it was the man he was supposed to meet. Seeing it was merely another wino, Lopez sagged and slinked back into the shadows.

The old wino stopped in front of Lopez, a whisky bottle swinging in his hand. "Evenin', sir," he slurred in an ancient voice.

"Fuck off, *viejo hombre.*"

"You the fella s'pposed to meet somebody?"

Lopez didn't tell the wino to fuck off this time.

I stiffened and leaned my head closer to the crack in the half-collapsed wall. Lights from nearby downtown and a half moon allowed me to sorta make out the wino. He wore dirty white hair and a scruffy beard and mustache. His long shabby coat was way too heavy for the warm evening, but then a coat was the one possession men in this part of town prized more jealousy than any other possession—short of booze.

"Who the fuck are you?" Lopez said.

"If you is the guy, he tole me to tell ya to meet him down by the tracks. He give me this for tellin' ya." The wino waved the bottle and took a healthy swig.

"Why down by the tracks? Why not here?"

"Dunno, sir. I jest tellin' ya what he tole me."

"Where down by the tracks?" Lopez demanded.

The wino shrugged and unsteadily pointed in the direction from where he had just come.

Lopez came out of the shadows and took several menacing steps toward the wino. "Go tell this fuck we meet here, like planned."

The wino backed away step for step with Lopez, almost reaching the corner of the warehouse. His free hand was up to ward off Lopez. "Go tell 'im yourself, jack. Don't make no difference to me. I already got me the bottle."

The wino awkwardly screwed the cap on the bottle. He glanced past Lopez, then behind him, as if searching for some-one. He put the bottle away in a coat pocket. When his hand came back out, it held a gun. He fired twice into Lopez, quick-ly. He disappeared around the corner of the building, heading down Inca Street.

Lopez staggered backward for a moment and then toppled over on his back.

"Fuck!" I yelled.

I ducked my way out of the shack into the street. Perdue emerged from across the way, his gun drawn. That was one of the reasons I had brought him along, in case I needed his marksmanship. That, and as a witness to what I had hoped would be the end to these weeks of madness.

"Joe, I'm sorry, it happened so fast I never got off a—"

"It's okay. Let's get him."

We hurried to the corner of the warehouse and peered around the side. The shadow of a man in a long shabby coat was well down the street by then. He no longer staggered like an old wino.

We took off after him in a run. I quickly left Perdue behind, who was not back to hundred percent shape. I hung to one side of Inca, along a strip of shanties, abandoned warehouses, and temporary metal fencing. Far to my left rose the Twentieth Street viaduct and the Pride of the Rockies flour mill in whose shadow we had found Art Red Owl. I slowed as I neared the end of the street. The shooter had vanished into the darkness of the railroad tracks. Several small buildings squatted along the tracks, most of them belonging to the railroad. The man could be waiting in ambush behind any one of them.

Or fleeing like the wind across the tracks and toward the river, and I would never get another chance.

I kept moving, faster than common sense dictated, although I slowed enough for Perdue to narrow the gap with me.

"Joe, look out!" Perdue yelled behind me.

Instinctively, I ducked. A second later, a gunshot roared out of the darkness, narrowly missing me. The rookie's warning had saved my life.

My attention had been so riveted on the end of the street where I had seen the man disappear, I hadn't spotted the shadowy figure rise behind the skeletal remains of a car two shanties in front of me. He must have doubled back to ambush us.

I ducked behind a large pile of broken concrete blocks as the rookie fired a shot. The shooter fired twice more. I heard a shriek behind me. I turned to see Perdue stagger and collapse into a stack of oil drums. His gun fell from his hands and he sprawled to the dirt on his back, motionless.

Shit!

"Moroni!" I started toward him but another gunshot ricocheted off the concrete blocks. I pressed the ground as low as I could.

I looked to where the rookie lay. Even in the sketchy light, I could see blood covering his face. I looked away. *Not again! No, no, dammit, not again!*

I half rose from behind my cover and fired three times in the direction of the shooter, blindly, as I had done so often in the war, shots more out of fury and desperation than purpose.

The shadowy figure of the wino bolted from behind the car and disappeared between two shanties, his long coat flapping behind him.

I glanced at Perdue's body, hesitated, then rose and hurried between the two shanties, hoping I wouldn't trip over trash in the darkness. I came out on Huron Street in time to see the wino fleeing toward the railroad yards.

I fired one shot and took off after him. I climbed an embankment and crossed two sets of tracks. I now was between the tracks and the river, at the edge of The Bottoms. North, I heard the rumble of a big diesel engine chugging its way in my direction. I ducked behind a stack of railroad ties. I had to make a decision. I could charge off into The Bottoms and risk trying to find the shooter in the thick underbrush, or I could hold my position. I figured he couldn't go far west into The Bottoms because the river would block his path. He could move north or south along the river, but that would be slow and potentially treacherous.

More important, these were not directions I suspected the shooter wanted to go. He was no ordinary wino. He no doubt had driven to this area to kill Lopez. His vehicle had to be close by. He didn't dare abandon it and risk it being found, for it would instantly identify him. He would need to double back across the tracks to get to it.

I chose to wait. I reloaded my gun. The train rumbled closer and soon its headlight caught the darkness above me. The ground beneath me trembled. I glanced back. It was a Union Pacific dragging a long string of boxcars, traveling on the set of tracks closest to me. I turned and watched south along the tracks as the lights of the approaching engine began to spray over the area. The train was a mere thirty yards away, the noise of the engine drowning out everything.

The wino made his break.

I spotted him twenty yards ahead of me as he bolted from behind a shed on my side of the tracks in an attempt to cross back over ahead of the train.

I hurriedly shot twice at him, missing. But he slipped slightly as he scrambled up the side of the railroad bed, and my third shot hit him. He grabbed his side, wavered unsteadily, and began to stagger painfully across the tracks.

The train was almost on us. In moments it would separate us and I could lose him, even wounded as he was. I bolted from behind the stack of ties and scrambled across the tracks just yards in front of the moving train. The engine blasted its warning whistle, its headlight silhouetting me like a target. The wino shot twice. I had no idea how close the bullets came to me. I couldn't hear them above the diesel.

I hurled myself off the tracks and rolled into the gravel bed between the two sets of tracks. I lay head down, the ground shaking, until moments later the front of the diesel roared by me. At that instant I was no longer visible in the headlights. The wino couldn't see me, but I could see him as plain as a noonday sun. I raised my head and my gun and aimed at the figure as he dragged himself across the second set of tracks.

I shot twice. I didn't miss this time. He sprawled backward over the embankment.

❧❧❧

The train was still rolling by when I reached the wino. His gun lay two feet from his right hand. I checked for a pulse. He wasn't going anywhere.

I picked up his gun in a handkerchief and pocketed it, so some passing hobo wouldn't steal it.

I hurried back to Perdue, praying there was a chance he was still alive and I could get him help. As I came up Inca Street, I didn't see his body at first, and then to my shock and elation I spotted him sitting up, leaning his back against the stacked oil drums, holding his head in his hands.

"Moroni!" I yelled as I hurried toward him.

He pulled his hands away and looked up at me, his face still bloody. I knelt in front of him.

"Grazed me," he said, touching a gash alongside the right side of his skull. "Head wounds sure bleed, though, don't they?"

An extraordinary sense of relief flooded over me. "I thought you were dead again," I said. I pulled out the handkerchief I'd wrapped around the dead man's gun and made the rookie press it against his skull.

"I was dreaming about this quaint cottage on a beautiful green hillside," Perdue said. "With a stream nearby where I could fish. In Technicolor, too. I wanted to stay there forever."

If the bullet had been one inch over, the rookie *would* have stayed there forever.

He looked up at me. "That guy who shot Lopez, what—"

"I got him. He's dead."

Perdue nodded approvingly.

"You saved my life," I said. He scrunched his bloody face in puzzlement. "You yelled about the man behind the car," I reminded him. "Your warning saved my life."

"Oh," he said, disappointment on his face. "I don't remember that. My head hurts like hell. This getting shot shit is for the birds."

What could I do but laugh?

I made Perdue stay while I went to call homicide and the meat wagon. We had come in my own car, so I had no two-way. Fortunately, I knew the location of a nearby call box. I shot the chintzy lock and called in. I retrieved a flashlight from my car and returned to Perdue. I told him I was going back to the body and he insisted on going, too. I helped him to his feet. He staggered and I told him to sit back down, but he refused. He walked with me all the way, leaning against me at first, then on his own, growing stronger each step.

The body was still there, undisturbed, even the shoes. You never knew around The Bottoms. The train was gone and the place was eerily quiet except for crickets. I reached into my pants pocket and took the gun out by the trigger guard. It was one of those small semiautomatic Colt Pocket Hammerless .32s. Like the gun Bonnie Parker supposedly smuggled into jail taped to her thigh and used to break out Clyde Barrow. I set the gun down near the body where I'd found it.

"Who is this guy?" Perdue said. "Why did some wino kill Lopez and shoot at us?"

"He's not a wino."

I knelt over the body and tugged at the head of shaggy white hair. It resisted, and for an instant I feared I was wrong. But I wasn't. The wig came off. Dark hair lay underneath.

"What the hell?" Perdue asked.

I tugged at the beard and mustache and they came off, too.

Below lay a pale, sharp-boned face I'd first met backstage at the Broadway Playhouse. A ripple of relief went through me.

I had shot the right man.

"Who is this guy?" Perdue asked.

"His name is Victor King. He's a theatrical director. *He's* the guy who murdered Seth Rawlins, and paid Lopez to kill the Indian and Moretti, and try to kill me."

Perdue glanced at me and said with disappointment in his voice, "You seem to have expected all this."

I hadn't exactly told the rookie everything going in. Yet another mistake. One should be upfront with a man when you're risking his life.

"I wasn't sure," I said lamely.

Perdue pulled the bloody handkerchief away from his head, examined it, and put it back. He stood silent for a few moments before saying, "All right, so why did this King guy kill Rawlins and pay Lopez to kill the Indian and Moretti?"

As we waited for the meat wagon, I quickly explained what I knew and what I suspected. It was King, not Terry Adler, who had blackmailed Rawlins over his daughter's true heritage. Rawlins confessed to Rachel that he was her real father shortly before he planned to take care of the blackmail problem. He sent his foreman out of town unexpectedly at the last minute on a chore, probably so Rawlins could confront King in secret at the banker's Lost Coyote ranch. When the banker told King he wouldn't pay any more blackmail, King killed him. Then King got a bright idea. He had learned about the banker's past conflicts with the Mexican lawyer, Estrada, and that they were secretly working together on the Ponderosa water case. He decided to frame the Mexican for the murder. He drove the banker's Roadmaster down to Denver and parked it near Estrada's office. His only mistake was leaving a thumbprint in the car.

"Wait a minute," Perdue said. "Presuming this King guy had to drive to the Rawlins ranch for this secret meeting, he would have left his own car there when he drove the Roadmaster down to Denver. How'd he get back?"

"Good question. I can tell you're not that badly hurt. Again, this is a hunch. Among all the useless tips on this case that came in to the dicks and the newspapers, one concerned a car stolen in Denver the same day Rawlins was murdered. A sheriff's deputy found the car at a roadhouse near the entrance to the Rawlins ranch. My guess is, King stole it so he could get back to the ranch and retrieve his own car."

"Okay. Where does the Indian fit into this? Why did this guy hire Lopez to kill the Indian?"

"Rawlins paid Red Owl to assault Villano Moretti, in an attempt to retrieve the blackmail photos Moretti had taken of the federal judge. My hunch was, Rawlins also had Red Owl tell Victor King, whom he worked for as a stagehand, to stop blackmailing Rawlins over his daughter. In fact, one of the actors overheard King and the Indian arguing shortly before the Indian disappeared. That's why when the news broke about the banker's disappearance, Red Owl got nervous and went into hiding.

He must have suspected King right away. King hired Lopez to hunt him down and kill him because the Indian could implicate King in the banker's disappearance.

"Why kill Moretti?"

"I'm not clear right now on that."

Perdue sat down on the edge of the tracks, looking woozy again. Hell, the chain of events was enough to make a healthy man woozy.

I told the rookie how I'd used Jesse Flores to instruct King to bail Lopez out of jail, or Lopez would squeal to the cops about the director hiring him to kill Red Owl and Moretti. The meeting Perdue had arranged with Lopez was so King could pay off Lopez to disappear—though Antonio Lopez himself didn't realize what the game was. "King shot the wrong Lopez," I said. "He didn't realize the Lopez he'd hired to kill the Indian and Moretti was a vegetable in the city hospital."

"Can you prove any of this?"

"The fact he showed up here in disguise and killed Lopez will go a long way to giving credence to my theory. Plus, I'll bet a month's pay the unidentified thumbprint detectives found on the dash of the banker's Roadmaster will match one of King's thumbs."

We both turned our heads in the direction of approaching sirens.

"You realize the captain is not going to like any of this," I said.

"You warned me about that, Joe. I said yes. I have no regrets. Except for my aching skull. We caught the banker's killer. Isn't that what we're all about—results. Catching the bad guys?"

"You would think so. But that's not always the case."

CHAPTER 40

Rachel Adler sat alone at an elegant table in the fifth-floor Tea Room of the Denver Dry Goods store, looking unusually reserved. She was drinking one of those fancy drinks that come in a large cocktail glass. She wore Katherine Hepburn pants and no gloves. Most of the other diners were women drinking tea, wearing fine dresses, strings of pearls, hats, and white gloves. The cavernous room was filled except for the tables immediately around her.

"Thank you for coming," she said as I sat across from her. She paused, as if summoning up words she was not used to speaking. "I wanted to properly thank you—sincerely—for finding my father's killer."

The young woman might be as crazy as a loon, but at least she remembered her manners now and then. Her invitation to lunch had been another one of her perfumed notes. This time it came to my home. The Tea Room wasn't the kind of place I would have chosen for lunch. Too much white linen and heavy cutlery for me. But I came anyway. A woman worth $26 million was buying. Besides, I had lots of time on my hands since I had been suspended from active duty while Captain Donlan investigated my insubordination and homicide investigated my killing Victor King.

Plus, I still had questions.

"You're not disappointed it wasn't your husband?" I said. "That would make your own case go away at lot easier."

"Maybe a little. But I still don't regret shooting Terry."

Rachel ordered lunch for us—the Tea Room's specialty, chicken ala king in a pastry shell. She didn't catch the irony of her order.

I ordered a beer and she ordered another drink—a cosmopolitan. Many of the older women in the place sat with younger women I guessed were their daughters. I asked Rachel how her mother, Mercedes, was.

She stared out the window overlooking Sixteenth Street. "I don't know. I—I haven't seen her since Pawnee Buttes."

"Don't you think you should—"

"I'm just not ready for it." Her fingers lightly touched the stem of her glass as if it were fragile. "It takes some getting used to, having a real mother after all these years."

The news of her true ancestry had finally surfaced in the press, though the reporters couldn't find Mercedes for comment. Perhaps she was lying low from her brother. He had been released on a personal recognizance bond from the Ponderosa county jail after a thumbprint from Victor King matched the mystery thumbprint on Rawlins's Roadmaster. Charges against the lawyer would likely be dismissed once the King investigation was completed.

We fell silent for a while. My beer arrived. A ten-piece orchestra at the far end of the room, all women musicians, broke into "In a Little Gypsy Tea Room." I wondered how many times a day they played that.

Finally, Rachel said, "I'm still shocked Victor killed my father."

I gave her the highlights of what had led me to deduce it had been the director—her "father's" odd visit to Estrada's office the weekend he vanished, the mystery appointment with Estrada who never showed, my being sidetracked by the blackmailing of the federal judge by her husband and others, and finally, the evening a thug beat his twin brother to a pulp. Seeing the Lopez brothers together in that alley, even with one almost unrecognizable, had made me ponder about how much they had passed for each other over the years. They never used their first names. Only their fingerprints could separate them.

It was then I got my first suspicion someone had masqueraded as Seth Rawlins, already dead and sunk deep in his own lake. Who better to masquerade as him than Victor King? As one of her fellow actors had told me, King had been a highly regarded character actor on Broadway "who could play anyone." I told her of seeing a tan cowboy hat in King's prop room where she had stolen the gun, the one sitting on some skull from a Shakespeare play—a hat resembling the hat her father always wore. It also had struck me as odd that no one at her playhouse reported seeing a man resembling Lopez asking around about Art Red Owl. Why would Lopez search everywhere else in the city for the Indian yet never ask at the very place where he worked as a stagehand?

Somewhere in the middle of my highlights, our chicken ala king arrived under silver-domed trays. The waitress draped my cloth napkin in my lap, as if I couldn't do it for myself.

"How do you think King came to discover you were your father's daughter?" I asked.

She had given that question a lot of thought lately, she said, but she had no firm answer. She admitted that, during her "fling" with the director, she had confided to him extensively about her strained relationship with her father. She had paraded out much of her family's history to him, including what little she knew about the range war with the Estradas. She had confessed some of her deepest secrets and fears to him.

I recalled King commenting to me that he tried to get his actors to pull their emotions, their own lives, into their characters. He was a very perceptive man, she said. Perhaps he had heard something in her words or saw a resemblance in her face she hadn't seen, a clue which told him she was more than an adopted daughter. Once he confirmed his suspicions, he had used it against her father.

Maybe, I thought to myself. But while she had claimed once she never had any idea she was her father's real daughter until the day he told her, I couldn't help wondering whether over the years she hadn't sensed the truth. It would have been a difficult truth for any father to hide from a child. The clues must have spilled out now and then in front of her—a look, a story that didn't quite match with a previous story, a picture full of resemblances on a fireplace mantel in an old cabin.

I could see where she might have been too afraid to confront her father—too afraid of the truth he might acknowledge. I could see her too afraid to speak her fears openly to herself. But I could see her, high on juju or alcohol, blurting out her repressed suspicions and fears to a manipulator like Victor King as he probed her soul in the name of acting. She may have been too afraid to dig for the truth herself, but King wasn't. He would have appropriated any juicy hints of Rachel's real parentage and dug around, played a "police detective" in Pawnee Buttes browbeating an ex-nurse into revealing the faked death of Mercedes Estrada's baby. He would have had no trouble blackmailing Seth Rawlins with that explosive secret.

I didn't ask Rachel Adler whether any of my speculations were true. She didn't need more pain in her life, guilt piled onto anger onto shame. I knew what that felt like. Maybe she would confront the truth someday. Besides, probing more would serve no purpose except to satisfy my own intellectual curiosity. Her father's killer was dead.

Case closed.

෧෩෨

Lou Sheppard sat in my backyard drinking beer and taking notes while I prepared to cook cheap steaks. Paula was still in Nebraska, so I figured I could safely have the reporter over for dinner.

I had promised Lou I would give him the inside scoop of what I knew once I had solved the case, and I was keeping my promise. He was busy these days, what with all the fallout from King's death, the Terry Adler shooting, and the increasing evidence that prominent citizens of Denver were linked to the blackmail of a federal judge. Even the police department couldn't ignore that. Yet Lou seemed more than happy to squeeze in another scoop.

As I set the picnic table, I told him what I had told Perdue on the edge of the tracks next to Victor King's body. Well, most of it. I left out the part about using Perdue and Jesse Flores to set up the meeting between King and Lopez. I'd told homicide I'd gotten wind of the meeting through an informant and secured the rookie's help since I didn't think homicide would assist. I didn't want us getting into yet more trouble with the department for arranging a sting that got two men killed—even if both of them deserved to die. I told homicide Antonio Lopez probably knew his brother Angelo had committed the killings for King, and when Antonio attempted to blackmail King over it, the director shot him.

They seemed to buy the story.

I threw the steaks on the grill and proceeded to tell Lou the stuff I had picked up from Rachel and Mercedes in Pawnee Buttes, and about my "tea" the day before with Rachel. I left out my speculation she had unconsciously confessed her deepest fears about her ancestry to King. I shrugged and said we would probably never know how the director came to learn her father's secret.

Lou scribbled furiously between gulps of beer. The man could simultaneously do both well.

"So King blackmailed Rawlins for money to operate his theater," Lou said, "and when the old man said he'd finally told his daughter the truth, King killed him to cover up his blackmail."

"That's part of it," I said. I pulled the steaks off the grill, and served them with ears of boiled corn and canned baked beans.

During my lunch in the Tea Room, Rachel Adler had speculated on an additional motive. Victor King hated living in Denver, a hick cow town in his eyes. He felt stranded here. But he had no choice but to live in the dry climate due to his poor health. The director was obsessed with theater and he wanted to build the finest theater west of the Hudson River. For that, he needed not only money but top-notch acting talent and thriving, sophisticated audiences. In short, he needed people, and lots of them. To help draw and support all those new residents, Denver desperately needed more water. King undoubtedly saw the Ponderosa reservoir as a future key to that. Yet her father potentially stood in its way with his lawsuit. Killing him not only covered up his blackmail, but also brought the reservoir that much closer to reality—especially if the director could pin her father's murder on the water lawyer he had hired, Emilio Estrada.

"Where does Moretti's murder figure in with King?" Lou asked.

"Moretti was a silent partner with Terry Adler in King's Broadway Playhouse. I also think the director supplied Mrs. Adler and the other actors with marijuana. I smelled it in the theater the first time I went there."

"You believe Moretti was King's dope dealer?"

I nodded. "When King needed a killer to go after Red Owl, who better to go to for names than Moretti. He probably didn't ask for a killer, exactly. Just some muscle. Moretti wasn't going to loan him his own muscle, so he gave him the name of one of the Lopez brothers. When I first confronted Moretti about Lopez likely being Red Owl's killer, he got a funny expression on his face. Moretti hadn't ordered the Indian's murder, so he probably suspected right then King was behind it. Then Rawlins turned up dead. I wouldn't be shocked if a greedy little hood like Moretti started leaning on King. So the director had Lopez kill him."

I didn't tell Lou that King also might have wanted Moretti dead after he learned from Rachel that Moretti had attempted to blackmail her with the photos of the federal judge. The director would not have wanted those photos becoming public and potentially losing the judge Lamprey and his buddies had in their pocket. Yet one more motive for having Lopez kill Moretti and burn his supper club to the ground.

We ate and drank for a while until I said to Sheppard, "I want to make sure you credit my partner, Moroni Perdue, for helping me catch King. He saved my life."

The reporter took a big swig of beer. "Is he in as much trouble as you with Captain Donlan and homicide?"

"He's a rookie. It'll be easy to fire him. And probably me. I embarrassed a lot of people in the department."

Lou Sheppard grinned. "The case is too big for them to fire you, Joe. You've broken this case wide open. They wouldn't dare fire either one of you, though I suppose they could make your life on the job hell. If they do, you tell me. The wrath of my pen will come down upon them. Hell, they not only won't fire you, they'll have to promote you to the dicks."

ᥱᢒᥱᢒ

I wasn't sure I wanted to be promoted to homicide. Hell, while I didn't want them to fire Perdue, a part of me didn't care if they fired me. Maybe that was what I needed, to be cut loose from my past. A fresh start. Run my own garage. I still had some of my secret stash. Yet a part of me wanted to remain a cop. The rookie's annoying enthusiasm and dedication had sparked in me something I had given up for lost—the belief that a cop's job meant something.

But I would worry about that later. I was still on suspension, so I got in my car and drove east, across the parched plains of eastern Colorado and the heart of Nebraska, toward Lincoln. I missed Paula desperately, and I sure as hell didn't want to miss the birth of my child.

THE END

About the Author

Award-winning author, Bruce W. Most is a mystery novelist and former freelance writer. His previously published novel, the award-winning *Rope Burn*, involved cattle rustling and murder in contemporary Wyoming ranch country. He's also the author of *Bonded for Murder* and *Missing Bonds*, featuring a feisty Denver bail bondswoman, Ruby Dark. As a freelance writer, he was published in such magazines as *Parade, TV Guide, American Way, Popular Science, Popular Mechanics,* and *Travel & Leisure*. He ghost wrote a self-help book, *The Power of Choice*, and wrote over 1,000 articles on financial planning topics for the Financial Planning Association. He and his wife live in Denver, Colorado.